# The Vegas Random

# Ellie Gerrard

ISBN: 978-0-6488796-0-2

ISBN: 0-6488796-0-2

Author: Ellie Gerrard

Publisher: Ellie Gerrard

Book Design and Formatting: Zoetic Words

Editor: Zoe Younger

Cover Artist: Kathryn Dee

## DISCLAIMER — READ THIS!

This is a work of fiction, written in first person from several different perspectives. It is written in Australian English, not American. It also has an HFN ending.

This story has more triggers than there are buttons in the cockpit of a 747 and the author is like an unattended two-year-old pressing every single one of them asking, 'What does this one do...'

### So, if you are under 18? PUT IT BACK!

If you are positively allergic to subject matter like, but not limited to:- explicit sex scenes, BDSM, lead characters that like threesomes (MFM), physical violence, swearing that would make a grunt in the army blush, rape, cancer and DEATH...

Then be warned. This is probably not the novel for you.

(**NOTE**: These are only some parts of the book, there is a beautiful story of love, acceptance, and peace intertwined through most of the book. But you gotta get through the rough stuff before you get the HFN).

*You may need a tub of ice-cream, a box of tissues and a teddy bear to cuddle when you have finished.*

This book is not all sweet and fuzzy. This book is a kick in the feels.

Readers don't call her **Ellie 'FUCKING' Gerrard** for nothing.

**Don't say you weren't warned.**

**PS.** If you made it through this warning and you have just accepted the challenge, buckle up buttercup. You are in for the emotional roller coaster of your life.

# Dedication

To Jody, my husband and rock. I couldn't have done this without your love and support.

To Paige, you are my pride and joy. This book is proof that you can make your dreams come true if you work hard for it and believe in yourself.

I love you both so much!

This book is for you.

## Massive Thank Yous to the Following People!

To my editor Zoe Younger, (this woman has the patience of a Goddess). https://zoeticwords.com

To cover artist Katheryn Dee, for the amazing cover, teasers, and swag. https://www.katdeezigns.com

To Nathan Hainline, for being the cover model.

To Cindy Barrett, for some of the best damn swag out there.

To Jodie Waters, my PA, she keeps me sane… ish. 😊

# TABLE OF CONTENTS

# *Main Character List*

**Kate**

Harry and Nelly Smith– Father-in-law & Mother-in-law
Brian (Smith) & Emma Smith– Brother-in-law & wife
Gerrard & Carrie Smith– Brother-in-law & wife
Billy Smith– Brother-in-law
Chris Smith– First husband (deceased)
Ryan and Ella– Adopted kids (Chris's)

**Charlie**

Ian Morrissey– Brother
John and Rachael Morrissey– Father and Mother
Richard and Tammy Morrissey– Siblings
Ben Henderson– Charlie's friend
Aria Morrissey– Ian's first wife (deceased)
Evie and Tim– Ian and Aria's kids

Sam– Charlie 2IC
Hannah– Charlie's doctor

# 1. Charlie

Waiting patiently was not in my skill set. I made people wait, not the other way around. Well not until I had to go to the doctor's. I had the man flu a week ago, it was so bad I had come to the doctor seeking medical intervention. While I was there, the doctor mentioned that I was due for a skin check. So, this week, I was back. Lucky for me this lovely doctor was hot.

I pretended to read a magazine so I did not have to pay attention to the receptionist who was giving me doe eyes. I could not help but think, *honey, I would ruin an innocent like you.* I sighed because she had beautiful skin that I would love to mark and a pretty face I would love to *fuck.*

Doctor Hannah came out, calling me in, breaking me out of my own thoughts. I followed her into her office as she apologised for the wait.

"Okay so skin check, let's get your shirt off and work our way down, shall we?" All business, as usual.

I took off my jacket and folded it trying not to smirk at the sexual innuendo of her words. Wanting to fuck this woman senseless was not helping. You should have seen her legs. They went all the way up 'til they made a cunt of themselves. I could see myself between them. I finished getting undressed, folding everything neatly.

Doctor Hannah looked at my reports while I completed my task. "How have you been feeling?"

"I am perfectly fine." *Now that the dreaded man flu was gone. For a couple of days, I thought I was dying.*

"You aren't tired or lethargic?"

"Only after a big night." I wondered if I could seduce her while the exam was conducted, she would have to touch me. I was not allowed to touch her. *Hmm, challenge? No, I had a meeting after this. I needed to be angry, not happy.*

Hannah asked me to sit on the bed before examining the few moles with her little camera, taking photos of each. I was thoroughly enjoying her gentle touch and she smelt good. I was wondering what perfume she was wearing…

Then she made a little noise.

I cocked an eyebrow before glancing back at her as she inspected a mole just below my shoulder blade. "Why did you make that sound?"

"This one has changed. Do you have a few extra minutes for me to take it out after I finish?"

"Is it that urgent?" raising my eyebrows, in surprise.

"I would recommend it. If you can't I will book an after-hours appointment later today."

While she finished inspecting me I sat there thinking that sexy doctor Hannah was overreacting.

"Are the rest alright?"

"Looks like it. I still don't like that one though." She was serious. I was going to make her wait but just her facial expression changed my mind.

I told her to take it out. I had back to back meetings and a new sub to fuck tonight, well if she dared… I needed to get this over and done with.

I got up, lay on the table while Hannah asked a nurse to come and assist her. I was warned about a sting. I grunted permission before it felt like I had been hit with a whip. *MOTHERFUCKER THAT STUNG!* Hannah kept poking me.

"Are you done?" I asked getting annoyed.

"I did warn you."

"You said a sting. Not multiple." Her no-nonsense tone did not impress me. "That hurt."

"Sorry Charlie. But I want to make sure you are numb." She touched the area she had just assaulted. "How does that feel?"

I told her it was fine. Hannah left it another couple of minutes while she finished getting ready. I lay on my front, listening to her banter and quickly realised this beautiful doctor might be gay, which I found perplexing, normally my gaydar was exceptional.

As she started to cut into me, I asked "Why women? Has a man never been able to do it for you? Or have you just never been attracted."

"Not really. I like women. I make no secret of it. Always have."

"So, have I." I smiled "But you didn't answer the question."

"I had a couple of boyfriends in high school, lost my virginity to a football player."

"Oh. Okay." *That made sense.*

Hannah laughed "What is wrong with a football player?"

"If you had lost your virginity to a musician, you would know." I grinned.

"Hmm, the thing is I don't find men attractive." Then she asked if I was feeling anything.

I told her no before I said, "I don't find men attractive either."

Hannah giggled. Laughter, one way into a woman's panties. She finished cutting the offending mole out of my skin then stitched me up. It was such a weird feeling. I couldn't really feel anything, but I could feel tugging as she closed the stitches. I hated local anesthetics. I handed her my phone and asked her to take a photo so I could see the damage.

THERE WERE TWENTY FUCKING STITCHES!

I looked at her as she informed me the biopsy would be sent away for testing. Giving the nurse a questioning look as this woman, older than the dark ages, looped a band around my arm.

"Just a quick blood test," she gave me a curt nod.

"You took bloods last week." I was tested regularly for STI's, even though I always—without exception—wore protection. If I picked something up, I wanted to know about it and deal with it as soon as possible. I needed to be responsible since I sometimes had multiple partners in one night. I liked my body and looked after it.

The twenty stitches were going to be a bastard. I loved to fuck in the little free time I had. This meant I would have to be careful. The last thing I wanted was a nasty scar.

Hannah gave me pain killers and a couple of dressings before I went down to my waiting driver. He opened the car door. I got in as my phone rang. "Ian, how did you go with your meeting?"

"It went as expected. I got my way."

I chuckled. "Good to hear. Are you going to the club tonight?"

"No, we have the fucking fundraiser you talked me into, remember?"

"Fuck! I forgot about it." It was for veteran's charity. I always supported vets when I could. More so when I knew the money was going where it was needed. Ian and I chatted while I was driven to the office. I finished the call as I walked into a meeting with my board.

## 2. Kate

The kids were in bed, the house was finally clean and quiet. I couldn't concentrate on work. Today was Chris and my wedding anniversary. We would have been married eleven years if things hadn't gone so wrong. It was three and a half years since he broke my heart. Three and a half years since a IED blew him into the afterlife.

I opened the box that held the photos from the few short years we had together. The first photo I picked up was of us kissing goodbye before he flew out for the last time. I remembered how that kiss made me breathless and my knees buckled. How good I felt in his arms as he held me. He had been happy because he convinced me to get out of the army, even though I was fit enough to go back after getting shot on my last deployment. As far as he was concerned, I was at home safe and sound.

He was going through training and then back to war. It was the last time I would see him alive.

Neither of us knew that he would cheat on me with the one person he swore never to touch again. Or, that he would get her pregnant. We couldn't know that I would be kidnapped, beaten and defiled before being left on the side of the road to die. Chris never found out about that. When I came out of surgery, Harry said the army was trying to contact Chris, but he had not long gone out on a mission. I told Harry not to worry Chris, that I would tell him when he was back safe.

I never got the chance; Chris was killed on his way back to base after completing the mission.

Emotions welled up inside me and tears came to my eyes. I put the photo down and grabbed a pillow holding it to my chest as the pain of the moment came back to me, fresh as the day it happened. I sobbed into the pillow. Three and a half years and I was still trying to glue my heart back together again.

I missed Chris so much! But I shouldn't be so sad. I should be picking myself up and moving on as I promised. But I just couldn't bring myself to do it. I don't think there was anything that could bring me to do it…

I cried myself to sleep. Then I got up in the morning and went to work the next day like nothing was wrong. I had training today so I would get through it like I did every other day. I was sitting in my panties and t-shirt, putting on my socks when the guys started coming in. Remy and Camo decided to start their bullshit early. They started getting changed. Until Remy stopped what he was doing, took my chin in one hand and made me look up at him.

"Why have you been crying?"

I pulled my head away and stood up to get my pants on. "I watched The Lion King. I hate it when Mufusa dies." I pulled my pants on and did them up.

"It was her wedding anniversary yesterday. Leave her alone. She will work through it like she does every year," Smith said walking in to get changed. "Did I mention that today is a joint training day?"

I glared at Smith, "No. You didn't."

"Probably because they want to test out our course and then do scenarios," Smith said it like it was nothing out of the ordinary.

"Who is coming in to play with us?" Remy asked.

"The not so secret service."

The rest of our guys came in and Smith briefed us as everyone finished getting dressed.

"Should we make them do it in weight vests?" Gerrard decided to be a smart arse. Everyone thought that was a great idea since most of us worked out in them anyway.

"No, today we are going to go with good old Kevlar. I want to run them through their paces." Smith grinned.

"How did you manage to wing it?" *Fuck he could be dodgy, I bet he was at the fucking pub.*

"I was at the pub, talking to a bloke who claimed to be secret service… I dared him to have his lot come play with mine and well here we are." Smith took my chin; his brown eyes flashed with grief for his brother. I didn't push him away when he gave me a hug and kissed the top of my head. "Are you alright to do this?"

I met Smith's eyes and nodded. "Yeah. My head is in the game."

After putting on our balaclavas, we went outside to where our playmates were waiting. Like every time when we did training, the second I came out, there was some arsehole commenting on my height. He got my standard response; I gave him the bird.

We didn't invite people here for the fun of it. We were training and pushing our limits. Our new friends apparently liked to play as hard as we did. Our course was brutal and there was always one wall that even I had trouble getting over. But not today. I lined up two guys as they were trying to get over it. I jumped and pushed off one guy's hip then used the second guy's shoulder to step up and grab the ledge before pulling myself over. Both men protested. I jumped off the other side and ran to the next obstacle.

They caught up with me two obstacles later and I smiled behind my balaclava as we approached the final sprint home. I only had to run along a hundred meters of narrow wood. It taught agility and was my favourite obstacle. This was my idea and every man in the place hated it. It was the one place in the course I could catch up time.

I dismounted and ran like the devil was after me. I got to the finish with men on my tail. I was nowhere near first, but I wasn't last and that was all I cared about. Being first was never my aim, not when there were men over a foot taller around you playing a game designed for the big and strong.

When we were all back, someone nudged me, and I looked up. "You are like a fucking jack rabbit," he said in his heavy Texan accent. "I have never seen a man run like you did on that wooden plank."

"And you never will." I said, patting him on the shoulder. As I walked away, wishing I could have seen the look on his face when he realised I was a woman.

"Hands up willing victims for the first scenario," Smith called.

My hand literally raised itself. I turned to see the Texan was holding my arm up. He winked at me then threw me over his shoulder. "I got a victim and I really want to be a bad guy."

Well the fuckery began. Missing my husband was pushed to the back of my mind while we played military fuck fuck games. There was nothing better than good company, problem solving, and physical activity that pushed your limits to help you forget your broken heart.

I felt human until I went home and saw my beautiful babies waiting, smiles on their adorable little faces. There was still a big hole in my heart. But something in their smiles that night, glued a couple of pieces back in place. That night, for the first time since Chris died, I slept with out nightmares.

# 3. Charlie

The location of the stitches made them a real bitch. They hurt. I was taking the pain killers prescribed, but only when the pain was too much. Being in pain made me more of an arsehole than normal so I used that to my advantage. It had been three days and I was just about ready to go home from work, when the doctor called asking me to come back in.

Hannah was waiting for me, looking hotter than ever. I was going to hit on her and try my luck, but she looked serious as she asked me to sit down. My beautiful doctor took a seat behind her desk, glanced at my file for a moment before she met my eyes.

I knew as Hannah watched me, I was about to get bad news. I took a calming breath and waited.

"Sometimes I hate my job," she said, giving her head a little shake. "The mole was a melanoma. I have already sent through an urgent referral to one of the best oncologists in the country. He is waiting to see you tonight to run a couple of tests."

I was stunned. "Huh? You took it all out."

"I did. But the blood tests I ran… showed that you still have cancer in your body." She handed me a piece of paper, a copy of the referral "You need to go there now. He will run the tests."

"I have other plans tonight."

"I pulled some serious strings to get you in to see him and have the tests done tonight. The melanoma is aggressive, Charlie. You have cancer showing up in your blood tests. The sooner we start treatment, the better chance of recovery you have."

I practiced self-control religiously. But, as I walked back to the car, though I wouldn't admit it aloud, I was having a brown pants moment. I gave my driver the address. Twenty minutes later, I was greeted by a man who looked old enough to have been around in the big bang. He held my file in his hand as he greeted me, before we walked down the halls following signs to the MRI.

I changed into a gown in the dressing room before I had a canular inserted into my arm. The nurse explained I would have dye injected into my vein while in the machine. The doctor asked if I was claustrophobic, and I answered yes.

I wasn't, not really, but in the last hour I'd gone from being a perfectly healthy, slightly annoyed man to a man who had cancer, being put through more tests. My nerves were shot. I was scared. The nurse gave me something that instantly warmed my veins.

When I had looked in the mirror this morning, I was sure I did not look sick. Maybe I had lost a little weight, but lately I had been more addicted to the gym. Or so I thought. Not quite set on handing over my man card, I went into the room with the MRI machine, in a gown barely covering my jocks. Being 6'6, I had all my own clothes tailor made.

I could feel the sedative start to work, my body slowly relaxing as I lay down on the freezing cold slab. The nurses covered me up because it was fucking cold. They put a blindfold over my eyes, then headphones over my ears. The radiologist asked me to stay still. I melted into the bed a little and relaxed.

Then the bed moved. My heart rate picked up.

The noise of the machine was fucking loud and not pleasant. Being a musician for most of my life, I tried to find a rhythm in the noise but could not. I was in there for so long that, had the sedative not been stronger than I originally thought, I would have been screaming for it to stop.

I could have sworn the machine was closing in on me.

"You are doing well Mr Morrissey, just a few minutes more. Nearly done." A man's voice came over the headphones.

*How the hell did they know I was freaking out?*

When the noise stopped, I took several shaky breaths. If I was not claustrophobic before this—

WELL, I FUCKING AM NOW!

A pretty nurse was the first thing I saw as the blindfold and the headphones were removed. The nurse gave me a kind smile as she helped me sit up.

"I don't like MRI's either," this little nurse confided. "You are a lot braver than I am. The last time I had to be put into an MRI machine, I had to be fully sedated." She touched my hand. I squeezed it gently. "Come on, you are looking a little drowsy. How about I help you get dressed and take you to the doctor's room?"

It was like slow motion. She was professional and kind. I wanted to spank her for it. I did not want her help. But right now, I needed it. Then she left the little dressing room drawing the curtain and saying she would be back in a moment. I was dressed before the nurse returned with a wheelchair.

"I don't need that."

"You are a little unsteady. Please take a seat. I will take you down to the doctor's office."

Sighing before reluctantly taking the seat, she pushed me up the hallway to the doctor's office. He had his back to the door, looking at scans on a lightbox. The nurse shut the door when she left the room. I stared at the scans and all the uneven white circles.

It was then I thought '*if that is me. I am fucked. I am going to die*'.

Instantly, I tried to talk myself out of it. I liked positive. Positive was good. Positive was not scary.

The doctor turned, glanced at me then looked through my file. My phone rang. "If that is a friend, you will need them to stay with you tonight after that sedative. If you can't, I will admit you overnight," the doctor said. I looked at him wide-eyed as I opened my mouth to tell him I was fine, right before he added, "I am serious."

11

"Charlie, I need a drink man. Where you at?" Ben sounded like he needed a drink.

I went to talk, choked on my words then managed to say, "Could you come pick me up? I um… I was given some medication… I'm not allowed to be on my own tonight."

Instantly, his tone changed, "Shit, okay. Where are you? Do you want me to call the boys or your parents?"

"No, don't call anyone. Just come get me." I gave him the address and hung up. I looked at my phone as I struggled with the conversation I was about to have with this archaic doctor. I scratched my head for no reason. "I have cancer."

"Yes, you do," he said gently.

"I am going to die."

His eyes were sympathetic as he nodded. "You need to make preparations…"

For a moment, my heart stopped… I wanted to be healthy, not DYING! Then I rallied. *Do not go down without a fight.* "Treatment?" I kept my hands moving as I texted my driver and told him he could go home for the night.

"Nothing that will work. I am sorry. The cancer is extremely aggressive. You are already stage four."

*Oh God!* "Would treatment give me more time?"

He shook his head, "No. I am sorry."

"How much time do I have?"

He made me wait a minute. "Maybe a month."

I looked at him wide-eyed, running my fingers through my hair and shaking my head in disbelief. "You have to be kidding."

"I am sorry." He shook his head. Though his demeanour was professional, his eyes betrayed the sadness he felt at delivering my death sentence. I wiped my eyes as the gravity of what I had just been told started to sink in. He handed me a tissue, then put a hand on my shoulder. "I wish I could help you. But it is too far advanced."

"I want a second, third and fourth opinion," I stated as anger set in. Good thing I was flying high on the sedative.

"I will send through the test results to my colleagues. They will contact you. But you really do need to prepare... I am so sorry."

I nodded and just sat there in my own head thinking, this can not be happening. It has to be a bad dream.

I didn't notice him move... A firm hand touched my shoulder. "Come on, I will take you home." It was then I realised that Ben had arrived. I thanked the doctor. Ben kept a firm grip on my arm as we walked out and he put me in his car. I covered my face and broke down. Unashamed by my tears for the life I would never get to live.

## 4. *Ben.*

Talk about an unexpected turn of events. I was in the mood to go out and get really fucking drunk, instead I had gone to an oncologist's office to pick up a sedated Charlie. He was currently sitting on the couch, the scotch in his hand completely forgotten as he stared at the coffee table.

When I walked into the doctor's office, one glance at his scans and I knew he was fucked. They were lit up like fourth of July fireworks. Charlie was still drowsy from the sedative, had tears on his cheeks and I don't think he even knew were there.

"Do you want me to put you in bed so you can sleep off the shit they gave you?" I asked.

He clenched his jaw, "I have a month to live."

*Holy fuck!* "Is that what he said?"

Charlie swallowed his scotch in one mouthful. "Yes. I have asked for more opinions."

"I don't blame you. Surely there is some new treatment or surgery?" I finished my scotch. Looks like I am going to get really fucking drunk, just like I planned.

Charlie shook his head. "No," he poured another double. "I am fucked. I will see these other doctors and hear what they have to say. Then I have to work out how the fuck I am going to tell my family." His eyes pleaded with me for help I could not give him.

Charlie's eyes showed the fear and longing for life every man I had seen dying on the battlefield had, before they accepted their fate. Not wanting to accept that they were going to die. Not willing to let go of hope. "How the hell am I going to tell them?" With that Charlie swallowed his scotch too, his eyes locked with mine, waiting for me to give him a miracle answer to his conundrum.

"Just wait and see what the other doctors say," I suggested, downing my scotch too. I poured another, shaking my head. "You don't look sick."

"I don't fucking feel sick." He snapped out of frustration. "I had a skin check twelve months ago, like always. Nothing was wrong! I have had blood tests. How come it hasn't been picked up before now?"

*Stop looking at me for answers. You are not going to get any from me because I don't have them.* "You will have to ask the doctors."

"They sedated me," Charlie grumbled.

"The doctor told me he did that for the scan because you are claustrophobic."

"I wasn't before the stupid scan. I am now. I swear it was closing in on me. Why did he give me something so strong?"

"Probably because you were freaking the fuck out."

He sat back, sipped his scotch, and sighed. "Is my Will up to date?"

I nodded, "Yeah. Any changes?"

"I don't know. I really do not want to break up the company and split it between the boys. Tammy is doing well but if I gave it to her she would not achieve her full potential as a designer. She has her own path to cut. I don't want to sell it either." He smiled, okay here we go. He has had enough scotch for stupid ideas. "Maybe I will give it away to a random woman who lets me in her panties."

I rolled my eyes. "Is the cancer in your brain?"

"I think that is the one place it isn't," Charlie muttered. "It's everywhere Ben. How the fuck does it spread and me not notice?"

I paused, trying to think of something helpful and came up with nada. "I wish I had an answer for you, Buddy, but I just don't."

"Do you want to watch a movie while this shit wears off. I will figure out what to fucking do in the morning."

I sat with Charlie. If he wanted to watch a movie and drink scotch… I was not going to tell a dying man 'no'. When he finished the bottle and finally passed out, I just sat, watching him, debating if it would be a good idea to call Charlie's father, John to come sit with him tonight. He needed his family but wanted to get all the second opinions, to get his own head around his diagnosis before telling them.

Getting up, I tried to wake Charlie, but it was a no go. Between the sedative and the alcohol, he was down for the count. I put him over my shoulder then I carried his arse upstairs to his room. The tall bastard was surprisingly heavy and that is coming from someone who benched 300 pounds with ease. I pulled down the sheets, then put Charlie into bed.

I took off his shoes and belt and put them in the closet. I liked things kept neat. So did Charlie. As I covered him, I decided to stay. The Doc had been clear he was not to be left alone. I took a seat in the corner of the room and started thinking…

*What would happen to Dad's business if something happened to me? I have no heirs; the company is private.* I did not want it split up any more than Charlie wanted his empire broken up and sold. Frowning, I retrieved my phone to bring up the background report on the little sister I had never met. The one that I thought came out of the woodwork when my father died, only to find out Dad had known about her all along. He had even left her part of the company. I didn't want her to get the company if she was a piece of shit.

I opened the report and looked at her financials and criminal history. Kaitlyn did not have a lot of money saved but she was stable. Her criminal history was clean. There was a flag though and I clicked the attachment.

I was sad about my friend's cancer diagnosis, so I used that as an excuse to indulge my mild curiosity about my little sister. The second the attachment opened, I went into a full-blown *RAGE*!

The first photo was of my sister in the hospital bed hooked up to machines, obvious stab wounds on her chest and belly and a slash on her neck where someone attempted to slit her throat. Her face was swollen, black and blue from the beating she had been through. And there were bite marks everywhere.

Her eyes were swollen shut. Her jaw looked broken. There were deep marks and cuts on her wrists and legs where Kaitlyn had been restrained. My sister had *fought*.

I read the police and the toxicology reports. Kaitlyn had been drugged with Flunitrazepam (Rohypnol) and didn't remember anything. She was lucky she didn't die of an overdose with the amount she had been given. I was less than impressed to find that the case was still open.

*That was NOT acceptable.*

Glancing over the rest of her background check, I soon learnt Kate had been married, but was now a widow. She had adopted two children. I was more than surprised when I learned she was now working over here in the States for Crosshairs.

Crosshairs primarily did security. There were rumours that they worked with the FBI, police and had a response crew that, if shit hit the fan, would respond in a joint task force. It was staffed by one hundred percent veterans, ex-military, and emergency services. They had soon become the best agency in the country for security and anything else they touched.

I was confused by this; Crosshairs was all veterans… there is nothing in her report about her serving…. How could Kaitlyn have gotten a job working there… Her name was Kaitlyn Grace Smith… What was her name before marriage…?

*HENDERSON!*

You had to be shitting me! Kaitlyn had been given Dad's name. I looked up Kaitlyn Henderson, why the hell it was not in the background report, I didn't know. Five minutes later, I did.

Her military files were sealed under her maiden name. A quick phone call and I found out my sister was a fucking war hero!

I put my head back thinking I probably should get in touch with her. Kaitlyn was my only living relation, after all.

## 5. Charlie

I woke up to find Ben asleep in my chair, his head resting against the wall. He had stayed all night, I did not know if that made me feel better or worse. I wanted last night's nightmare to be over. Ben being here, meant it was all real.

After I thanked him, he had gone on his way. I showered and got dressed like it was another day. As I walked into the office I pretended it was just another day. I would have to wait for the other doctors to call me with appointment times.

I hoped they did not fuck around. I wanted yesterday to be a nightmare I could wake up from, for the oncologist to ring me to say he had gotten everything wrong, that everything was fine. I threw myself into work. I was still sore from the damn excision. I would have to get the dressing changed later today. Yet another thing I did not want to think about.

My day progressed well, feeling almost normal. I had a meeting with a good friend and first choice lawyer, Larry. I told him about my diagnosis. He was shocked but got down to business. We were quick to put a DNR in place. I did not want to be left on life support. If I was supposed to die, then let me go when I was called home.

"I am thinking about finding a random and giving the company to her." I smiled knowing that this would piss him off to no end. Larry groaned loudly, rolled his eyes as he shook his head. "What? Don't you think it is a good idea?"

"I think that if you did that it would throw into question your mental state and there would be a legal fight over the Will."

"Not if I could talk everyone around before I went." I grinned.

"Whatever Charlie. But you pay me in advance. But what do you want to do if you don't find a random?"

"Then give it to Sam. God knows she has done the work." I shrugged as he smiled. For a lawyer, he was an alright guy if you were lucky enough to be his client. We went through, tidied up my legal affairs before adding stipulations to the Will regarding the media release and the funeral arrangements. It would be hard enough for everyone when I went. Mum and Dad especially, so I wanted to do as much as I could in advance.

Over the next couple of days, I went to the funeral home, picked out a coffin and flowers. I would deal with the church later. It was on the third day that I got a short notice appointment from another oncologist.

When I walked into his office, he was nice, asking me questions about what I had been told. I thought it was going well. I had hope.

Just for a second...

"What you have been told is correct. If you had surgery, you would not survive it. If you went for aggressive radium and Chemo—you would have no quality of life. I am happy to try it if that is what you want. But my advice is to go make your arrangements. Enjoy the time you have left and make peace."

I sat there stunned, *again.* "So, you want to do nothing."

"I want to help you. I would love to cure every person that comes through my door. But your cancer is at a stage where I can't do anything without decreasing your quality of life and possibly kill you by doing so."

I do not think it was something that I could get used to hearing. You are forty years old and you are dying of cancer. I nodded my understanding of the predicament I was in and thanked him for his time before leaving. I wondered how many times I had to hear it before accepting my fate.

Later that afternoon I went back to Doctor Hannah so she could change the dressing on the stitches. Hannah was professional as she went about her work, I was happy when Hannah told me a couple more days and I could have the stitches out. I was healing up nicely.

"You're not flirting today. Are you okay?"

"No. I was planning on living to a hundred. I am going sixty years too early." I gave her a little smile.

She nodded he understanding then out of nowhere, "I am sorry."

"Don't be. It's my hand."

"About being gay, I have seen the way you look me over. I am really not attracted to you." She looked away.

"Don't ever be sorry for who you are." I took her hand before kissing her knuckles "I will never apologise for who I am. I will see you in a couple of days."

"I want to kiss you." Hannah blurted out, then turned scarlet. I cocked my head to the side and waited. She bit her lip hard, then sighed. "I like your lips, their shape." Her eyes dropped; Hannah touched my hands. "I like your hands. The way they held mine. I just don't like dick."

It did not take a genius to figure out something had happened for her to not like dick. Brian would be getting a phone call after this. I lifted her chin gently.

"Look at me." I commanded softly. Reluctantly, she lifted her eyes to mine. "Who hurt you? Tell me."

Hannah shook her head. "It was a long time ago, it doesn't matter." Trying to dismiss the conversation she backed up. "I will see you in a couple of days." She chewed her lip nervously then walked to the door and opened it.

Long time ago, my ass. I left her and called Brian.

## 6. *Brian*

That mother fucker was the cock block of all cock blocks! I had just seduced Emma, finally talking her into office sex when Charlie called. Emma motioned that we would have sex when we got home before leaving the office as I listened to Charlie's predicament. "So, let me get this straight, your doctor is gay because she was hurt by someone and… you want to know who?" I rubbed the bridge of my nose then smiled. Shorty had been giving me the shits. I would give this little assignment to her.

"Yes, that is what I want you to do." Charlie snapped. "Someone hurt that woman. I do not care how long ago. I want your assurance that you will bring him to justice if he hasn't been already."

"I will bring him to justice if he hasn't been already. Send me the details. I will take it from there." I promised—instead of telling the domineering fucker to pull his head in before I knocked his block off.

There was no point arguing with Charlie when he got like this. He had a ten-million-dollar loan hanging over our heads. He hung up saying—with a huff—he would get it to me then disconnected the call. My phone pinged a minute later, as the information came through. I sent it to the printer, then picked it up. I walked it straight down the hall to Shorty who was investigating a vehicular manslaughter cold case. That too, was one Charlie had sent through.

"Don't you fucking dare." Shorty snarled like a vicious little dog. "I am about to have a breakthrough on this." Leaning forward, studying what she was looking at as I put the paper on her desk.

"It is another thing from the boss," I told her. "You can do it when you finished that case."

"I really don't fucking care, that man *OWNS* our company. I am not his little investigative whore," Shorty snarled. She really was a cranky bitch today.

"You are the best we have Shorty. Just suck it up."

Shorty wasn't like other women. She didn't like dresses or skirts, couldn't put on make up to save her life, didn't watch TV or read magazines to keep up with the latest on the rich and famous. She honestly couldn't give a shit about money. She just wanted enough to pay the bills.

As for rich and famous? Well everyone was her equal until they proved themselves to be a complete and absolute cunt. Then you were forever in her shit books. She had no fucking clue who gave us the loan and didn't care.

"Smith, you really fuck me off with this shit."

"Love you too, finish up and go home for the day."

Shorty glared at me. "I am about to get a breakthrough. I am in the zone."

"Your babies are at home. Mum is waiting on you so she can go home too. This will still be here on Monday."

Her jaw ticked, as she saved her work and then glared at me. "You give me the shits. I love you. But you are giving me way too much work. I am burning out. This is a murder; it wasn't an accident. That means a piece of scum is out there." Shorty motioned to the case she was working on.

"And you will get them, Shorty. Just go home and chillax with the kids. It is the weekend so take some time to ride and play with the animals." I put my arm around her shoulders. "I know things are hectic, but I promise you some time off soon." We walked out of the office.

"We need another investigator. I need more staff."

"We can't afford it," I told her. "We have some big contracts coming up that will bring in more money but until they do, we have to play it safe."

"Let me look at the contracts before you go putting them out. I am sure there is money going astray. We seem to be losing money like water through a sieve."

"Don't you trust me?"

"With my life. But you need to trust me when I say something isn't right," she said. "Trust me to go through everything."

"I do trust you. This is your baby."

"No. This is your baby. I just want the background stuff; I keep telling you. Give your job to Harry if you don't want it."

I rolled my eyes. Shorty was burning out. Her workload had been huge. I would see what holiday time she had owing in the morning.

## 7. *Charlie*

Four separate opinions. All of them told me the same thing. It had taken two weeks but now I knew... I was *fucked*.

I was going to die.

I had a lot to do, a lot of loose ends to tidy. A lot of life to live.

I went back to my sexy Doctor Hannah and sat down with her. I would not come back after today. There would not be any need.

"You had your stitches taken out days ago. Why are you here? Are you in pain?"

I shook my head, "I hired an investigator."

"Why?" Hannah looked surprised.

"Because I won't be around. The people I hired will find whoever hurt you and bring them to justice. I want to make sure that when I am gone no one ever hurts you again."

Hannah bit her lip as she lied, "No one hurt me."

"You have been good to me Hannah. You put up with years of sexual harassment on my part." I leant forward and placed Brian's card on her desk. "Anytime you have trouble, you call him. Tell him I told you to."

She shook her head. "You don't have to do that. I won't ever call. My problems are mine."

"No one fucks with the people in my life. I might be about to check out but I sure as fuck will not go out without ensuring everyone will be okay. That card is me, looking after you. Just like you have cared for me."

I watched her struggle; I had always let her have the upper hand. Hannah was the doctor, not me. But today I was here as a friend. She had already told me what she wanted from me and had chickened out. I suspected the problems were more current then past tense. I would be putting this at the top of Brian's list. Aria's killer had been loose for long enough, a few more days wouldn't make a difference while I protected this woman from more hurt.

"Your problems are current. If you tell Brian, he will stop them," I said firmly. She shook her head. "Hannah, he can stop them." She teared up and shook her head, not meeting my eyes. I got up, walked around the desk ignoring the fact she started to run away and could not because the corner desk was against the wall. Her squeak of alarm, her chest heaving. Her eyes terrified. It broke my heart.

I pulled her out of her seat into my arms, Hannah's body went limp. I looked at her unconscious face as I lifted her gently.

Whoever hurt her so bad that she passed out from fright when about to get a hug, was a fucking dead man.

After locking the door, I sat down cradling her. Holding her. Protecting her. I stroked her hair as I felt her wake. I pressed record on my phone. If Hannah talked, I wanted to be able to send it to Brian.

She did. Two years of being stalked. Two years of phone calls, until the last month when it had escalated. Her apartment had been broken into six times. In the first two there was a rose left at the end of the bed. Twice she woke with cum on her bare chest.

But just before my cancer diagnosis she had woken with him in the bed on top of her. Hannah had been bound roughly with duct tape and gagged before being raped all night. She was clinical with her delivery. Not a tear was shed. I was officially worried about this woman. Hannah should have been a sobbing mess.

"He treated me like I was a kinky lover." Hannah whispered, "If I fought… he would hold my nose until I blacked out."

"Do you know who he is?"

"No, he smelt sweet like he ate fruity gum. He was not fit like you. But I never saw him. He was dressed head to toe in black, he even wore sunglasses." She lifted her head. "I don't know how he is getting past the doorman." Her brown eyes searched mine. "I don't understand why he is doing it to me."

I stroked my thumb across her face tenderly. "I don't know why. But I promise he is going to be stopped."

"Why are you doing this for me? I am just your doctor. You don't love me. I am not anything to you."

"Because you need help. I have never been in love, this is true. Yes, you have been an exceptionally good doctor to me. But you are closing my file today. I won't be returning."

"What about your family? Have you told them?" she changed the subject.

"No, not yet. I have had four other opinions; they all say the same thing. I have my test results and I am going to show them, then talk them through it."

"Have you written a bucket list?"

Smiling sadly, I shook my head. "No but I think I will do that. It sounds fun. What do you think should go on the list?"

"Anything that you haven't done or swore never to do. How about get married?"

I think the look on my face said how I felt about that. She smiled, then laughed when I shook my head.

"No, getting married isn't on my to do list. Well not unless I can divorce her the next day." I grinned wickedly at her. "Are you putting your hand up for the task?"

The fear in her eyes put ice in my gut. My beautiful doctor had been really hurt. She put her head against my chest.

"I will never be able to have sex again." She whispered. "If people find out, I will never date again. I feel so dirty and disgusting. I have had myself tested. So far, I am clean. I think he used a condom. But I feel so... filthy..."

"If you weren't so fucking vulnerable, I would put you up on the table and show you how wrong you are." I took a fistful of her hair so she would look at me. "You are not disgusting. He is. You are beautiful, independent and a success. He is a piece of shit that is not worthy of you."

I meant every word I said. Hannah looked surprised when she realised it.

Then she looked at my mouth. My cock twitched.

*Oh, come on, Hannah! I am trying not to be a bastard!*

"I let you think I was gay so you wouldn't hit on me...I...I know you sleep around... I just did not want to be used like that. Just to be another one-night stand."

"That is all it will be now. I am dying Hannah. I respect you enough to not take advantage of you while you are hurting and vulnerable."

"I know. But you could wash him off me."

"I don't do Vanilla. I am a Dominant." I wanted to fuck her senseless, but I need to talk her out of it.

"I know." Hannah turned away but I turned her back toward me again. Her unspoken words were loud and clear. She trusted me to keep her safe knowing it was for one night, that we would not see each other again.

"Okay. If you choose to come to my place, then we will see what happens. But Hannah, it is one night." *Make it clear, crystal clear.* "That is all you will get in my lifetime. I need you to promise that after, you will not be scared or worried anymore."

She hesitated, then nodded. I let go of her hair before kissing her forehead. "Which nights did he sneak into your apartment? Do you remember the dates?"

She gave six dates to me. Hannah looked at my mouth again as I helped her stand. I stood to my full height so she could not kiss me. I was going to leave her on a professional note. I held out a hand she took it. I shook it gently.

"Thank you, Doctor. Your care for me has been exceptional. I wish you all the best for the future."

"It was my pleasure Charlie. Good luck with your bucket list."

I nodded and unlocked the door then whispered in her ear. "I hope you come. If you don't, I won't be offended. Just do not ever go off finding love because you have been hurt. You are stronger than that." I kissed the very side of her mouth. "Good-bye, Doctor. I wish you nothing but happiness in the future." *Maybe not so professional.*

I left her, turning off the voice recorder as I walked.

## 8. *Brian*

Charlie walked into my office like he owned the place. I wanted to be pissed off but technically he *did* own the place. He threw himself into a seat like he was only just keeping his temper…

"Nice to see you Charles, what can I do for you?" *Play nice.*

"I have a recording of a discussion I just had with the woman I asked you to investigate. I want to give it to you and speak to the investigator. I thought it was past tense, it is not. She was raped last night."

There was a terrified scream down the hall that made Charlie jump and look around for the distressed woman.

"BRIAN SMITH! You mother fucking cunt of a man!" Shorty yelled from down the hall. I grinned, honestly, I could not help it. That was the first time she had talked to me in days.

Charlie cocked an eyebrow. "You let your staff talk to you like that?"

"When I do things like that, just to piss her off? Yes, I do. I asked for that." I chuckled as I watched her come out of her office. "That is your investigator."

"I want someone sane." Charlie said, completely serious.

"Oh, Shorty is sane. She is the best I have, just a little over worked is all."

"Then employ more people." Charlie snapped as Shorty opened the door, mad as a cut snake and twice as mean.

"Thank you!" Shorty exclaimed. "I told him the same fucking thing a week ago." She marched past Charlie without looking at him and threw the rubber snake I had hidden in her paperwork at me. I laughed as I caught it. If Charlie weren't here, she would probably have beaten me with it. "I'm gonna have a heart attack when you do that to me one of these days." She yelled, getting up in my grill.

*Fuck, she really is pissed off.*

"Well if you talked to me, I wouldn't have to do that to get attention. But since you are here, I am about to send you a voice file. You are going to add it to the file that I gave you last week. It needs an urgent stamp on it."

"The doctor with a stalker?" Blunt as always. She only ever pretended to have tact.

"Yes," Charlie said. She ignored him and focused her evil glare on me.

"He is breaking into her apartment raping her." I noted how bad Shorty was looking. She looked like she had attempted a mum bun but most of her hair had fallen out. She wore a DILLIGAF shirt, old fitted jeans and sneakers. Her clothes... the rips were not from the manufacturer. They were from wear.

She could have tried dressing up for work but nope. It must have been a rough morning with the kids.

"Fine, send me the voice file. I will sort it out." Shorty marched out of the office. I watched her walk down the hall into her office... and smiled as I waited. Then there was another scream.

I burst out laughing. Holding my gut. *I had managed to get her twice and... there was still one to go!*

"She found the other one," I told Charlie.

I was still laughing when she returned with this snake cut in pieces. "You're a cunt. You do that again and I will slash your fucking tyres!" When she tried to hit me, I only just managed to block it.

"Alright, alright." I held up my hands in surrender. "There is another one in your desk."

I got up "Give me a moment, please." I said to Charlie as I led Shorty from my office. "That is the big boss. Please dial down the crazy."

"Fuck you." She snarled.

I got the other snake, she punched me in the gut as I left her office. It hurt enough for me to grunt. She slammed the door behind me.

It always surprised me how vicious Shorty could be, and it made me smirk as I rubbed my sore gut on the walk back into my office. The little bitch hit like a sledgehammer. I shut the door. "Office shenanigans. Gotta love it."

"I sent you the audio file," Charlie stated, not impressed.

I nodded and moved the mouse as I sat down.

"Okay, I sent it on to Shorty. She will deal with it."

"I don't really want a woman near a rapist..." he started.

"Well assuming she is your average woman was your first mistake. Thinking I would let her do anything without back up is your second. Relax, we got this."

Charlie sighed, still not looking happy. "Do you play pranks on your staff all the time?"

"Only Shorty and only when she won't talk to me." I chuckled. "Now she is talking to me again. Communication is open."

"She could have you up for harassment," Charlie warned.

I smirked, shaking my head. "She is more likely to walk in and tell me to get on the mats so she can beat the shit out of me."

Charlie changed the subject, so I took the opportunity to show him the progress we had made since our last meeting six months ago. Everything was looking fantastic; we weren't bleeding money like Shorty suspected. I was being frugal. We could afford another investigator; I just didn't want to spend the money yet. He went from pissed off to looking happy, maybe even a little impressed, which was hard to do with this man. By the time he and I finished talking there was a soft knock on the door.

"Smith," Shorty was back, softly spoken. Not good, she was wild and on the hunt. Whatever had been on the recording must have been bad. "I have contacted the client. I am going to go chat with her now."

"Sure. Are you going in as her decoy?"

"I am going to set up cameras. Billy is coming with me. Tell the boss, we will get it sorted." With that the door shut.

"She sounded perfectly reasonable then." Charlie sounded surprised.

"Yeah... that wasn't reasonable. Her tone sounded reasonable because you are here. Shorty is now one extremely dangerous woman and I will do as I am told." *Seriously, whoever was on Shorty's bad side was about to get fucked up.*

"Look you are not giving me any reason to have any faith in her. I think I want another investigator on the case. I want this bastard caught."

There was a knowing smile on my lips as I winked at Charlie. "You trusted me when I said this place would work. Trust me when I say she is the best for the job. She is going to go after this guy."

"Who is Billy?"

"My brother."

"I thought you only hired vets?"

"I do."

"What about that crazy woman?"

"That woman is a vet."

"What as? An office bitch? Brian the guy she is after is dangerous." Now he looked angry again.

Without a word, I pulled up a video of Shorty and me having it out on the mats. I turned the screen on, pressed play, and enjoyed the look of shock on Charlie's face. "This was the last time she was pissed off with me. Still think she is going to need help?"

"You aren't holding back." Charlie watched the screen intently.

"No, because I don't want to get hurt. She goes alright, huh?"

"She is completely insane."

"Actually, Shorty is one of the loveliest women you could ever meet. That is just the side you don't want to be on."

## 9. Ben

I was getting too fucking old for this clubbing shit. But I wanted to pick up but it was not going well. The girls were easy enough, but way too drunk. I wanted a woman who could fuck back. I was about to leave when I saw Tammy Morrissey walk in.

She was on her own, stupid girl. Beautiful, so damn beautiful. Her long dark brown hair, her blue eyes. Her body screamed sensual woman. I was completely in love with her, but she was off limits, thanks to her brothers. I wondered if stealing a kiss from her would be worth it.

I smirked because it would be. I had been in love with her since the moment we had been introduced.

Tammy was at the bar getting a drink when Vince appeared out of nowhere. His hand went onto her shoulder. Instantly she tensed up. Her body language changed from relaxed and happy to fear.

When the fuck did Vince manage to get his hands on her?

Vince was a violent fucker and suspected rapist. But he never got caught, he always had an alibi, and the girls always 'magically' dropped the charges. I watched Tammy and Vince for a good twenty minutes before he grabbed her arm so hard that she cried out. He walked her toward the door. I followed at a distance.

He got her out of the club. I could see how tightly he held her arm. She would have bruises. He marched her down the street despite her protests. I followed, pretending I was drunk. When Vince turned to see who was behind him, I pretended to bump into the wall and laughed. The laugh was genuine, I was happy because I was about to fuck him up. I quickened my step when I saw Vince steer her down an alley. I made sure no one saw me follow them. I checked for cameras, ATM's etc. I did not need evidence of what I was about to do. I called my driver, telling him where to meet me.

31

I could hear Tammy crying and begging before I rounded the corner. He had her on the ground. I stayed in the dark, moving fast. But not fast enough.

He hit her and she went limp before he pulled out his cock and got on top of her…

I saw red.

I pulled him off her, swung him into the wall and held him there. The first punch ensured his eye would be black for weeks. The second knocked him the fuck out.

I let him crumple to the ground into a pile of trash because that is where the fuckhead belonged. He didn't get a good look at me, *gotta love shadows*. I kicked him hard in the guts for good measure when I saw Tammy was still unconscious.

I bent down, gently scooping her up and carried her quickly to the end of the alley as Harrison pulled up. He got out and opened the door. I put her in the back of the car. We drove away under ten seconds later.

"Do we need the hospital boss?"

"No, back to my place. She is okay." Tammy moaned softly, as I stroked her hair to keep her calm. "Tam, it's Ben. I got you babe. Vince isn't going to hurt you again."

"Ben?" She opened her eyes and dissolved into tears.

"Tam, are you hurt bad enough to need a hospital?" I asked.

"I am okay." She cried, looking at me with wild eyes as though remembering something. "He is going to kill me. I told him I didn't want to go on a date and now he won't leave me alone!"

I held her to my chest to comfort her. Careful of any injuries she might have sustained. Harrison drove into the underground carpark, opened the door and I got out with Tammy still in my arms. By the time we made it up to the apartment, Tammy had told us she did not want to involve the police or her brothers because Vince had threatened to kill them all if she did.

Tammy obviously still did not know about Charlie's diagnosis. I had secrets coming out of my ears. While she talked, I tried to decide if it would be worth telling them about what was happening with Tammy. Maybe Vince would be smart and back off now that he had his ass handed to him.

Tammy calmed down and stopped crying, but she was still in shock. I got her an icepack for her jaw before leading her to the bathroom. I ran a bath, adding lavender bath salts to help calm her. It was not often I had women over, I much preferred to go to their place so I could leave while they were asleep. But I was always prepared for the odd woman that made it past my front door.

Leaving her to bathe, I half wished I were in the tub with her.

Harrison was less than impressed as I entered the kitchen. "You have to tell the Morrisseys." he said softly. "They will sort it out."

His advice was solid, normally they would sort it out. But Harrison didn't know the bomb that was about to be dropped on them all, so I shook my head.

"If he doesn't back off after being mugged then I will mention it."

"Mugged huh, is that what we are calling it?" Harrison smirked at me. I was sure he didn't believe me.

"Yes, I found him crumpled in the garbage. Poor woman was on the ground beside him."

"If he saw you, or you were caught on camera, then things could get interesting."

"For him. He would have to explain what he was doing down that alley and why he knocked out Tammy. He was in the process of pulling his cock out when he got jumped."

Harrison did not look surprised. "Shocking when karma gets you. Would you like me to do up the guest bedroom?"

"Yes. I think I want her to stay here 'til I am sure she is out of danger. If not, I want you to shadow her."

"None of the Morrisseys are going to be happy with this being kept a secret."

I knew that already. "They have other things to worry about."

## 10. *Charlie*

I had all my medical files in my briefcase. I was about to sit down with Mum and Dad to tell them about my diagnosis. I did not want to do this, but it was time I told them. It had been over two weeks since the original diagnosis. Time was ticking. I had decided on my bucket list, all I needed to do was tell my parents and then my siblings.

We sat down and had a lovely lunch. I enjoyed their banter for the first time in years, sitting back with a smile. They had taken me in when no one else had. My own parents were lost to drugs; my mother was Dad's sister. He and Mum took me in before my junkie parents died from their addiction. They had saved me from the hell of neglect.

To be honest, over the years Mum and Dad had not really changed. Maybe they were closer. Mum watched me for a moment then clasped her hands together, placing them on the table.

"Okay, you have been on your best behaviour. What's wrong?"

Suddenly I felt tight in the chest. I did not want to do this but not because I didn't want to be honest with them… but because I didn't want to be rejected. That was pretty much my entire life. Fearing rejection. Everyone at arms-length. The two people who loved me enough to take me in included.

I went and got my file from the briefcase. Taking a calming breath before walking it back into Mum and Dad, I could not look at them as I sat down. I avoided their questioning gazes before getting the balls to meet their eyes.

Both waited 'til I was ready. Neither pressed. They just waited.

"I went to the doctor and had a mole removed." Fuck, looking at them was hard. "It was a melanoma." I swallowed. "I have been to oncologists and had a heap of tests." I shook my head before putting the file on the table, sliding it toward them. "They all told me the same thing."

"Which was?" Dad asked carefully, reaching for the file.

It took a moment for me to get it out, *fuck this was so hard*. "I have terminal cancer."

Both blinked, obviously shocked. Then Mum's mouth set.

"No." Mum snatched the file. "No." She opened it and started reading through it. Dad was right there with her. "No," she kept saying.

I was all good until I saw the moment, they realised I was going to die. The look on Mum's face. Pure devastation. I had thought they might be glad to be rid of me.

Apparently not.

Dad sat back in his chair and stared at me, shaking his head. "We would have come to every doctor's appointment. Why didn't you tell us? I bet you did this all on your own."

"I didn't like the answer I got. I went to those doctors and hoped one could give me something different. But they all told me the same thing."

With that Mum broke down into tears, covering her face sobbing into her hands. It was like watching her heart shatter. I teared up before getting up to hug her. Pulling her onto my lap to hold her, I glanced at Dad and he was only just keeping his shit together. He got up and went to the scotch decanter before drinking from it.

I chuckled softly, rubbing Mum's back, "The last time I did that you smacked me up the back of the head and told me to get a fucking glass."

Dad looked at me as he took a defiant swig. "My son is dying, there is nothing I can fucking do to save him. My wife has a broken heart and there is nothing I can do to fix it. I have a broken fucking heart. There is nothing I can fucking do about it. So, *fuck the glass.*"

"If you have told the boys before us…" Mum sat back her hands cupping my face, dear God, the pain in Mum's eyes cut me deep.

"I haven't told them. They know nothing. Ben knows only because he picked me up after the MRI. I freaked out and had to have sedation. He stayed with me all night to make sure I was okay."

Mum smacked my arm. "You should have called us. We would have come, or you could have come home."

"I know but I just wanted to be alone." I wiped her tears as she wiped mine off my cheeks. "Mum, I am getting my head around it. There is not a thing I can do. So, I am going to get my affairs in order and have fun."

"Charlie this isn't a joke." Mum cried out pointing to the files. "You haven't gotten married or given me grandbabies or…" She buried her face in my neck, sobbing as her tears soaked through my shirt. "Was I that bad of a mother?"

I hugged her tight, refusing to cry and doing it anyway. "No, you were the best Mum I could ever want. I know I haven't gotten married, that is why I have written a bucket list." *Fuck, getting married has just gone on the fucking list.* I would do it for Mum. *If I could find a half-sane woman insane enough to do it with me.*

Dad handed me a scotch and sat down beside me, tears on our cheeks. Shoulder to shoulder while Mum cried herself out. We sat like that for nearly an hour in a bubble of mutual grief. *This was fucking awful.*

"I never said thank you." I said softly. "For everything you did for me."

"You never had to." Dad answered, taking another drink from the decanter. Dad's eyes met mine. It was then I decided that looking into Dad's eyes was worse.

## 11. *Shorty.*

I had been sitting watching Hannah for three days. Sitting in Hannah's apartment looking at screens, displaying images captured by the cameras that had been placed around the building. Being set up in a small closet had been the only subtle option. Hannah moved around like nothing was weird. Billy was playing her boyfriend while he got her to and from her surgery but did not stay. Nothing had happened during the night.

But three nights in a row on stakeout and I really needed a day off, Billy was now sitting in the closet in case the son of a bitch made a move. Although the police were happy for us to stake out and try to catch the fucker in the act, they said there was not enough evidence to get a warrant for our suspect. Franks begged to differ, but it wasn't his case.

Working flat out for months with little down time had worn me down. The kids were full-on, no matter how cute they were or how much I loved them. They had three million questions, each. I was tired and wanted to sit down and breathe for a minute. Regardless, I was spending it with my babies. Exhausted or not, my children deserved all the time and all the love I could possibly give them... for they were my miracles.

We played with our menagerie of animals while we washed and cared for them. Ryan and Ella loved to be wet. They were loving the fact that they could wash the animals and have a bath too. The dogs loved the water as much as the kids.

The cats were...tolerant. I washed them so I could make it quick. They stood there giving me a filthy look while I did. The kids told me a million little stories while they watched, what they did with Nanny and the imaginary friends they had and not forgetting, the funny farts the dogs did.

Tired or not, I loved every moment of it. I was blessed to be a mother. It had not happened the way I had planned but I had a part of Chris with me and that was all that mattered. My children were my saving grace.

They had saved me when I thought I would put a gun in my mouth to stop the pain of my broken heart and betrayal.

Ryan turned, smiling at me. He was Chris through and through. His brown eyes, blonde hair, and his smile. Even the way he moved and the way he laughed. Ella looked like Chris except her green eyes are a similar shade to mine. Which was weird because Vanessa's eyes are brown like Chris's.

The animal husbandry took a good four hours to complete but we had a lot of fun doing it. Food and water bowls were cleaned out, the cages and stalls cleaned. The kids were buggered by the end of it but they both got a second wind when I told them it was time for lunch.

Days like this, even though there was a lot of work and play, bought me back to center. The work I did would always be important, but it would never be more important than my family. After quick showers and a healthy lunch, we sat down to watch a movie and veg out.

A daytime nap was a rarity but, apparently, we were all tired. The dogs and cats joined us lay around us like a sea of fur. When I woke a couple of hours later, I didn't even know what year it was. It took a couple of moments to work out what woke me. I reached for my phone and groaned when Brian's caller ID came up. *What now!*

"You know I used to love it when you called. I got excited and couldn't wait to chat," I told him without saying hello. "I am not working. I am napping with the kids. I am tired. I have been working 16-hour days. I haven't had a fucking day off in four weeks. I need a fucking break."

"I was going to ask if you wanted to go to Mum and Dad's for a barbie?" Smith sounded a little concerned. "Shorty, why are you working after hours? You work investigations. All of them are cold cases and can be worked on weekdays."

"I am trying to get on top of my workload. And this thing with the Boss's doctor, it's serious."

"Then get someone else working it with you. Other than Billy."

"I have told her I will need to, but Hannah is a rape victim, her trust is fucked. Billy managed to talk her around, but she only wants me there at night."

Brian sighed. "Why didn't you tell me?"

"Because you just put it on my desk telling me to sort it." I grumbled, knowing I was in the wrong and should have told him.

"Yeah well Emma or one of the other girls could keep watch at night." I could hear Smith was annoyed with me.

"Only Emma might have a hope of stopping him." I looked around me at the sleeping kids and animals. I didn't want to go out. "What time is the barbie?"

"Well I am going to cook at five. Do you want me to just bring the party to you?"

I looked around my house; the dishes weren't done, toys were everywhere, the floor hadn't been vacuumed in God knows how long... Tuesday I think... "Um... No. I have washed the animals. I haven't even started on the house yet..." I sighed rubbing my eyes. "Smith, I will give it a miss. I will just hang with the kids and get the house cleaned up. Then I will call Billy and see how he is going."

"You are just mumbling things you still have to do today. Don't worry about work. Just go finish your nap. I will bring you some tucker later and save you cooking dinner. I will see you soon."

With that he hung up. I teared up. I was tired. I hadn't had a holiday since moving to the States three years before. I had weekends off until a month ago. In the army I had worked hard, but this had been so different. The only days I felt sane were the ones when we ran drills.

39

I got up, loaded the dishwasher, and wiped down the benches before Ryan lifted his head and grinned at me. I grinned back as he got up and came to me. I put the dish rag down, squatting down to get my cuddle.

He wrapped his arms around my neck as I hugged his little body.

"Mummy?"

"Yes, my boy?"

"When you go on holiday, can we stay at Nanny's?"

I smiled and kissed his cheek. "Don't you want to go on holiday with me?"

"No, you have fun in Vegas on holiday. You bring home new Daddy."

"I am not going to Vegas." I told him.

He looked confused. "How you get us a Daddy?"

Kissing Ryan's cheek, "Your Daddy was the best."

"I know dat." Ryan kissed my cheek. "But new Daddy will be cool. I gotta pee." He wriggled and I put him down. He ran off to the bathroom. When he came back, after one reminder to wash his hands, I asked who told him he was getting a new Dad. *It was amazing what you could understand when kids were little.*

"Dad did in my dream," he said and woke Ella with a shout, "Ella! Come play!"

Ella grumbled, lifting her head. "Why you waked me up?" she got up. "What we play?"

They ran off to their room as I started picking up all the toys scattered on the floor. The kids did jerry on to what I was doing and helped for a little while but they got distracted and made a mess again. By the time I finished vacuuming and sat down to draw with the kids, Brian, or Smith as I called him most of the time when he gave me the shits, had arrived.

Smith put food on the bench as the kids ran to maul him with hugs and kisses. He returned all of them, showed them the food he bought before he sat down to colour with them. They decided that they wanted to go down to their rooms and destroy them more before dinner was served.

Ninja lay down beside me, putting her head on my lap. I loved this Doberman.

"Shorty?"

I looked up at Smith and waited. I must have fucked up something.

"You really need a holiday. I am going to pull you off this case with Billy."

"No, the client only wants me."

"That is all good if you can sort this in a week, but this really should be handed over to the police…"

"I'm working with the police. We're keeping watch on her because they are understaffed. I have a feeling this guy is going to try something again soon. I want to be there to stop him."

Smith rubbed the bridge of his nose before sitting beside me. "You are exhausted. I am sending you on holidays. I am just finalising bookings. You will be on holiday for two weeks."

This should have had me cheering for joy. Instead I covered my face and started to cry. "Have I fucked up?"

"NO!" he exclaimed as his big arm went around my shoulders. "Of course not. You haven't had a holiday since we got here. You are tired. You need some time off." Smith stroked my hair. "Stop it, I hate it when you cry."

"I'm sorry. I had a nap today and I didn't even know what year it was when I woke up."

"You used to do that when the twins were born." He sighed. "One more shift, I will get you out of here and send you on holidays. You just pack your bags to go away."

41

"I don't need to go away; I am happy to just chill at home."

"I know. But, getting away and recharging might just be the ticket."

## 12. Ian

We had just finished an awesome lunch with Mum and Dad. The kids had stayed with Rita, so it was nice just to have the adult family conversation. Charlie was smiling and animated, which was odd, he usually hated Sunday lunch.

We all moved into the sitting room, drinks in our hands. I glanced at Mum who had been okay for most of the meal, but now looked like she would be sick.

"Mum? Are you alright?" I asked, putting a hand on her shoulder.

She looked up at me with heart-broken eyes and nodded. I didn't understand why she was so sad.

Charlie cleared his throat, getting our attention. "I have some news." He looked each of us in the eyes, Tammy, then Richard, Susan, then me… "I have started working on my bucket list."

"Why the fuck would you be working on your bucket list?" Richard voiced my thoughts.

"Because I have terminal cancer. I am dying," Charlie responded casually. "So, I need help with my bucket list. I was thinking a week in Vegas with the boys then Tam and I will do a few things…"

He waffled on about what he wanted to do. Richard, Tammy, and I stared at each other before Mum covered her face and cried into her hands…

"What do you mean you are dying?" Tammy asked softly, her voice ready to crack.

Charlie shrugged, "I had a melanoma. It has spread right through my body. It will kill me."

Tammy took Charlie's face between her hands. "No. No! You cannot die! This is a really fucking mean joke. Take it back!"

I could not have agreed with her more as I stood up, walked to the wall, and leaned against it feeling like I would be sick. It had to be a joke. A wrong diagnosis or something…

"It is not a joke." Dad said, hugging Mum with tears in his eyes. "We have seen his test results. He has been to the top doctors in the States… There isn't anything that can be done."

I turned and put my fist through the wall in frustration before sliding to the floor. *How the hell could Charlie be dying when he looked perfectly fucking fine! I cannot lose my big brother!* Only three years ago I lost my wife. I had only just survived that. I do not know if I would have if not for Charlie. I could not do more death. I needed him.

I noted then that I had busted my knuckles and sat watching the blood drip onto the leg of my pants. Now I understood why they asked that the kids stay home today. So, he could tell us. My heart thumping in panic and grief made my chest ache. I wanted to vomit. Richard looked like he wanted to hit something too but was only just maintaining control.

*How the fuck, were we supposed to deal with this news?*

## 13. Richard

Charlie sat there looking perfectly fine. Ian had just destroyed one of the walls… He had not done that since he was sixteen. Tammy got up and sat on Charlie's lap. As the youngest of the four of us, she was the only one who could get a hug out of him.

First Aria, now Charlie? *What the fuck?* Anger rose inside me. Susan reached out to touch me then thought better of it. Thank God she knew when and when not to touch me. Now was not the time.

I turned to Dad and Mum; they had obviously known for a couple of days. Mum had already started to calm down. Charlie held Tammy as she sobbed softly into his collar.

Anger and frustration filled me. I reacted without thought as emotion gave way to a physical need to break something. I kicked the coffee table, *hard*. A split second later... pain registered. I grabbed my foot, hopped twice and...

I fell over the fucking coffee table, bounced off it and landed on the floor. Susan was with me a moment later. I swore loudly as the pain in my foot exceeded the pain in my chest. Susan looked worried for a moment... then I heard Charlie roar with laughter.

I turned my head and stared at the big goof. This was the Charlie we had not seen lately. His face was bright, so full of life. He laughed so hard that Tammy nearly fell off his lap. When she started laughing, he laughed harder as he tried to stop her falling.

Slowly, I smiled. Then I chuckled before I met Susan's eyes and started to laugh. Poor Susan was somewhere between grief and finding Charlie and me funny. She smiled then put her head on my chest laughing, or so I thought. She had started to cry.

I put my arms around her to give her comfort and a moment of privacy as I laughed with my brother and sister.

"I hope you didn't break your foot, you idiot. I plan on going to Vegas in a couple of days." Charlie laughed. "And, I am taking you boys and Ben with me."

Ben? Why is he taking Ben? I don't mind him, but he is so... *straight*. Like a line straight. Do no fucking wrong straight. Excellent lawyer but there was something about him... Maybe it was the puppy eyes he had when Tammy was around...

"Why Vegas?" I asked as my foot throbbed and my wife sobbed.

"Because that is where I want to go." Charlie grinned looking at Susan, his face fell when he realised, she was crying. He told Tammy to move.

He got up, plucked Susan off my chest, sat down, and cradled her in his lap. Susan wrapped her arms around his neck. "Shh, don't cry. It's alright." He stroked her hair glancing at me with a little smirk... This prick was up to something. "Gees, the amount of times Susie wanted to fucking kill me over the years... I didn't think she would be this upset."

She slapped his chest. "I wanted to strangle you! You idiot! I never did it because you like it rough!... We can't lose you too."

"I have about as much say in the matter as you do," he said softly. "But I am going to go out, hopefully on a good note. So... can you, my beloved, most beautiful, and wonderful sister-in-law, give your husband a free pass for a week? Susie? Can Richard come play with me?"

She nodded. "He can have a free pass."

Charlie beamed a naughty smile at me; this fucker was going to get me divorced!

## 14. *Charlie*

Well I did it. My family now knew about my diagnosis and bucket list. Susan, the one woman who never succumbed to my charm, broke down. Honestly, I was surprised but not as much as her hugging me right now, her tears were for me and I didn't know if I should be feeling loved or terrible for kicking her while she was down after scoring Richard a free pass. Tammy of course had to have a hug, she could be a real sook but today the hug had been warranted. Richard in the most slapstick moment of pure comic genius had not only kicked the solid wooden coffee table but fallen over it! I hadn't laughed that hard in forever! He better not have broken his foot. We had a lot to do in Vegas.

I glanced over toward Ian, sitting against the wall, his knuckles dripping blood onto the carpet. I had to think before asking…

"Isn't that the same wall you hit last time?"

Ian did not even crack a smile, just nodded. He looked like he had been gut-punched as he glanced at his hand absently then went back to staring at the back of the couch, off in his own thoughts.

I knew this would be hard on him. Three years ago I had managed to get through to him when no one else could. After his wife died, I was sure I would find him dead from alcohol poisoning after the way he tried to drown his sorrows. After three weeks of bullshit and a genuinely concerning call from his housekeeper and groundsman… I had made him get out of his funk.

Yes, the way Aria died was horrible. It was disgusting that the driver had never been caught. No, she did not deserve what happened. It was terrible that Ian did not get to spend the rest of his life with her. But Aria got to spend the rest of her life with him.

She would never have wanted him to fall apart. Even after the wakeup call I gave him, he had not really come back. He was a shell with no intention to move on, just going through the motions. His focus was his kids, his family and working on his empire, not necessarily in that order.

With any luck, the Vegas trip would fix this.

I hoped Ian would get his head around my dying and be okay by the time I was gone. With that thought, I put Susan down and got up.

I clapped my hands. "Right. Well, now this horrible business is all out in the open, let us have a drink. My life is a celebration, not a commiseration. I do not expect you are happy with the news. I am a bit pissed off myself, but I do have a little time left and I am going to make the most of it."

"How long?" Ian did not bother to look up.

"Well, they told me a month, two weeks ago." I delivered this news gently knowing this would hit them hard. Ian groaned, his eyes brimming with tears. "I didn't like the answer, so I went to other doctors until it was pointless."

The shock and pain in Ian's eyes were enough for me to turn away to get the scotch decanter. I looked at Dad, grinning before taking a big slug from it. Dad gave me a sad smile.

"Come on! It is no fun if you don't yell at me." I protested with a grin.

## 15. Billy

I wasn't even out of the car before Brian was on my case about the doctor's investigation. We went straight into the conference room and shut the door.

"Has Shorty been operating effectively?" he asked straight out.

I swear I looked at him like he was losing his fucking mind. "Of course, she is. When doesn't Shorty function in the field? Her investigation load has been heavy, but she is above board on everything, running it by the book as always. Other than being a bit tired and more of a bitch, she is normal Shorty."

Brian thought about it for a moment. "So, she is showing no signs of PTSD, anxiety or depression?"

"No. Shorty is tired. That's all." I gave Gerrard an up nod as he walked in. "Why is Brian worried about Shorty? She hasn't screwed up."

Gerrard sat his big arse down and folded his hands, "Well, when we asked Shorty over for a barbeque on Saturday, she mumbled about housework and didn't want to come."

"When we went over, the little cow had obviously been cleaning like a demon trying to catch up because all the stuff she had mumbled about was done. She's either working too much or she isn't coping. We are trying to work out which. Because she was not herself. She even cried. Shorty doesn't cry."

That was a good point. I considered whether Shorty had done anything weird to indicate she wasn't quite right. I shook my head. "She works a lot and often takes work home. She has been brilliant with this lady doctor. We think we might have worked out who it is, but proving it is a pain in the arse. We have to wait for him to make his move."

"Have you got the police involved?" Gerrard asked, watching me like a hawk.

"Of course, we have. They have been since day one. The client only trusts us because Shorty had a little talk with her."

Brian nodded. "I am thinking about pulling her out and sending her away for a holiday."

"Thinking about it? Or have you already booked? Brian, she needs to be with this woman 'til the end. She won't relax 'til we have him. The client is only good with our involvement if Shorty oversees it…" Then I remembered, and chuckled. "When she met Hannah, it was so funny hearing her introduce herself as Kate. For a minute, I was wondering who she was talking about!"

Both of my brothers laughed at that. We talked for another ten minutes before Shorty walked in, unannounced.

"Which one of you fucks told my kids I am going to Vegas to get remarried?"

That was Shorty in a nutshell. Said what she was thinking. Brutal, in your face and uncensored. A house brick to the face had more tact than she did.

"Don't look at us." We held our hands up. "We know better than to mention fucking Vegas or remarrying. I saw Hannah today; she says someone tried to get into the apartment last night."

"Get anything on camera?"

"Yeah all in black, nothing to go on. I reckon he is getting antsy."

Shorty nodded. "Alright, we will set up for a sting for tonight then. Maybe we can get this bastard. I will call up Franks and see if we can get some uniforms close by for an arrest. I want to go through the rest of the cameras to see if we have missed something."

"I haven't seen it yet but it's all on file." She nodded and squinted suspiciously at the three of us.

"What's with the secret squirrel business?"

Brian grinned, "Thinking about going on a boy's night in Vegas. Check out the boss's motel and casino."

She sighed and shook her head as she left the room. "You are so full of shit." She shut the door behind her.

I smiled. "See? Normal bitch Shorty."

Brian gave me a smirk. "I am sending her to Vegas."

Slowly, I smiled. "She will go off."

"She will be in a completely different state." Brian smiled like a Cheshire cat.

"But we should have a good view of the mushroom cloud from here." Gerrard grinned. I loved having brothers who loved shit stirring as much as me. When Chris died, he broke Shorty's heart and left a hole in our family. We lost a brother and gained a sister we all loved dearly, even when we were being shit stirring arseholes.

## 16. Charlie

Now that the important people knew, it was time for me to have fun. Inspecting my reflection in the mirror. Immaculate. Not a hair out of place, my beard short and neat to hide my baby face, suit tailored and looking sharp, cufflinks, plain gold with a matching tie pin were classy not ostentatious. My shoes shined to perfection. I looked good and knew it. I picked up my flogger, phone, wallet, and keys, making sure there were condoms in my wallet before heading off to what would probably be my last visit to the club.

Walking in with my flogger in hand and let every ounce of Dom ooze out of my being. I loved this. After being vanilla with a woman only a handful of times, it had been enough to know it wasn't for me. Then I discovered handcuffs and spankings and my world changed forever.

There was one little sub that I wanted tonight. I just hoped Nathan had not got his hands on her first. She saw me and there was a shy smile on her lips before she fell to her knees at my feet. My cock went hard as I looked down at her bowed head. I glanced at Nathan who gave a slight nod.

Turning my attention back to the woman, I asked her "Would you like to have a private session?"

"Yes, Sir," she answered softly.

Very quickly, I went through her hard limits and found them satisfactory. I held out my hand. "If you want to come with me, Princess? Take my hand."

With only a slight hesitation, she took my hand. I had a reputation for being extremely hard on subs who dared come with me to the private room. Mostly because none of them walked out. Ever. I always drove a sub home and put her to bed. Smiling, I pulled her to her feet and threw her over my shoulder in one smooth movement.

She let out a squeal of surprise then giggled. This would be fun. I smirked as I strode toward the back rooms. I gave Nathan an up nod as I did. I had been hoping this woman would come to the party for weeks. I knew Nathan had been grafting the same girl, I was sure he succeeded too.

Walking down the hall I asked, "Are you collared by anyone?"

"No." Infringement one.

"Are you seeing anyone out in the normal world?"

"No." Infringement two.

Her hands went on my arse. Infringement three.

I walked her into my room, locked the door and put her down. I cupped her face making her look at me. She had brown eyes, brown mousy hair, her body had lovely curves. Her tits were fake, her arse though was not as toned.

"Do you find it acceptable that I will be taking you home to care for you 'til dawn?" I stalked around her like a lion who had caught his prey and was now toying with it.

"Yes."

Oh, this girl had no manners. She would learn. This made me smile for I was an excellent teacher. I stood behind her.

"You are going to be marked for a few days? Are there any uniforms I should be mindful of?"

"My calves and my forearms, everything else is covered."

"What is your name?" I asked softly in her ear.

"Daphne." She said softly, I do believe little Daphne just blushed as I moved around, facing her so I could tease her.

"Are you ready to be mine for tonight?" Gently I ran my fingertips up her arms until she gave a little shiver as I moved close enough to kiss her. Her breathing spiked with excitement.

"Yes." She tried to kiss me, and I stood up to full height. Daphne looked up at me with doe eyes, obviously disappointed.

"Get undressed. Kneel at the door," I commanded turning my back to prepare for the rest of the night. She was a naughty one and needed to be taught manners first.

"Have you been a sub long?"

"No. I have always been different. I hooked up with a Dom, he showed me stuff and... I liked it. So, he suggested I join."

"So, you have had very little training? Have you had any of what we discussed used on you?"

"Yes."

The infractions just kept coming. "Tonight, I want you to refer to me as Sir. So, when I ask you answer, Yes, Sir or No, Sir. I would love more, Sir. Please Sir? Do you understand?" I glanced at her while I found a butt plug with a red jewel.

Daphne nodded, smiling as she looked me in the eye, "Yes, Sir."

"You will not look at me unless directed. Do you understand?"

She lowered her eyes. "Yes, Sir."

"You will not try and touch or kiss me without permission. Do you understand?"

"Yes, Sir."

"If you need to pee, go now."

I directed her through the door. While she got her business done, I selected hand and ankle cuffs before picking up my whip, placing it on the bed. Daphne came out, I pointed to the floor by my feet. She knelt without a word and did not look at me once. She was a fast study and was starting to impress me.

"Daphne my beautiful woman, I want you to go to the table. Write down your address and place your house key on it."

She did so without hesitation, when the task was completed, little Daphne was back at my feet. I was impressed. This could be a good night.

I picked up the hand cuffs. Squatted in front of her "Are you ready, Princess?"

"Yes, Sir."

"What are your safe words?"

"Red and Yellow." She said softly. "He told me that was what everyone used."

"Would you like to use something else?"

Daphne shook her head. "No, Sir." She offered up her wrists to me, I wanted to smile when I noticed her hands shaking a little.

I put the cuffs on her, "Are you nervous?"

"I have heard rumours, Sir," she whispered. "Sir. Are you going to hurt me so bad I won't be able to walk?"

"The reason I will take you home is because I am about to fuck you so hard that you will feel boneless. There will be some pain, but I always outweigh it with pleasure. Do I scare you?"

"A little, Sir."

I took her ankle and cuffed it. "Would you like to stop?"

"No." She caught herself, adding quickly, "Sir."

"How much lying have you done tonight? Have you really tried everything we discussed?"

She hesitated again before admitting, "I haven't lied. He was cruel. He didn't care if I wanted to stop. He didn't care if I cried. But for some reason, I still liked it."

I cuffed her other ankle. "Did you use your safe words?" I asked her and she shook her head. "I will make you cry. I will make you cry out and scream. I will mark your body but not permanently. It will please me to do all of that. Does this bother you? Do you feel safe enough to share this with me?

She nodded, "Yes, Sir."

"Daphne, if you call red, I will stop, I will take you home and I will care for you. But do not for one second forget that tonight— you are mine." I placed her feet wide apart, exposing her cunt. "I want you to leave your legs wide. I want you to masturbate. I want you to cum for me." I relaxed back in the chair watching her hesitate before she wet her fingers and put them over her vulva. Her fingers began to move. "Look me in the eyes."

She lifted her eyes. I watched her take her orgasm. It was quick. Sweet little Daphne knew how to get herself off. I asked her to come to me before I sucked on her fingers, cleaning them one by one.

I pulled her into my lap, straddling me before I vivaciously assaulted her breasts. I squeezed them, bit them, pinched, twisted, sucked, and nibbled 'til naughty little Daphne went to run her fingers through my hair. I connected the cuffs behind her back. No touching.

I grabbed a handful of her hair, her head back, her breasts forward. I continued watching all of her tells. Daphne was new. I didn't want to scare her, but she was officially in school. My free hand went down to her dripping wet slit and pressed a finger deep inside her.

I finger fucked her and edged her for half an hour. Being an evil bastard, I did not let her cum. I put her over my knee proceeding with a spanking that started gentle and worked up to hard. I tied her to the ceiling, picked up my whip and gave her twelve strokes for the twelve infractions. She cried out and tears fell.

While I worked, I talked to her, instructing her on how to make it easier. How to enjoy it but most importantly, told her how beautiful and how proud of her she made me. I pushed her limits.

When I was sure she'd had enough, and she had pleased me immensely, I tied her up to the bed and fucked her six ways to Sunday.

As with every other woman I had bought to this room, she was sated and boneless, deep in subspace. I bathed her, rubbed cream into the welts on her body before dressing and taking her home.

Her home was old and her bed uncomfortable. But I spooned her until daybreak, listening to her soft breath.

Daphne opened her eyes as I was about to leave. "You were not as bad as the girls said."

I smiled and kissed her forehead. "I took it easy on you. Are you okay?"

She nodded, "The best I have been in a long time. Thank you, Sir. I feel again."

I smiled and stroked her face with my fingertips. "Rest up beautiful. Remember your lessons. I might just invite you back into my room again."

"I will take you up on the offer, Sir."

"Good night, Daphne."

"You remember my name?" She genuinely looked surprised.

"Yes, of course. Take care." I kissed her forehead again and left. There would not be another offer. Not in this lifetime. The night had been epic. I was exhausted, sated, and I could not wait for Vegas.

I made a mental note on the drive home... sleep before ringing my brothers and Ben to make sure they had their shit sorted so we could go to Vegas in peace. Then thought... I probably should tell Sam that I am going away too. She would be in charge 'til I returned... or until I found someone to take my place.

## 17. Hannah

After being dropped off at home, I unlocked my door and stepped into my apartment that felt more like my private hell than my home. Knowing Kate would be in the closet waiting was small comfort. I could not help but hope it would be tonight that he came. That tonight they would stop him, and this would be over.

I put my bag on the kitchen table just like I did every evening before opening the fridge. Inside on the top shelf was a home cooked meal in a Tupperware container.

"Kate? Did you cook for me?" I asked softly as I walked past the closet to the loo.

"No, Billy did," Kate responded. "Relax, I will be with you all night."

We had discussed at length what would happen. Everything would be caught on tape. My account of everything that had happened until tonight was recorded with the police and I could not have asked for a better support person. Charges would be laid now I had a better case with the rape kit being positive for his DNA. The bastard didn't already have his DNA on file so we would have to catch him to find out his identity. Kate arrived the morning after he had managed to get in again and had known with just one look what had happened. She had taken me straight to the hospital. Kate was so lovely, staying with me start to finish. They had stayed with me every night since.

I heated up dinner and sat in front of the TV to unwind. Like most nights, I ate while watching a movie. This was the life of a doctor. I did not have time to date. By the end of my workday I was exhausted and just wanted to relax.

I got bored with the movie, getting up to take a shower as I turned the TV off. Scrubbing myself clean like every other night was not just routine, it was therapeutic, for a few minutes after I got out of the shower, I felt clean.

Not just from sick patients but from *him*. I now understood why women said they feel dirty. I put the loofa on the rack to drain and stood under the water that was way too hot.

Routine got me through, the things I could control kept me sane. I turned off the water and dried myself. My skin was pink from the shower. I dressed before wandering around the apartment, turning off the lights. Finally crawling into bed and snuggling between the clean sheets. Taking a couple of deep breaths before staring at the ceiling. I prayed for this to be over before rolling over to look out the window. It took a good twenty minutes before my eyes drooped. Every little sound, no matter how familiar, took me from nearly asleep to fully awake.

But like most nights when overtired, I dropped off without knowing it. Only to wake up the next morning feeling rested. I sniffed, smelling coffee. I took my time stretching, Kate had gotten up early. Routine… I went to the toilet then wandered out into the kitchen, rubbing my eyes sleepily.

The realisation Kate was not the one who had made coffee, stopped me dead in my tracks. It had been my doorman, Steven, mid-thirties, red hair, polite, he'd never set off alarm bells. He sipped coffee looking over the top of my cup, pale green eyes watching me. My heart tried to jump out of my chest. I did not know what to do. Where was Kate? And why the hell was Steven in my kitchen, staring at me like that?

"Did you sleep well?" He put the cup down. "I have watched you for an hour. I wanted nothing but to fuck you, but I had issues."

"What are you doing in my apartment Steven?" I asked coolly.

"You see, you thought I didn't know about the mole you had staying here. I know everything about you."

*Oh no! Kate!* I glanced back at the closet where Kate had been.

"She is still in there. Would you like to see her?" He sneered; his offer sent a chill through to my core.

With my heart pounding in my chest, I walked back to the closet and opened the door. Praying Kate was ok. She was crumpled on the floor. I rushed to her side, feeling for a pulse. It was weak, but there. She needed a hospital. I left the closet and grabbed for my phone.

The next thing I knew, my back was on the bed, he was on top of me, holding my nose. I opened my mouth to scream... He poured liquid down my throat... the bitter taste barely registered before everything went black.

## 18. Kate

I blinked a couple of times trying to focus my eyes. I felt like I had a motherfucking hangover. My body was sluggish, my mouth dry and fuck my head hurt! I went to move into a more comfortable position, and I couldn't... *What the fuck?*

Opening my sleepy eyes, fighting through the cobwebs in my head, I tried to get my eyes to focus... It took me a moment to comprehend that I was looking at Hannah. She was naked... bound... and unconscious!

*Shit, this is not good. Why the fuck can't I think properly?* I tried to move only to realise that I was bound too... naked... and gagged. *FUCK!*

*Motherfucker! Really? How the fuck did you manage to get me down like this?*

I felt for the ring on my finger, I can't describe the relief I felt when it was still there. I pressed it hard as I heard footsteps coming into the room. I lay still as he moved around the bed. *Hmm, play sick and try to get him to release me? Maybe, I can't fight him with my elbows, wrists, knees and ankles bound. Pretty fucked right now. I must be if I thought playing possum would work. It never fucking works!* I pressed the ring again.

I opened my eyes. He was dressed head to toe in black, had sunglasses on so I couldn't see his eyes, rubber gloves on his hands. He came close inspecting me. I didn't have to fake the eye roll. It just happened. A strong hand grabbed my jaw, he inspected my face, blowing sickly sweet breath over me. *Yuck.*

"Starting to wake up, huh? I wonder if you realised that I watched everything that went on in this apartment. I know you found my cameras and disabled them. You didn't know I put in more."

Um, yeah. We did.

"I disabled your little network. They can't see you. Or hear you scream…"

Hmm buddy, I don't scream. And they can see me. They know I am in trouble and they are coming.

He checked my restraints. It was then I realised how truly fucked I was. There was no way I was going to get out of this without being cut free. He walked to the other side of the bed and I opened my eyes to see how my client, Hannah, was bound. I'd thought she just had her hands bound above her head.

No, she had her legs and knees tied open. He touched her breast, fondled it for a moment before he got out some duct tape.

"Hannah is so beautiful. I was so excited to make her my lover." He taped her breast up into a peak, which looked tight and painful. *Thank goodness, she is unconscious.* "Then you showed up." He reached over and slapped my tit. *THAT FUCKING HURT!* I

58

grunted, looking down at my tits. He didn't hit me that hard but it felt a lot harder. I was greeted with a shocking sight.

*THEY WERE NOT JUST BOUND! THEY WERE FUCKING TURNING PURPLE!*

I darted him with my best I may be drugged and bound but when I get free, *I am going to kill you* look. He chuckled as he taped Hannah's other breast. I looked down at *my poor boobs!*

"They won't fall off." He said, picking up a remote and pressing a button.

My arsehole started vibrating! He'd put a vibrating butt plug in my arse while I was unconscious!

He picked up another remote, clicked it. I jerked as I realised there was something in my vagina as well.

I gave him a death stare. He was a fucking dead man. I was going to get loose and kill him. I pressed the ring again and this time held it. Apparently, he wasn't worried about the buzzing in my nether regions or the glacial death stare I was giving him. He climbed on top of Hannah.

I growled at him not to through the gag.

He stopped, took the remotes, and the buzzing increased. *Oh no. I was going to orgasm.*

He came over to my side of the bed again, pulled my hair and he touched my nose. I breathed in as he forced me to look at him and coughed. He put something up my nose.

"A little cocaine to help that orgasm." He chuckled and put more up my nose. "It will wake you up."

Then he touched the plugs and made sure they were in. The cocaine hit me like a freight train. I started to jitter because suddenly I had energy and couldn't do anything about it. He laughed and shoved more up my nose before crawling over me to get to Hannah.

I shook my head and told him no. He put on a condom and positioned himself over her as my body reacted to the stimulation. He slammed into her. He put a hand over my nose, squeezing as he raped my client. It didn't take long to start blacking out. My lungs burning, my head pounding, I did struggle. I blacked out as Hannah started screaming. I couldn't help wondering where the fuck was Billy. He only went out to get coffee.

# 19. Hannah

This had to be a nightmare. Please, oh please, let it be a nightmare!

I struggled but could not move. I lifted my head, my breasts! OMG! I looked around for Kate, she was on the bed beside me. Her breasts purple, Steven pinching her nose. Kate could not breathe. Her body convulsed a little, he let her go and laughed.

He was inside of me. He was raping me. Again! Kate had not been able to stop him. I was going to die. Kate was not moving. This was horrible. Poor Kate. I glared up at him, shouting through the gag. I could survive being raped. What I could not accept was someone dying because of me. I tried to struggle to move but I was bound too well to allow that.

When he came close, I head butted him. Fuck him. Filled with rage I did not care. If I got loose, I would break my Hippocratic oath and kill this man. He needed to be stopped. He slapped me hard for my effort. His hand went around my throat in a vice grip. I would not die being weak. I defied him with everything I had through the pain. The last thing I heard was a loud bang.

## 20. Billy

Raging. I was like an absolute mother fucking raging bull. There was no police support. They were dealing with something downtown. All we had was Franks. I had been having a break, getting a coffee with Brian, Gerrard, and Franks when Shorty's alarm went off. With the traffic fucked, we had just run three fucking blocks, got out of the elevator to hear muffled screams.

We drew our guns, kicked in the door, ran into the bedroom. *Fuck me dead!*

Hannah and Shorty were bound on the bed. That fucker was on top of Hannah until I ripped him off her, throwing the gutless piece of shit to the ground. When he started to fight I was more than willing to oblige, if he wanted a fight he had one. Dragging the shitcunt to his feet and throwing him into the hallway to get him away from the women. *I was going to kill him.*

Franks was with me a moment later. When we got the fuckhead cuffed, Franks pushed me off him. I fell on my arse, glaring, ready to ring this cunt's neck. How Franks held him down and pushed me off him a second time, I didn't know.

"I got him. Go help the boys." Franks snapped at me. "Go. I got him." He grabbed his radio, calling for backup and ambulances.

I walked down the hall Gerrard and Brian were treating the women.

"Get photos." Brian said, not looking at me. "Get them now. We are going to have to move them."

I went to the closet and checked the cameras; it was all on tape. "Got it all on tape."

"Then get the fuck back out here," Gerrard snapped.

"Tell me they aren't dead," I said walking back into the room.

61

"Get the tape off their tits." Gerrard was all business. I shook my head and did it quickly. "Brian, how is Shorty?"

"Breathing. I think she has been drugged." Brian removed Shorty's gag and white foam came out of her mouth, he was quick to clear her airway. "Fuck, hang on Shorty, I got you."

"Hannah alive?" I checked.

"Yeah. Just." Gerrard nodded.

Quickly, I cut the restraints off their arms and legs. "How far off are the medics"

"Coming. Sit-rep?" Franks called from the hallway.

Gerrard took over and within ten minutes of kicking down the door, the scene was covered with medics. Gerrard, of course, would go with Shorty. Brian got the unenviable job of calling the big boss. I downloaded all the surveillance to a USB and gave it to Franks.

The doorman hadn't gotten Shorty easily. But by the look of it he tap tased to to drop her and pinned her long enough to drug her. Everything recorded went straight to the work server, so I wasn't worried about disk integrity as I gave the police a copy of the break-in and attack. When they took the red headed fucker out, the fucking doorman just as we had predicted, he looked straight at me and grinned.

"I fucked your girl."

He got no reaction from me. I knew better than to be stirred up by a sly prick like that. I did make a phone call to sure that the fucker would have a welcoming party in prison. I grinned as I hung up. Franks was right there and didn't stop me.

"He deserves what you did."

"He shouldn't have fucked my girl," I responded.

## 21. Charlie

It was not a call I wanted. It was not one I expected. Dear God, I was fucking furious as I marched into Brian's office and slammed the door behind me. He was on the phone. When he looked up, he was deadly calm. I seethed while he finished his call. He put down the receiver and stood up.

"I have fucking bigger problems to deal with than you right now," he started. "I don't want to hear I told you so's or any bullshit. We got the guy. Hannah is going to be okay. My staff member is going to be okay... well until I go out there and kill her for coming into work despite being told to stay at home."

"Hannah is not okay. SHE GOT RAPED AGAIN!" I shouted.

"I suspect not, but she will be. I have linked her in with a great counsellor and Billy will work with her to improve her self-defence. I called to tell you only because you brought the case to us and you are paying for our services. Hannah is our client, not you. Her confidentiality is paramount. I am going to need you to give me a statement stating why you hired us on her behalf. This will go to court. I want every fucking T crossed and every i dotted. Because this fucker is not getting off."

I was going to yell at him but right now, he seemed even more dangerous than me. I tried to remember what he did in the Army again. He walked past me and opened the door leaving his office.

"BILLY! TAKE THIS LITTLE WENCH HOME! PUT HER IN BED AND SHOOT HER IF SHE THINKS ABOUT DOING ANYTHING MORE THAN READING A BOOK OR GOING TO THE TOILET!"

"FUCK OFF SMITH. I AM JUST FINISHING MY REPORT!" A woman's voice shouted.

"NO! YOU ARE NOT! YOU ARE ON FUCKING LEAVE!"

"I wasn't raped I was just drugged a bit."

"You were sexually assaulted, and you overdosed!" he snapped. "It took them an hour in the ER to work out what the fucking buzzing noise was."

"Smith, don't you dare! MOTHERFUCKER!" she screamed.

My jaw dropped when Brian came out with her over his shoulder. "You are going home. I am going to book you a holiday and you are going. You need to rest and recuperate."

He physically threw her to another man, "I mean it. Put her in bed or on the couch, shoot her if she so much as looks like she is working."

The other man smirked as he held the little woman who was still weak after her ordeal. Poor little woman covered her face.

"I am fine, just let me work," she sobbed.

"Oh, stop fake crying." Brian rolled his eyes. "Go home. I will be over to debrief you a little later"

Lifting her head, her hair pretty much covered her face as she gave Brian the bird, a scowl on her lips. "My report is finished. Save it for me." With that the second man carried her out.

Brian sighed and rolled his eyes up to the ceiling, "Some days I want to kill her." He gave me a filthy look. "You don't know how fucking frustrating it is to love that woman."

"Is she your wife?"

"Sister-in-law."

I sat down. "She was assaulted?"

He sat down behind his desk, rubbing the bridge of his nose. "I thought I could hear something when we were with her but it wasn't until they went to do the rape kit that they found a large vibrating butt plug in her arse and a vibrator in… well you know where." He leaned back and shook his head, "That woman is the toughest bitch I know."

"Is he being charged with her assault?"

"Yes. I don't know how her tits didn't fall off."

"I don't understand." I think Brian needed debriefing too. He was not making sense.

"He bound their breasts. They were purple. I don't understand why he did that."

"Makes them hypersensitive. To cause pain. I am not really into that; I like breasts a normal colour."

"Me too," he muttered "Okay, proceed to yell at me if you have to. I have work to do."

"What other things have you set in place for Hannah?"

"Hannah wants to move out, as soon as she finds somewhere we will set up security and help her move."

"I have a spare apartment she can have close by."

"That is good for the interim but…"

"I mean she can have it. I will put it in her name It will be all hers."

Brian blinked, watching me for a moment before responding. "Must be nice to be rich."

"Sometimes. Other times it is a pain in the ass. What are you going to do about your sister-in-law?"

"I am going to book her a holiday, put Shorty on a plane without telling her where she is going."

I nodded, took a note pad off his desk and wrote down the address of the apartment. "This will be ready in three days. I will have it professionally cleaned and that will give you time to put in security." I gave it back to him. "You do a great job. I was hoping Hannah would not be hurt but according to the detective, the case is solid. Send me an ongoing contract for security on her home and, if she needs it, personal protection. I will put the money aside for her."

Brian nodded as I got up. I went home wondering how the fuck I had seen Brian's sister-in-law twice in a couple weeks without seeing her face properly— and whether she owned a hairbrush.

## 22. Hannah

When I knocked on Charlie's door, I was shaking like a leaf. I wanted to check that he was okay and thank him for his help. At the time I was more worried about Kate than myself.

I knocked again. Maybe he was not home. I frowned and turned to leave. I heard the lock click. I stopped, turned back to the very sexy ex-patient who would die well before his time. He looked me over and then he moved. His arms went around me, locking me in his warm embrace as my feet left the floor.

"I am so sorry," he said softly against my neck. "I asked them not to put the woman in with you. I thought they could stop him."

I held him, enjoying his cologne, "They did stop him. They were brilliant. Thank you so much for getting me out of that nightmare."

My feet went back on the floor and I gazed up at him as he shut the door. I did not even feel him move. Now I was inside his apartment with this beautiful man, safe. He took my chin and inspected the hand marks on my neck.

"I am going away tomorrow… to cross some things off my bucket list." Charlie sounded guilty.

When did I decide to sleep with him? Oh, like a second ago. "I am so glad."

"Are you okay?" He cupped my face, his eyes searching mine. The concern on his face was as real as the guilt in his eyes.

"I wasn't scared this time. I am more angry about the fact he hurt Kate. We will survive. I am okay."

He frowned, "You don't look it. I hate how he marked you." He touched my neck, "I hate what he did."

"So do I, but he won't do it again." Gazing up at him, he looked so guilty when he had no reason to. "I came to talk to you about this ludicrous idea about me moving into one of your apartments."

He smiled, there was no guilt now. "I have already gifted it to you. I do not need it anymore. You need a fresh start. Somewhere safe. I promise it is beautiful."

He touched my face and then my neck, I watched his eyes. He was just being himself. Not trying to control me. Not trying to get me into bed. Just concerned about my welfare.

"You are very generous. Thank you." I said softly.

"You have scrubbed your skin too hard." His eyes studied me. "Please don't hurt yourself. You are not dirty."

I gave him a wry smile and nodded, "I feel it though. I would love nothing more than for it to go away but it will not. Brian has set me up with some really good support… eventually I will be okay."

Charlie nodded, "I know you will."

I would not have come if I didn't want to sleep with him. So here goes nothing. "Will you help me forget? Make a new memory?"

He did not look surprised or disgusted. He held out his hand, "One night."

"It's all I need." I took his hand.

He walked me through to what was a beautiful bathroom. Everything from the tiles to the towels was beautiful. He flicked on the taps to fill the bath. I was kind of hoping we would just have sex with the lights off. My breasts were still discoloured. I had bruises everywhere and suddenly I did not want him to see me naked.

He turned his back, unbuttoning his shirt. I watched in the mirror. His body still beautiful, strong despite the cancer ravaging him. The cancer which would soon claim his life. He took off his shirt, throwing it on the floor, stepped out of his shoes, removed his socks before slipping off his suit pants and boxers in one go.

He stood bare before me, watching like a hawk for a minute. Slowly, he reached out to unbutton my top. I did not stop him, but I looked away. I did not want to see his reaction.

"Why did you look away?" he asked softly. "Do I frighten you?"

I shook my head, "I thought we might just have sex with the lights off."

He chuckled. "When I am done with you there won't be an inch I haven't touched." He slid my shirt off my shoulders, "I have waited years to see you naked. Do you really think I would turn off the lights when I have someone as beautiful as you to look at?" He reached around and unclasped my bra, letting my poor boobs free. I shook my head.

"I hate what he did to you. But even with a few bruises you are beautiful." Charlie bent down removing my skirt and panties. "Look at me," he commanded softly. I shut my eyes, and gathered my courage before obeying.

With his eyes on mine, he leaned forward and ran his nose up my slit. I gasped at him, shocked. He winked at me then grinned as he stood up smoothly. He picked me up and got into the tub with me safely in his arms.

The water was the perfect temperature and being held against his chest was divine. I lay there listening to his heart. He held me for a few minutes before moving me off his lap. Using the liquid soap that smelt of ylang ylang and roses, he washed every inch of my skin, massaging my sore, bruised body gently.

I went to get the soap and return the favour, but Charlie shook his head, "This is for you. When I am done you will never have to scrub yourself again. He will be gone, and you can move on."

I let him wash me. I relaxed and before I knew it, I was begging for his touch. Oh my, it had been so long since I was last seduced, I hadn't even realised it was happening!

Out of the bath, he dried me gently then himself quickly as I panted for him.

"If you don't want sex, say so now,", his eyes dark with lust.

"Be gentle, don't hold me down." I almost choked on my words, "And please don't choke me."

He scooped me up and took me to his bed. "I want to fuck him off you. I want you to orgasm 'til you pass out. I want you to be happy. Do not let that fucker hold you back from finding someone nice and settling down. One night, Hannah. That is all you get."

He was begging for understanding. He wanted me to know that this was going to be it. I would never see him again. Slowly, I nodded. He looked pleased then put me on the bed and picked up a tie hanging over the bed end.

"Hands out. I am a Dom, some things I can't change. I will be the one touching. Not you. Understand?"

I held my wrists out, in answer to his question. He wrapped it around my hands almost as if he were bandaging them together, but he left it loose without a knot before he kissed me.

Fucking hell, I got wet, my breath kicked up a notch and I could not touch that handsome man because he wrapped my FUCKING HANDS!

He chuckled as he broke the kiss, laying me back on the bed. "You are so beautiful Hannah. I have wanted to do that for years." He kissed along my jaw and neck holding my arms above my head gently. "You taste even better than I thought you would."

Damn… it felt *good*. No fear. Nothing but him. He was attentive, careful of my bruises, gentle on my body as he touched me everywhere, kissed me everywhere. I was fine until he went to kiss my lower lips… I flinched.

He kept his cool. "Trust me?" His hands stroked my thighs. "I won't hurt you."

"I know. I want this."

He nodded, still stroking my thighs. He kissed from my knee up toward the apex before repeating on the other leg. I thought he would do it again, but his hot mouth went over my clit, licking me deep. My eyes rolled before I lifted my head to look at him. He

69

winked before he really got to work. My eyes rolled; my head went back against the mattress and I panted.

The orgasm built and I was so ready for it, then he changed what he was doing… *What the hell?* He did it again. I gave him a '*what the fuck* look'. The bastard winked and did it to me again. He was driving me out of my fucking skin!

A finger went in and I didn't flinch because he made me want to cum. *But NOOO! That would be too much to ask!* He did it again, another finger, and he did it again.

"Charlie, I need to cum," I begged. I was losing my mind.

"Not yet," was all I got right before I went to grab him by the hair. He laughed and grabbed my hands. "Not. Yet." His fingers inside me still moved at a maddening pace, hitting every spot that made me hot. "Put your arms above your head, Hannah. I am only just starting."

"I am going to rip your hair out," I threatened.

He just smiled, "Really, you want to rip my hair out?" He moved and then kissed me deeply…

His FINGERS CHANGED THEIR MOVEMENT just as I was about to CUM AGAIN! *HOW DID HE KNOW!*

"Hannah, I know you are getting sensitive. But you are going to just have to roll with it because when I put my cock inside you, you will be ready."

"I am ready now," I mewled pathetically.

"No, my dear. You are not ready. Relax, we have all night."

Well, he drove me insane. When he finally let me have his cock he stopped moving until the orgasm stopped again. He kissed me to stop the abuse raining from my mouth.

"Hannah?"

"Yeah?"

"I am going to fuck you now."

His cock hit deep inside me three times as the orgasm started to build. The sixth stroke landed sweet. I detonated. He swallowed my cries, his big body impossible to move off mine as he drove into me and the orgasm built again.

The third time he flipped me over and drove into me from behind, going deeper. He pulled my hair, slapped my ass, and rode me like a bucking bronco while I was helpless, screaming with pleasure. Completely overloaded. He swapped and changed positions, my body a slave to his.

Around four in the morning, I lay with him spooning me. Completely wrung out but the best I had felt in ages.

"Promise me you will find a nice guy who treats you like a goddess and fucks you like I did."

"Any tips on where to find him?" I smiled looking out the window.

"I have no idea." He kissed the back of my neck. "But if he doesn't fuck you like I did—he isn't the man for you."

Time would heal me properly, but Charlie had made me feel clean. He had washed that bastard off me. I smiled as I fell asleep.

## 23. Kate

I had been babysat and debriefed. I was not overly concerned about a butt plug or a dildo. He hadn't touched me other than to tape my tits. I had gotten over the drugs. Now, I was officially on holidays. I had cuddled my kids goodbye before I was put on a plane wearing headphones and a blindfold.

Yes, this is how I was flown to wherever I was going. Completely oblivious to what was going on around me. So, I chilled out to my favourite tunes. I jumped when a hand touched my shoulder and the earpiece was removed.

"We have arrived," a woman's voice said. "This man will take you to the motel." I was then instructed to put the earphone back into my ear. I thought I would be helped to stand but nope. Plucked out of my seat and carried like a child.

I was put into a car, a short journey later I was again picked up and carried. When I was finally put down, it was on to a bed, the earphones were removed, then the blindfold. Blinking, I looked at the man who had carried me—obviously security.

"Hi."

"Your room card." He handed it to me. "Welcome to the Diamond. Your bags are in the closet. Enjoy your stay."

With that he left hastily. I looked at the card key. There was no clue to where I was. I got up and went to the window and opened the curtain, praying Smith didn't just send me to Vegas.

HE SENT ME TO FUCKING VEGAS!!!! My phone rang and I smirked as I glanced at the caller ID.

"Real funny cunt aren't ya! What the fuck am I supposed to do in Vegas?"

Well the laughter said everything, back home I was on speaker. I smiled despite myself. *Wankers.*

"You have fun, get drunk, have sex, maybe find a new husband," Smith suggested as the rest of the zoo laughed.

"I think the first thing I am going to do is sleep. Then I will see."

"Sleep is a good start. Have fun." He hung up on me. I giggled looking out at the view.

"Chris, I can hear you laughing. I love you. Please keep me out of trouble."

## 24. Charlie

Ben, Ian, and Richard just agreed to do whatever I wanted before showing them the bucket list. Good thing I got Richard a free pass, huh? Now we were walking around looking for number one on the list.

*Pick a random hottie.*

Ian and I were going to have a threesome with this chick if we could find someone to agree. We hit up a couple of women who were happy to do the sex part of the list… but nothing else. We walked onto the casino floor laughing about the last chick who had crazy written all over her and how she had been more interested in Richard than us.

"It is a good thing you are married," Ian teased. "She is exactly the kind of crazy you used to like."

"Shut up," Richard grinned. "Go on, pick your victim."

Ian had stopped laughing. He was staring across the room. I followed his line of sight.

"The single woman at the blackjack table?" I asked.

"Nah. You don't want her. She looks rough and a fucking ten on the crazy scale," Ben said. "Come on, there are plenty more fish in the sea." He went to move on but stopped when we did not budge.

I cocked an eyebrow. That was weird. I looked at the woman then at Ian then back to her. Her eyes met Ian's then, ever so casually, she turned back to the dealer, checked her cards, and put them down.

"She didn't mean to look you in the eyes," Richard noted then he looked at Ben. "She is a pretty, little thing."

"She looks like trouble." Ben muttered, watching Ian. "Really? You like her?"

Ian nodded. "Yep, Charlie? Thoughts?"

I looked her over, she was beautiful. Ian had not taken his eyes off her. If I couldn't talk her into the list, maybe he could talk her into bed, and I might get my brother back.

"Yes, let's go have a chat." I added, "She looks just like your kind of crazy, Ian." *Holy shit, he wants a woman!*

"Yours too." His eyes not leaving her.

I studied her as I approached, Ian was right.

Then Ian did something I would not have expected in a million years. He took my arm and snarled in my ear… "We might share her, but she is *MINE*."

## 25. Kate

It was hard to turn off your training that had you scanning for threats even when you managed to get out and go on a holiday. When you wanted to drop your guard, relax and be normal. Like right now, I was dressed up, hair done, makeup on, even wearing heels that were surprisingly more comfortable than the combat boots I was so used to wearing. But it didn't stop my awareness of who was around me, what they were doing and where the exits were.

I was staying in one of the best hotels and casinos in Vegas, The Diamond. Everything sparkled, there were mirrors everywhere. The lighting was bright, the punters were happy and well looked after and the service was exceptional. The security was brilliant, moving around casually; the patrons hardly noticed they were there. I noted that they were all ex-servicemen.

I sipped a mojito as I walked around, looking for something exciting to do. I was bored. Why the hell my beloved family thought it was a great idea to send me on holiday on my own, I had no idea. Maybe it was because of what I had told them about Chris and his vision… that I would meet the new husband in Vegas. I wandered past some slot machines and put money in random ones and lost, of course.

It was an interesting experience, watching people get drunk and blow their hard-earned money. It was even more interesting to watch the whales make stupid bets with stupidly high amounts. I shook my head disgusted. Must be nice to have so much money that you can be so irresponsible. I went to a free table and tried my luck at blackjack.

"It's not a lucky table tonight," The dealer told me as I put my chips on the table.

I smiled, "It's alright, luck can always change."

I sat there winning some and losing others so that it didn't become obvious that I was counting cards. Still bored, another mojito later, I was two hundred grand up. I would be debt free by the end of the night if I stayed on this 'streak'. It was a good feeling but drinking and gambling was only fun to a point.

Where the hell was the action happening? Where was all the fun?

Laughter got my attention as four men came in. They were all tall, three had to be closely related but there was one with lighter brown hair who looked a lot like my estranged half-brother, Ben. The chances that it was him was like one in seven billion. I had seen him once, from a distance.

The taller of the men had a styled beard, not much more than a five o'clock shadow. I bet he had a babyface and this was his way of making him look his age. I smirked, Chris had been like that, hence he had loved his beard. This man's eyes were light blue. His smile lit up his face. He was relaxed and seemed happy. He had an air of old money about him, but it was his dominant undertone that I liked. He was powerful.

The man to his right was clean-shaven. Not a hair out of place. Like the man with the beard, he carried himself with an air of dominance and the grace of old money. His eyes were a medium blue, his hair was brown. He smiled and laughed as they stood talking.

I turned my attention to the man with hair colour close to my own colouring, a light brown with golden sun highlights. He really did look like my half-brother. I quickly concluded he was ex-military and well-schooled in the art of social etiquette.

I wondered if this was someone's buck's night as I deliberately lost a hand and pouted. I watched the man with almost black hair out of the corner of my eye. He had to a be a brother of the first two… and he was looking directly at me. He was tall, around my age and carried himself with the grace of the first two, only I bet this guy did some sort of martial arts. I also noted he hadn't taken his eyes off me since they stopped.

Being discreet when observing people was a skill, I was well trained in. The one with a beard, glanced at me, inwardly I smiled. This could be interesting. They were up to something and I was now apparently in their sights. Playing my next hand, I wondered if they would come over. He was talking to his friends, especially the one that had the dark hair. He needed a name, so he was dubbed TDH (Tall, dark, and handsome). Lifting my eyes for another scan of the room and I locked eyes with TDH. I didn't mean to do that! *FUCK!*

TDH was hot. Scratch that, he was hotter than a solar flare. I looked back at the dealer and then my cards pretending my heart rate hadn't just gone from a relaxed 60 beats a minute to 120, that my skin wasn't flushed with adrenalin because I had been caught looking at possibly the hottest man on the planet. Out of the corner of my eye, I saw the men debate as I took a breath to calm myself. The last thing I needed to do was look like a deer caught in headlights. *I was no prey.*

TDH and the beard watched me before both smiled. They looked as if they were discussing the rules of engagement before shaking hands. They made their way toward me with their two mates following behind. Both smirking.

Things were about to get interesting. Finally, a bit of fun. Maybe, let's see what they put on the table.

They all parked their arses on the empty seats beside me. I was between the beard and TDH. The dealer was waiting on me to make my move. I tapped the table and the man beside me muttered something like, you will lose your money…

Apparently, I wasn't stupid because I won the hand. I didn't smile or look at him when I muttered back. "You were saying?"

"I admit it, I was wrong." He turned to me. "Would you like to play a game?" He watched me, reading my reaction, noting he wasn't the only one. TDH was being discreet, but he too was looking me over in that good way. His presence made my spine tingle with awareness.

"What kind of game?" I asked as the dealer took out a new deck of cards and dealt. I didn't look at him, I just waited. The ball was in his court.

"The kind that involves you hanging around with us while we tick shit off my bucket list," he shrugged.

I frowned, 'bucket list' was not a term I liked. I held out my hand. "Have you got the list?"

Mr Beard put a piece of paper in my palm, and I opened it carefully to peruse a list of thirty items including kinky sex, getting head, threesome and then making love. That was weird.

I made a face and folded the paper before putting it down to think. Checking my cards, twenty-one. I stayed and went back to the list. There was nothing about drugs but there was a lot of dancing, drinking, paintball, skydiving, firing a gun, getting married and then divorced.

I had to smile at that. I bet he swore never to do it. Now making love made sense. He had never been in love and wanted someone to show him. Maybe he wanted to fall in love? My heart ached at the thought of falling for a dead man. I wasn't healed enough for this. Come on man, give me a reason to turn you down.

"Are all those activities and shows pre-booked with proper instructors?" I wanted to make an informed decision, casually looking back at the cards on the table.

"For the dangerous stuff, yes." He nodded and pointed at my cards. He had beautiful hands. They were big, like him. His fingers were that of a musician's. He had to be six feet six inches tall. "Are you going to show your cards?" I flipped them and he groaned. "You just took me for twenty grand."

"Well it sucks to be you," I smiled sweetly before I issued my dare. "Would you like to play again?"

"Hell yes." He laughed as the cards were dealt. He waited 'til we were halfway through the hand before casually asking, "Are you interested in playing with us?"

Was I interested! But sex? Sounds fun but nah. Not real interested in that.... Fucking hell that TDH is sexy... Mr Beard was one hot man too... No, remember you didn't come here to hook up. You came to relax... I wonder what his cologne is... *SHORTY! STOP IT! FUCK!* You were toast after one look. One sniff and you already have to hold your knickers up to stop them falling off.

*NUN STATUS BITCH! THAT MEANS NO SEX!*

"You have an interesting bucket list." I concentrated on the dealer instead of being in my own head and the internal struggle of my sexual attraction to a man for the first time in over three years.

"Yes, I have a lot of boxes to tick." He agreed with a nod, now concentrating on his hand. Apparently, he didn't like to lose.

"How sick are you?" I asked, please don't say terminal, please don't say terminal...

"Terminal," he admitted with a nonchalant shrug. "Got a month max. I could go anytime though."

*FUCK!* I was a hard woman, battle worn, three and a half years ago I had my heart broken and I never thought I could put it back together. If it weren't for the kids, I wouldn't have. The marriage and the sex part of the list was something I didn't want to do, but the man was dying. I can't have pity sex, that would just be mean. I am sure you must like someone to have sex with them. But what if I liked him....

I started to weigh up how bored I really was because as much as this could be a lot of fun, I could end up hurt emotionally…. Was it worth the pain? Could I do it again? Are you drunk and seriously considering it? Shorty? *What the fuck are you doing?*

"You have someone in mind for fourteen through to twenty?"

"Yes. She is kicking my ass in a game of cards," he said with a cheeky grin. *Oh, you are a smooth fucker.*

"Are you always this random?" I turned toward him. He was handsome, his eyes had a touch of yellow in the whites but otherwise he looked okay.

"No. Never. If you hadn't noticed, you are number one on the list. Pick a random hottie." He pointed at his list.

I smiled and handed the list back to him, "You may want to consider someone else for fourteen to twenty but the rest of it I would be happy to do."

We played cards in silence and then he turned to me, "How long since a man touched you as in nineteen, Make love?"

Too long. Only because I want Chris back. Not that abstaining would bring him back. "Five years," I said, not looking at him. Every man including the dealer gasped in surprise and disapproval before the dealer composed himself. "You all right there?" I glared at him in warning. "Don't repeat it."

He nodded. "Yes, Ma'am."

"No. I don't understand," Mr beard beside me exclaimed softly, turning to look me over. "I don't get it. How can you not do that in five years'?".

"It is your bucket list. How can you have not done that in a lifetime?"

"Touché," he muttered to himself. "Yeah okay. I will give you that one because the only answer is I have never been in love. To me it was an inconvenience and having one woman in bed every night sounded like a nightmare. I only had to look at the level of crazy my brother's wives bought out from time to time to decide it was not worth it."

It was an honest answer. I pondered it and decided that he must never have found the girl to make him drop his guard enough to fall. I won another hand. His mate, Mr TDH, seemed to think this was funny. I glanced at him and smiled, when his eyes met mine, so full of life and so blue, sparkling like the ocean at midday...

*Oh, that smile could turn your panties to ash, spread your legs and hope he pulled down his zipper...*

*How many drinks have I had? Am I doing this? Yes, alright. But make him work for the sex. What the fuck was in that drink?*

I stood up, collected my chips, and thanked my dealer. Mr Beard watched me, mouth open, almost panicked. He stood up. He was well and truly taller than my five-foot two-inch frame.

"Where are you going?" he asked.

"I am going to go and cash in these chips. That is what you do in a casino," I said walking toward the cashier.

"Are you going to help me with my bucket list?" he asked as he followed me. The way he said it had me turn to look up at him. He was handsome. He was tall and his body still strong enough for shenanigans, but now he was worried he just spent the last hour laying the groundwork for someone to play with, only to be turned down. No doubt he rarely got turned down and didn't like the feeling.

"What made you pick me?" I needed to know.

"You were on your own, looking bored," he said, studying my face, not my chest. *Good move.* "Will you help me with my bucket list? You do not have to do it all if you don't want to. I am not going to promise not to try to seduce you though. Until I do, you can just be one of the boys."

His eyes stayed locked on mine as I nodded, "Alright. One of the boys it is. Everything else we will see."

## 26. Charlie

My eyes went wide as I stared at this beautiful little pocket rocket after she said she would help me. I could not help being extremely happy. I thought for sure that she would turn me down. My list was ludicrous. I mean the things that were on my bucket list were not for pretty and petite little women. They were rough and scary.

But I had to ask myself why would she go five years without sex? She was beautiful. I looked at Ian who would be part of the threesome if she went through with it. He looked pleased. *Very pleased.*

Ian smirked at me then he turned his gaze to her. I saw his eyes flash. I realised he was more than a little attracted to this little pocket rocket. Ian had not looked twice at a woman since his wife died, well not like he was looking at our new friend. It had not been a figment of my imagination when he claimed her an hour ago. Both Richard and Ben looked as surprised as me. Ian had never done that. Not even to Aria. Maybe I would sneak another thing onto the bucket list. I wanted to see him remarry. If I did not put it on the list, he would never do it. He had been alone too long. It was time for him to move on.

We took her to cash in her chips. She had managed a three hundred-thousand-dollar win. I was impressed but, watching her play, I figured she was counting cards. Not that I would say anything. Her clothes and shoes were nice, but not expensive. My guess—she was here just for a holiday, to get away from things.

I owned the Diamond and did not mind that she could potentially take me to the cleaners. "That is a nice little win," I commented. "Have you got plans for it?"

Smiling up at me "Yep, that just about paid off my house. Just a car and a couple of student loans to go."

She was not being greedy; just paying off her debts. I hated being stolen from, but she was doing it to ease financial burden. I took her hand as we went upstairs.

"So, what's the first thing we are going to do?" she asked.

"We are going to a private party," I smiled at her, looking her body over.

We got to a room where one of the whales was partying. He was a douche who loved high end hookers, escorts and paid for the best. He also wanted a contract with me, and this was his version of smoothing the path. He was smart, good at his job and kept his parties like this discrete. Which was the only reason I was turning up.

I glanced at Ben who was watching our new friend, not looking at all impressed. I had to wonder what his problem was. Ben had tried to talk us out of approaching her. I looked back at my pocket rocket and wondered how she would react to what was ahead. There was no end like the deep end. She would either chuck a tantrum or walk away.

This was going to be full on—even for me. Ian was chatting to her, looking happy and relaxed. If I was not mistaken, he was pulling some subtle moves on her. I glanced at Richard and Ben who indicated that she would walk out, disgusted. I bet them she would not, just to be a recalcitrant. *Game on.*

We arrived at the whale's room only to be greeted by two bouncers. We were frisked. Kate gave me a questioning look. I just shrugged as we were let in.

Inside there was so much naked flesh walking around it was insane. Even at the club where clothing was optional, but here there were some of the most beautiful women I had seen naked— all in one suite. The women seemed not to care, for them it was work. And work it they did. The men openly looked and touched as they pleased. The women flirted and encouraged them.

The host had a woman in his lap riding him, she had the best set of fake tits I had ever seen. He looked up at her, lips parted, one hand on her hip, the other on her tit squeezing her nipple with no skill at all.

He smiled and waved us over. He shook our hands as the woman worked on his lap. She was going through the motions, but he was getting off. I felt sorry for her. He was high, and she was not having fun. Our host looked at my little pocket rocket then at me as I bent down and kissed the hooker's ear and neck before I nipped at it. She sighed and moaned.

I reached around and ran my hands lightly over her nipples. They responded, going hard.

"Fuck she just got so wet," our host groaned, holding her hips as she moaned softly to my kisses and nips. He held her hips as he pumped into her. I reached for her clit and although he was useless, I was not. She came before he did. She collapsed on his chest panting hard as he finished.

He looked up at me, touching her ass, "You bought a woman to the party? You know this is full participation or get out."

# 27. Kate

I had never seen so many naked women in my life. Every one of them was damn near perfect with arses and tits that could make an onion weep with joy. Now, I was informed of participation. Considering I just watched him fuck a woman who looked like she wanted to be anywhere but on top of the host, before Mr Beard worked his magic, it didn't take a genius to work out what was going on.

This had to be a test.

"She is one of the boys tonight," Mr Beard said to the host with an up nod. The host shrugged and told us to enjoy ourselves. We got drinks and sat down on a couch.

"Charlie," Mr Beard introduced himself, holding out his hand with a panty melting smile.

"Kate." I shook his hand, his handshake firm but gentle. There was a little bit of buzz in the contact too. Okay, this is a good sign.

Then I thought… *is that the hand he touched the hooker with?*

"This is Ian," he introduced Mr TDH. "That is Richard, and over there, is Ben," he finished.

The one who reminded me of my brother Ben was called Ben! *What the fuck?* He didn't want to know me, so I guess it didn't really matter. Can't be him. What would be the odds?

"G'day boys. Soo... What is the point of all the naked women?" *Please don't say I have to fuck one.*

"We are going to get blowjobs," Charlie said matter-of-factly. "The girls here are clean, well paid for their efforts and their discretion. After this, we are going to go and drink and dance."

Blowjobs? Seriously? Oh, okay. I was the one about to get fucked. What the hell did I agree to? Bored now Shorty? "Why blowjobs?" I s'pose that isn't too bad… How many fucking drinks did I have? I did complain of being bored… Well I'm not fucking bored now! Get up and walk out, you can't do this!

"Why not? I am dying and I want one. I have paid for them and that is what we are going to do." Charlie stated. He thought I was going to run. *Fat chance buddy, I walked into war zones, I can do this. You wanted a playmate Shorty? You got four. Have you gone insane? Looks like it.*

"Are these guys helping you with the bucket list?" I pointed at the men either side of us. I was sandwiched between Ian and Charlie and not feeling at all uncomfortable.

"They made the mistake of saying 'whatever you want to do, we will do'. Minus me having sex with them," Charlie smirked.

"Yeah you can keep your cock away from us," Ben stated. "I want none of that action."

Charlie laughed, "You are safe."

"I haven't agreed to that either," I stated firmly. "There is no guarantee I will."

"No, but I think you will." Charlie smiled confidently, giving me a wink as a woman approached him with a wicked grin.

"Oh, hello trouble." He was seriously smooth as he patted his leg. "Take a seat for a moment." She straddled his lap and kissed him. Charlie let her have the upper hand for a second before his hands went in her hair and he took control.

The man must have had some talent—she melted with a moan of surrender. He was a seducer. An incredibly good one. He broke the kiss, "Blow me, beautiful."

This just got really fucking awkward. Smiling wickedly, she got on her knees. All eye contact as she undid his pants, releasing his big cock in her little hands. I was going to look away, but she effectively swallowed it.

My jaw dropped, "Well, that is fucking impressive. I did not know anyone could swallow that much cock so easily. Well done, love. You put the rest of us to shame." The young woman pulled her head off his cock and laughed at me. She was quite pretty.

"Thanks." She looked up at Charlie. "You have a very handsome cock, Sir," then swallowed his cock again. He growled and his head went back as his eyes rolled.

Must have felt good because it was fucking impressive to watch. Soon, all four men were being blown (I tried not to look at Ben. He wasn't my brother but yeah nah. Not watching, just in case).

I sat there feeling awkward, completely captivated by the woman who could swallow a cock that well. Seriously, it was cool. I never got past the gag factor. Charlie did have a handsome cock. As did Ian. His was slightly bigger and circumcised. Hmm, very nice cocks. I absently wondered what Ian's tasted like.

I had come out of my thoughts for a moment to check the exits and see who was around, when a soft body moved on to my lap. She was beautiful, seductive, with hazel eyes and an amazing body. She took my hands and ran them over her tits and belly.

She was seducing me… well this was different. I had never been seduced by a woman before.

"Before you decline, you are one of the boys, remember," Charlie reminded me with lusty eyes.

"I can't do that here." I whispered to him in protest as the woman got off my lap and knelt on the ground in front of me. She parted my legs and I closed them, pulling my skirt down to cover myself.

"You are one of the boys," Ian said as he and Charlie took one of my hands each, linked their fingers with mine, and the woman smiled and parted my knees again.

"Trust me," she said, reaching up my skirt and feeling my panties. "Hmm lace, very nice." She moved my panties aside, winked at me and pulled my butt, so I was slouched on the couch. Ian and Charlie hooked one of my legs each holding them open.

At this point my heart was hammering. I had never had a woman touch me like this before and I hadn't been pinned by two men while she did it either. A flashback to a week ago entered my mind for just a moment. I kicked that thought in the balls and sent it packing. It had no place here.

She gave me a wink and her head went under my skirt; her mouth was where no one had touched me in over five years. She was hot, wet, skilled, and made my eyes roll just a little.

"Fuck," I swore softly, my head going back. She giggled under my skirt before licking up my inner flesh then moving me again, spreading me like a feast. This woman was surprisingly strong.

Charlie and Ian still held my hands and they chuckled. I glanced at Charlie who grinned at me. Eyes heavy with lust, he concentrated on the woman getting him close to orgasm. Ian stroked the woman's head bobbing on the end of his cock. He was tender and gave her his attention, looking her in the eye as she worked. But he also held my hand firmly, as did Charlie.

Hazel eyes was down there working incredible magic. It wasn't long before I was panting and swearing, not giving a shit about who watched. The orgasm rolled over me and though I tried to be quiet, a throaty moan escaped as I tried to arch my back. But I couldn't because of the way I was sitting on the couch. Panting, watching her as I came down. She put my panties back into place then moved out from between my legs and closed them. She grinned at me and I gave her an embarrassed smile. I can't believe I let her do that, and I enjoyed it!

"You are yum."

"How yum?" Ian asked as he was about to come. She smiled and leaned over me to kiss him. He sucked on her top lip and groaned. Charlie reached across me and took her hand. She went to him. He kissed her too, sucking on her bottom lip. *They were tasting ME and using her to do it!*

Ian was sexy as he came. His cheeks flushed and his beautiful lips parted for a moment before he threw his head back and growled, his jaw clenched. But not once did he stop stroking the woman's hair. When he returned his attention to her moment later, taking a few deep breaths he have her a tiny smile as thank you. She gave him a coy smile as she licked her lips.

On the other side of me Charlie was about to come so I turned to watch. He was sexy when he came too, only he didn't break eye contact.

There was something satisfying about both men getting off. I turned my attention back to the woman with hazel eyes who had moved back into my lap.

"Come here. You girls did so well, I am going to give you both an orgasm," Charlie said with a wicked smile. He helped the girl that just swallowed his load up onto his lap before he turned to hazel eyes. "You wait right there."

"Waiting patiently." She smiled and grabbed my hair before putting her mouth over mine, delivering my first female kiss. I couldn't stop her because Charlie, and Ian, still had my hands. I kissed her back. She really did have a wicked tongue. She broke the kiss. "You haven't been touched for a long time have you." She touched my face tenderly.

I shook my head, "Shit happens, and you don't want to anymore."

She nodded. "You did enjoy it though, didn't you?"

"Yes, I did." I smiled and she grinned. "I think you might have just got me back in the game."

"I hope so, you taste too good to be out of it." Her eyes were sincere.

I had to ask the question, so I whispered, "Why are you doing this?"

"Because it pays well. At the end of the year I will have my debt paid off, my children's education paid for and be able to buy a house. Then I can retire into a normal boring job that will pay the bills. That and I am a nympho, so it scratches the itch."

I laughed as the girls near us were ready to cum. "You get a little of that next. Are you excited?"

"Hell yes." She grinned. "Can I kiss you while he does?"

Well I had gone this far, why not! "I want to watch you cum." *I wonder if my drink was spiked.*

She nodded as the woman on Charlie's lap came like she was hit by a freight train, crying out her ecstasy before collapsing against his chest. He held her, stroking her back as she regained normal breathing. She opened her eyes after a minute and sat up. He smiled and she blushed.

"Thank you, beautiful," he said and kissed her sweetly. She gave him a wink as she got off his lap and walked to the bathroom. He sucked his fingers then looked at my girl. "Come here, I have wicked and wonderful things to do to you." He plucked her off my lap and put her on his. I smiled as she gave him her attention. He whispered in her ear and she listened as he stroked her body.

Ian's girl was now mid throes of an intense orgasm. She collapsed against his chest, breathing hard, her body jittering with aftershocks. He looked pleased with himself as he held her 'til she calmed, then he spanked her on the bum. She giggled before she lifted her head to look at him.

"You have amazing hands." She smiled and got off his lap and she too went to the bathroom. Ian tucked his handsome cock away. He smiled at me as I openly watched.

"Do you like what you see?" he asked casually.

I would have answered but an unsteady hand went into my hair and I was turned toward hazel eyes heavy with lust, her mouth parted to allow for her ragged breathing. Her hand in my hair pulled my mouth to hers and she kissed me hard. Moaning as whatever Charlie was doing got her off.

She broke the kiss, swore and moaned, coming toward orgasm. I held her face between my hands.

"Look at me," I demanded softly, and her eyes locked on mine.

I watched the changes in her face as her orgasm approached, then rolled over her as she cried out. I hoped I looked that pretty when I came. When she started to calm, I kissed her again as she let go of my hair. Charlie put her head against his chest. She looked at me and I smiled.

"That was the most intense finger fucking I have ever had." She sighed and then she turned her face to Charlie "You Sir, have some serious talent."

He grinned, "Like that, did you?"

"Loved it." She smiled and kissed him briefly then kissed me a little longer. "Bye beautiful."

"Take care, Lovely." I smiled and she got off Charlie's lap disappearing into the crowd.

"Alright what is next?" Ben asked, clapping his hands together, ready for the next activity. I wouldn't get a crush on him anytime soon.

"Drinks and dancing," Charlie said, getting to his feet. I smirked and got up too. "You are the fucking jackpot. I am so glad I picked you."

"Really?"

"Yes," he nodded "We are going to have a lot of fun." His arm went around my shoulder, so I put mine around his waist. "Come on. Let's go drinking."

# 28. Charlie

We went downstairs and walked into my favourite bar in The Diamond. It was time to get drunk. I honestly didn't think Kate would go through with receiving head, but she did. Ian's choice of woman so far was exceptional.

Kate went to the bar to get drinks while we got a booth.

"Well, I thought she would walk out. but you were right, she stayed." Richard sat back watching her as she spoke to the barmaid. "I wonder how much she has had to drink?"

"I wonder how much she is going to drink. What's to bet we have to take her back to her room because she gets messy before us?" Ben muttered, still not impressed with our random.

*What the fuck is his problem?*

"What's to bet she puts out tonight?" Richard smirked looking at Ian. "You want to fuck her. Charlie wants her as a toy, but *you* want to fuck her."

Ian shrugged, "I don't think she will put out tonight. As for me wanting to fuck her. Yes, I do. I am not going to deny it. But she is Charlie's random, not mine."

That was a complete 180-degree turn, he had claimed her a couple of hours ago. I squinted at Ian. "You agreed to it and to her. Hell, you are the one that chose her." I am going to give this little fucker shit.

Richard and Ben smiled as Ian shook his head in pure denial. "No, I am happy to share. Just while we are here. Just a fling, that is it."

We would have given him more shit, but Kate returned with drinks and put them on the table. "There ya go boys. Drink up."

I took a mouthful and nodded, "Thank you, Kate."

She smiled and sat down. She took a sip of her mojito and sighed, "Yum."

"Have you always been into girls or was that your first time?" Richard asked, keeping it casual.

Kate shook her head, blushed, and tried to cover it up with a shy smile. "First woman. Never really been attracted to chicks. Too soft."

Interesting... "That is exactly why men like women. Because they are soft, as you put it." I told her.

"Then, if I were a man, I would be gay. I like big, tough and hard."

"And that is why men are attracted to you, you are small, soft and sensual," Ian informed her.

Kate gave me the weirdest look, "Huh?" She really did look confused and patted her stomach. "You are going to find nothing but a six pack there, buddy. I am not soft."

"You are still a woman." Ian reached over and put his big hand on her belly. "Wow you really do have a six pack under there, don't you!"

"Yeah, as I said, not soft."

Little fucker is seducing her. Okay, let's see how far he gets.

"Women, even with bodies like yours, are soft. Their skin," he touched her neck, "Their hair..." Ian ran his fingers through her hair lightly, for a moment her eyes closed before locking eyes with his, her lips parted. Ian watched her reaction intently. "See, you want to relax and just let me take the lead. You are a soft and sensual woman. That isn't a weakness."

"It is." There was a little quiver to her voice.

91

"It isn't, that is every woman's superpower. It brings men to their knees." He took all contact away from her and picked up his drink. "You have forgotten that, and that is probably why you haven't had sex in five years before tonight."

Kate shook her head as though to clear her thoughts. Then took a big sip of her mojito. "I don't need you to take the lead on anything. I have my life in order. I don't need a man to do it for me."

"I never said you needed me to take the lead," Ian stated before clarifying. "I said you wanted me to."

Kate gave him a nasty look then pointed around the room, "You could have any woman in the room. Go try them. Easier prey."

Ian smirked and leaned forward into her personal space. Kate held her ground as she looked into his eyes. He was being a mischievous little fucker tonight. Generally, he calmed down once his balls were empty. "I like a challenge."

I watched her take a shaky breath then to my surprise, she flicked him on the nose, he flinched but did not move back.

"Stand down, you horny fucker. I am one of the boys."

He gave her a smile that always seemed to get him his way. "Ah, technically yes you are, for Charlie's list. You didn't say that I couldn't try my luck."

"How do I know you aren't just trying to smooth the way for his list?" Kate challenged.

For a moment it looked like he would kiss her, but he stopped just short. "You don't. But as a rule, I don't share."

I watched Kate smile cunningly, "So you just want to get in my panties huh?" She leaned forward; her lips so close to touching his. Ian's eyes darkened. I do believe these two have more than just a little chemistry.

"Uh huh." He nodded his lips brushing hers. "I want to start with your mouth first."

Her little hand went over his mouth and pushed him back, "Not tonight, mate. Nice try." She picked up her drink and took a sip. Kate gave me an up nod. "He's a horny little fucker, isn't he?"

"Only because he knows you are a nympho who could probably keep up with him." Richard sat back looking relaxed.

Kate threw her head back and laughed. Her whole face lit up, her eyes bright. In that moment, I didn't think I had seen such a beautiful woman.

"Ha! You are funny." She got up and pointed at Richard, "Come on, I wanna dance."

Richard got up with a smile and went to dance with her. As soon as she was out of earshot, Ian groaned, running his hand through his hair.

"What's wrong?" Ben smirked into his drink. "Don't tell me Kate is getting under your skin."

Ian took a long drink and put his hand up for another drink. "No, she isn't getting under my skin. I am smoothing the way for this threesome." That might have sounded plausible if he did not sound like a brat when he said it.

"Sure, sure." I used my wise man tone, "You have some serious chemistry happening between you."

"Yes, they do." Ben agreed watching her for a moment as she danced. "She is going to be a handful with a couple more drinks in her system. She is a wild one."

Ian nodded, "I wonder if she would sub out?"

I shrugged; I already knew she would, just from her reaction to Ian. But I doubted she was a true submissive. "I don't know. Is it going to worry you if she can't?"

"No, I like sex vanilla maybe with a few add-ons. I am not like you. I don't need the dungeon."

"You have lived as a Dom for years, Ian. You might find it hard to let go of the reins," I said.

93

Ian shrugged, "Are you going to be able to let go of the reins for one night?" he made a good point. "You have never done it."

"I have a few times. I have let female Doms have a go," I admitted.

"Right before you topped them." The little shit smirked.

## 29. Kate

I danced with Richard and had another drink before we moved to another club where we did a lot more drinking and dancing… I got very drunk. *Very, very drunk.* I was slurring my words and starting to stumble when I walked. All the boys were playful in their teasing even though they were just as drunk as me.

"I need to go to bed," I slurred when they told me we were about to go to another bar. "I can't drink anymore tonight."

"I will take you." Ian smiled and I shook my head. I have to say he looked hurt. Ian pouted; he was so cute I had to stop myself reaching for his face. "Why not?"

"I can take myself to bed," I slurred insistently.

"Then we will all take you," Ian said, putting his arm around my waist.

I pushed him off. "I am a big girl. I will take myself."

After an argument, which I lost, they walked me back to my room. They told me they would see me in the morning. I patted Charlie's arm. I liked him. He was nice. Ian made me want my panties to fall off. Richard was cool because he didn't hit on me… and Ben, *well* he was good for conversation. I shut the door leaving them outside, went to my bathroom and bought up all the contents of my stomach.

I wasn't sick. I just preferred to empty my gut after the night of fun and fill it with something a little better. I went to my bar fridge

94

where I had some cheese, got out a couple of slices and a bottle of water. Then I picked up my phone as I went to sit on my balcony.

"Shorty, its fucking three in the morning," Brian answered the phone sounding half asleep.

"I know. I'm drunk."

He chuckled sleepily, "Are you now? Are you drinking on your own?"

"Nah, I made some friends. I think… I have a crush. He is really fucking hot, as in, I think… I want to have sex."

"Well fuck me dead. About fucking time. So, you have fucked him then?"

"No!" I made a face. "I am going to make him work for it. I don't know, give it a couple of days. I might just discover he is the hottest fucking arsehole I have ever met. But I am thinking about it."

"Well that is good. It's about time you got back in the saddle."

I sighed, "Brian, how are the kids?" *I missed my babies.*

"They are fine. We have been hanging out and having quality time. You just relax and have some fun. And sex now that you have found someone worthy of getting into your panties."

"I don't know if he is worthy yet. We will see. Not really cool with a holiday fling."

"Well you should be. Life moves on. Chris wanted you to move on. At least have sex and clear out some cobwebs."

I laughed. "Okay I will think about it."

"Alright, I am going back to sleep. Have fun."

"I will. Night," I said as I looked out over my view and sighed.

I sipped the bottle of water slowly and the cheese—well I scoffed it down and then got a couple more slices because I was hungry. When I made my way to bed. I stared at the ceiling thinking about the weirdest night I had ever had.

I wondered if I dreamed the bit where I got head from a woman. Or that I had flirted with Ian. Not just played, flirted, something I hadn't done in years and only ever done with Chris who had always wanted a threesome. It was on that note, I went to sleep.

## 30. *Charlie*

Kate danced like a stripper, drinking with us 'til the early hours of the morning before we took her back to her room, very drunk and even more insistent that she was perfectly fine to get to bed by herself. She flirted with me a little, the more drunk she got. But it was Ian she seemed to like.

I think I underestimated just how much I had to drink because I woke up with the mother of all hangovers. After a bottle of Powerade and a hot shower, I felt semi-human. Today we would go to a few shows and drag Kate along for the ride if she was up to it. A knock at the door got my attention. Richard was outside waiting.

"I thought you would be hungover," he said as he came in.

"I am very hungover," I muttered. "I didn't think I drank that much."

"I didn't either." Then he chuckled. "I wonder how your random is feeling this morning."

"Not very well I would say. We should probably go check on her."

Richard shook his head, "Leave her sleep."

"How is Ben this morning?"

"Pissed off because he is hungover." Richard laughed then grabbed his head wincing in pain. "This is bullshit. I think that little bitch was feeding us doubles."

I nodded. "That would make sense." I rubbed my temples, got more water and handed Richard a bottle as we sat down. "How have you been feeling about the news? Are you alright?"

Richard took a long drink, not meeting my eyes, shaking his head. "No. I'm not alright. But there isn't anything I can do…" He shook his head again. "I am gutted. I thought we would be old men causing havoc."

"You will still have Ian." I tried to be positive. "He will be worse than me."

Richard tried to smile and just could not quite make it happen. "Yeah, but I thought it would be the three of us. I thought you would settle down with some wild woman and have a couple of kids. We would live as neighbours and have our yards together so our kids could play."

I watched my brother who had always planned life and the happy ending he wanted. "I threw a spanner in the works, didn't I!"

"Not you, the fucking cancer!" Richard snapped then motioned at all of me with a wave of his hand. "You don't even look sick. You have lost a bit of weight that is all. Are you in pain? Like, are you hurting bad enough to just want it to be over?"

I shook my head. "I am not in any pain at all. Except for this fucking hangover that little bitch is going to pay for with a red ass." I smiled but Richard did not. "I am going to play up, sort out my shit and have fun for as long as my body lets me. If I could go out surrounded by my family with a glass of good scotch in my hand–that would be the end of a happy and successful life. If not, I just want to go in my sleep after having some wickedly wonderful sex."

"Knowing your luck? You would go while your sub was still tied to the ceiling." Richard muttered and I burst into laughter. He was right, that was my luck. He watched me. It hurt knowing he was memorising the sound of my laugh.

It was hard, knowing I am going to die. Watching the people, I love, mourn me before I go, desperately try to memorise my voice, my laugh, my smile. It was hard watching their hearts break. I wanted to go out being me. I wanted to go out giving them happy memories. Not of a sick and decrepit man who was a shell of my former self.

People who die fast and unexpectedly seemed to be given this mercy. But I was glad I had time to say what I needed to. To have them say what they needed me to know… even though mostly, I already knew.

"You are the reason I didn't kill Ian when he was a boy." I gave Richard a playful punch in the arm. "He was such a cocky little fucker."

"He turned out alright. Considering the floggings we gave him."

"There were a few. You will have to keep up the good work."

"Nah, might adopt Kate and let her do it."

I laughed. That was a good idea. "You think she could take him? I think he would wriggle his way out of it. Ask Ben to help you."

"Speaking of Ben." Now Richard looked me in the eye, "I think he is trying to get into Tammy's panties."

I sighed. "Trying or already in?"

We debated for a few minutes before Ian joined us, looking physically green.

"If I remember correctly, she bought the drinks last night. I think she was giving us doubles on top of the shots." Ian rubbed his head as I got him a Powerade and water. I handed it to him. "Thanks Charlie."

I nodded as I sat down. Richard told him about our debate about Tammy and Ben.

"He'd better not be. I will track down his so-called sister and fuck her six ways to Sunday." Ian looked at Richard. "I warned him about it."

"I think they would actually make a good match. Ben is a good man. Respectable, good in business, self-controlled, dedicated. I think we should give him the go ahead and see if she wants him." I said, using my eternal wisdom tone. "He is ready to settle down and so is she."

Richard looked thoughtful and nodded. "I agree. She is starting to date some real losers. That Jeremy, for instance. That fucker is trouble."

Ian sighed and nodded, "That is a good point."

There was another knock on the door. I got up and let Ben in, he looked not only fine but perfectly healthy. He looked around at us and smirked.

"You," he pointed at me, "I can understand being unwell. But you two? That is just fucking weak. I have been to the gym this morning."

Ian gave him the bird, "Fuck off soldier boy. You didn't look that great when I saw you before." Then he asked him, "Are you fucking Tammy?"

Ben cocked an eyebrow. "Am I fucking your baby sister? No. Tempted to, if only to take her off the market so Vince doesn't come near her again but, no. I am not fucking Tammy."

The mention of Vince had us all sit up and lean forward, paying attention. Ben watched us, cool and calm as always.

"What do you mean Vince was near her?" I growled, I hated Vince. He was a vile piece of shit. If there was one person in the world I could be tempted to destroy, it would be him.

"Near her? No, he roughed her up when she wouldn't put out."

"He is a motherfucking dead man when I see him next," Ian snarled.

Ben's mouth lifted with a little smile. "I heard he was mugged. He still has a decent black eye for a while there."

Ian eyed him, I smiled slowly. Richard sat forward, "Got mugged, eh? You didn't happen to have anything to do with it, did you?"

"I plead the fifth." He sat back and directed his next question to me. "Would you have a problem with me taking Tammy off the market?"

I considered it for a few minutes, Ben was a good guy. He did not slut around and was good to the few women he did go out with. I shook my head. "No complaints from me. Mind you, I won't be around long enough to have you as my brother-in-law." I asked Ian and Richard, "What do you think?"

"I'm good," Richard said. "She could do worse."

"Yeah, me too."

"What about you fucking my sister?" Ben looked at Ian.

"Well you don't want to know your sister and don't really give a shit about her so why do you care?" Ian challenged Ben.

"You would fuck my sister just to fuck with me. I am not cool with that. I would fuck yours and make her my wife. There is a big difference."

"How? When you do not know her, don't want to know her, and she has no part in your life?" Ian asked. "I would just be a one-night stand, she wouldn't even know who I was."

"I do know who my sister is. Since I did a lot of research into her, I don't think she is the money grabbing bitch I figured she would be."

"Well she did come out of the woodwork after Don died," Richard pointed out.

"No, she didn't. Dad knew about her, just did not tell me. He died before he got to read the last letter from her asking to meet."

"But she wrote that letter to you. It was all mushy and full of 'concern'." Richard said.

"Yeah. But no word of money. I think I misjudged her."

I watched him, "It's because I am dying, you are wanting to connect with your sibling."

Ben shrugged, "That's part of it I suppose. But now that I have met her and hung out... I think I want her in my life."

This was news to all of us. "When did you meet her?" Richard exclaimed.

"Why didn't you tell us?" Ian added.

Ben looked at Ian then at me, "You have spent a good portion of last night hitting on her. Didn't you think it was slightly weird that I never once hit on her and actively tried to convince you not to choose her? Kate is my sister and you two have her lined up for not just a one-on-one but a fucking threesome."

He pointed at us, "I don't care, I won't think less of her because hell, I am no angel. That and she will have two nice men looking after her." He sighed, "Kate is my kid sister. She does not know it. I do not plan on telling her. But either one of you hurt her and I will rain pain all over you."

We sat back, digesting that little bit of information. We stared at each other and Ian shook his head. "I will back off. We need to find another girl. I was fine with a random we would never see again but I can't do that to Kate."

I frowned, "You sure? Because I like her. She is nice and spunky."

"I like her too. But you don't really think she will go through with it, do you?" Ian was backing down, and I felt deflated.

"Enough seduction and if you can convince her that you will respect her after, she would." Richard said. "But the whole idea is to dump her and run after, isn't it?"

"She doesn't know who I am. I will not be telling her. You can all do what you want. I just ask that you are good to her," Ben said. "I will stay in contact with her regardless."

## 31. Kate

I spent the day by the pool getting some sun, relaxing, just doing nothing. I didn't remember the last time I got to do that. The kids had called, and we had a face time chatting about everything and nothing all in one. They were happy. They even thought that the pool looked nice before telling me Nanny's was better.

I went back to my room for a nap and slept for four hours! I woke up with energy to burn so I went down to the gym and did a workout to get the alcohol out of my body. The PT was in there, working with people who wandered in. He told me he would be with me in a minute to help. I stripped to my gym clothes and flicked on the treadmill to warm up before my workout. A couple of times he looked as if he was going to tell me to take it easy or that I was using too much weight but stayed silent. When I was done and leaving, he held out his fist and I bumped it. We grinned as I left. It was a productive day.

Now, I was dressed up, ready for another night of fun. Except the boys never called. I hated to admit it, but I was disappointed, I'd had fun last night. Then I had a thought, maybe they were picking a random hottie per night to share the fun around.

So, I went downstairs to have dinner on my own. My dinner had just been served when I saw my playmates moving through the casino looking around the same way they had last night, discussing before hitting on a woman.

I must have been a one-night thing. Or maybe they were mad I gave them all a big hangover? Did I play too hard to get?

I dismissed the thought of having sex, I had gone years without. Then I decided that last night was a mistake. Fun, but a mistake. I suppose I could say that I ticked something off my own bucket list.

I ate my dinner watching them fail with the first woman whose friends came along and all started hitting on the men.

I finished my dinner paid and slipped unseen by them into the hall. If they didn't want to hang out, that was cool. I wasn't going to hang around hoping they would. I walked to the craps table and watched for a while. Old mate was on a winning streak and he had chicks all over him.

I left when he started to lose and kept betting. If he wasn't smart enough to stop while he was ahead then I wasn't going to watch the impending train wreck. Moving to the slot machines with a sigh, I got some change out of my purse and sat down. A hundred bucks would be my max in this machine.

I lost it all. Then I moved to another. Same thing. I decided that I had a three-machine limit and I was bored with the flashy lights. I wanted to move on to blackjack so I picked an older looking machine and just threw the whole hundred in and pulled the lever. I was going to walk away when I heard it slotting into place and sat back down. My eyebrows went up as alarms started going off and gold confetti fell from the ceiling.

"You have got to be fucking shitting me. You little beauty!" I laughed and caught a little of the confetti before looking back at the machine.

The next thing I knew, I was pushed from my chair and landed ungracefully onto the floor. There was yelling and some yahoo was saying he won it. I was nearly to my feet when I was shoved against the machine so hard that I bounced off it, ending up on the floor again, this time with people standing all over me. All happy for the 'winner'.

While on the ground getting trampled, I wondered why they were all so excited. It was probably only a couple of thousand bucks. I tried to get up but was kept down. I couldn't have been down for more than a couple of minutes, but I got kicked a few times and stood on a dozen or more. Then people scattered, shouting their protests.

"Move!" a man shouted.

There were more protests, then movement. A man crouched in front of me, a member of security. I went to get up, but he stopped me.

"Stay there a minute, I want to make sure you are okay."

"I am all good, Mate. Let me up," I said. "What are all these yahoos goin' on about? Anyone would think I won a million bucks."

He spoke into his radio then helped me stand up. "Fifty actually."

I looked at him shocked, my knees not real steady. "What?" He took my arm to walk me away, but I stumbled. He didn't hesitate, picked me up and carried me away from the crowd. I reckon right now I looked like a stunned mullet. "What did you just say?"

"You just won the fifty-million-dollar major jackpot," he said as another security member opened a side panel in the wall. Hmm, I never noticed those doors. I might have to have another look around. *Wait what? Did he just tell me I won fifty million dollars?* The world spun. "Woah little lady hold on. I will be able to lay you flat in a minute and put your feet up."

"Do we need an ambulance?" Another man asked.

"No, we don't need a fucking ambulance," I snapped. "I'm fine. Just put me down and repeat that ludicrous bullshit you just told me."

## 32. Charlie

I heard the fifty-million-dollar jackpot go off. We had been open for four years and this was the first time it had been won. I looked around at the boys with a big grin on my face.

"I hoped I would get to see it go off." We looked up at the crowd of people who were jumping for joy and then the fight started. I rolled my eyes. "I knew that would happen."

Ian shrugged watching then pointed. "Security is on to it."

I nodded and went back to the fourth woman I was trying to convince to do my list. She wanted the sex but nothing else, just like the other three. I wanted someone to do my list with.

I really looked at her this time. To be honest. She was not even my type. "So, you won't do the rest of the list?"

"Honey I will fuck you and whoever you want for a threesome, but I have no interest in jumping out of a plane."

I sighed, "Well you have a good night then." I looked at the boys. Ben was still watching the fuss upstairs. I turned my head and saw security carrying a woman away. "Aw shit! Don't tell me someone got hurt. Last thing I need is a fucking lawsuit."

I went to walk out the back. "Charlie leave it. You are on holiday," Ben said.

I shook my head, "I will go check everything is okay. I probably should congratulate the winner."

"It was Kate," Ben said. "I am sure she is fine. Just leave it be. If she sues then I will know she is nothing but the no-good money-grabbing bitch I first took her to be. Come on, let's find you another girl."

I had felt deflated since he had dropped the bomb on us that Kate was his sister. I had been looking forward to seducing and fucking her brains out. I wanted to see her cum from my hand and my cock but now she was off limits. I felt bad because we gave her no explanation why we had not picked her up as promised. I raised an eyebrow at Ian who shook his head and scanned the room.

"How about her?" he asked. I checked out the woman and shook my head.

"Charlie, just put banging my sister on your bucket list." Ben shrugged. "You and Ian have looked like I castrated you ever since I told you. I should have shut up and said nothing. I just did not want to get dragged into some fucking orgy and have to fake erectile dysfunction to get out of it. I won't touch Tammy as I promised."

I smiled and patted him on the shoulder. "I thought we decided you were going to take Tammy off the market."

"When she is ready." Ben shrugged, "I'm not going to rush her. And while you are sick isn't the time to be hitting on her."

"You know, I think you just got my absolute approval. I hope you live a long and wonderful life together." I patted him on the shoulder. My phone rang and I shook my head as I looked at the caller ID then up at the camera "Yes?"

"Sir, the Jackpot went off. Did you want to talk to the winner? Hand over the cheque?"

"Does the winner want the publicity?" I asked the question before...

"*NO!* I don't want any fucking publicity! I don't even want that much fucking money!" Kate exclaimed.

"Go on. We will go with her and take her out to celebrate." Ben gave me a nudge.

"You sure?" His friendship was important to me. Ben nodded. "Don't tell me to do this just because I am dying. I would not extend the same courtesy to you if it were the other way around."

"Come on. Just don't let on to who I am and please, look after her."

I took the boys out the back to the control room. We heard Kate before we saw her.

"I told you. I just want enough to pay off my fucking house! What the fuck do I want fifty million dollars for?" she shouted.

We all chuckled as we walked into my office. She looked up at us, her hair was a mess, her face pale, and frustrated, though now that she saw us—she looked angry.

"What the fuck are you doing here?"

"I came to give you your winnings." I rubbed my hands together, thoroughly enjoying her reaction. "Now, do you want a big cheque in front of the press or for me to give it to you here, nice and quiet."

The look on her face was priceless. Absolute shock. She looked from me to the boys behind me. "Don't be a wanker. You can't just sign over fifty million bucks! And how the fuck did you get back here?"

I was handed my iPad and sat down beside her. As I opened the account for the winnings, she watched me silently. When I bought up the spot for her account details, she shook her head.

"No."

"Yes. Put your account details in here please."

"This is a joke."

I rolled my eyes and glanced at my security, "Get her details. She is in shock."

"She got slammed into the slot machine and trampled, I am surprised she is conscious," I was informed as he handed me her background check with her account details on it. I started putting in the numbers.

She took a moment to realise what I was doing, "What the fuck? Charlie NO!" She tried to stop me but was restrained by my security. She swore at me to stop. Fiery little bitch was making my security work, it took three of them to hold her.

"You won it fair and square." I smiled as I checked the numbers and then put my thumb print to it, sealing the deal. "There. All done."

She stopped fighting, "I don't believe you." Her voice sounded weaker. I showed her and her eyes went wide and stared up at me in absolute shock as all fight left her. Her eyes rolled and her body went limp.

My security team lay her back down on the couch. Ben chuckled and took a photo on his phone before taking a selfie with her unconscious body. He put his phone away as she came around. Richard and Ian were trying hard not to laugh. Covering their mouths like juveniles. I had to admit, it was something we would have done to Tammy and have done to each other while passed out drunk.

Kate took a couple of deep breaths and opened her eyes, meeting mine. She almost looked lost...

"How does it feel to be a multi-millionaire?" I asked, caressing her cheek softly. "How about we go out and celebrate?"

"I want to go back to my room."

"Sir, she got slammed and trampled. That is twice she has fainted. I think she needs to be checked by a doctor."

"I told you I am fucking fine." She snapped, glaring at him, eyes wild before she redirected the glare at me, "Take the money back. Now."

"Did she win it fair and square? No cheating?" I asked security, not breaking her eye contact.

"Everything was as it should be with a genuine win," he stated. With the number of gadgets and security devices in this place to pick up cheats, I believed him.

Holding up my hands, I shrugged. "Then I can't take it back. Come on, I will escort you back to your room if that is where you really want to go, or we can go party and celebrate."

Kate covered her face and shook her head. I motioned for the doctor on call for the casino to be called in, only to be told she was already on her way.

The doctor arrived ten minutes later. Kate had not moved, nor would she show her face. We left the room to let her be examined. I watched the footage of Kate's win and her subsequent assault.

"Did you get him?" I asked.

"We did. He is chatting with police. This would be great publicity if she would have a photo for the press."

"She won't do it," I said and looked at Ben. "Do you think you could do up a press release?"

"Do I look like your PR person?" He rolled his eyes. "Yeah I will put something together."

The doctor came out a couple of minutes later, "She is going to have a couple of bruises, but she hasn't got a concussion. She is just very overwhelmed."

I went into my office; Kate was waiting.

"This is your office."

"It is when I am here." I held out my hand. "Come, let's go have a couple of drinks."

Kate hesitated, then took it. She stood up, still a little shaky. "I will just go back to my room thanks."

I walked her from my office. The boys followed us silently. We went straight to her room where she got her door card out of her purse and swiped it.

"Are you sure you don't want to celebrate?" Richard asked.

Kate shook her head. "No. You guys go have a good time."

Ian took her hand, pulled her against him and hugged her. "Congratulations. On your big win."

She slowly put her arms around his waist and then stood there with her head against his chest. "Thanks."

We all took turns hugging her, I went last. "Can I explain why we didn't come pick you up today?"

"No need. I figured you wanted a random hottie per night." Kate let me go. "I don't want any press. It will make my job incredibly hard and I have a past that would become a very fucking big nightmare if it got out. Please, don't let it get out."

The look in her eyes made me nod and agree. "We are going skydiving in the morning. Are you still up for a bit of fun?"

Kate stepped away. "I thought you wanted another woman to help you. New random hottie each night."

"Well as it turns out, every woman I asked wanted the sex and not the rest and you are the only one that wants the rest and not the sex. So, are you still one of the boys?"

She looked up at me and bit her lip, rejection in her eyes. She nodded. "Alright."

She said that and I realised she thought I was asking her because I did not want to have sex with her. I stroked her cheek before taking the back of her head and kissing her. My lips met hers and it was as if I were struck by lightning. Normally I could kiss a woman, enjoy it and have nothing but the small tingle of attraction.

This... this... I lost my train of thought as I claimed her mouth again. She tasted like lolly pops. Her mouth was greedy, her body melted like chocolate. I regained control right about the time I realised I had her straddling my hips, pressed against the wall. My cock was hard as stone. I broke the kiss and took some shaky breaths to get the strength back into my knees.

Kate's breathing was shaky. She looked shellshocked. "What was that for?"

"I always said I would kiss the winner of the jackpot."

"Lucky it was a woman."

"I am lucky it was you," I breathed, not putting her down. "Are you sure you won't come out for a drink to celebrate?"

She nodded, "If I am jumping out of a plane tomorrow, I don't want to do it hungover."

I put her down, "See you in the morning then."

Kate nodded, went into her room and shut the door. I ran my fingers through my hair giving Ben a silent apology. He patted my shoulder. We walked up the hall to the elevator. Inside I looked at Ian.

"She tastes like lolly pops."

"She melts like butter." Ian said.

"And she will sub out," Richard added. "I thought she would be a Dom like her brother, but she is a sub."

"Charlie just kissed the hell out of her! That doesn't make her a sub." Ben rolled his eyes. "If she isn't an alpha-submissive, I think she might be a switch."

And that started the debate of the evening.

## 33. Kate

Inside my room I gathered my senses. Being kissed like that had set my whole body on fire. I could still taste him on my lips. I could still feel his lips against mine, his hips between my legs, his hand in my hair and the lightning bolt of attraction that zapped me the second his lips met mine. I pulled out my phone and called Brian.

"Shorty, you are making a fucking bad habit of ringing while drunk. I love it, keep it up."

"I'm not drunk." I told him sitting down beside my tablet. "But I do need to talk. Are you half asleep or should I call back in the morning?" I opened my tablet and got into my banking. I felt nothing but panic as I stared at the fifty million in my account.

"I am at my desk, working from home because it is the end of the month. What do you need to talk about?"

"How much do we owe on the loan you took out with Morrissey?"

"The loan you are still shitty about?"

"Yeah." I wasn't going to be baited into an argument.

"Ten million. Slowly paying it off."

"Am I correct in saying that when that ten million is paid off you will officially own the business; we won't be under his umbrella?"

"We will own the business and yes, that is what the contract states." Brian confirmed. "What are you doing?"

"Well I just won fifty million on the fucking slot machines and I am paying off the loan right now," I said as I pressed in the details. "I am also about to pay off everyone's houses, cars and put money away for the kid's college funds. And I am going to buy shares. After that there should be enough for everyone to go on a holiday."

The silence on the other end of the phone was deafening. I just let him process it. I wasn't processing it. The only way I could cope with it was to get the money away from me as fast as fucking possible. If Kym found out, she would be all over me like a rash. I had finally gotten rid of the bitch and I did *not* want her near me.

"Shorty?"

"Yeah?"

"Did you just say you won the fifty-million-dollar jackpot at the Diamond?"

"Uh huh."

"You are going to get press."

"They promised. None."

"Well you should be putting that money away for safe keeping."

"I am. I just put H&S Crosshairs into the black with a nice little fund for in case. It's now in the black. Your house is paid off. Gerrard's house is paid off, Billy's house is paid off, Harry and Nelly's house is paid off. Cars are done, a million in each of the kid's trust funds for college… a million each… Yep we are now debt free."

Brian muttered and I could hear him typing. He swore and then called Emma. I heard him explain to her what had happened. I had to pull my phone away from my ear as she squealed. I smiled. It was nice to do something so good for my family who had helped me through so much. They thanked me and informed me they were going to dob on me and tell the others. I just smiled, hung up, and waited for the calls.

I bought stocks and was in the process of looking at property when Gerrard called me.

"What's this shit I hear you been up ta? You better not have done it Shorty. I will bring the smack down on your arse."

I decided to play dumb, "Done what exactly?"

"Paid out debt that wasn't yours to pay."

"No, I didn't do any such thing," I said with a smile and he sighed with relief.

"Thank God for that."

"You don't have any debts to pay out," I added.

"SHORTY! FUCK IT! WHY WOULD YOU BLOW YOUR WINNINGS ON US?!"

I laughed; he was a monster of a man. A huge wall of muscle intimidating as fuck to everyone—except me. I saw him as a teddy bear. Carrie saw him as the hottest man on earth. But to me Gerrard was a big ole teddy bear.

"Because I love ya."

"Then give me a fucking hug. Don't pay out my debt. I don't want your money Shorty."

"You don't have any debt to pay off!" I laughed. "But I love ya G, I do."

"Aw don't go getting all lovey at me. I can't stand it," he grumbled. He really didn't like it when I was nice.

"G. You are welcome." I knew he was absolutely chuffed and overwhelmed with the very extravagant gift. None of us were struggling for money. Since we had started the business, it had given us a decent wage but still, the bills needed to be paid.

"You know I have never met a more infuriating woman."

"Love you too. Talk later okay?"

"Yeah Shorty. We will." He hung up on me because he didn't like saying 'bye.

Billy rang before I could put the phone down. He went fucking postal. Ranting at me like a mad man. I just sat and laughed at him.

He called me a bitch, told me he loved me and hung up before I could say anything.

Then Harry and Nelly rang. They were the closest things to parents I had since my parents had died when I was fifteen. Harry was Dad's friend and when I told him I wanted to join the army, he and Nelly had signed me up. Harry was Chris, Brian, Gerrard and Billy's father. Nelly was Chris's step-Mum and mother to the other three.

I answered "Oi."

"Oi yourself."

"I hear you came into a bit of money."

"I heard the same rumour." Harry said softly, his voice full of emotion.

I teared up, "Are you happy?"

"Yeah." He said, "You are a good girl Katie. You didn't have to do that for us."

"I know. But I wanted too." I heard a sob in the background. "Oh, don't tell me Nelly is crying! Why is she upset?"

"She isn't crying because she is sad. She is happy the mortgage is paid."

"So are the cars and the boat," I smiled.

"Oh, you little cow. We didn't need you to pay all that off! What about your own debts?"

"Done. Paid for. Just trying to put the money to good use before I put the rest into stocks that Kym can't touch. If she finds out, she will be back."

"Well honey, think about it and spend it wisely. You have a lot of life ahead. It would be nice to see you not have to struggle."

"I am putting it away. I'll be okay. I am going skydiving tomorrow. I need to be up early."

"Okay honey. Have fun," And he hung up.

I went and lay on my bed wondering if I was dreaming about completely eradicating the biggest stresses in my families lives—house and car repayments and the fear that we would never afford for our kids to attend college.

Oh, and the business debt. It would be nice to see Morrissey sign it over to us in full, now that the debt was paid. Hell, even my debts were officially gone. I smiled as I shut my eyes happy, confused, and overwhelmed. As I fell asleep, I thought about the breathtaking kiss Charlie had delivered.

## 34. Charlie

By the time I got up the next morning, it was time to go jump out of a plane. Ian had already brought Kate from her room. She seemed calmer, like she had gotten over the shock of becoming an instant millionaire. I, though, had not gotten over the shock of my reaction to kissing her.

Ian was openly hitting on her; he could not help himself. He was pulling all his old moves and some new ones too. I smiled when he told me he was laying the groundwork for the threesome. But he was full of shit. Ian liked her as much as I did. I still could not get that kiss out of my head. I had gone back to my room and masturbated to let off some steam.

We drove to the airport and had a briefing before our tandem jumps. Kate looked calm and happy. We got on the plane and half an hour later we were at 14,000 feet, ready to jump. The plane's engine was surprisingly loud, the air rushing past was noisy and cool.

Kate was the only one who looked relaxed. I personally, was shitting myself, and by the looks on the boy's faces, they were too. Well except for Ben, but he was ex-military. He had done this before.

I planned it, it was my idea, so I went first. Leaving the plane was the most terrifying thing I had ever done in my life. The free fall had me completely disorientated. I looked up at the sky, watching everyone else jump from the plane. It only took a minute to start enjoying it. I was weightless. This was the most freeing experience I had ever had. Kate and Ben jumped before Ian and Richard. I waved to them with a big smile on my face. This was great fun!

Only when Kate and her instructor were right with us did I figure out something was wrong. She grabbed my hands and flipped me, so I was facing the ground. She pulled me to her and reached behind me… it was as if I was shot up into the air. She was below me now and her chute deployed a second later. Then I realised the instructor behind me was kind of just flapping around. That was not comforting.

Kate was back and to my absolute fucking horror she hooked her legs around my waist and her instructor released her from his harness. She grabbed on to some handles that had been useless until she got a hold of them and then her instructor was gone. She took control of our descent. I held on to her, afraid her legs would weaken, and she would fall. I would never let that happen.

She was calm all through our descent, even smiled at me comfortingly. A few minutes later she reached around me as we neared the ground.

"Legs up. This is going to hurt. When I release the chute let me go!" she ordered and then she shouted… "NOW!" The 'chute released. I let her go and we tumbled. When I rolled to a stop, my instructor was on top of me. I could not move; he was too heavy. A moment later she was there, releasing him, rolling him off me.

"Charlie! Are you okay?" Kate asked, now tending to my instructor.

"Yeah. You are fucking insane?" I shouted as I got up. *Fucking stupid woman could have been killed!*

"Yeah that's what happens when you pick up a random. That'll learn ya," she said as she started to give him CPR. I would like to be able to say I helped but I felt ill and sat watching her. Then Ben was at her side helping.

"What do you need me to do?" Ben asked.

"Get his shirt open. With any luck these blokes have a defib," she said. Ben worked beside her as if they had done it a million times before. Ben shouted at our instructors to get a defibrillator only to be told they didn't have one, but EMS were on the way.

Ian and Richard came into land along with their instructors and Kate's. When they were down safely, they all ran toward us.

"Charlie! Are you okay?" Ian said panicked, sitting in the dirt to check me over. "You are bleeding." He got a hanky out of his pocket and pressed it to my brow.

"I am okay," I said, patting his arm.

"I thought you were going to die," Ian said, looking like he was having a heart attack. Richard sat with us but watched Kate and Ben.

"I am dying, Ian. There is nothing going to stop it. If it had happened then, I would have died happy, feeling free."

I worried about Ian and what he would do when I died. He was struggling. Richard was too but he seemed to have accepted it, like I had. Kate's instructor called her *batshit crazy*. She shook her head as Ben assisted her.

There were things happening around us that I could not pay attention too. I think I was in shock. My body shook from the adrenalin. Soon the medics arrived, Kate did a whole heap of medical speak as she assisted them to get my instructor on a stretcher and loaded into the ambulance before they rushed off with lights and sirens blazing. While all this happened, another crew checked me over.

Kate stood back watching as they worked on me. Ben stared down at his little sister for so long that she looked up at him. After a moment Ben gave her an up nod and she gave him a little nod. It was the weirdest thing, watching them. I turned my attention back to the medics as they cleared me. Other than a cut on the head and a few bruises, I was fine.

When we got back to The Diamond Richard, Ian, and I were all shook up. We went up to my room dragging Kate with us. I was beginning to think she *was* as batshit crazy as her instructor had said. I called room service and had them deliver food and drinks. I was trying to keep busy so I would not yell at Kate for being so fucking stupid.

I turned to Kate, grabbed the back of her neck, and snapped her to me, kissing her so hard it was nearly violent. She whimpered in protest, trying to push me away. I put her against the wall, pinned her arms with one hand and moved her head with the other so I could deepen the kiss.

After a minute, I settled down and kissed her more gently, 'til she responded. I took my time making out with her for a moment before pulling away, breathless. Kate gazed up at me, her green eyes full of confusion.

"Don't you ever do anything so fucking stupid again," I growled. "I am a dead man. I am dying. You just put yourself at risk for absolutely no fucking reason!"

"I beg to differ. So, I suspect, do the boys." Kate eyes were defiant as she met my glare with one of her own. I saw that she would have died trying to save a dead man and not have thought twice about it. She was not batshit crazy. *She was insane!*

"How did you even know what you were doing?" I growled still pinning her against the wall.

She took a moment to answer, "I have done it before."

"You have unclipped your harness and hooked your legs around a man while he fell to his death?" I asked. "Then gave CPR like you had done it a million times. No normal person does what you just did!"

"No, I kept my harness and strapped him to my chest while falling to our deaths."

I blinked and let her go. "You are fucking insane."

118

Kate smirked, went to sit on the couch, then touched her lip. "That's what you get for picking up a random," she muttered under her breath.

"Did I hurt you?" Shit, I did not want to hurt her. If I fucked her trust, I would never get her into bed.

She shrugged, "I'm good." She looked across at the boys. "I'm starving. How 'bout you?"

"I feel sick," Richard shook his head.

"Ah, that is just the adrenalin. You'll be right, tiger." Kate said, sympathetically patting him on the shoulder.

## 35. *Kate*

Well after such an eventful jump that really should have killed Charlie and then debriefing them in his room, they decided that I was right, and it would be a good idea to rest before we continued our shenanigans tonight. I went to the gym and worked out, though not as hard as yesterday. I was sore and just wanted to walk some of it off. I did five miles before I was ready to go back to my room, get a couple of icepacks and have a nap. The gym instructor again gave me a knuckle bump as I left the gym. Back in my room, I ordered six bags of ice and had a cold shower to wash the dirt out of my hair as I waited. The ice arrived as I was wrapping a towel around my body.

Every ounce of ice went into the bathtub and I filled it with water before I got in and lay in it for as long as I could stand. Then I dragged myself out and got dry. I snuggled into bed and had a sleep after a morning that could have gone a whole lot worse. It would have been bliss if I weren't so sore.

When they didn't pick me up by eight, I thought they must have decided against going out. Or they decided that I was too crazy and really were letting me play on my own tonight. I was having another ice bath when there was a knock. I answered the door in a towel. Ben and Richard stood there. Richard looked me up and down. Ben averted his eyes.

"I thought you would be ready by now. We are going to a strip club. Are you up to coming out?" Richard stared at my shoulder where I was bruised. "You never said you were injured."

"I wasn't. Just a bit bruised is all. Nothing got broken." I rolled my eyes and sighed like he was making a huge drama over nothing. I was sore but wouldn't admit it. "Give me ten minutes to get ready. Come in." I stepped aside.

Both came in and took a seat. "I wasn't sure that anyone would be going out tonight after this morning's excitement. I thought you would rest and recover." I went to my suitcase and picked out panties, shorts and Emma's favourite fitted top that showed off my cleavage. Most importantly, it would cover my new bruises. "You especially Richard, you went quiet." I felt sorry for him. He had struggled this morning.

He shrugged, "You scared the shit out of me."

I laughed softly as I found my favourite bra and picked it up. "Sometimes that happens." I walked to the bathroom to get dressed, "Where are the other two?"

"Charlie is sleeping. He is going to come out later. Ian is video chatting with his kids, and we are bored." Ben gave me the rundown. "So, since you are such a good sport. We thought you should come out with us."

Smiling, I dressed and, put my hair up in a ponytail "How are you both after this morning?" I couldn't help myself, I wanted to make sure everything was okay.

"After seeing you have a fight mid-air with your instructor and everything after that, I think you are a nutcase," Richard said.

That made me laugh out loud. "Is that so?"

"Absolutely. Nice girls do not do that," Richard continued.

"I never claimed to be a nice girl, Richard." I put on some mascara and lip-gloss.

"Yeah well, you look it," Richard said as I walked out of the bathroom and put on some heels. "Especially looking like that."

I looked at him as I got my little bag and checked I had everything I needed. "Looking like what?"

"Woman, you have the best set of legs I have ever seen. My wife is a ballerina so that is saying something."

"How did you get free rein to be out visiting strippers then?" They both gave me weird looks. "What?"

"Are you only wearing mascara and lip gloss?" Richard asked.

That was about all I could do without looking like a clown. "I told you ten minutes to get ready. I have done it in five."

"You are naturally very pretty." Richard touched my cheek, studying me. A blush heated my cheeks, so I stepped away from him. We got out of my room and went downstairs. "You know they plan to tag team you."

*Holy fuck, not really the conversation I want to have.* "It bothers you?"

"Only that I am not invited." Richard shrugged making me I laughed at his feigned indignation. He smiled easily and draped an arm around my shoulder. I winced but left it there. "Oh, don't pretend to be prim and proper. You are one of the boys."

"Yes. We are going to take you to the strip club and drink you under the table," Ben smirked.

I laughed. "Okay, well make sure I get back to my bed in one piece. Alone."

"That can be done," Ben nodded. "What state you are in when we get you there though, we can't promise."

"So, this threesome and sex business. You all know about it."

"Yes," they both confirmed with nods.

"So, who will the three consist of?" Might as well find out.

"You, Charlie and Ian," Richard said as we walked. "Ben is a prude and I am married."

This was good, I liked both men. We got to the strip club, got a booth, and sat down.

"Have you decided to go through with it?" Ben asked as the drinks were served.

I took my shot and then shook my head. "I haven't. It's not something I normally do."

"Women say that shit all the time. Oh, I do not do that, or no I wouldn't do that. Generally, when they do." Ben said.

Nodding, "I absolutely agree. But I was a virgin bride and other than a night I do not remember, well, I class one man as having touched me. We had great sex, but I've only known one man in the bedroom. Taking on two after such a long time..." I shrugged, "I don't know if I could do it. I need safe and secure. It's been a long time since a lover saw me naked." This was something I had a problem with.

Ben watched me. "You were raped?"

Ben has as much tact as me. Maybe we are related. "I don't want to talk about it. I was drugged and don't remember. So, in my books, it didn't happen." I turned to Richard. "Do they like to tag team or is this just a one-off bucket list thing?"

Ben shrugged but Richard answered, "One off, I think. Charlie and I did it, years ago. The women never had any complaints. But Ian? Nah, he does not like to share. If you are comfortable, you should step out of your prude box and give it a go. You would have a lot of fun."

I took a sip of my drink. "Are you two trying to talk me into it?"

"No, I don't want you to do anything you are uncomfortable with," Ben said, and I believed he was being honest. "Saying that, sexual experimentation is always fun and a good way to grow."

I rolled my eyes, "If I was to do something like that, then no one would know about it."

"We would find out about it. Not details, but we would find out," Richard shrugged. "We are brothers. We talk."

"Then that is why I won't do it. Men talk more than women. I wouldn't tell a soul."

"Because you would be disgusted by your behaviour? Or that you were brave enough to go through with it?" Ben asked.

What now we are getting psychological. Oh, come on. I rolled my eyes.

"No, because she would be ashamed of enjoying her sexuality," Richard stated, pretty much nailing the issue on the head. That and the issues I had from a couple of weeks ago, but I won't think about that. "Put it on your bucket list and then you can say you have had one." He waved his hand as if, by giving me a solution, it could be dismissed.

"Did it ever occur to you that maybe I just don't want to have sex?" I suggested, even though that was a rather good idea to put it on my bucket list.

"I watched you cum," Richard said. "It was sexy as fuck. You meant it when you said you were back in the game. There is nothing wrong with having a little fun. And they are two nice men who will look after you. You should at least consider it."

"We won't think less of you if you do or if you choose not to. You will find no judgment here. We have had threesomes. You will not lose respect for it, especially after what you did today. I don't think I will ever not be friends with you."

I smiled; this was an interesting. "Why is that Ben?"

"Because you are way too fucking full of surprises," he grinned.

I thought about this, then pulled a page out of my late husband's book and started buying them doubles. If we were going to talk about this shit, then I was going to make sure they woke up with hangovers tomorrow. Now I was a fucking millionaire, I could afford it.

## 36. Charlie

Ian and I arrived at the strip club to find Ben and Richard well on their way to being hammered. Kate was tipsy but far from being drunk. I got my first drink and soon worked out it was a double. Kate sat there looking innocent. She even batted her eyelashes at me. Cheeky little minx.

I leaned over to speak into her ear. "You are feeding them doubles." Oh, she smelled good.

She looked at me with feigned shock and pointed to herself. "Who me? I have no idea what you are talking about."

"I have been doing that to them since I got to Vegas. Good work." I bit her neck gently. She gasped. I sat back. I needed her to relax. I fucked it last night and needed to rebuild her trust if I was to seduce her into the threesome.

"Did you just bite me?"

"I did." I nodded with a seductive smile. I could see the pulse in her neck jumping a little faster. Nice, just what I want to see.

The seduction started tonight. Threesome tomorrow night if I played my cards right. This woman would have literally died to save my life this morning. There was no way I was leaving this earth without being inside her, thanking her properly.

FIVE YEARS WITHOUT SEX! I was going to end her Nun Run and turn her into the sexual being she obviously had forgotten she could be.

Ian gave her an easy smile that made women swoon. She sipped her drink and cocked an eyebrow, watching him before she put her drink down.

"How much does it cost?" she asked him with a straight face and an up nod.

He laughed and winked before eyeing off a stripper with nice tits.

I swear I heard her mutter under her breath, 'I am so fucked.' She managed to keep her demeanour cool. But the pulse in her neck was jumping. Richard who had seen the exchange, watched her with a smirk.

Ian turned back to her. "I have no idea what you are talking about."

"Hmm, you either want something or you are in trouble for something." She sipped her drink watching him. "Which one is it?"

He grinned. "Maybe I want to get in trouble."

"Then put a hand on a stripper," Kate dared.

We laughed, and she sipped her drink with a little smile then shook her head. "So, tonight is about strippers?"

"Well no, we are going to a club to sing karaoke and dance." I tracked my eyes down her legs to her feet. "You are not really wearing walking shoes." Her legs were amazing. I could totally see myself between them.

I got the boys up and we went for a walk down the Strip hoping to sober them up a little. I held her hand as we walked. She was so like Ben it was weird, both of them always scanning. Always watching. Ben, I do not think he even knew he did it anymore. But Kate was always hyperalert. Ben noticed too after a block and cocked his head to the side.

"Are you always on alert?" he asked her.

"Huh?" She looked up at him confused. "I am checking out the sights."

He shook his head. "You are on alert. Who do you think will hurt you? Or are you scared of us?" Fuck, he could pull the plug on us.

She scoffed, "I am not scared of anything out here. I am not worried. I am just looking around like the tourist I am."

Ben looked over at me and then continued giving shit to Ian about his newest car, a bright yellow Maserati. Ben hated the colour and Ian loved it.

We walked into what was considered a dive bar where there was not Karaoke but an amateur band competition. The band on stage sucked.

"Do you like Halestorm?" Richard asked Kate.

She nodded. "This is a band competition. I don't play."

"Do you know the words to Freak Like Me?" Ben smirked.

She shut her eyes and pursed her lips. "Yes." She did not want to do it, but she was going to. I grinned as the band on stage got booed off. The MC looked around, frustrated.

"Nice try guys but is there anyone in here that can actually play? Anyone?" He did not look hopeful.

"Yeah, here." Ian put his hand up. The audience groaned. We walked up on stage, picked up the instruments and tuned them.

"I can't sing," Kate warned.

I smiled, "Just do the best you can." I waited until the boys were all comfortable and had checked that the mics worked. I nodded at Ben who counted us in.

When we started playing the crowd looked relieved and when Kate started to sing the patrons got up and cheered. Kate told a lie. Couldn't sing my ass! She fucking owned the stage as we backed her up. When the song ended, she did the girliest thing I had seen her do. She curtsied to the crowd before turning to us with a big smile.

The MC came back looking absolutely over the moon. "The last band of the night just made this fucking worth it! Anyone think they didn't win it?" he asked the crowd who shook their heads. "Good cause I am giving it to them."

The crowd cheered and the MC handed Kate a thousand dollars.

As we left the club, Ian threw her over his shoulder, and she laughed as if it was the funniest thing in the world.

"What are you doing you idiot?" She laughed and looked to me for help, "Make him put me down! He is acting like a caveman."

"No, just be glad you don't have to walk in those heels." She smiled and nodded before I added, "And I like the way your tits are busting out of your top."

They were straining against the shirt but not popping out. Relieved when she checked, she gave me a dirty look. "That was mean."

## 37. Kate

The next morning, the boys were on my doorstep bright and early, demanding that I get dressed in jeans. Today we were going shooting, then to skirmish... and then whatever the hell Charlie felt like doing. Last night had been epic. We had danced and played as a band. I hadn't sung since Chris died. I did try once but had just burst into tears. When I got home it might be time to get the band back together.

I was surprised everyone was in such good shape, considering the state we were in when they dropped me off to my room late this morning. We were all very drunk when we went to bed. When I mentioned it, Ben glared at me from the rear-view mirror as he drove.

"You were feeding us doubles, you little bitch."

I gave him my most innocent look, he glanced at me a couple of times as I went to answer but I got a slap on the leg. I glared at Ian.

"Don't go giving us that bullshit innocent look. You were feeding us doubles on top of the shots."

"Oh, come on I was drinking the same." I waved my hand. "You all pulled up alright. I went to the gym this morning."

"I didn't see you there." Ben said.

"I was there at six." I shrugged.

Ben huffed. "I was there at seven."

"We must have just missed each other." I had decided to be good then I thought I might shit stir a little… "Or you are just bullshitting me."

"I work out every day." Ben said, "Hence I look as good as I do."

I huffed. "You look like you used to work out and now are just fucking trying to not get fat."

Charlie smacked my other leg. "Be nice."

"What! He does." I picked on Ben not even really knowing why. I grinned at him. "You are getting soft in your old age."

We arrived at the range and when I got out of the car Ben lifted his shirt and asked, "Where exactly am I soft, Kate?"

He was ripped. I giggled and put my hand over his heart, "Right here." I looked up at him and the look on his face made me take my hand away and step back. When I took another step back, he stepped forward. I giggled. "What are you going to do?"

He moved like lightening and after a short scuffle I ended up under his arm, carried into the range like a pet. I laughed so hard, even harder when my butt got smacked.

We were greeted by the instructor who was obviously ex-military. He was not overly impressed by Ben's and my shenanigans. Ben dropped me and I managed to land on my feet.

"Don't go pulling any bullshit on my range. I will shoot you myself," the instructor warned.

"Understood," Ben and I said in unison.

I was trying to work out which division our instructor was from. A glimpse of a tattoo on his arm and I tried not to grin as I realised, he was a retired seal. He was particularly firm ensuring I understood what was being said. I played dumb. He got the boys through with no issues, all a little shocked at the power in their hands. Except Ben who was a good shot, further fanning my suspicion he too was ex-military.

When he got me to the line, the instructor was all business. "Right now, fire it once and see how it feels."

I bought the gun up. "Like this?" He improved my stance for me. I smirked and let off one shot off as instructed. "How was that?"

He looked down the range, "Not bad. Do you want to stop fucking around now? Empty the magazine."

I smiled and did as I was told. "I wasn't fucking around." I cleared the gun out of habit and put it on the stand.

"Yeah you were." He eyed me suspiciously before walking us to the long range. Oh, there were a few guns to choose from but that .338 had my name on it... When he got out the .308, I pouted. The instructor got us all down on the ground in prone position. He showed us how to load it and then let off a shot to show us what to expect.

They went through one by one. I watched as he talked them through it all. Charlie didn't really enjoy it; I think it might have hurt him a little, I don't think he had it shouldered quite right. I wasn't going to call him a pussy though. He was sick and that recoil could have broken his clavicle.

Ian surprisingly did enjoy it. He would get a little smile of satisfaction. Richard didn't like it at all, but I think it was more the fact he wasn't comfortable. Ben, now he got on the ground and lay prone, he got comfortable and the way his hand went on that rifle and loaded it so smoothly, I knew he was ex-military, though he hid it well behind a veil of smooth and suave.

"Right girl get down on the ground. Show me what you got. Target five."

I smirked and looked at Ben's target then back at him. "Alright, looking at your target, I want to know, where did you serve?"

Ben gave me an up nod, "SEAL. You?"

"Army," I said turning and looking down the scope, lining up the fifth target. "Charlie, do you reckon I can beat his score?"

"If you don't, it's consent for fourteen to twenty."

"And if I do?"

"Then you marry Ian in white."

I took the shot and checked it. "And if I shank it on purpose?" There must be a way out of it. *Marrying Ian? Where the fuck was that on his list?* I did like Ian, he was hot and all, but who would wish a hell on wheels like me on a good man like him?

"All of the above."

I turned and looked at Charlie, "Fuck, you are not giving me a lot of options." I turned back to the job at hand and reloaded as he laughed. "What if I shank it and help you win?" I checked out his target, "No forget it. That is shocking. There is no saving that shit."

I looked over at Ian's target. "Ian, you did alright."

I looked at Richard's, "No love in that at all. Absolutely crap."

I went back to my target, checked the wind and took the shot. Then repeated three times.

The targets arrived and the instructor graded the groupings. It came down to Ben and me, as expected. I pursed my lips. This was closer than I figured. I had tried to recreate his grouping with the thought that if I got the same then I was out of a wedding or the sex or all three.

"It is damn near identical." The instructor said with a smile. "But your grouping is slightly tighter, so you beat Ben."

"You tried to shank it and get out of it… so it is fourteen to twenty and a wedding in white to Ian." Charlie smirked. I protested and he just covered my mouth. "Deal is a deal."

I looked up at him with my mouth covered —a Mexican stand off and I was losing. Fuck! I did not want to do that part of the list. Not really. Maybe I did a little… No, I did not want to have sex with these men. One that I would have to bury, one I would marry and the other two I'd have to look in the eye afterward. I begged Ian for help with my eyes but he just shrugged.

Charlie smiled at me. "We are going to paintball next."

"Then I suggest you wear your cups." I said sweetly, "Because I am going to shoot all of you in the balls."

130

## 38. Charlie

Paintball was officially one of the most vicious experiences of my life. After finding out Kate was ex-army, she and Ben ended up having a full-blown battle that we civilians ended up stuck in the middle of. I got shot in the ass and the arm and then as promised, I got shot in the balls. Ian and Richard got hit with a few body shots. Ben was spattered with bullets and paint.

But when Kate came out of her cover when we all ran out of paintballs, a little calmer because she had been really pissed off, I did not know how she was not crying. She was covered in paint from our retaliatory fire, grinning at her win. I was hurting. I did not realise how much paintball would hurt. I had no idea how she could smile.

We went back to The Diamond, dirty and covered in paint. When Kate went to her room Ian and I followed her. She bit her lip when we stepped inside her room.

"I am okay. Just a bit of paint and a few bruises."

"Tonight, I want to run through most of fourteen to twenty," I told her, watching her reaction.

"How the hell will I look at you two, Ben and Richard in the morning?" she growled. She was not really upset, more frustrated. "I am not a slut! I have had one man and now one woman touch me my entire life. Can you seriously say that you are going to respect me in the morning?"

"Yes," Ian and I said at the same time. We were sincere and she looked surprised before lowering her head and shaking it.

"You don't know what you are asking of me," she said softly and turned away, but not before I saw a tear fall down her cheek. "I need a shower. Where are we going to start? Threesome then kink, wedding, making love and then divorce tomorrow? Next day a white wedding?"

"You don't have to consent," I said, touching her shoulder.

"I lost a bet," she mumbled softly. "Do you want me to shower here or get clothes and come to your room?"

She did not let me answer but gathered a small bag of her things and we walked back up to my suite. She went straight into the bathroom. Ian and I looked at each other.

## 39. Kate

I went into the bathroom, shutting the door softly before leaning against it as the minimal memories I had of what that fucking son of a bitch doorman did to me flashed back... causing me to shudder involuntarily. I shut my eyes and took a couple of calming breaths. I dismissed those memories with a right hook. They had no business trying to live rent free in my head.

Taking another shaky breath, I opened my eyes to meet those of the woman in the mirror opposite. I was tired and sore. I just wanted to have another ice bath and go to bed. Instead I was attempting to summon the courage to go through with whatever came next. I was in two minds, once I fucked Ian and Charlie, the last time Chris touched me was gone. He was *gone*. I didn't think I would ever be ready to let Chris go. Sometimes I felt like he was just out of reach...

I was attracted to both Charlie and Ian. I did feel safe to do this with them, to share my body with them and with it, a part of my soul. I couldn't sleep with a man if I didn't have feelings for him. But I was scared they wouldn't call in the morning. That everything was only for tonight. That this was just a game. That I would be thrown into the trash before it started—when they saw my body.

I set my jaw and stripped naked, pulled my hair out to give it a quick brush as I surveyed the damage to my body in the mirror. I was bruised from skydiving, I had welts all over me from paintball and the scars of a lifetime ago were faded. But the damage I had suffered was painfully clear. But other than that, I had a slight six pack. I had a nice shape, nice tits, and bum. My eyes dropped to the apex of my legs, before looking away. I had been waxed before I left home, thanks to Emma and Carrie's insistence on following the six P's. Prior preparation prevents piss poor performance. The doorman entered my mind again for just a moment before I dismissed the fucker with a swift kick in the balls. He had no place here. Nothing to do with what I was about to do.

I was uncertain, a little afraid, self-conscious, and my nerves were frayed but something in me wanted this. I was just worried they would see me naked and turn me down. I could hear them talking so I opened the door quietly and went out to listen.

Naked as the day I was born, hoping they would still find me beautiful.

## 40. Charlie

Ian looked so uncertain that he was giving me doubts. "Why do I get the feeling Kate is just going to scrub her skin until it's raw when we are done? Charlie, she is carrying baggage we know nothing about. I am not sure I can do this to her. You have had threesomes. You have had your kink. I am not sure she will handle what is about to happen."

I watched him. "Are you thinking she will change her mind halfway through and we will be looking at rape charges?" The last thing I wanted to do was go out on a bad note.

"I think that we are going to take that woman and break her. She is more fragile than she wants us to see."

Movement got our attention. We turned to see her standing in the doorway, naked in the darkness of the bedroom. "Thank you for your concern but I will be fine. Are you two coming for a shower or not?" She turned and went back into the bathroom. Ian and I stripped off our shirts as we went after her.

Kate was under the water as we undressed. We looked her over, well tried to, her long hair was wet and covering her up. I noticed a hair tie on her wrist and took it as we joined her in the shower. I was going to braid it so that we could look at her, Ian shook his head, pointing to the shampoo and conditioner.

I did not expect to see the damage on Kate's body. I did not expect to see so many welts that we had caused with the paintballs and bruises that would have to be from skydiving. I could not help myself as I gently stroked the black bruise on her shoulder. She had said nothing about being hurt… But it was the damage from before these last few days that shocked me. How was she still alive? There were what looked like bullet, knife and shrapnel scars. Then I saw the burns and five marks on her lower back and buttocks that looked like whip scarring.

What scared me more than the damage on her body was my reaction to her. I was semi-hard, and every time I touched her, I felt a little zap of lightning at my fingertips. I was overcome with a fierce instinct not just to mate, but to protect her. I had planned to whip the hell out of her for shooting me in the balls, but I could not whip her now.

I glanced at Ian who was inspecting her body. He was really attracted, his dick was hard, his eyes inspecting every inch of her. He was completely captivated. This woman had him intrigued.

Kate's head was down, seemingly waiting for us to say something before she got restless enough to take the soap to wash herself.

## 41. Kate

Charlie took the soap out of my hand gently. "Let me." He lathered his hands and waited for me to give him a slight nod before washing my body. "Ian will do your hair." Now they were in the shower with me, I was nervous. Both had waited for me to give them permission before they began to touch me so intimately. It was a move that gained my trust.

OMG, I had hands everywhere, one pair washing my body and the other in my hair. They were gentle but firm with their every touch. Ian, scratching my scalp like he was, oh it felt so good… I relaxed into it. This was going to be fun.

This little adventure was going to rub against my prude bone badly. But the way I was feeling right now—I didn't care. I was feeling so wanted and beautiful. My body was coming alive for the first time in what felt like forever. I could tell by their touch that they wouldn't hurt me. I almost felt revered. When my head was directed under the water to rinse off, I was ready to drop control and to give them my all.

## 42. Charlie

We washed ourselves as we watched Kate rinse off. Oh, that muscle tone on her beautiful hourglass figure. Her tits and ass were amazing. Her skin was smooth. She would have been flawless without those scars and bruises. Ian washed quickly, he bit his lip and mouthed the words, 'Fuck she is so hot!'

Kate got out of the shower when we finished and picked up a towel. She waited for us, dripping wet. We dried her before we let her dry us. A little exploration was in order before we took the next step.

"What happens now?" she asked as she finished, trying and failing to hide her nerves.

"Is there anything you don't like during sex?" I asked.

"Anal," she said softly, looking ashamed and a little frightened.

"So, we don't go there." I promised, the protective feeling intensified. Kate had gotten that bruise on her shoulder saving my life. We would have to be gentle. "If we are doing something you do not like, tell us and we will stop. You are completely in control."

"Threesome tonight. Might throw in a little bit of bondage if you are okay with that." She shrugged but would not look at me. I took her chin, looking her in the eyes. I could see she was turned on, but I wanted her completely with us. "Neither of us will hurt you. But I want to know that you are really with us on this. It is going to be intense, but I promise, it is going to be fun. You do not have to sleep with us because you lost a bet."

Kate's green eyes would not show me what she was feeling. Her body language said it all when she tried to cover up. "I want to be here." I kissed her gently, stroking her body with my fingertips. I asked her again, watching the walls in her eyes come down a little. Kate said, "Yes".

Ian was still not convinced and did the same thing. It was the first time he had kissed her and the chemical attraction that had been brewing for days was blatantly obvious. Kate would have lost herself to him. Ian only just managed to control himself. He broke the kiss and asked her if she wanted to sleep with us. Again, Kate consented.

Ian took her to the bed. I went to my drawers and got out some rope while Ian swept Kate off her feet and laid her on the mattress as if she were a bride. He stroked her face and then whispered in her ear as I tied her limbs to the bed frame. She watched with interest as I tied the knots while Ian decided to get out the rabbit fur and run it over her. She looked up at him with a smile.

"What is that?"

"Rabbit fur."

"It's so soft." She smiled, biting her lip.

"Yes, your nipples seem to like it." He smiled. I glanced at her pink nipples, all puckered up tight. They made my mouth water wanting to suck and bite them. I finished tying her leg to the bed then Ian and I stood back to admire her. She tested the restraints.

"Why are you smiling?" Kate bit her lip.

I moved toward her, "Now we play."

"You make me sound like a new toy." Kate was a little more nervous.

The mattress dipped as Ian joined us on the bed. "Yes, you look like a lot of fun." Ian kissed her.

Now we had her tied spread-eagle on the bed, it was play time. We teased, kissing her mouth, nipping, licking then blowing on her neck. Stroking her skin, not once touching her nipples or the wet heaven between her legs, teasing every single erogenous zone she had. She swore at us for teasing her. We did not stop, even when she was reduced to begging. And I do mean begging. Her whimpers and moans, how she wriggled and threw her head back in frustration just made me want to tease her more. It was obvious that she had never been in this situation before. Kate was getting her very first taste of being a sub.

I grinned at Ian then went and got some nipple clamps designed for pleasure. I showed Ian and he plumped her breast before sucking hard on her nipple.

Kate's body bowed, her mouth open and her eyes wide. I bent down and did the same thing to her left tit and she did it again. With every kiss, and every touch she responded. I loved the way she did. She was untrained, so when she dropped her guard she acted out of her own need, reacting with total abandon. Normally, I avoided untrained women but Kate's natural response to our seduction was an aphrodisiac that ought to be bottled, its potency was like nothing I had ever experienced.

I wanted to taste her, but Ian beat me to it. He got comfortable between her legs and put his mouth over her pussy, growling as he did. I settled for putting the nipple clamps on firmly and kissing her beautiful mouth. Not with the bruising force I had yesterday. But with gentle licks as I stroked my hand lightly over her body.

"Please," Kate begged softly.

Ian growled as he started to finger fuck her. Kate's body bowed as she fought the restraints, not because she was scared but because she wanted to hold something. I took her hands and a moment later she gripped the ropes. I kissed her blind, then kissed her harder through her orgasm, swallowing her cries. It had not taken Ian long to get her off but then, we had laid the groundwork.

Ian moved, kissing his way up her body, tightening the nipple clamps before he kissed and nipped her neck. I went down between her legs to eat her out. As I got comfortable, my mouth watered at the sight of her flesh, I blew on her pussy gently. She responded by trying to shut her legs. Her pussy was beautiful, soft folds of perfection. With gentle intrusions, I used my fingers to spread her flavour over her folds, her smell made me pull myself back into check before I lost my control... I wanted to be gentle, but I was starting to feel like an animal.

I rubbed her clit with my thumb, she lifted her head and tried again to close her legs. But, since I had her attention, I put my mouth over her, thrusting my tongue into her dripping cunt, licking her deep. Kate's eyes rolled as her head dropped back to the sheet. My eyes rolled at her flavour. Very rarely did a woman taste this good. I could spend a month eating her out. She was sweet and addictive. I went back to teasing her. I wanted her to cum like an imploding star, but only when I demanded it of her.

I watched Ian make out and touch her. He used ice on her before putting the ice in her belly button. Kate growled at him before glancing at me for help. Her head fell back as she panted, testing her restraints again. Her eyes were so beautiful as she lost herself in sensation and pleasure. Her brain comprehended only our touch and the feeling it gave her. I was pleased when Ian put a blindfold on Kate. Instantly, every sensation we gave her was heightened.

Ian was having a great time. Poor fucker was toast. He liked her. A lot. I pushed a finger gently into her, surprised at how tight she was. I worked her and sucked her clit until her orgasm hit, making her cry out and fight the restraints again. I pressed two fingers into her and she detonated again. Ian kissed her as she cried out until she went lax on the mattress, chest heaving, body jittering with aftershocks.

I sat up and wiped my mouth as Ian took the blindfold off her, then sat back and we watched her as she stared at the ceiling. Slowly she blinked before her eyes fluttered shut.

"Kate, we are not finished with you yet." I dragged my thumbnail up the instep of her foot, but she did not flinch.

Ian laughed, took the nipple clamps off and released her arms while I released her feet. She moaned softly when Ian put her arms at her side. "Don't you dare go napping, we are just getting started."

"Give me a minute! I haven't had that many orgasms in a row for five years. You start and I will gather my senses and be right with you." She waved her hand and sighed as her hand flopped to the mattress. She was sated. I grinned at Ian.

"Next bit involves sex," I warned her. "You sure you want to come into it mid-way?"

"Just use protection," she mumbled, then stretched like a lazy cat.

Ian chuckled as I knelt on the bed and pulled her to her feet. Her face lit up as she laughed. She took me by surprise when she wrapped her arms around my waist putting her head against my chest. I glanced at Ian, unsure what to do, then took a handful of her hair so she would face me. Kate's smile was bright enough to light up every dark corner of my soul. My heartbeat just a little faster as I realised, —I had feelings for this woman.

*That was not the plan.*

Still holding her hair, I bent her over, holding my dick out. Like a good girl she opened her mouth. Ian put his hands on her hips before caressing her ass as I put my cock into her hot mouth, thrusting gently to see where her gag reflex was.

I hit it and her hands went to my legs to push me back. Ian leaned over and took her arms. I kept my thrusts shallow until I made her gag again. She went to pull back and Ian spanked her perfect ass once before teasing her entrance with his cock.

Kate made a noise as Ian pressed into her slowly. I took my cock out of her mouth and watched the emotions on her face as he filled her. She was looking at me but at the same time she was somewhere else. In her eyes, every wall she had built was down. Every safety net she had made was ash. Her eyes rolled as a moan escaped her beautiful mouth.

Ian stilled; his breathing harsh as he stared at the back of her head. Lightly he ran his hands over her body and pulled out. Kate whimpered and Ian grabbed her hair and twisted her to him, his mouth just brushing hers. I took her hips and eased myself into her tight, wet cunt.

Watching Ian, I knew he was seeing what I did. Only now I was watching the same emotions on his face. He was dropping his guard. I filled her tight cunt and thrust up just a little as her mouth touched his. Ian's hand in her hair tightened and tipped her head back and he kissed and bit at her neck as I kept my movements slow and deliberate, thrusting in and out.

Kate's breathing was harsh. She gasped as she touched his chest and then his face, then her hands went into his hair. Ian snarled and bit the base of her neck making her moan, her grip on his hair tightened.

"We are only just getting started, Kate," Ian snarled.

"Shut up and kiss me," she moaned, trying to pull him to her. I was a little firmer as I entered her. Ian gave her a wicked smile. She tried to kiss him again.

"No, I want to fuck your mouth."

"I will bite. Kiss me first," she said, her voice breathy.

Ian kissed her 'til she tried to pull away. I held her hip and reached around to massage her clit as she fought the overload of sensation.

"Kate, Ian, is going to keep kissing you until you come on my cock. You will come only when I tell you."

Kate let go of Ian's hair. He caught her arms and held them in one hand while the hand in her hair moved her to show what he wanted from her. Her body was ready, primed for orgasm. "Don't you dare fucking come Kate," I quickly swatted her ass and gripped her hip again. My fingers on her clit made her legs shake.

This was almost as painful for Ian as it was for Kate. They both needed air. They both needed more. Ian glanced at me and I nodded.

Ian broke the kiss and pushed her head down. She took his cock between her lips.

"Come for us Kate." I demanded.

Her body shook as she detonated between us with a muffled cry. Ian threw his head back, breathing hard through an animalistic groan before he looked back at her with a satisfied smile. Her pussy clenched around me. She was not done so I fucked her harder and this time the build-up was faster.

Ian took her head off his cock giving me an up nod. I pulled out and he bent her over backward and put one of her legs up on his chest, she looked gorgeous doing the splits on him. I filled her mouth with my cock as Ian fucked her. I held her shoulder and head, keeping her steady, my strokes in her mouth shallow until I felt the orgasm hit her and then I pressed into her throat.

## 43. Kate

Now one man who was an insatiable fiend in bed was a task...
But two? HOLY FUCK!

Good thing I was fit, flexible and light. Well, Ian made me feel
that way because he just picked me up, bent me how they wanted
me before they fucked me again. They were teases. They made me
beg and honestly, I'd never begged before. But these two had me
so heightened with no release that I felt like I had two choices.

I either begged, or punch one of them out of frustration.

I didn't have a talent for deepthroating, never had. Once I threw
up in my mouth, it was all over red rover. No more head for the
night. That had always been the way. I don't know what these two
did to me.

After swallowing Ian's cock during an orgasm, I think I heard
my husband cheering from beyond the grave. Even I was proud.
Even more so when something similar happened as I swallowed
Charlie's. Considering how big their cocks were—Ian's
especially… He had such a handsome cock.

If I didn't have one leg up on Ian's shoulder, the other on the
floor, bent over backward with him holding both of my hands in
one of his. Charlie supporting my head and shoulders as he thrust
into my mouth, I probably would have done a happy dance. Now
that was an achievement.

And filthy mouths, that was something new I had never
experienced. Never had I ever been so completely dominated or
cared for with such dirty things said to me.

Chris was an amazing lover. But this was primal, dominating.
These men giving and taking pleasure from me, was something I
could never have imagined. All I had to do was listen and obey. I

had never been submissive. I took orders in the army as part of a job, but I was my own boss.

I felt thoroughly fucked by the time I lay between them. The warmth of their bodies, their gentle caresses. Tonight, hadn't been about love. But as I lay there, I felt cared for. They hadn't done anything that hurt, nor had they touched me where I asked them not to. I had no fear, being with them. I thought I would be at least a little frightened after what happened a couple weeks ago, but I wasn't. Nobody could have wiped the smile off my face as I fell asleep, snuggled between them.

## 44. *Charlie*

Between us we fucked Kate six ways to Sunday. She lost all her inhibitions and gave herself to us with more trust than I had ever experienced with any sub. Hannah had been vulnerable when she came to me, her trust fragile, but that was nothing compared to Kate's. When she finally lay asleep between us, we were exhausted. I grinned at Ian.

"That was absolutely incredible."

"And flexible. Wow. I have never had a woman do that."

I had, but she had been a dancer. "I will marry and divorce her then I am going to take her to get a white dress. Ask her to marry you. She is a good girl."

He nodded and moved some hair out of her face. "I don't want you to die. I do not know what I would do without you. It scares the fuck out of me. You are acting like the normal you and it feels like there is nothing wrong."

I stroked Kate's back. "I don't want to die." I looked at him. "But Ian, as much as I am playing up and doing all this?" I am going to lie now so he will think it is a blessing when it happens. "I am in pain all the fucking time. I am tired and, when death comes for me, I do not want you to be angry. I have lived my life my way. I have accomplished almost everything I wanted to. Mum and Dad will be here tonight to see me marry. This one is for Mum. She always wanted me to get married and settle down."

He met my eyes, "Who is going to keep me on track?"

I pointed to Kate, "Why do you think I chose her?" He looked at her sadly, stroking the scars he could see. "She hasn't been touched for a long time. When you make her your wife, you are going to have to fuck her 'til she fits you like a glove."

He shook his head. "She doesn't want to get married. She will because she lost the bet, but I don't think she will let me touch her."

I put my head on the pillow and stared up at the ceiling. It sounded more like he feared the connection he had with her and wanted to run. Even I was a little scared of the connection I had with her, but you would not see me running away. I had a bucket list to complete.

"Ian, seduce her, make her feel safe and beautiful. She wants to be loved."

"Then why is she running from it?" he asked.

"Brother, that is the million-dollar question."

## 45. Kate

I woke up between two men who seemed intent, even in sleep, to protect me. It was a good feeling. But the prude in me needed to get some clothes on and get back to her room for some space. Carefully I extricated myself from their hold, redressed before doing the walk of shame back to my room. I had enjoyed what we did but I didn't have a slut bone in my body, and this was rubbing the wrong way. I didn't feel rape dirty, I felt slutty. Naughty.

I had been a virgin bride and had never had a one-night stand before, so last night had thrown me for six. I never knew that having two men all over me like a rash could be so sensual or feel so good. My inner nympho smirked because I had loved every single second of it. I showered in hot water 'til I felt less naughty. I went to the gym when the thought entered my head that they were not going to call so I worked out 'til my legs were jelly. After getting another knuckle bump from the trainer, I returned to my room, had another shower and a long nap. When I got up late in the afternoon, I got ready to go out for the night. Apparently, I would be getting married and I didn't want to look like shit.

I picked out a dress, from my closet, white satin underneath with a navy-blue lace overlay and a white ribbon around the waist. It had a tulle skirt that flared out to just above my knee. The fitted top covered my bruised shoulder. It was perfect for a Vegas wedding, especially with the silver heels I put with it. I looked up into the mirror to see if it looked okay and wondered where Emma got this dress. I had just finished brushing my hair and putting on mascara and lipstick when there was a knock on the door. I opened it to find, Charlie and Ian looking absolutely edible. They looked me over as Richard and Ben stood back.

Charlie growled, "I loved you in shorts, but I think that is my favourite dress."

I blushed. "What's on tonight? Dancing, drinking and fun?" Charlie took my hand as we walked down the hall. Ian put his hand on the small of my back, both checking I was okay.

"Actually, we are going to dinner with my parents" Charlie said casually as if that were a perfectly normal thing to do if you hadn't just met your wife for a night four days ago! "You know, I didn't ask if you wanted anyone from your family to be here, especially for two nights time."

"My parents are dead and everyone else is working. My kids are going to be pissed at me but that is for me to deal with," I said as we walked down the hall. Hmm, didn't want to explain this to them.

"You have kids?" Ian sounded surprised. I nodded. "How many?"

"Fraternal twins. Ryan and Ella are two," I said smiling. "Have you got kids?"

"Evie and Tim," Ian said with a smile. "Four and six."

Charlie took my hand as the elevator doors opened. "Tell me you aren't married."

"Not anymore," I said softly and so began our night of drinking and, not surprisingly, fun. His mother, Rachael and his father, John were an absolute hoot. I had a good old chat with Rachael and his sister Tammy about being a mum and my kids. Rachael and I talked about raising boys who were just like their fathers and daughters that were more like us than we liked to admit.

I felt like we connected which was nice, considering my last mother-in-law was, and still is, a fucking nightmare.

Charlie played host for the night. He was jovial as he got us all in the back of a limo and ten minutes later, we arrived outside a little chapel. My heart kicked up a beat and I glanced at Charlie. We were really going to do this... He smiled as we got out and he calmly explained to his parents his bucket list item of marriage and what he was about to do before he told them about the divorce that would happen in the morning. Then he described more fun and games he had in store. Then he dropped the bombshell that the day after, I would marry Ian so that he would get to see Ian move on.

His parents looked at him like he had hitched a ride on the crazy train and had gone batshit insane. I glanced at Ian who had no readable emotion on his face. That worried me. He was about as keen on the idea as I was. I was bought out of my thoughts when his mother glared at me.

*Shit, here we go.*

"What is your angle?" Rachael snarled, getting up in my face pointing her finger. "Are you after their money?"

What? Huh? Why is she all up in my grill? What fucking money? I was laughing with her literally two minutes ago!

"No Mum, Kate was a completely random pick. She knows nothing." Charlie said holding up his hand. "Ian and Kate have agreed to it. I have things in the works to make it nice and respectable. But tonight, it is my turn. She likes me enough to go through with it."

"She feels sorry for you," Rachael snapped at Charlie.

Now that just made me angry. "Oi, I don't think you know me well enough to make that judgement," I snapped back at her. "I have been hanging with him for four days and we have been through some serious shit that has bought us close. I am doing this bucket list for a little fun and to help Charlie. There is no money involved. If there was –I would have told him to find someone else."

I was over Charlie's shoulder half a second later. He carried me into the Chapel. I laughed as I looked at Ian who smiled back but shook his head. What the fuck was that man thinking?

Ben and Richard grinned. Charlie and I signed the paperwork before I walked down the aisle to him in a shitty veil with a bunch of roses as a bouquet and Ben on my arm to give me away.

Charlie looked nervous. I gave him an equally nervous smile and kept my eyes locked on his. I bet he was doing this for his mother.

I wasn't, I was doing this for him.

The service was short and sweet. Elvis did a good job. Ian handed Charlie some rings. Charlie's hands shook as he put a ring on my finger, taking me as his wife. In his vows, he gave me the opportunity to say no. But I could see he meant his vows. For right this minute, for tonight, he loved me. I was never going to run from him. He had chosen me to share this. When it was my turn to take him as my husband, I put the ring on his finger with steady hands. I gazed up at him and he looked like he was going to faint. He had lost a bit of colour but gave me a goofy grin.

When he lifted my veil, he did so with shaky hands.

"Is this what it feels like? I am so fucking nervous right now." He gave a nervous laugh. The boys chuckled as Charlie looked into my eyes. "Had I not met you I would never have done this. Thank you." He bent down and kissed me sweetly and then passionately. I returned it. He broke the kiss and stood up straight and went white.

"Hold him, he is going to faint," I said before Ian and Richard grabbed him as he fell backward. Once he was on the floor Charlie opened his eyes almost immediately. I smiled and touched his cheek tenderly, "Hello Husband." He looked at me wide-eyed for a moment, then his eyes rolled again.

"Come away from him for a moment. He just did something he swore black and blue he would never do." Ian helped me stand before we stood back and let Charlie come around with John and Rachael fussing over him.

I glanced at Ian, went to say something and then couldn't, the words lodged in my throat. He put his arm around my shoulders, seeming to understand. Even if it was only for tonight, I was married. When Charlie was okay again, we went back to The Diamond to have a few drinks and dance. John and Rachael were *not* happy but played along.

At some point Charlie figured out I was wearing a garter and put his head under my skirt taking it off with his teeth. He flicked it at Ian who caught it out of reflex. He laughed when he saw what it was.

Charlie spoke to the boys and his parents and then took my hand, walking back to his room. He surprised me by carrying me over the threshold. Inside, once the door was shut, he put my feet on the floor, stepping back to look me over.

"You look so beautiful. Thank you for being my wife for a night." He bit his lip. He had something to say and I was going to let him say it. "I wish I had met you sooner. I wish I had longer, but I feel the grim reaper in the room… and he is telling me I do not have long. I have nearly ticked off my bucket list. I am not scared because I look forward to not being in pain. But I am sure wishing I had more time to be with you. You made me an incredibly happy man tonight. I can't ever thank you enough for what you have done for me."

I went to him and touched his chest before unbuttoning his shirt, I needed to do something, or I was going to cry. "Put more on your list." I kissed his chest as I bared it. "I will be your wife for as long as you need me."

"Only for tonight." He stroked my shoulders. "Any longer and I will fall in love with you. I need you to love my brother more, to look after him. He will need you when I am gone."

I took his hand and led him into the bedroom; I didn't want to talk about this now. I needed to show him that my attention was focused solely on being in this moment with him, that I was his tonight. We undressed each other slowly. Kissing tenderly.

Touching, exploring without rushing. The need to mate was there, the attraction was there… but tonight, neither of us was going to rush. We didn't need words. Everything was said in a kiss, a look, a touch...

I could tell he had never been this intimate. Our lovemaking was intense. He looked me in the eyes, something I felt he did not do often for he kept shutting his eyes, shaking his head, then looking back. I gave him everything I had; Charlie was a good man. He had been dealt a harsh hand with an early death sentence. But this wasn't pity I was feeling. I had fallen in love with him. I told myself I was loving him for just a night. But I opened my heart to a man who would leave me, knowing that I would love him for the rest of my days.

When we finally lay sated, holding each other, he wanted to talk.

"Is that really what making love is like?" His hand absently stroked my arm.

"Yes, we made love. Because I love you and just for a night, you love me too." I kissed him. "I couldn't have done it if I didn't."

He touched my face gazing into my eyes. "You will love him, won't you?"

"Tonight, can I just be in love with you?" I begged. This was eating at my core, and I was really trying not to let it.

"This is important. I need to know."

"I will try," I whispered.

"That is all I ask." Charlie kissed my forehead.

## 46. *Charlie*

I woke with Kate in my arms. Her soft breath tickling the hairs on my chest. I looked at her and wondered if she really did love me. I do not think I had ever felt so content. She sighed and stretched and rubbed her eyes before cuddling into me again, her arm over my chest.

I took her hand and kissed her fingers. "Come on, beautiful. It is time to get up and get divorced."

She giggled. "Don't you want morning sex? It is a marriage thing that only happens on the rarest of occasions."

I chuckled as she gave me a cheeky grin. "Now that is not an offer I can pass up." I put my hand between her legs and massaged her clit. She was already wet and ready.

I always thought making love was a stupid thing to say. People fucked. Sometimes gentle, sometimes hard. But it was just fucking. Last night, I finally understood what it meant. Well I thought I did, until five minutes ago when she topped me and rode me with that beautiful body, her eyes locked on mine. Through the sex haze and lust… I could see she honestly did love me. She gave me her body and bared her soul shamelessly.

That was when I fell. The phrase, 'falling in love' was scarily accurate. There was nothing you could do to save yourself.

The realisation that I would do almost anything to protect her and look after her hit me hard. I played with her hands, staring at the shitty ring I had bought her. For her it was enough. She did not want my money, she just wanted me… it was something I had never felt. Women wanted me for something, my money mostly. They had never wanted me for me.

I was a stranger who had walked up to Kate and made a completely ludicrous proposition. She took the challenge and was one of the boys until Ian and I had slept with her yesterday. Now with me, in this moment, she was completely mine. The feeling was overwhelming. I wanted to bury myself in her. I wanted to go nowhere else. I was hungry for her touch. But it was the feeling of being 'whole' that floored me. I had always felt like a part of me was missing. Now with her—I had the missing piece.

I pulled her to my chest and rolled so I could kiss her 'til I saw stars. It was like my whole world opened. I hated it when women looked me in the eyes but with Kate, I craved it. This was better than anything I had ever experienced. This was love—what sex should have felt like. The connection of souls I had denied myself for forty years, I had run from it fearing the commitment I now craved.

Kate quickened under me before she shattered, her eyes on mine. Her walls completely down. I swear I could see her soul as I came, filling her with my seed. I had never done that with another woman. I was not even worried or panicked that I might possibly have gotten her pregnant. I was glad I could share a part of me I had not shared with another woman in my lifetime. I kissed Kate tenderly. I was in love with her. I did not pull out because I didn't want to break the connection. She touched my face gently with her fingertips making my skin burn. She did not push me off or go to sleep. She stayed with me, in the moment, staring into my soul with such love in her eyes that my soul burned at a new level. I felt *alive*.

When we did break the coupling, I held her in my arms, spooning her protectively as she went to sleep. I heard my door open and pulled the sheet over us as Ian came in. He glanced at Kate then at me.

"Are you okay?" he asked softly. "Mum insisted I check." I motioned him over and he sat on her side of the bed, he looked down at Kate and smiled. "She looks exhausted. Big night, huh?" He touched her cheek moving some hair out of her face with his fingertip.

"Ian, I fell in love with Kate." I whispered and he looked at me as he tried to work out whether I was joking. "She is wonderful. Please marry her and do not dare let her walk away from you. I will haunt you if you do. She will love you completely."

"She will drive me insane." Ian was serious...

"That too, but she will look after you and kick your arse if you need it and hold you. Please Ian, be open to loving her and fall like I did. Do not let her go, I am begging you. Look after her for me. Tough as she is, she needs you to have her back too."

He watched me for a moment. "You really did fall for her, didn't you?"

I had tears in my eyes as I nodded, "Yeah. And I am going downstairs to divorce her so that I can see her in white and married to you. Then you will have her when I go."

"You still have a few weeks." Again, he feared my death, sounding desperate.

"Ian. Promise me to love and to hold her until your dying breath." I whispered as Kate stirred and mumbled something incoherent. Then she jerked.

"Jesus Ian! You scared the shit outta me!" she exclaimed and we both laughed. She turned, glanced over her shoulder then rolled over. "What's wrong? Why are you crying?" She touched my face, wiping my tears. The concern in her eyes was a punch in the guts.

"I am not crying," I denied pointlessly.

"Don't start your macho shit with me. What is wrong?" She touched my face. Her eyes reading mine.

"I want to know why it took 'til the end of my life to finally fall in love only to have to leave. Because you are really in love with me and I am going to hurt you. I do not want you to hurt. I need to get you downstairs and divorce you so that I can see you in white and happy with my brother so that I know you will both be okay. I want to meet your children and your family."

Yes Sir, I broke down like a babbling idiot.

Feelings? Eww. I needed to control myself before I was asked to hand in my man card. Kate sat up and pulled my face against her bare chest and held me... I did not remember the last time I was the one being held.

I feared dying but I was not going to go out like a fucking sook. I lied about being in pain just so they would feel the end to be a blessing. The truth was that other than feeling a little tired, I was not in any pain at all.

Kate rocked me gently, stroking my hair. "Because it is better late than never. Because the stars aligned. Whatever reason makes you happy. Charlie, I am never going to forget you. You are going to live in my heart. You have bought me on this wonderful crazy adventure and had me do things that I will never do again."

"Like take off your parachute?" I asked being perfectly serious.

"I didn't take off my parachute, I took off the instructor. I can't make promises on that, shit happens, and must be dealt with. I was talking about the woman giving me a blow job and the threesome." She scratched my scalp, calming me. "That is something only you two will share with me. As for me getting hurt. Fuck yes, it will hurt. I will grieve but one day the clouds will lift.... And... I will be okay."

"I want you to be okay. I don't want to hurt you." I touched her face looking her in the eyes. "Will you marry Ian? Will you love him until you die?" I asked.

"Charlie, of the three men who have touched me in my entire life, two are in this room. If Ian wants me, I am sure he will ask. But you don't need to worry about anything except having a good time and enjoying life. I need you to know that I am completely honoured you chose me to be your wife. I will never regret falling in love with a man who loves to pick up Randoms to do crazy stupid shit with."

"You really do love me for me, don't you?" I said, gazing into her eyes.

"I don't know you as anyone other than you." She smiled touching my face. "It would be hard not to love you…you are pretty awesome."

Ian wiped a tear, "Fuck you. You two are going to make me cry with all this sappy shit."

I laughed, "How about I suggest that when you two are married, you fuck like rabbits as often as possible—minimum three times a week."

"What, now you are stipulating what we will do in our marriage?" Ian asked and lay down beside Kate, "Okay, let's hear it." He let me change the subject.

"Okay sex, lots of it. If proven wrong, you must give head as an 'I am sorry'. You must go on dates, go out and have fun. Oh, and more babies. And I want you both to love and accept each other as you are. And never lie to each other."

"That all sounds fairly doable," Ian said with a nod.

"Except that minimum three times a week sex thing. Hell, marriage equals no sex," Kate said with an outright cheeky smile. Ian and I looked at her as she turned to Ian with a grin, "Morning sex is a rare thing, isn't it?"

"I love morning sex. It is the best. But rare? Yes. Exceedingly rare. Even more so when you have kids."

"I want you to have morning sex at least once a month," I said.

Kate giggled, "Is that what we would have been like?"

"Woman, I would tie you up in my dungeon, locked the fuckin' door and only let you out to feed and water you," I chuckled.

"What about Ryan, Ella and my job?"

"You could have time to play with the kids. But the second they were in bed I would be all over you. Oh, okay that is another thing—no frumpy unsexy pyjamas. Sexy stuff to bed."

"What! No jammies! No way. Next you will tell me I have to wear dresses."

"You do wear dresses." We both exclaimed.

"I am wearing dresses because Emma and Carrie friggin' repacked my suitcase. I am a jeans, shorts, boots and t-shirts kinda girl. I have no reason to dress up."

Ian and I looked at each other. "What do you do for a living??"

"I work cold cases mostly."

"And you were in the army?" I asked, surely not.

"How do you think I got most of the damage?"

"Are you out?" I asked.

"Yeah. Got out twelve months ago after…" she moved the sheet and pointed at four scars, "I got shot. Didn't hit anything major so it was an easy recovery. When I got the kids, the in-laws came over here and started a business. I have worked with them since then. I had a really shitty week at work, so they insisted I have a holiday for a couple of weeks since I haven't ever taken one. So, they sent me here."

"Where are your parents?" I asked.

"Dead."

"Your husband?"

"Killed in action." then it hit me why she said that I did not know what I was asking of her.

"Oh Kate, I am sorry," I said, sitting up. "If I had known…" I was making this poor woman a widow twice!

"You would never have fallen in love? No regrets Charlie. Absolutely none," she said with sincerity.

"Why were you shot?" Ian asked.

She looked at him, "Classified. But I can tell you this one passed right through me and went into my brother-in-law, Brian."

I got out of bed. "Come on wife. Get up and have a shower. I am about to divorce your beautiful ass and you are going to call your family since they are here, not in Australia and invite them to your wedding. I have things already in place and when I have divorced you–I am going to take you dress shopping."

"Can't I sleep another half an hour?" She grumbled.

"No," I laughed. "Time is ticking; I will sleep when I am dead."

## 47. Kate

Charlie had a way of throwing his weight around. I wondered what he did other than manage The Diamond. I watched him smooth the way with the judge for an actual divorce. Not an annulment.

The judge smirked at me. "So, are you going to be the bitch that goes after everything or are you going to let him steam roll you?"

I looked up at Charlie. "You want to role play or just have it signed off?"

"No, I want a divorce. But I want a bit of a fight. You walk away with yours and I walk away with mine. No exchange but I want a fight."

I nodded. "Alright then."

The judge sat in his chair as Charlie yelled at me about the parachute and shooting him in the balls at paintball. I shouted at him for the money I won and how I didn't know who he was.

"Hold up a second!" The judge stopped us, and we turned to him.

"Oh, come on, it was just getting fun," I grumbled.

"No, do you really not know who you are married to?" The judge questioned me, pointing to Charlie.

"Well, no. I met him five days ago and have been pretty much drunk for most of it." I questioned Charlie. "What does he mean who you are?"

"Ma'am you are married to a multibillionaire," the judge informed me.

I cocked my head to the side. "So what? He has a bit of money, good for him. I am sure he worked hard for it."

"Are you sure you don't want to at least get alimony?" the Judge asked.

"Huh? Why would I do that?" I was confused.

"It would set you up for life," the judge stated.

"I don't want his money. I have a job," I said softly to the judge then looked at Charlie as panic started rising in my chest. "As much as we are play acting, we are getting a real divorce. I don't want your money. I would rather have a miracle cure for cancer and have you here for the next sixty years."

"I would be a hundred!" Charlie laughed.

"I mean it. I don't want your money. If you force any on me through this process— we will not be play acting." I was serious, then he smiled slowly.

"I don't know what the judge is going to do."

"Damn it, Charlie! What the fuck have you been up to!" I threw my hands up, I wasn't acting now. "Don't be deviating from the list."

"You told me to add more on to my list!" He shouted back.

"I don't want your money! Miracle cure for cancer yes but you have a family that you can give it to. Don't make me the bad guy and set me up."

"I will do whatever the fuck I want," he smirked. "If I want you to have everything then you will have it."

I went absolutely fucking postal. This was a real fight now. I was upset and angry at things that I had no control over. I didn't want any money. Hell, I hadn't even managed to spend the money I'd won yet.

Someone jumped the barrier and got a hold on me. I fought until I realised, I was restrained by Ben. Why did he do that? I looked up at him tears on my cheeks, my chest heaving as I sobbed. His hand in my hair hurt as did the way I was restrained. If I fought him, I would break an arm.

I was helpless.

"Calm down. Before you get locked up for contempt of court!" Ben snarled and tightened his grip and I whimpered involuntarily. "I mean it. Calm the fuck down. Charlie is fucking with you."

"Make him stop or I won't sign the papers. I didn't do this for money. I did it because I fell for him."

Ben stared at me, I flinched when I saw sympathy in his eyes. "Would you do it again?"

"Yes," I whispered. "I don't want to get divorced. I am his for as long as he has."

His big hand pressed my head against his chest but instead of nearly ripping my hair out, he stroked my hair. It felt like Dad doing it and with everything going on, suddenly I missed him and Mum. Oh goodness, I was turning into a mad woman. I was so upset I wanted my MUM!

I started sobbing again. Ben's grip on my arms though, didn't loosen. Then he said, "Okay, enough play acting. Get the papers and let's just do this. She has had enough. I didn't realise she had fallen for you."

I didn't know why he was being so kind to me, but I was glad. I felt so alone. "I fell for Ian too," I sobbed. "I am such a whore," came out of my mouth before I could stop it. When I realised it was true it hurt more. Charlie never would know what it was like to be loved by a woman who was wholly and solely his.

That was one thing I couldn't give him.

## 48. Charlie

She was happy to play and pretend. But the second I hinted at paying alimony, she lost it and went a level of crazy that I had not seen. I looked at my brothers and parents for help. I wanted to give her a gift, so she knew that I meant my vows and that this had not been a joke; that I loved her. I knew she had money now but more never hurt.

Kate physically launched herself at me and Ben got a hold of her. She fought him for a moment, but he held her roughly, restraining her painfully. She whimpered in pain when she moved slightly. I felt bad for her. I did not want her to get hurt. I motioned for Ben to be gentle, but he shook his head before returning his attention to his sister.

I was done playing. I had been trying to play up because I was protecting my heart. I did not want to get divorced. I wanted her to be mine. This hurt. I did not realise how much. It was made worse because she wanted me and not my money. She wanted me healthy and for me to have more time.

When Kate confessed to Ben that she had fallen in love with me and with Ian right before she called herself a whore, my heart broke. When I glanced at Ian he turned away.

Ben glared at me and told me to wrap it up. I nodded and turned to the judge who was now looking sympathetic now that something fun that had begun as a game had become very real with our hearts involved.

The judge motioned me over. "Do we go with plan A or B?"

"B. I will find another way to give her my gift."

"I see a lot of antics in my court room and you don't want to divorce her any more than she wants to be. She is not kidding when she says she loves you. Why not just keep her 'til you go?"

I watched Kate in the arms of her brother and then turned back to the judge. "Because I refuse to make her a widow twice."

His eyebrows went up and I handed him the background report I had done on her. He read the first few pages and said, "I remember this." He looked from her to me.

"I need to see Ian move on. We both know he won't if I don't force his hand," I said softly.

"Okay, but I wish you would reconsider. It is nice to see you in love, Charlie. You are glowing."

"Thanks. She isn't going to get into trouble for losing her shit, is she?"

He shook his head. "I will call order and we will get this signed off so you can get on with your plans. I wish you the best of luck and hope you get everything you want so you can rest in peace. You are a good man; I have always respected you."

I smiled. It was nice to hear. "Thank you. I wish you the best too. Just give me a moment to kiss the hell out of my wife before we do this."

I took back the background report and handed it to Ian before I turned to Mum. "I told you she wasn't in it for the money."

I looked at my little wife who had calmed but was balanced on a knife's edge emotionally. Her emotions boiling close to the surface. Her eyes closed, accepting the pain her brother was inflicting on her. Ben released her and I took her shoulders, massaging them. He stepped back as she turned and wrapped her arms around my waist.

"I am not sure I like your level of crazy." I said softly, "Ian, on the other hand, has a raging boner."

She looked up at me with sad eyes. "That is very reasonable grounds for a divorce." Her bottom lip quivered. "I am sorry I lost it."

"I am sorry for pushing you past your breaking point." I wiped her tears, "We are going to sign the papers now. You get nothing, I get nothing."

"Are you sure? I will be yours for as long as you have got."

I stroked her face. "Yeah. There is no way I am going to make you a widow twice." I hugged her. This hurt. I wanted her.

I wanted her to be with me when I died, by my side. But if I chose that, I knew in my heart, she would not move on. And Ian would be alone. I needed them to be happy. I needed their chemistry to take hold and burn for the rest of their lives. She looked up at me when the papers were put on the table in front of us.

This was the moment when I could stay married, live my happily ever after in the arms of the woman I loved, with her as mine every minute—or enact the dare, have her marry Ian and hope like hell the marriage worked and they lived the happily ever after they both deserved.

She was so beautiful as her eyes begged me not to do it. I cupped her face and kissed her. My last kiss as a married man. The best kiss of my life. This was how I should have kissed her when I said I do. This was how I would have kissed her for the rest of my life. Her lips were soft, her tongue like candy, and her taste was going burned into my brain. I ran my hands over her and then broke the kiss.

I cupped her face and looked into her eyes, "I love you." I hoped she knew I meant it.

Her eyes teared up. "I love you too."

I kissed her again then signed the paperwork with tears in my eyes. She followed my lead. We both looked at the papers that ended our marriage, then at each other.

"We did it."

"Yeah." Kate bit her lip.

"That hurt like hell," I admitted.

She nodded. "What now?"

"I get you ready for your happily ever after." I hugged the love of my life and thanked the judge with a nod.

## 49. Kate

Charlie walked me into to a bridal boutique and took off his tie. I watched him walk toward me. I held my hand up to stop him when he went to blindfold me. He cocked an eyebrow.

"You are going to have to trust me."

"I want to see the dress. I am not a girly girl."

He laughed. "I don't want you to see the price tags on these dresses."

I looked around. "What do you mean the price of these dresses?" He smiled at me as the tie went over my eyes. "Charlie, what are you up to? I can't see a bloody thing!" When I tried to take the blindfold off, my wrists were bound behind my back. "Charlie!"

He chuckled and kissed my mouth chastely before giving me a little push, so I sat on what felt like a couch. I could hear him talking and sighed. I took that couple of minutes peace to come to terms with what had happened at the courthouse. Before coming here, Charlie had spoken to his family briefly while Ben sat with me.

Ben just sat beside me. No contact, no words. Just a weird solidarity. I would forever be grateful for his support. Charlie had family there and I didn't. I would thank him later. I couldn't believe the way I reacted. Or how much it hurt to sign that paperwork. It was the ultimate rejection.

I tried to rein myself in. I had known Charlie six days. Was I really in love? Was I loving him in the hope it would save him? Was I feeling sorry for him? For myself? No, that wasn't it. I was in love with him because he gave enough of a shit to make a list of things that he had not done, or sworn not to do, and do them. He was living every day like it was his last. I loved him because he stole my heart.

He took my arm, scaring the shit out of me... He laughed, "Are you okay?"

"I was just thinking about getting out of the bullshit tie you have around my wrists."

He chuckled, stood me up and a moment later when my wrists were untied, he tied my elbows together. "You won't get out of this."

I giggled, "Kinky prick."

His breath was hot in my ear a moment later, the smell of his subtle cologne filled my nose. I breathed him in.

"I never showed you how kinky I really am. Would you like to find out?"

I shivered; his breath was hot. "Uh Huh."

His tongue went into my ear "Okay. I will show you when I get you home."

"Why don't you just show me?"

"Because I am a Dominant. I like whips and canes but I would never use any of that on you. I have other ideas for you." He whispered, "Now trust me, I am about to undress you and put you in a dress."

A Dom? Huh? I thought he was just a kinky fucker!

## 50. Charlie

I picked her up and she flinched "What's wrong?"

"You have taken my sight. Everything else is heightened," she said softly.

I chuckled, "Ever had sex blindfolded with earphones in?"

"Like in Fifty Shades?"

"Yeah."

"No."

"Maybe, we could do that." I kissed her cheek and put her down, instructing her to stand still while I undressed her. The assistant stared at Kate's body and turned away, pity on her face with a little disgust.

"I know it isn't pretty." Kate sighed, "But I am alive, and I am grateful."

"No one said anything," I said giving her a weird look.

"The lady gasped a little. It's alright. I am not ashamed of it."

"Nor should you be," I said and gave the assistant a warning look as we got Kate into the dress.

"You better not be making me wear something really girly. I don't like lace or beads or frills or dresses."

I laughed. "Shut up."

"I'm serious. I don't like looking girly."

I smiled as the dress went into place. She looked like a bound-up bride—sexy as hell. The dress though was not the one. We got her out of it and the next dress on her. The more I saw her in white, bound and blindfolded, the more it became a fantasy.

I really needed to talk to Ian. Maybe he would share her 'til I went? Maybe I could take her to the club and parade her all in white, restrain and fuck her. How sexy would she look in lace-top stockings?

I got my head back on track long enough to realise that the fifth dress we put her in was perfect. It was corseted, it was full of everything she said she despised. It was white and pure, like her heart. I thought of Ian and how he would react to seeing her like this. Then the assistant got a full-length veil and put it on her.

"Are we done yet?" she asked. "Because this is boring."

"Soon, I think I found your dress," I mumbled, walking around her, running a critical eye over her from every angle. Nodding my approval, I glanced at the woman. "That is the one. Is it the only one?"

She nodded, "Yes, I think it was made for her because there are no adjustments needed."

"Okay well let's get this off her and out of here so she can get dressed."

Five minutes later Kate was back sitting on the couch, still bound and blindfolded. She grumbled.

"Kate, keep it up and I will gag you as well," I snarled, and she giggled. I had her dress delivered to my room and another to my home. That one I would rip off her before I fucked her and showed her who I really am.

I am not married to her. She is not mine. I needed to collar her the only way I knew how, but first I needed to talk to Ian. For a moment, the thought entered my head that I had made a mistake by divorcing her so soon. But with everything going on behind the scenes to make their wedding happen and knowing the attachment she already had to me, I had to believe this was right for her. Kate's happiness was the most important thing on my list.

I took the bindings off Kate before we left the shop. I took her shoe shopping then back to The Diamond where her family were waiting for her in her room. A welcome surprise for her, I hoped.

Ian, the boys and Dad were waiting in my room. I took them to Tiffanies.

Ian sighed, "You have been busy. I don't even know how you have had the time to organise it all."

"Yeah well I am hoping that you will propose to her, marry her and get the happily ever after you both deserve. I am also hoping that you will share her until I go, or until my dick does not work. It isn't the traditional start to a marriage… if you don't want to share her, that is cool."

Ian glared at me, "You shouldn't have divorced her."

I looked at my little brother and my heart rate kicked up a notch, "What?"

"You should never have divorced her. Neither of you wanted that. She would have been yours 'til the end and you divorced her."

"Ian, you like her. I would love to see you move on and be happy. I know she could do that with you."

"Chemical attraction like ours will burn out. There is no way it will last." He shook his head, "Remarry her..."

"I will not make her a widow twice! I cannot and will not do it. But if you don't think she will make you happy then I will cancel everything now."

"I will go through with it. I will share and play happy families with her until you go. After that we will just have to work it out between us. If you can live knowing that, then I will go through with it."

I could not believe my ears. I asked Ben. "She is in love with both of us. I know I love her. Do you believe for one second that he isn't in love with her?"

"I know he isn't in love with her." Ben shrugged. "He likes her but to him she is just a fuck."

"Hey! I wouldn't go that far." Ian objected, "She is beautiful, smart and brave as hell, but she is a level of crazy that I don't think I can handle."

I smirked at Ian, "You were hard at the courthouse watching her."

"I get turned on by tears." He shrugged.

"You get turned on by crazy. That is why you put up with Amy," Richard snapped.

"I have never fucked Amy," Ian snarled.

"But you have fucked Kate." Dad glared at Ian. "I bet you and Charlie fucking tag teamed her." Ian went to deny it and Dad pointed a finger in his face. "Don't fucking lie to me. I know you are all filthy fuckers. Charlie and Richard tag teamed girls more than once."

I do not believe any of us knew that Dad knew. We all looked at each other. "We aren't that filthy," I shrugged.

Dad rolled his eyes. "Bullshit. You idolised Don. That fucker was even kinkier than I am..." All of us stared at Dad. I started to grin slowly as Dad realised, he had just let the cat out of the bag... So, he got back on the subject. "Kate fell for both of you." Dad pointed at Ian then back at me, "You randomly found a really nice girl and you are both going to break her heart. You better hope like hell her father is easy going and she doesn't have any brothers because if they find out what you did, you won't have time to finish your bucket list."

"Her brother is right here." Richard pointed at Ben.

Dad looked at Ben with disbelief. "What?"

Ben shook his head, "Don't John, Kate will be fine. I will make sure of it."

Dad shook his head, "If Ian marries her, he is going to break her heart. He doesn't love her."

Ben nodded. "She will go through with it because she lost a dare. I can't tell her what to do because she doesn't know who I am."

"Would you tell her not to be so stupid as to go through with it?" John challenged.

"No. Because she would do it anyway." Ben sighed "In that respect, she is just like me."

## 51. Kate

I walked slowly to my hotel room. I was emotionally wrecked. Charlie knew his clock was ticking and seemed to be just getting the bucket list ticked off. I was just the fool going along with it. By the time I got back to my room, I was ready for a shower and a sleep. I opened the door and stopped dead in my tracks.

My kids and in-laws were waiting inside. *FUCK!*

I hugged them all tightly and broke down like a complete sook as I filled them in. I left out the sex, but I told them everything else.

Each of them told me off. We had a family shouting match that had security come up to check everything was okay. Twice. My family all made good points about the weddings but then they shouted about my using the money I won to pay off their debts. I got angry and shouted back.

"Look, I know I am a fucking idiot and you all think I am a fucking fool, but I did it because I love you all and you put up with me. Stop shouting at me about the money! I didn't fucking want it! Charlie just put it into my account! Blame him! Please just get off my fucking back. IT WAS *NOT* MY IDEA TO COME TO VEGAS! IN FACT, I TOLD YOU *NOT* TO SEND ME HERE! YOU ALL SAID OH RELAX SHORTY IT WILL BE FUN! GO HAVE SEX AND FIND A NEW HUSBAND. I DID AND NOW I'm THE FUCKING BAD GUY? GO FUCK YOURSELVES!"

Well we sat glaring at each other while the kids watched us. They both look like they needed popcorn for the show they were watching.

I was wiping my eyes calming down when there was a knock at the door. Brian, still fuming, opened it and Charlie came in and was instantly greeted like a brother. I looked at my family opened mouthed as they did. They just spent God knows how long chewing me out like the bad guy and here they were treating him like a brother. I felt so alone. I shook my head and went to the bathroom to wash my face and to listen.

I needed to find some fucking composure!

"You know how fucking mean it is that we didn't get to give you a buck's night," Brian started.

"Yeah, it is tradition." Billy got in on it.

Charlie laughed, "I would have asked you, but Kate would have not played up as much."

"Who is Kate?" Ryan asked. I frowned and walked out of the bathroom. Charlie looked confused when he pointed at me. "You are nuts mate! That is Shorty."

I glanced at Brian and the rest of my family, realising at that moment the kids had only ever heard me called by my nickname.

"Ryan, Ella, Shorty is my nickname. Like when I call Emma, Red," I explained.

"So… your name isn't Shorty?" Ella clarified, omg two-year-old attitude.

"What is it then?" Ryan exclaimed.

"Kaitlyn Grace. Or Kate for short." I told them with a blush. Both kids made a face "What?"

"My whole life is a lie!" Ryan threw his hands in the air dramatically. "It is just so girly. Like a princess name or something." He shuddered.

Thanks son, way to make Mummy feel gross.

"Yeah." Ella sighed, obviously loving it. "You should be called that more often. It is pretty. You could wear dresses if you were called Kaitlyn."

Charlie smiled as I introduced him to the kids. They sat on his lap and told him stories about the real me. He listened and laughed. I doubt he understood a word they said. There was another knock on the door. I opened it to find Ian was there with two little kiddies who were as adorable as mine.

"This is Evie and Tim. They just arrived and want to see Uncle Charlie." Ian looked apologetic.

"He is inside, go get him." I smiled at them and they burst past me into the room.

"Hello Monkeys!" Charlie exclaimed as Ian and I went to the bedroom shutting the door so we could talk.

I couldn't face Ian. I was too emotional. "Are you okay?"

"Are you?" he asked. I shook my head and I bit my lip to stop it trembling. I didn't want to cry. "Come here." I face planted his chest and hugged him, trying desperately to compose myself. His arms held me tight. "Do you want to come sit and process?"

I shook my head. "All my family are here."

"Do you want to sleep with Charlie tonight?" he asked.

"I don't know what he wants."

"He wants us to get married."

"Ian, after the things we have done, I don't think you really want someone like me as a wife."

"Actually, I do. My wife was a princess. Delicate, petite, with not a violent or retaliatory bone in her body. She always worried about her weight and to be honest, was a little too skinny. She was not adventurous, would not go camping or try different things. She could not see the bad in anyone. I suspect that is what got her killed."

He tilted my chin up so I would look at him. "When Charlie picked you, you looked beautiful and petite and like every other girl. Then you took up the challenge of helping him with this bucket list. I thought you would moan and complain. But you did not. You stepped up to every challenge. Watching you get head was sexy as fuck. I love watching you come."

I blushed. "I watched you too."

"I know." He smiled. "But I think it was when you saved Charlie… I watched you argue with your instructor, even he did not want you to do it. On the ground, he called you batshit crazy."

I giggled, "It is just me. I haven't acted anything else. What you see is what you get."

"What I see is a beautiful, elegant woman. What we got was a little badass dressed like a princess. That excites and scares me."

"Why? I would never hurt you," I said softly.

"Because getting put in the doghouse could hurt. Why do I get the feeling you could kick my ass?"

"Because I could." I winked at him.

"If you two are in there doing wicked and wonderful things to each other, would you please open the door so I can watch?" Charlie called and I giggled as I met Ian's smile.

"Charlie! I am trying to propose," Ian called back.

*Wait what?* I looked up at him, panicked. My heart started pounding through my chest.

"She will faint," Gerrard called as the doors opened. "I love it when she faints. Proceed."

I looked at Gerrard and my family and then over to Charlie who just smiled, he was obviously feeling how I was. A little heart broken and overwhelmed after the last few days. I looked at him for help and he mouthed, *'Just say yes'*.

I turned back to Ian as he took my hand. He was on one knee. He held out a ring with a diamond so big I was sure I would never lift it. I looked into his blue eyes which were uncertain but set on his decision. He didn't love me but would marry me to make his brother happy.


## 52. Charlie

Kate's eyes rolled and her knees gave out. Ian grabbed her, looking a little surprised. He glanced at me as he put her on the floor gently. Her family stood around laughing. I smiled; I had not expected that. She looked so small on the floor. It hurt that she was not my wife. I reminded myself that I was making arrangements for her when I died. I had more plans for her.

"Dad? Why did the lady faint?" Tim asked as he went to Ian, patting him on the shoulder.

"Well I am hoping she will be your new Mum." Ian smiled.

171

*Oh no Ian. Please do not say this and break their hearts later. If you do not love her do not do it!*

Ian glanced at me as though reading my thoughts. His face said he would marry her for me and look after her, but love was not a promise.

"You want to be our Dad?" Ryan asked wide-eyed.

"Yep." Ian looked at him and Ella then at me checking I was okay. I nodded. There were children involved. He looked back to Kate who opened her eyes. He held up the ring. Her eyes rolled and she went limp again.

"Get the ring out of her face. Ask her the question and then give her the ring," Brian chuckled. I had not expected to see half of Crosshairs in Kate's room.

"Fucker makes us all look bad," Gerrard grumbled shaking his head. I looked at him wondering why he would say that.

"I wouldn't change the ring you gave me for the world." Carrie said, "Having you is enough."

He smiled and kissed her. She wanted him regardless of the size of the diamond. Only Kate had ever been like that with me. I looked back at Ian and Kate. Kate had opened her eyes and he smiled at her.

"I was in the process of asking you to marry me." Ian chuckled.

"Is this forever or 'cause Charlie made you?" she asked softly.

"Forever." Ian looked like he meant it. He was acting and deserved an academy award for his performance.

Ian sat Kate up and hugged her while he whispered in her ear. She was reduced to tears and then met his eyes and nodded. He went back to whispering in her ear and she looked over at me. I was the most loved man in the world. I smiled and nodded. I needed them to move on. I had to believe he would fall for her. Time was ticking.

Kate and Ian looked into each other's eyes for a moment before she nodded, "Yes." My heart felt shattered for a moment. Now she was not mine. Then it filled because Ian had finally moved on. Kate would make Ian happy and look after him for me. All the kids started cheering and piled on top of them. I sat back and sighed. This was fucking awesome. A glimpse of the future. One I would never get to see.

A hand touched my shoulder and I looked up to see Brian as he sat beside me.

"Hard not to love the little bitch, isn't it?"

I looked at him. nodding. "Yeah."

"How long you got?"

"Grim reaper is stalking me. The doctor gave me a month. I don't think I that have long," I said softly. "If Ian tries to divorce her, beat him to his senses and tell him it was from me."

He smiled. "Done. Anything else?"

"Are you her brother?"

"Charlie, you have met her before, remember the investigator you thought was crazy? Shorty? That is Kate."

I turned to stare at Kate, again her words came back to me and I realised; only a couple of weeks before she had been hurt by the same man who had hurt Hannah! I turned back to Brian who just finished answering my question.

"We are technically in-laws but when Chris died, we made her our sister." When he smiled at her I could see how much he loved and respected Kate. It was the same love and friendship I had seen at the office. How the fuck did I not know who she was?... It might have helped if I read her background check properly.

"She doesn't have any blood relatives?"

"Well she is the product of a one-night stand between the man who raised her and her mother who died when she was just shy of 15."

"So, she doesn't know who her biological father is?"

"Yeah, she had a photo. When I came to work over here, she asked me to track him down."

"Did you find him?"

"Yeah. He died twelve months ago. She has a brother but when we contacted him, he didn't want to meet her."

"What is his name? I will make a phone call." I grinned.

"Ben Henderson. Supposed to be some hotshot lawyer." Brian sighed. "I think he thought she was after money. She just wanted to know him."

I looked at Brian, deciding to drop Ben in it. "Well that is just too fucking funny."

"What is?"

"She has been hanging out with him for the last four days. He likes her, thinks she is a bitch, but he likes her, and he hates pretty much everyone." I got out my phone to text Ben and my family *'party in Kate's room'*. "Want to meet him? And not tell him who she is?"

"I like games but if Shorty finds out. She won't forgive me."

Brian and I sat debating until everyone arrived. We looked at Ben, at Kate and then back at each other.

"I don't know how I didn't notice; they have the same eyes," I whispered to Brian.

"She has got her mother's height," Brian whispered back. "But yes, their eyes are remarkably similar. Was her Dad tall?"

"Bit shorter than Ben."

I introduced everyone to my family and Mum—well she had her eyes locked on Ian, the ring on Kate's finger and the kids all over them. I took her hand and she looked at me. I got up and gave her a hug and then kissed her cheek.

"Please, accept it. She will look after him when I am gone. I need to see him move on. I want him to be happy."

Mum looked up at me, opened then shut her mouth. I could pretty much get away with murder right now. I gave her another hug as Brian slapped Ben on the shoulder in a brotherly way.

"So, Ben, do you like to drink?" Brian asked as I tried not to smirk.

"I love to drink," Ben grinned.

"Good, cause that fucker looks like he needs a hangover." Brian pointed at Ian.

Ben nodded thoughtfully, "He does, doesn't he…"? He looked across at me. "How much shit have you got left on your bucket list?"

I smiled, "Those two getting married and a few other things." Like the house I had bought for Ian and Kate to live in. I had put it in their names and literally had an army of workmen repainting and furnishing it as I sat here.

"Well come on then. Rita and Joe have unpacked. We can leave the kids with them while we go play." Richard rubbed his hands together and said to Kate, "You hold your drink well my girl but tonight you might be out of your league."

Kate laughed, "Honey, I will drink your arse under the table and still be up at the gym in the morning."

"You didn't go to the gym this morning." He smirked.

"I had a personal trainer give me a cardio work out." She grinned at me. I smiled. "What do you say Charlie, they should have given you a buck's night too."

"Oh, this is going to be epic." Billy rubbed his hands together.

"Hey, we are coming too." Emma said.

Billy looked at her. "No."

"Yes." She contradicted.

"It's a buck's night." Billy growled at her. I would say they fought like siblings.

"Yeah well, I want to party, and Shorty is too much trouble when she is drinking. We are going to need help." Carrie crossed her arms.

Billy pursed his lips, "Alright, just dress hot so you drive the boys nuts. Hey kids, do you want to have a sleepover?"

## 53. Kate

Emma and Carrie were going to get dressed with me, but we ended up having another fight. I kicked them out of my room so I could have some time with Ryan and Ella. They sat on my bed and we checked out the selfies and photos that I had taken so far on my holiday.

"You didn't tell us that you were coming to find us a new Dad?" Ella scowled.

I kissed the top of her head. "I didn't plan on it."

"Is he going to be our Dad forever?" she asked.

I shook my head "I don't know. But I can promise, I am going nowhere."

"Does that mean we don't have to listen to him?" Ryan asked.

"You do have to listen to him." I said, "He is an adult, so you need to respect him."

I got dressed with their help. Ryan kept telling me how pretty I looked, making me blush. When Nelly and Harry arrived to pick the kids up for the night, they couldn't wait to go. Harry had another quick dig at me. I just shook my head because I didn't want to hear it.

On my own at last, I sat in silence with my head in my hands. I was an idiot. Ian didn't love me. I knew in my heart that he was only doing this for Charlie. So, I had to ask myself, why was I going along with it? I owed Charlie nothing. I could be there for him through his last days and not pretend that Ian and I would have a happy ending.

Ian arrived to pick me up and we walked in silence. I suppose when you lose a bet you are too stubborn to back down from, there isn't much to say. In the elevator, I looked up at him.

"You don't have to marry me. We can do the wedding but not sign the paperwork. Charlie would never know."

"Have you got cold feet?"

"You don't love me. I don't want you to feel trapped." I turned away.

"We are getting married. Charlie will share you until he goes. We are going to play happy families and when he goes, we will work it out."

"Are we even going to try?"

"We will work it out," he said softly.

He took my hand as the elevator doors opened to our waiting families. Everyone seemed to mix well. I didn't want to do anything but go hide in my room. It only took half an hour for Ben to pull me aside.

"Are you alright?"

"Yeah, I am fine."

"This is supposed to be your bachelorette night," he pressed. "You aren't talking to anyone."

"That is because everyone on my side spent a good two hours pointing out how stupid I am and well everything else… I am fine. I will smile. Will that get you off my back?"

He shook his head. "Nope. Do you want to pretend to be sick and we can go gamble and get drunk then come back when you are in a better mood to party?"

"I am okay." I patted his arm. "You are the only one not calling me a gold-digging fucking idiot who is out of my mind. I am not sure I even deserve your good graces."

"Yeah alright, now I am worried. Come on." He took my arm, pulled me to my feet and walked me toward the door.

"Oi, where you goin' with Shorty!" Billy called.

Ben turned, "I am going to see if we can have more fun drinking and gambling together."

"What? Do you want in her panties now?" Billy smirked. I turned and looked at him feeling more hurt than I had in forever. The look on Billy's face a second later, he realised what he said. "Shorty, come on, that wasn't directed at you. I was kidding"

I held up my hand and shook my head. "I will be back. Ben and I are going to gamble for a while."

"Shorty, I am sorry." He touched my arm. "I know we were a bit rough on ya before…"

"Yeah, it's all good Billy, I wouldn't expect any less from you. You all said what I was thinking anyway. Well except for the money stuff. I just need a little time out. It's been a big day. I will come back and play up later."

## 54. Charlie

Ben walked off with Kate and I almost followed. I turned to Ian and pointed.

"What did you say to her?"

He held up his hands "I didn't say anything that would make her feel like that."

"No, that would have been us," Brian admitted. "She came clean and we went off."

"Had security come up to the room twice to check we were okay." Carrie shrugged.

I cocked an eyebrow, "Why did you let her have it?"

"Because she is an idiot." Brian pointed at me. "She loves you; I don't doubt it. And you…" He pointed at Ian, "You are under her skin in a big way and you only want to fuck her. You put on a fucking good show but that was all it was."

Ian took a long drink, his eyes flashing with anger. "Who the fuck are you to tell me how I feel about Kate?"

"I know love when I see it. Charlie loves her. You don't." Brian wasn't about to back down.

"It is my fault." I said, feeling like shit. "It is my fault." I ran my fingers though my hair in frustration. "Call it off."

Ian shook his head, "I have talked to her. We have worked it out. It will be okay. I asked her. She said yes, she will be my wife. I will look after her and be open to loving her as promised. You do not need to worry about anything except having fun. Everything else is on me."

"Is it her scars that bother you?" Emma asked softly looking up at him.

Ian looked at her. "No! Her body is amazing." He meant that. We could all see it.

"So, it's because she works a rough job?" Carrie nodded understanding.

"I don't even know what she does for a living. After winning that fifty million the other night, I would think she would retire." Ian said with a smile. "I wonder what she will spend it on."

"She didn't tell you?" Gerrard asked, we shook our heads. "She paid out our collective debts, set our future kids up for college and paid off our business loan."

I smiled at Brian. "You finally own it."

He nodded, "She bought a heap of shares or something and put some money away for a rainy day and then gave the rest to charity."

My jaw dropped. "She spent it?" Her family nodded. "How the fuck did she manage to spend fifty million dollars in five days? How much did she give to charity?"

"Oh, she um put it in the charity she started. She has had trouble funding it for a long time." Emma shrugged.

"I don't understand. Why she would just go spend it all! I was going to sit down and talk to her about investing in stocks and property."

"She did all that." Billy shrugged. "She didn't waste a penny."

I looked at them. "How? We have been with her most of the time."

"How have you managed to plan a wedding, a house and everything else?" Richard countered. Ian looked at him with a WTF expression. Richard looked calmly at Ian. "He bought a house for you and Kate to live in when you get back."

I could have killed Richard, but I held my tongue and energy because they all started arguing. Ian growled at me and I sighed.

"Well don't go through with it. It really is that simple. If you do not love her and feel nothing for her. Do not marry her. You both deserve better." I gave up.

"I feel for her Charlie. You know I do. I just do not think I can love a woman after five days! I need time. As I told you, I have talked to her and she is alright with it."

"Hey! This is supposed to be a joint bachelor night. It is supposed to be fun." Susan stopped the conversation. *Great now she was about to get pissy.* She took Tammy's hand. "How about we get back on track and actually get drunk and party? We are going to go find the bride-to-be and take her dancing. Because this sure as fuck is about as fun as fucking a cactus."

She glared at Emma and Carrie, "If someone had just gone and paid out my debt, you can bet your ass I would be fucking grateful. Not bitching about it. If you come with us, then you better remember it is Kate's night. She shouldn't be fucking miserable."

Then she turned and glared at Ian. "And you… If you marry that woman and try and measure her by Aria's standard, you will fail, the marriage will fail, and you will hurt not just her, but all the kids. You need to let Kate sit on her own pedestal with her own standards. She cannot be Aria. So, don't expect her to be."

Emma and Carrie looked at each other. "We weren't all that rough on her."

"Charlie flew you in because she needed her family here for support, especially after this morning's events and the first thing you did was kick her in the teeth to make sure she stayed down. Kate raved about you all, how much of a support you were to her and how much she loved you all. I honestly can't see why."

"Susan, this isn't your place," Richard put his hand on her shoulder.

She shrugged him off. "Richard, I am going to go find Kate. I am going to get her drunk and I am going to make sure she has some fucking fun. Because I really am over the drama."

"Ben said he will be back with her." Ian said, "Just leave them chill."

Susan glared at Ian. "Ben did that thing he always does when he has no intention of returning. He gave her an out and she took it. So, I am going to go find her, get her so fucking drunk that she will be so sick tomorrow that she won't care that the marriage is a sham."

## 55. Kate

Susan and Tammy found Ben and me sitting at the blackjack tables losing money, Ben was being a fucker. Apparently, he counted cards as well as I did. I didn't mind losing to the house, I just didn't like losing to him. Susan fed us drinks before conning me into going to dancing. She made me laugh. Even Ben was smiling when we made our way to the club. I was finally starting to relax and have fun.

That was before I saw that the rest of them were at the club too. But they all seemed content to dance and drink and have fun. Emma and Carrie joined me when Ben disappeared to the bar. My two best friends were being their normal cheeky selves. I was still hurt from our fight, but I'd had enough shots to relax.

We played up like two bob watches for four hours and the boys were suffering for it. Emma, Carrie, and I had fed Susan and Tammy enough shots that they were dirty dancing with us. The boys watched us, drinks in their hands and lust in their eyes.

Ian looked like he wanted to fuck me six ways to Sunday, Charlie looked at me like he would spank me and then fuck me. I turned away from both of not really wanting to touch either of them. Charlie had broken my heart and Ian… He would eventually work out that he really didn't want me and leave.

Emma was stirring Brian who was devouring her with the same carnal look Chris used to get.

"He is going to fuck your brains out," I said in her ear, trying to be heard over the music.

"I know, I can't wait." She smiled. "You might just end up with a threesome with Charlie and Ian if you keep going."

"We already did." I said.

Shocked and bright eyed she demanded, "Details now."

"No, I can't." I blushed then realised she probably already knew that.

"Well are you going to do it again?"

I shrugged. "Maybe. I kissed a girl too."

She went wide-eyed. "Was that on his bucket list?"

"Well, it kind of just happened."

"What was it like?"

"It was okay, she was a good kisser."

"Was it different though?"

"Yeah, well her mouth was softer, different, still nice though." I really shouldn't be having deep and meaningful conversations with Emma while I was still angry and bordering on drunk…

We danced a little longer. "Will you be my first girl kiss?" Emma asked with a filthy grin.

I was surprised by that but shrugged, why the fuck not. We were about to kiss when Carrie butted in to ask what we were doing. Emma explained.

"I always wanted to try that," Carrie said.

"Try what?" Tammy and Susan asked.

After another explanation, they grinned too. "We have done that. It drives the boys insane." Tammy giggled.

"I'll kiss you Carrie. The boys get weirded out when Tammy kisses a girl." Susan offered.

"You still keen?" I asked Emma.

She nodded, "Hell yeah." She bit her lip and we moved in slowly, brushing our lips together. "Oh it is soft." Emma said, looking into my eyes.

"Yeah." I said, knowing that the alcohol was fully to blame for my behaviour right now. Oh God this was so naughty.

As she pressed her mouth to mine, I put my hands in her hair. She wrapped her arms around me. I claimed her mouth as she kissed me back. Kissing a woman was different. After a little while Emma giggled and broke the kiss. I opened my eyes to see Brian who had lost his self-restraint.

"We are going back to the room. Now." He told her, trying to glare at me, but his eyes were sparkling as he pointed. "Naughty girl. You should be spanked for that."

I giggled and felt a hand on my shoulder, I looked back at Ian, "Am I in trouble?"

"Yes, you are." I smiled and took his hand with one hand waving 'bye to Emma with the other.

When Ian and I made it upstairs Charlie was waiting with the door open. When the door shut behind us Charlie took my face and kissed me while Ian undressed me. If the first threesome was intense. It had nothing on this one.

When we finally lay on the sheets Ian kissed me with a tenderness he had not shown before, like a promise. It made my belly flutter. It shouldn't have fluttered. I had been feeling like shit for most of the night knowing I was about to marry a man who didn't love me. Now that I had fucked the alcohol out of my system, I felt slutty. Connection or not, I had just been used and I had let it happen.

"I'll see you tomorrow. Bad luck to see the bride before she goes down the aisle. You two enjoy the rest of the night."

Ian gazed into my eyes before touching my face, concern in his eyes. "Are you okay?" I simply nodded. "You sure? You didn't have that look in your eye the first night."

"I am fine," I said softly looking away from him and his beautiful blue eyes.

He took my chin gently and moved me, so I met his eyes for a split second and then had to look away again. He stroked my cheek. "It isn't traditional Kate. I admit I am not in love with you. But that does not mean I will not fall. Fuck everyone and their opinions. We will work it out, okay? We have time."

I nodded but didn't give him my eyes. "Okay."

"Look at me," he snarled softly. I shook my head. "Look at me."

Slowly, I lifted my eyes to his. I dropped my walls and let him see how I was really feeling but I could not face the intensity in his eyes.

"Kate, look at me." His hand cupped my face, he was surprisingly gentle which weirdly hurt more. Not many men had touched me with such tenderness. "We will work it out. I promise. We will work it out." I could see he believed it and wasn't just saying it to make us both feel better. "Stay with Charlie. After the last twenty-four hours, I don't think you should be alone."

"Ian, are you sure?" Charlie asked.

"Yes, we have to make the most of the time we have. Kate can't help loving two men." Ian kissed me again then got up and dressed. He winked before he left the suite.

Charlie pulled me into his arms, and I snuggled against him. "Tonight turned out better than I expected."

"Me too after the way it started." I kissed his chest. "Thank you for bringing me on this crazy adventure."

"Thank you for being you." He kissed my forehead. "Are you okay?"

I shook my head. "No, I should have turned him down, I should have turned you both down so I could gather my thoughts and get some sleep. But I gave in like a little slut."

"You feel used? By him or both of us?" Charlie's concern flipped my heart. I didn't want to upset him.

"Him. I mean if you hadn't have picked me, he wouldn't have looked twice. I mean who wants to go to bed with Frankenstein and Deadpool's love child every night for the rest of their life?"

He pulled me into his arms spooning me. He bit my neck gently, whispering in my ear, "Me. I would. I want you until my last breath. But I won't make you a widow twice." He sighed. "Can I tell you a secret?" I nodded "He saw you first. I saw your eyes meet and how you played it cool. But you didn't hear his reaction when he first saw you."

"What do you mean."

"He stopped walking and when I asked what he was doing he said 'Mine. We might share her. But she is Mine.'" He paused for effect. "I haven't heard him effectively claim a woman ever. He wants you but does not want to. This means that what he had with Aria is officially finished. He has to move on."

185

I shook my head. I couldn't believe that Ian's issue was pretty much the same as mine. Chris was gone and now I was moving on. It scared the hell out of me. I wondered whether Ian ever considered that I was in the same boat. First with Chris and now with Charlie—and he wasn't even dead yet. "Can we make love again? Before you are going to have to rest because tomorrow is, I hope will make your dreams come true."

I touched his face and nodded, "I love you, Charlie." He eased himself into me, my body bowed and clenched down on him. I took a couple of deep breaths. I was a little dry.

He reached down to manipulate my clit. I wasn't dry for long.

"I love you, Katie." The way he said it broke my heart. He meant it. He really, truly meant it.

We made love 'till we were exhausted then we cuddled, looking deep into each other's souls until we fell asleep.

## 56. Charlie

I woke with Kate in my arms, at peace. She opened her eyes. I smiled.

"Good morning."

"Good morning, Charlie." She sighed and touched my face. "You look happy."

"I am. Today I get to pretend you are my daughter and give you away."

"Did you want kids?" Kate asked.

"Before you, no."

"Go jizz in a cup and I will have one for you. You can leave your legacy." She got up on her elbow.

I stroked her face with my fingertips as I felt tight in the chest. She would give me everything I ever wanted and not think twice. "Are you on the pill?"

"No, but you and Ian have used protection."

"I haven't," I admitted, watching her reaction because Kate was either going to be happy or kill me. "If it happens then it happens. If it doesn't, it wasn't meant to be."

She stared at me as that sank in before she whispered, "Jizz in a cup in case it doesn't."

"Charlie Johnathan for a boy and Alexia Rachael for a girl, okay." I kissed her with the tenderness I had never felt for another woman. "Get up and get dressed. You have a wedding to prepare for."

Kate made no move to get up and smiled at me instead. "Before I do, I have a secret to tell you."

"What is that?"

"There is another rarity in marriage I want to share with you."

"And what would that be?"

"Charlie, I am pregnant." She looked so shy as she said it.

I am sure my eyes damn near bulged out of my head with surprise as excitement and love flowed though me like an unstoppable river. I kissed her belly where they would be growing if this were real, then kissed her mouth. "Oh, I hope so! Swim you little fuckers swim. Find a couple of nice eggs and fertilise them. Boy and a girl please. You are going to have the best mum in the world and dad. I am going to be your guardian angel. CJ please do not be a slut. And Lexie you either. I love you both. Somehow, I just know you are in there."

I went back to kissing her belly. Kate stroked my hair with a contented smile on her face. I moved up the bed and kissed her again as my heart wished this were real. "They are in there. I know it. Thank you, Kate."

## 57. Kate

Part of me just wanted to have Charlie hear the words just so he could feel the elation and another part of me knew he was right. I got dressed and kissed him once again before I went back to my room. It was empty and for once I just enjoyed a shower and prepared myself mentally for the day ahead.

There was a knock on the door an hour and a half later. Ben entered with Ryan and Ella. I hugged both my babies fiercely.

"Ben and Charlie made us buy dresses and stuff and he is making me wear a suit." Ryan rolled his eyes as if it were the biggest drama in the world. "I hope you look pretty Mum 'cause if I have to wear a suit you should look like a princess like Ella and Evie."

I smiled, "How about I get some food bought up and you guys can chill?"

They ran off to turn the TV on and zoned out. I looked at Ben. "I hope they were okay?"

"They were absolutely hilarious." He grinned. "Charlie was trying to convince Ryan that a suit was the way to a woman's heart."

"We all know it is a uniform," Ryan shouted.

I laughed and Ben chuckled before he said, "Ella had a dress allergy until Charlie convinced her to try on something and now you may have issues with her and fashion."

"Dresses are awesome. Charlie said I was pretty," Ella blushed, her hands behind her, moving as if she were swishing a dress. I asked her to go watch the TV and when she ran off, I looked up at Ben.

"Thank you for last night. For getting me out of the mood I was in."

"Don't mention it. I am glad you ended up having a good night."
He pulled out an electronic document reader and papers. "Ian
wants the paperwork signed before you go down the aisle to save
time for photos and the reception." We went to a table and he put it
all down.

"There is a prenup and a couple of other things to sign too. The
gist of the prenup is no alimony, 50-50 split on kids should you
have any together, shared holidays and birthdays etc, no money
exchange. Put your thumb print here." He pointed to an electronic
document. I did and put my thumb where he asked me to. "Okay,
sign these and we are done."

I checked the paperwork and saw Ian had already signed. I
signed it all and asked Ben, "Has Charlie finished his bucket list?"

"Just the wedding, the reception and a few things he needs to sort
out for work. He will probably add more to the list. He said he is
going to walk you down the aisle and pretend you are his
daughter."

"He told me that." I bit my lip. "What is your take on the last
week?"

He thought about it for a moment and sat back. "It has been
interesting. We have each had a conversation with him and pretty
much said our goodbyes. I think you are exactly what Charlie
needed. And I think you are exactly what Ian is going to need," he
said firmly. "I have known the family a long time. When Ian lost
Aria, I thought we would lose him too. He went to a dark place. I
think if he didn't have the kids, he would have killed himself."

I could totally relate to that feeling. "So, is Ian only going to
marry me because Charlie wished it? Am I going to be hurt at the
end of this?"

He cocked his head to the side. "Is he just doing this for
Charlie?" I nodded slowly; I wasn't sure I wanted to know the
answer. "No, Ian wouldn't marry anyone because his brother
insisted on it. He likes you. He is a little worried for the same
reason only the other way around. Are you marrying him for
Charlie's sake? There is no money involved regardless."

"I don't want money. I have a job. I am marrying him with the hope of growing old together. I really like him but..." I bit my lip and my eyes welled up. "I fell for Charlie; he is going to die, and I only just survived Chris. I am worried that when all this is done, Ian will realise he doesn't want me."

I turned away from him and shook my head. "I wish Mum and Dad were here to talk to. But I already know what they would say. Everyone made it perfectly clear yesterday."

"Haven't you got anyone else?" he asked.

I shook my head. "I have the kids and I have the Smiths who love and accept me. Most of the time that is enough."

"What about aunts, uncles or siblings?"

"No. I am the product of a one-night stand. Mum had a photo of my Dad. When we moved over here, I thought why not? I could go and meet him and see what he is like and stuff." *Why the fuck am I telling him this? Am I so emotionally fucked that I can't shut my mouth?*

"Did you find him?"

"Yeah, I was three days too late. He died. I went to the funeral. I stood back from the crowd because I didn't really belong there, but I did go. He has a son, so I have a half-brother."

"Did you try and contact him?"

"Yeah, he wanted nothing to do with me. Probably figured I was after money or wasn't worth the time." I shrugged and sat on the bed, running my hands through my hair. "I just wanted to check he was okay after losing his Dad. When he responded saying he didn't want to meet, I respected it. I am not everyone's cup of tea and that is okay."

I changed the subject. I didn't want to talk about this anymore. "When am I supposed to get ready?" Where the fuck was this leading? We had not really spoken other than to talk shit, now we were talking family.

"Well now. The girls should be here soon." He stepped forward and sat on the bed beside me. "What is your brother's name?"

"Doesn't matter. If he is anything like me, once his mind is made up then he won't change it."

"I am trying to have a moment with you." He grinned and I must have looked as confused as I felt.

"I am not going to screw you even if you are dying." I held up my hand, shaking my head.

Ben laughed, "No, it's nothing like that."

"I am not kissing you either." I got up and moved away from him.

"I will not be doing that either." Ben laughed more.

"I like you man, but you are friend zoned like Richard. Yuck."

"Brother zone me and I will feel safer."

"Billy, and Gerrard are in that zone. Friend zone is appropriate."

"Kate, I am your brother. So please, brother zone me."

I blinked as I looked up at him. I was right? I mean I did think he looked like him but then I had only seen him from a distance at our father's funeral. I opened my mouth to talk, but nothing came out. I was gobsmacked. *I had been given head within a meter of him! OMG!*

My vision started going dark and for the third time in two days, I fainted.

## 58. Charlie

I talked to Ian; he was in a much better frame of mind about getting remarried. Then I stopped in to see Mum and Dad. They shook their heads and said they accepted the impending wedding, but neither were happy. Thankfully, they were not going to try to stop it. When I stopped in to check on Kate's parents, they were having a family meeting and greeted me like a brother. They were all dressed for the wedding and looked great.

"As if I didn't wreck her enough, you all finished the job yesterday," I told them. "Please, I am asking you to be supportive. Ian is in a good frame of mind now and so is Kate."

"You wouldn't know what is going on in her head," Harry said softly. "You haven't got a clue. I think this is a big mistake."

"So, you yell at her?" I asked. "You all ganged up on her. All of you. There wasn't one person in her corner."

"Yeah well Ben seemed to be in her corner. Is she fucking him too?" Billy muttered.

I cocked an eyebrow. "He is Ben Henderson, her brother. Yesterday, he was the only one who was in her corner."

"I forgot to tell you all that." Brian shrugged. Everyone glared at him, "Ben is Shorty's brother."

Harry recovered and turned back to me. "Look, I know that you and Ian have been tag teaming my daughter and I am not happy about it. I am sorry you are ill Son…"

"I am dying. I was given a month nearly three weeks ago." I said flatly. I did not like admitting my time was nearly up. "I love your daughter. I promise you she will be well looked after when I am gone to make everything worth it."

"She will never accept it." Nelly shook her head.

"She already has. She thinks it was part of the prenup," I told her. "I hope to be nothing but a happy memory for Kate. To go out as I am. Not some sick and decrepit man she felt sorry for, but the man she fell in love with."

"She doesn't feel sorry for you." Brian said, being sincere. "She loves you. She loves that idiot brother of yours too."

"He is going to hurt her," Gerrard muttered before shaking his head.

I shook my head. "He is massively attracted to her. They have great chemistry. He saw her and… I have never seen him like it. The second she lay eyes on him it was the same for her. Give Ian time to get his head around it. He has been in a bad way since he lost his wife."

I spent five more minutes making sure that they were not going to cause trouble and would be supportive before I went to Kate's room.

I had so much fun with Ryan and Ella earlier. They were great kids and could not wait to see them all dressed up. I was all suited up, ready to walk my Kate down the aisle. When I knocked on her door Emma greeted me with a big smile, looking beautiful in her dark blue satin bridesmaid's dress.

"Did you really pick the dress?" she asked. I did not think she could look much happier. *Good, she was supporting Kate, just as she should.*

I nodded as I walked in, "Does she like it?"

"Come see for yourself, I believe that she is your daughter for the day."

"Yes, she is." Ella came over and did a spin. "Well now, don't you just look like a perfect princess. You look beautiful."

Ella blushed sweetly. "Thank you, Daddy."

My heart melted. Then Ryan walked through the door in his suit. "Now, there is a smooth, good-looking man."

"It does look good." He looked impressed.

See, little man, suits do make you look good.

I gave both kids a hug and then went to the bedroom where Kate was eyeing herself nervously in the mirror. I could nearly picture my daughter standing there. I teared up. I was not used to warm and fuzzy feelings like this, but I was sure, this is what I would feel if she were my daughter. Technically, I was walking my daughter down the aisle, she was inside Kate… I hoped.

The A-line gown fell gently off her hips with very little flare, full of lace and jewels, it had a cathedral length train on it, the corseted bodice tied up perfectly. Kate looked like an angel.

"You looked beautiful when I married you but, as my daughter for the day, you look absolutely stunning," I said softly going to her.

Kate looked at me in the mirror. "Ben is my brother."

"Yes I know." I took some earrings out of my pocket and put them in her ears.

"I fainted when he told me."

"I know that too." I chuckled and put a necklace on her. I stroked her neck. "Are you ready? Ian is as nervous as the first time."

"So am I."

I held out my hand. "Come on, the paperwork is signed, let's go get you married." Kate took my hand and I realised she was trembling. I lifted her chin and looked deep into her eyes asking the question I would ask my daughter. I did not want her to do something she didn't want to do. Last night, she had felt dirty and not in a good way.

"Is Ian who you want? Is he who you love? Kate, you need to take me out of the equation. If you do not want this, please don't go through with it because I have a fairy tale in my head." I was serious. I would pull the pin now if this were not what she wanted.

"Yes Dad. He is." She spoke softly, her eyes welling. "But I love you too…"

I nodded and hugged her. "I know. Today though, love me like my daughter." I touched her tummy. "And lay off the drinking. My babies are inside you."

"I hope so." Kate touched her belly.

We got to the roof where I hoped to give Kate the wedding of her dreams. I had thrown my cash around and had it decorated with white roses and fairy lights. The white wooden chairs had small bows of white satin on their backs. It looked perfect.

Kate gasped and glanced up at me. I smiled and squeezed her hand. All the kids walked down the aisle first, then the bridesmaids. With Kate on my arm, shaking like a leaf, her veil down, she was ready. We walked toward Ian. I watched his face and saw what I wanted to see.

Wonder, excitement, nerves, and a little love. That chemistry that I had been telling her family about was kicking in. In that moment, I do not think I had ever felt so proud. I gazed at Kate and she was right with Ian. I do not think I could have wiped the smile off my face if I tried. Give it time and this love would grow.

I gave Kate away, kissing her mouth one last time softly, like her dad would have before putting the veil back in place. I gave her hand to Ian with the look I would give to any man I deemed worthy of marrying my daughter and he nodded his understanding. I sat down next to Mum and Dad to watch.

They were so shaky on their feet, a few times I thought Ian and Kate might faint. They said their vows and exchanged rings. Their hands shook, I smiled. I knew how that felt now, how much those vows meant to the people saying them. The only difference was, when I got married, my hands had shaken because I realised Kate promised forever. I only ever promised her a night.

Then it was time for the kiss, and they were husband and wife in the eyes of God, not Elvis. Ian lifted Kate's veil, his hand still shaking. When they kissed, they held onto each other perfectly, as though they were holding on to life. Ian lifted his head and when they both smiled—wow.

"I thought you were going to faint," Ian hugged her.

"I thought you were too."

"It is my privilege to introduce you to Mr and Mrs Ian and Kaitlyn Morrissey," the Minister announced.

That was the moment Kate realised who I was, that until a few days ago the business she worked for was owned by me… Her eyes snapped to me, Brian, then up at Ian who put his arm around her waist and steadied her.

"Yes, Shorty, you just married another billionaire." Brian smirked.

It was a good thing Ian had hold of Kate, because her eyes didn't have time to roll. Her knees gave out and he swept her up into his arms. Ben was quick to get in another unconscious selfie which all the brothers, including me wanted in on. Then Ian took her to a quiet corner of the roof and sat down with her in his arms. When she woke up they held each other, it was beautiful how gentle Ian was with her. I noticed Harry watching them and saw a tear in his eye. I put my hand on his shoulder. "Are you okay?"

He nodded "You said he lost his wife."

"Yes. He did. Three years ago. I thought we would lose him too."

"I thought the same thing about Shorty when we lost Chris. That moment there isn't because she just married a billionaire."

"No. It isn't." I shook my head. "They are saying goodbye and moving on."

## 59. Kate

I was now a Morrissey! I married the man that had given us the loan to start Crosshairs, the man I had been so mad at for owning our company was Charlie! I had been married to one fucking billionaire and now I was married to a second in as many days.

Oh, my goodness you should have seen the roof. How the hell did Charlie pull this off! I didn't have a clue.

I was a grunt. I didn't know fancy. I rarely wore dresses and he had me looking like a princess walking down the aisle to prince charming in a wedding gown so beautiful I could never have dreamed it. I was married to Ian, feeling overwhelmed, more so when I glanced at Charlie who looked so happy. I could see that he had ticked off an important item off his bucket list. The joy in Charlie's eyes when he looked at me… I wanted to run and cry in a corner.

We had family photos taken before going downstairs to the reception. They were very formal photos, no fun ones. Now that the wedding was over, the deal was done, everyone seemed to come off the knifes edge and relax into the party ahead. Though I was sure the photos would show the emotional strain everyone was under. But then it might have just been me who was overly emotional.

If I thought the rooftop was beautiful, it had nothing on the reception. It was a fairy-tale come true. The flowers on the tables were stunning. The rings on my finger... If these were real diamonds I was going to have a heart attack. I was grateful that my sham marriage looked like my dream wedding.

The kids were on their best behaviour during dinner and managed to sit still for the speeches, which were thankfully short. But not once was anything said about all of this being Charlie's idea or that he was sick. I cut the cake with Ian and danced the first dance with him.

Ian smiled when we got on the dance floor and he pulled me into his arms. "He overdid it."

I smiled shyly, "It was more than I could have ever dreamed."

"Are you happy?"

I gave him a slight nod; I was happy though I felt ripped in two. "Are you?"

I watched Ian as he answered yes. He meant it, but Charlie was weighing on his mind too. This was for him not for us. We stopped talking and just danced.

Charlie scored the next for the Daddy Daughter dance. He was tired. Pulling off a wedding like this after fucking my brains out last night, I wasn't surprised. Man, I really was a slut.

"How are you holding up?" I asked.

"I am the happiest man alive. How about you? Is it the wedding of your dreams?"

"It went beyond." I smiled up at him. "Thank you. You didn't have to."

"I did. Our wedding, though fun, was a travesty. I should have done this for us."

"I just needed you," I said, feeling my heart break. "It was just as memorable as this one."

He kissed my forehead.

## 60. *Charlie*

"You are the most beautiful bride in history." I was so proud of Kate right now. She had carried herself flawlessly. Lady to the first degree. And not a drop of champagne.

Kate blushed, shaking her head, "Only in your eyes."

"You really are the fucking jackpot Kate." I held her to my chest as we finished our dance with tears in our eyes.

I danced with Ella and Evie after Kate. The look on each of their little faces as I did my best to make them feel like princesses made me feel like a million bucks. Little girls who were unjaded and innocent are the most precious thing in the world. Their smiles were enough to wrap my heart around their little fingers.

The boys though just liked to rock out and dance. They were just as precious as the girls in their innocence, but they both had a cheeky side that I related to.

Harry danced with Kate before Brian pulled her into his arms talking to her and managing to make her laugh. It was good to see her finally relax.

Emma was dancing with Billy watching Kate and her husband without an ounce of jealousy. She adored her friend.

Kate had wonderful in-laws who loved her dearly, even though they fought like cats and dogs. It made me believe her first husband was a good man who did not hold back when he spoke his mind. I wondered what he would have thought of the last five days and what we had done to his little wife.

If it was me who died and Kate had not moved on— and Chris had got his hands on her and talked her into what we had—I would have be cheering. She was a sexual being. And so damn flexible. We had been good to her and made sure she was satisfied long before we were. Kate deserved to be satisfied in bed as much as she deserved to be held in loving arms, more so since she seemed to run from it.

I never really liked weddings and now I did not understand why. Probably because monogamy had seemed boring and not for me. Now it was. I still had a few girls at the club I had promised to whip the next time I went in, but Kate was the only woman I would touch with my cock until the day I died.

I danced with Mum, Susan, and Tammy. Then Carrie and Emma wanted to dance too. I was having a ball. I even got Nelly up to dance. Then I went to have a few drinks with the men. I decided weddings were a lot of fun. The promise of forever in the air. Both Ian and Kate had been hurt terribly but I hoped that today was the beginning of their happily ever after. Even if they did not recognise it yet.

The night was perfect. We drank and I managed to talk to everyone who mattered. This was my farewell to a lot of people. When the night ended, the kids begged for a sleepover in my room. I had rarely babysat so this was a novel treat.

Kate and Ian smiled as I went upstairs with all four children. I helped them get undressed and pulled the pins out of the girl's hair. They chatted happily and told me their secrets. (Kids are so weird; their secrets are so tiny but to them so huge).

The kids thought it was hilarious when I gave each of them a shirt of mine to sleep in. They did look funny since they were so little, and my shirts were so big on them. I lay in the middle of the bed and the girls snuggled into me before the boys lay beside them.

I watched as they finally settled and went to sleep. I had never seen anything so beautiful. Their innocence was just so rare to see in this day and age. All of them had lost a parent yet they felt peace when they slept. Not like their surviving parents who could not find peace in sleep. Both had looked haunted, alone, and carrying heartbreak I was glad I would never know.

I lay watching the kids, thinking about my life. I had done well for myself, managed two degrees, built an empire and had the pleasure of bedding more than my fair share of women. I had a great family who had supported me.

Then I thought of my cancer diagnosis. I still did not understand how I was dying or what I had done that I deserved to die before my forty first birthday. I did not understand how I could be dying and feel so alive. How I could be dying and only just now finding the love of my life. I did not even feel sick! I still did not feel sick!

My thoughts turned to Mum and Dad, the looks on their faces when I broke the news. Their utter devastation. Completely different from when they adopted me at ten. It showed the level of love that they did have for me. Though I had never really doubted it, this proved that I was their son, full-blood or not.

I remembered telling my siblings and the fucking seven stages of grief party that followed. How I almost fell off my chair laughing when Richard hurt his foot kicking the coffee table while Tammy cried in my arms. That memory made me chuckle again. Then I remembered Ian's reaction and how after putting his fist through the wall, busting his knuckles, he had just sat there looking lost and heartbroken. I teared up when I remembered how I physically kicked him when I found him passed out drunk in the bathroom with his kids being looked after full time by Rita and Joe after Aria was killed.

I had been so angry with him. Disgusted he would be like that around the children. I had kicked him so hard in the guts that Ian vomited. I did not understand his pain. Not even after taking him to see her after the accident. I did not understand how you could love someone so much you would want to die. Now, I understood. If Ian walked in my door right now and told me Kate had died. I would want to die too. The world would be a dark place without her in it.

I thought about it and it made me both smile and cry. I asked myself, could I have done more? Settled down and had a family?

What was success? I pondered that for a while until I realised that I was happy with giving 70,000 people a job that earnt them a decent wage. I was happy with my charities and the work they did with veterans, the homeless and underprivileged children.

If I could go back and do it again, I would have had kids. They were cool. But maybe I had done it. I hoped Kate really was pregnant. That thought made me smile. They would be good kids. I made a note to write a letter for a boy and one for a girl. Lessons from the grave from their father.

I thought of Kate, how glad I was to have met, had the pleasure of having her in my bed, the honour of having her as my wife for just one day. I fell asleep feeling uncomfortable amongst the little bed hogs but happy with a life that though short, was very well lived.

## 61. *Kate*

The next morning, I woke up to the phone going off. When I found it I answered it sleepily.

"Hello?"

"Hey, just letting you know that I have the kids," Brian said. "Charlie is alright. He just needs to have some rest."

"What do you mean?" I asked sitting bolt upright.

"He is just a bit tired from the shenanigans. Ian's kids are with Richard."

"Where is Charlie?" My voice had a note of worry to it.

"He is having a sleep Kate; he is tired. The kids hogged the bed all night." Fairly sure I just heard his eyes roll.

"Where are you?"

"Having breakfast in our room. We are still hungover so we will chill for a few hours and watch a movie. Let you and Ian relax."

I thanked him and hung up the phone, rubbing my eyes. I sighed, got up and went to the loo before having a shower. Ian and I hadn't consummated the marriage opting instead to go to bed and sleep. When I went back into the bedroom Ian was sitting on the bed rubbing his eyes like a sleepy child. His hair was a mess. Ian looked adorable as he tried to wake up. Then he stretched like a lion with a big yawn, his muscles rippled and I leaned against the door having a good perve. He looked me up and down, then smiled, holding his arms out. "Come here."

I gave him a shy smile, walking toward him. "Why? Whatcha gonna do?"

"I am going to kiss you good morning then have a shower." Ian surprised me when he grabbed my arm and pulled me onto the bed before rolling on top of me. I laughed as he pinned my arms above my head. He kissed my jaw and neck. "How are you feeling today? You were overwhelmed yesterday. So damn beautiful but overwhelmed."

"I am going to need a holiday to get over my holiday," I said breathlessly, thoroughly enjoying his attention... "I want to go home and hug my dogs and go for a ride."

"Charlie bought us a house for when we get back home. You are going to bring your animals over, aren't you?"

"Yes of course. My animals and I are a package deal."

"Inside or outside?"

"Inside."

"I don't like inside pets." He growled.

"Do you put your clothes in the hamper?"

"No." Honestly, he looked at me with a why would I do that expression.

"Then we are even."

Ian's hand tracked down my body "Is that so?" I nodded. "Putting clothes in the hamper is important to you?"

"Yes. As is putting down the toilet seat." He stroked my body lightly; maddeningly it burned.

"Well I do that. Do your dogs sleep in your bedroom?"

"Only one. She has a bed in the corner if she wants to sleep in it."

"But not on the bed?"

"No, not on the furniture," I confirmed. "The cats try, but they have beds."

"So just cats and dogs?"

"Two tortoises, birds, horses, dogs and cats. Do you have any pets?"

"No, never really had time. You talk too much."

He shut me up with a kiss that had me melting into the mattress.

"I love how you respond, so sexy." He smiled with his lips against mine. "How about you have a little more sleep while I shower and get us some breakfast."

That sounded like a great idea. Ian gave me another kiss and got off me. "Ian, you are married to me but we know nothing about each other. Doesn't it worry you?"

"I knew you were batshit crazy before I married you. I am good." He gave me a cheeky grin and walked into the bathroom.

## 62. *Charlie*

I had spent a good part of the day sleeping off the epic night before. But now I was ready for a little bit more fun with the new members of my family so long as the drama of the bachelor/bachelorette night was finished. Everyone had dropped their differences and concerns to come together for the wedding and it had gone off without a hint of drama. The press had not got wind of the biggest wedding of the year.

Brian worked for me, so it was going to be interesting seeing him play. Workwise, Brian was a weapon. Calculated, smart, precise, and brutal. I had funded his business proposal and smoothed the road in some places for that reason. Over the years I had a lot of people come to me for help starting up a business. I had not helped many. Most had come in with half assed business plans and attitudes of entitlement.

Brian had walked in with neither. He put his cards on the table with a short sweet briefing on the business. He put the proposal on my desk asking if I wanted time to look it over. He said he would be happy to come back at my convenience to answer any questions I might have. Then he left the ball in my court. I left the proposal on my desk for a week before I even bothered to look at it.

The detail was incredible. It was the best business plan that had ever crossed my desk. For the first time since Richard, Ian, and Tammy, I handed out the start-up funds for a business. The first time I had done it for a stranger.

Even my siblings' proposals had needed more work before I signed off on them. I only really signed off on theirs because I was their big brother. My siblings had paid back their loans in five years. Brian had done it in three, thanks to Kate's win.

I had liked Brian the instant I met him. Now, watching him relax and tease Kate, I liked him more. Then I realised that Kate's demeanour did not change around them... She did not lie about who she was. She did not pretend to be someone else.

I leaned over and whispered in Emma's ear, "Is she always like this?"

Emma turned her pale green eyes to me. She was possibly the most beautiful redhead I had ever met. She smiled. "Yeah this is her when we aren't working. When we are working though she's a different woman, as brutal as the boys. She just doesn't give a fuck. I mean, Carrie and I fight and shoot but nothing like Kate."

"How do you mean?" *Fight? Huh? Oh, the video Brian showed me...*

Emma smiled, "If she goes off, she can make the boys back down. The crazy just isn't worth it."

I laughed, "I can't see it. She is too soft and sensual."

Emma cocked her head to the side then gave Billy an up nod. "Hey Billy, you were in the bomb squad, which is more volatile? A bomb or Shorty?"

Billy smirked, "Out of the two going off in my face I will take the bomb, Shorty would still nag and remind me about it ten years later."

Kate turned and glared at Billy. "Oh, we goin' back to that, are we?"

He held his hands up and then pointed at Emma. "Red asked me which was worse, a bomb or you."

Emma smiled innocently as Kate squinted at her. "I am trying to behave. Stop trying to get Billy in trouble."

Emma sipped her drink before smiling. "Brian took Gertie to the range before coming to Vegas."

I swear I did not even see Kate's hand move before Brian blocked it. How the fuck he blocked it I do not know. Kate and Brian glared at each other with wild eyes. It was a standoff.

Ian stared at his new wife wide-eyed before looking at me. I tried not to smile.

"Why?" Kate snarled at Brian. "You know not to touch her."

"Because you weren't there, and I wanted to use her." He said, still holding her wrist.

"So, you touched my stuff because I wasn't there. It's a habit of yours, isn't it?"

"You would never have taken it to even try." He smirked, I do believe they were no longer talking about Gertie, whatever the hell that was.

"I would have when I was ready." Kate snapped.

"Well you've got a job now because I did." Brian said, not sorry at all, in fact he looked quite happy to stir her.

"Yeah but now you want me to fucking run it. Buddy that is on you." Kate pointed at him. "You deal with the fucking drama. You are just pissed because you want to be in the field more. I keep telling you, put Harry at the top and get back in the fucking field. I won't bitch about kicking your arse more often."

I stared at them as I realised what they were talking about. "Brian, who did that business plan up?"

Brian smiled as the rest of his family pointed at Kate. "Shorty did."

"I keep telling you it was Chris. He was the brains." Kate rolled her eyes.

"The man had brains but that was all you. Your random questions, our answers and ideas magically end up in the final product. Chris might have put in his two cents, but that business plan was all you." Brian smirked.

"I am not that smart." Kate rolled her eyes and my hand itched to spank her.

Brian smirked, "No, you are smarter."

"That was the best business proposal I have ever read." I meant every word. "I thought you did it, Brian."

"I did up the second one." Brian grinned "But I handed it to Shorty to look it over before I did."

Cocking an eyebrow I asked, "Why did you give it to her?"

"Because she is the one with like four degrees." Brian smirked.

I thought I had done well with two. I was really going to have to sit down and read her background report. I sipped my drink, staring at Kate. "You must have student loans coming out of your ears."

"Nah, I paid them off the first night here counting cards." She smiled cheekily "Paid off my house the second night when I won the fifty."

"Well this one," Carrie said, "The other one was paid off with Chris's insurance."

"I am becoming a little real estate queen." Kate looked proud.

"With two properties?" Richard huffed. "It's a start."

Gerrard looked at Richard. "She has a house on 6000 acres in Australia, the one here is on 200 acres and I have a feeling she was trying to buy the one next door which would have added I think another four hundred."

Kate nodded. "I put in an offer but someone else made a better offer."

"Are you going to make them move?" Gerrard looked at her with a glint of mischief in his eye.

"If they are cunts, absolutely."

Ian laughed, "How do you make someone move."

I was not sure I liked the way Kate smiled. There was cunning in it. She had a vicious side. "I don't do anything, really."

"She hated her neighbours in Australia so much that she wired their house to play a barely audible frequency which put them on edge. Then she randomly picked their windows and left them open. They thought the house was haunted." Emma smirked at Kate. "Like seriously, they bought in a psychic and everything."

Kate batted her eyes at Emma, "It probably wouldn't have been so effective if they weren't using LSD. Just sayin'."

Ian smiled slowly, glancing at me. I was impressed. Richard sat back in his chair watching.

"I would never have picked you as one for psychological warfare."

"I'm not really. I just did not want to go in, bust them up and give them their marching orders. I thought I would be nice and let them make up their own minds." Kate tried and failed to look innocent.

Carrie was watching the bar. Billy was right there with her. I turned to see the beginning of a bar fight. No-one seemed concerned. They kept on conversing until things got very loud behind me and I went to turn.

"We are going to get out of here. Is there anywhere we can sing karaoke or something?" Emma stood up.

I nodded. "Yeah we know a place."

# 63. Kate

Charlie took us back to the bar where we had won the band competition. The management seemed to be having a lot of trouble finding people who weren't tone deaf. But that was what happened when you were dealing with amateurs like the punk wannabes on stage. Billy shook his head, glaring at Charlie.

"You are fucking kidding yourself if you think I am going to sit here and listen to that shit." Billy indicated to the band on stage with his thumb. "Fucking teenagers."

Charlie smiled. "Scare the living shit out of me."

I smiled as I sat down with the girls as the men plotted to take over the stage.

"Control freaks, all of them." Susan grinned.

This was going to get interesting. When the boys began, I leaned back to watch them. The other night we had sounded good but with both sides of the family playing together—wow they sounded fucking incredible.

"You know they would sound better if we helped them out." Emma said looking around at the women at our table.

"You think they need help?" Susan grinned.

Emma and I went up with the boys, grabbed the two spare mics and yes, we made them sound a lot better. Now we were rocking the joint. We girls played up like two bob watches. The boys grinned and encouraged us. People came in the door to listen. Charlie was having a great time and man; he was great on the bass. And man could he sing; his voice was incredible.

I caught Ian's eye, and he gave me a wink. We played for close to an hour before we decided to get drunk, much to the disappointment of the now packed bar. Outside, we walked back to the casino. A big arm went around my shoulder.

"Fucking jackpot." Charlie kissed the top of my head.

I put my arm around his waist, "So are you."

"You know it sucks that we are going home tomorrow." Gerrard said, "When are you going home?"

"Tomorrow." Charlie said. "I need to sort out my business and make some preparations. Most of it is done. Just gotta hand it over to the COO until the new CEO steps up." He gave my shoulder a squeeze. "You have a big job ahead of you."

I kind of ignored it for a moment but everyone stopped walking. "Ha ha Charlie, very funny." I patted his back.

## 64. Charlie

Leaving Vegas was hard. I had so much fun there and it would be the last time I would ever visit. It was a last, not a first. I loved Vegas mostly for the fun I had there over the years, and The Diamond had been one of the most lucrative investments I had ever made. But I still had so much to do. This was moving-in day and getting Ian and Kate settled in together was number one on my list.

I double checked the house, making sure everything was in place. This was the house I hoped Kate and Ian would make their home while they got back into the swing of being married.

After our last night on the town in Vegas, I had gone back to my room alone. I needed sleep but I did not want to be alone. Kate was married to Ian now, so I said goodnight to them. To my surprise, Ian and Kate had knocked five minutes after I closed the door. What surprised me even more was that Ian lay down on the bed and told me to have my way with his wife. I had been tired, but he just touched her and told her she was beautiful while I made love to Kate like a starved animal.

Stepping out of my memories for a moment, I realised Ian had just arrived with the kids. I got a heap of wonderful hugs and kisses when they got out of the car. Tim and Evie were both overly excited running around exploring. More so when they heard what sounded like a removal truck arrive. They ran out the front door. Ian looked at me as Joe, his groundsman and his wife Rita Ian's housekeeper looked around the property with wide smiles.

"This is over kill."

"This is my wedding present." I smiled, patted his shoulder and went outside to watch Kate get out of a truck. She waved at us and smiled before opening the back door. She helped Ryan and Ella out, both of whom held a tortoise and had a bird on each shoulder.

Then four huge Maine Coon cats followed the kids out. She went to the back of the truck, tapped the side and six dog heads popped up. Three black German Shepards, a Doberman, a beagle, and a fox terrier.

She lifted the smaller two dogs out and then told the others to get out. They all obeyed except the Doberman who stood looking at Kate.

"No, Ninja, you are a big girl, you can get out." The dog whined at her. "Ninja, we talked about this. Get out of the ute."

Ian chuckled as he sat on the steps to greet the kids and animals. I sat beside him. Kate gave up on the Doberman, went to the huge horse float and opened the door. She disappeared and a moment later the first horse walked off closely followed by a second, third, fourth, fifth....

210

"Oh, come on Jet! Fuckin' Molly forgave me for moving you again!... Nah now you're just being a fuckin' arsehole...DON'T FUCKIN' BITE!"

Ryan covered his mouth and started laughing before he looked at Ian and me.

"She says a lot of naughty words." Tim noted.

Ryan pointed at him "They are big people words; kids get their mouth washed out with soap."

"Your Mum is short." Tim stated, "I'm not scared."

"Don't start on me, Timothy," Kate called from the horse float. "JET! Right get off the trailer or I am not giving you treats this afternoon."

"Mum has ninja hearing." Ryan whispered.

Kate appeared with a horse that had to be sixteen hands and black as midnight. He got off the float and whinnied in her ear.

"Mate, you have had a bee in your bonnet since I told you I got married. They are both on the step. Go say hi. But, if you bite them, I will put you in the back paddock away from happy time with Molly for a month." The horse huffed. "And be nice to the kids too."

Jet huffed and shook his head as he walked toward us. Then he whinnied loudly, letting everyone know he was not happy. Ian stood up. I joined him.

*Were we about to argue with a horse?*

The horse looked me up and down and gave me a nod, then turned his attention to Ian. Looking Ian in the eye he pulled himself up to his full height. He was taller than me—and I was up on the step.

"I take it you are going to be pissed off if I hurt her." Ian said and Jet huffed. "Consider me warned." Jet nodded, looked me in the eye for a while then gave me his side, waiting with a sigh.

I glanced at Kate for help. "What does he want?"

211

Kate looked perplexed. "He wants to talk to you. Get on. He will take you for a walk."

The horse wants to 'talk' with me? Okay then, never talked to a horse before. Ian gave me a leg up. I took a handful of his mane to keep my balance. Then the horse walked off, leaving everyone else on the steps. I hadn't ridden a horse in over fifteen years, so I was a bit nervous. After a few minutes I relaxed and pondered what Kate had meant when she said her horse wanted to talk to me.

Something like a movie began playing in my head. I stopped thinking so I could watch. It was like having a vision.

So, this is what Kate meant…

## 65. Kate

I watched Jet leave with Charlie, knowing he would come back in a better headspace. But that didn't stop the uneasy feeling I was having. Ninja howled until I gave up and lifted her out of the back of the ute. Then she nuzzled me and goofed off as I went to greet Tim and Evie before kissing Ian. We still hadn't consummated the marriage but there had been plenty of kissing and touching. I didn't push him for an explanation and he never offered one.

"Your horse thinks you are his girlfriend." Ian was serious.

"My horse is magic. Don't try and ride or pat him unless he offers it to you." I looked up at him in warning. "He will hurt you. Okay, I have to put these guys away." I walked down the steps and let off a low whistle and walked around the house.

Ian joined me a moment later, taking my hand. "Are you okay?"

"No, but I am trying to get my head around it all. How are you feeling?"

"Like I am in over my head." Ian shrugged.

"Well warn me before you go off to your mancave to think." I said softly. "I am going to need a little time out too."

"Good plan. We will just take it easy."

I nodded and glanced up at him, "Yeah, we are married. We don't need to stress about the little shit. We just concentrate on open communication and compromise."

He let go of my hand and put his arm around my shoulders. "I have been married before. I think I was a good husband. I know how it works."

"Good, then teach me. Chris and I didn't have a traditional marriage. We had an army marriage. We spent a lot of time apart, so we didn't do a lot of things traditionally."

Ian kissed the top of my head. "Well if it helps, I am always right. The toilet seat stays up and if you are on your period and don't want to have sex, I get to have head all week."

*Smart arse!* I laughed "Get stuffed. If I sit on a cold porcelain bowl then you are in the doghouse. You are not always right. If you are game to stick your cock near my mouth when I have PMS? Then sure, you can have head."

Ian laughed, kissed the top of my head and let me go so I could get the horses stabled. When I was done, we went inside to explore our new home. The cats had made themselves at home laying anywhere that suited them.

The dogs were still sniffing everything, and the kids were running around crazy. Ian walked me up to the master bedroom. The bed was big enough to be its own state. Ian shut the door and locked it before looking under the bed. He stood looking around, perplexed. I asked what he was looking for.

He stopped, smiled, went to the wall and pushed a barely perceptible button. A door slid open and, being the curious kind of woman, I was, went to see what had put such a big smile on his face. I kind of had a heart attack when I spied all sorts of tables, chairs and eyelets in the roof. It was a fucking dungeon.

Ian took my hand, pulled me into the room and before I could protest, I went over a padded semi-circle. He put his pelvis firm against my arse. He ground into me, his hand holding me head down, pinned. *Holy shit, I knew Charlie was Dominant, I didn't know Ian was too… Surely not!*

"You and I are going to have a lot of sex. I would love to use this stuff with you. I am more about pleasure than I am about pain. I am about control, but you know that already. I don't expect you on your knees, I don't expect you to call me Sir. You are my wife. My equal. I saw the look in your eyes when you saw all this so you need to know, I will never hurt you beyond giving your skin a few pink marks."

He lifted my shirt and traced the whip scars on my back "If you don't like it, I will shut this room and never open it again. I think we have awesome sex and I would not change a thing. But if you are feeling daring… This is something I would like to share with you."

As he spoke my heart hammered with a mixture of fear and excitement. His hands were firm and the longer he spoke, the further his hands moved over my arse, my hips, waist, sliding up under my shirt, moving it up.

"You are a dominant like Charlie" I decided to clarify in case this was a joke.

"I am." Ian confirmed, making my heart thump as I wondered what the fuck I had just gotten myself into.

His touch made me burn. When he stopped talking, he let me up and we walked from the room. He shut the dungeon door before he unlocked and opened the bedroom door. A moment later we were walking down the hall as if nothing happened.

Ian started to chuckle, and I asked him. "What's funny?"

"You have no idea how close you were to being taken like that. And we cannot just run off and do that until Rita and Joe get to meet your kids."

"Who are Rita and Joe?"

"My housekeeper/nanny and my groundsman. I am not firing them; they have worked for me for nearly ten years."

"Okay." I wasn't going to argue. "We should find the kids and check on Charlie too." We went downstairs to find all the kids playing with the kids under the supervision of an older woman. She gave me a knowing smile and then asked the kids who was hungry.

## 66. Charlie

Kate was right, the horse did talk. Now I knew I was on the right path. I played with the kids for an hour before leaving Ian and Kate and their family to settle in.

Next, I visited Larry to ensure everything I had put in place was iron clad. The meeting ended with us drinking and talking shit until midnight when my driver took him home.

The next morning, I took Kate to my company headquarters. I warned Ian I was going to fuck her into acceptance. He just smiled and told me to have fun.

Walking Kate through my building, telling her my hopes and dreams when I had started my business. Then I told her my plans for the future. I watched her, closely. She took it all in, listening to me before she asked questions. She was interested, not just pretending. She even suggested some good ideas. I told her they should be implemented.

I introduced her to Sam who had been with me almost from the beginning. She was brilliant and upheld my values. Kate seemed to take an instant liking to her and Sam, though threatened by the prospect of having a woman boss, seemed to like her too. Sam and I would have a meeting after I spoke to Kate.

I shut and locked my office door before turning to Kate. Finally, I had her alone… Kate looked around my office before she went to the window and looked out at the view.

"You have worked so hard for this. You should be so proud of giving so many people a job."

I nodded as I moved toward her, taking off my tie. "I am." I put my hands on her hips and turned her to me. She looked up at me with those beautiful green eyes as I walked her back to the couch and sat her down. I loved the rise and fall of her breasts when she got excited, I loved how her eyes went a darker green as she became lustier. I loved the way her tongue darted out and wet her lips in anticipation.

I got on my knees in front of her. I parted her legs so I could get between them. I cupped her face; my thumbs stroked her cheek before I kissed her blind. I dropped my hands to her legs, lightly stroking her inner thighs. Kate's breathing was already harsh, her hands in my hair before touching my face.

I hooked my fingers in her panties and snapped them. I moved my hands up her legs spreading them wide for me. I broke the kiss and whispered as I fingered her gently, she was not wet. She was dripping... I grabbed her hair in one hand making her gasp. "I have given you my company."

I pushed two fingers deep inside her pussy and kissed her deeply, stopping any protest she might have made. Oh, I loved this woman. Once she turned off her head, she responded naturally. I pulled my wet fingers from her and she whimpered as I put my other hand in her hair, lifted my mouth from hers and put my fingers covered in her juices into her mouth.

"Suck," I instructed as she looked both a little grossed out and shocked. "See how good you taste. Why I am addicted to you. Now, suck." I fucked her mouth with my fingers and after a moment she did as she was told. Her eyes though were locked on mine, asking questions. "Undo my belt."

I smiled when she did not need to be told twice. Once my cock was released, I removed my fingers and turned her, so she was laying on the couch, legs on the back rest, her head over the edge of the seat. She opened and I pressed my cock into her mouth. My eyes rolled; she could suck a cork through ten foot of garden hose.

I spread her legs and curled her up to my mouth. She was pretty much upside down now. My mouth watered at the sight of her flesh. She had a pretty cunt, pink, soft and wet. I put my mouth over her and ate her out like I was starved. I ate her out and fucked her with my fingers while I fucked her face. When she came, she jerked, and her muffled cry went silent as I pushed deep down her throat. I pulled out a moment later and she gasped, her chest heaving.

I sat her up and kissed her hard. "I gave you my business Kate. I gave it all to you." I kissed her again. "The best thing is you can't say no. You already accepted it." I got on top of her and pushed my cock just inside her soft, tight flesh, her mouth beneath mine went slack as I did. I put her knees to her chest and grabbed a fist full of her hair before slamming my cock deep.

# 67. Kate

Charlie had my feet over his shoulders, balls deep inside me, fucking me senseless. He dominated my body and kept me from thinking about the bomb he had just dropped on me. Loving me like he was starved, I loved him the same way in return. His time was ticking. I wouldn't have him much longer. I shouldn't be having him now. But Ian had told me he was okay to share while Charlie was here.

I was in love with two men. One who had a few weeks and one who said we would sort it out.

My body raced to orgasm and like every time, I shattered with a strangled cry. My body losing control, but he didn't stop. I was so sensitive, I started building again. Charlie's grunting and heavy breathing said he would cum before I got there. Well so I thought, until his fingers started massaging my clit.

Detonation. Blinding fireworks.

We went at the same time. He slammed deep as we did, and he didn't move. He looked into my eyes as we caught our breath. I looked up at his pale blue eyes, memorising every detail of them and of his face. His short beard and the bow of his lips.

"Why would you give me this?" I whispered, not able to talk. I had so much emotion boiling inside me. The orgasms should have calmed me, but they had just made me emotional. Tears slipped down my temples as we stayed as connected as two people could get.

He wiped my tears with a sad smile in his eyes. "Because you are everything, I could have dreamed of having in a woman. You were my wife…"

"I would still be your wife." I said but he kissed me quiet, my eyes shut, squeezing out more tears as he broke the kiss by lifting his head.

"No, I needed you to move on. I do not want you to mourn me like you did your husband. I want you to be happy. I know in my heart that is exactly what Ian will do." Charlie stroked my face and gazed at me so lovingly. "I also want to be sure you never want for another thing in this lifetime. That is why I gave you this. It is my empire, my legacy. I do not have children. This is all I have to give."

"I am glad you think so much of me that you would trust me with this but what about your family?"

"They all have money. They all have their own businesses. I willed them the few things I thought they might like but you are the one I need to look after. It's for you that I need to ensure security."

"I don't understand why?" I really didn't.

"Because you are the only woman who ever stole my heart by wanting me for me," he said softly before sitting up with me straddling his lap. He didn't leave my body though, not for one moment. "Because I love you Kate. My insane, tough and beautiful Vegas random."

"I don't deserve this." I told him, "I did nothing to deserve this. I would rather you spend every cent you have on getting better…"

Charlie's big hand covered my mouth, his eyes sad but intense. "Kate, I am not going to get better. I am going to die. You cannot stop it. I cannot stop it. It is my time. That is why I need to make sure that my business will be okay, so that my employees will be okay." He searched my face. "You do understand, don't you?"

"What if I fuck it up?"

"You won't." He said confidently.

## 68. *Charlie*

It had been two days since I told Kate she was the new CEO of my company. Apparently even after being fucked into taking it, she had gone home, pretended nothing happened and had been distant toward Ian since. But not to the kids. Ian had been the one to suggest that Kate sleep over at my place. I told him it was only for one night so she would know exactly who I was. He said that that was fine. They had a dungeon in the new house, and I could stay over any time I liked.

Ian parked his car in my front yard while I stood on the front steps watching. Kate was relaxed, obviously clueless about what I had planned for her. Ian was grinning because he did know. We had discussed at length what I would do with Kate —make her cum until she was brainless and then put her into subspace so deep that no problems were going to touch her tonight.

They got out of the car and Kate gave me a suspicious look then glanced at Ian. "What is going on?"

"Well, remember in Vegas when I said I would like to show you the real me?" I asked.

"I know the real you. You mean the one you show everyone else."

I did not have a comeback for that. Because she was right. Ian and I walked her inside my home and straight into the spare room where there was a beautiful but skimpy wedding dress on the bed.

"What the fuck?"

"Ian will help you get changed," I said, shutting the door. I went to my room, took off my shirt and undid the top button on my pants. Kate had been through hell only a few weeks before, so I needed to be careful how I proceeded.

Ian came in with a smile on his face. "Well, I will be leaving now."

"You can sit in the corner and watch if you like."

"Watch the master at work? You sure?"

"If you want to." I did not want him to. I wanted Kate to myself, for one last night.

Ian nodded, "I would love to watch her cum like I know you are going to make her, but I promised the kids a movie night. Have fun."

I nodded as Kate walked in, fidgeting nervously with the dress. "I am not sure about this dress. It's too tight."

"It isn't tight enough." Ian kissed her forehead. "See you tomorrow when you get your brains back."

"Huh?" Kate watched him leave looking confused. "Ian?"

"Just have fun," Ian called back.

Kate turned to me for answers as I heard the front door shut. Her mouth opened and shut as she looked me up and down. "Why are you half dressed?"

I held my hand out. she took it without hesitation at all. I pressed the button on the wall and walked her into my dungeon. Kate's breath hitched. "Ian has a room like this." Ian did have a room like this, but she was yet to find out what fun this room could be.

"The door swished shut. "Do you want to explore?"

"Honestly, I find it all a little scary."

So, for an hour, I walked her through all the equipment, and she experimented with the different sensations. I talked about what I wanted to do and what I wanted her to do particularly concentrating on what I wanted to use on her. All while my cock yelled at me to fuck her out of that dress. But I needed her to relax first.

I seduced her with touch, I seduced her with my voice. I seduced her with kisses. Then I told her what would happen after the scenes and what might happen when she went into subspace and might come after with sub drop.

That got her talking medical speak as she tried to understand. I gave her two minutes before I shut her up with a kiss. She was ready.

"So, if I want to slow down, I say yellow and if I want to stop, I say red? Can't I use something else?"

"Would you like to pick a word?" I was interested.

"No. You pick one." She shrugged but would not look at me.

I took her chin and searched her eyes, "If you want to stop? I want you to say 'Jackpot'."

"Okay. So, what do I do first? Kneel or something?"

"I know what happened a few weeks ago. I want you to tell me if I scare you."

Her eyes flashed with uncertainty. "Do you want to stop?"

I held her hand and kissed her palm, "I want you to trust me."

"You have a fantasy about tonight. You should do what you like."

I kissed her with hunger that boiled over at those words. She would have gone along with anything I wanted to do thinking that she did not matter. That her needs did not matter. When to me, it was her needs that mattered most.

This was why I had given her my business and everything else—to ensure that she would want for nothing again.

I broke the kiss and showed her who I believed I was as I peeled her out of that dress, inch by inch revealing her stunning body. When she was finally naked, it was play time. I stayed well with in her hard limits. But I pushed her sexual limits. Kate was beautiful.

Responsive. Painfully trusting. The most beautiful sub I had ever been with.

I used rope and suspended her, used different kinds of nipple clamps on her. I spanked her ass with my hand and with a paddle 'til her juices dripped down her legs. I tied her to a table and finger fucked her with a wand held to her clit. I overloaded her with sensation as I let my Dom out to play. He was a bastard and she found out why women never walked out of my room.

When the scenes were done for the night. I put her on the bed, pulled her ass into doggy style and slammed my cock into her. She held herself up perfectly, her arms rigid. My hand rained hard slaps on her ass as I pulled her long hair roughly. Her juices covered her thighs and mine. Then it happened. She orgasmed hard, gave a strangled cry as her arms gave out and she face planted the mattress. Kate was in subspace but her greedy cunt did not want to stop playing. She gripped and rippled around me. So, I fucked her until I came so hard I went blind with pleasure. I fell on the bed to catch my breath pulling her into my arms.

Her body limp completely wrung out. Her eyes glassy, but she looked at peace for the first time since I met her.

Then she started to shiver, and I realised she was going into shock. I wrapped her in a blanket, got her to eat some chocolate and ran her a bath to help bring her down. When I carried her to my bed and cuddled with her, she started to cry.

Any other time it would have been a turn on. "What's wrong?"

"I love you."

She was asleep five minutes later. I held her protectively to my body, we would have sex again. But we would never have another night alone like this. I turned my head and eyed the little ring box on the nightstand. I reached for it then opened it to look at the diamond ring inside. The platinum band with three radiant cut diamonds representing the three loves of her life. Chris, me, and I hoped, Ian. She loved us and had wrapped us around her finger without even knowing it. I had meant this to be my collar for her.

But she would have promised forever again. I could not do that to her.

I slid the ring on her finger gently not wanting to wake her. It was a perfect fit. For a couple of minutes, I admired my collar on the love of my life before I tried to take it off. Kate's hand closed into a fist. I checked to see if she was awake, but she was not. I waited a few more minutes and tried to take it off her again. This time I took it off her gently and cried as I did.

*Why the fuck did I have to be dying? I wanted to live! I did not want this to be the last time I would sleep with her in my bed.*

"Put the ring back." Kate whispered.

"It was a collar."

"Put it back."

I put it back on her finger and she made a fist before she went back to sleep. It meant the fucking world to me that she wanted to wear my collar. So, for one more night, Kate was mine.

I went to sleep holding her. I woke up the same way, feeling loved and refreshed. She was still asleep, her hand still balled into a tight fist. If I left her to wear it as my collar, she would never take it off. Gently I opened her hand, took it off her finger and put it away. I lay holding her, enjoying every moment I had with her because I was now going to have to start pulling away and letting her move on.

Kate woke up an hour and a half later and looked down at her hand.

"Where is it?" She sat up like she had lost the most precious ring she owned.

"Where is what?"

"You gave me a ring."

I gave her what I hoped was a weird look until she started to doubt herself. She stared at her finger, made a fist and pouted. "Did you have a dream?" I asked. Kate nodded and cuddled into me. "How are you feeling?"

"A little bit sore."

I smiled. "Yes, well your pussy got well used. How's your head feeling?"

"I just kind of went brainless. I feel like I am still there."

I checked her eyes and moved down the bed. She shamelessly opened her legs to me. "You know, I think you and Ian were telling me lies about morning sex. It's not rare."

## 69. Kate

After our night in the dungeon, I spent the next week under Charlie's wing, getting to know his business inside and out. I watched him during the few meetings he went to and got the hang of his paperwork. I started noticing discrepancies. When I pointed them out, we investigated them.

What we found wasn't good. It was then I saw Charlie morph from a fun, sexual man to an angry powerhouse who would rip these fuckers a new one. He paced his office pulling a level of crazy that might have rivalled mine. I was impressed.

Ian and Richard came into his office because apparently, Charlie was sick of blowing his stack at me. I sat with my feet on his coffee table, which he had told me several times not to do, while I made a case against the fuckers stealing from him, laptop on my lap.

"Kate, get your fucking feet off my coffee table," he snapped at me when he had finished filling in his brothers. I gave him my best resting bitch face before giving him the bird. His face changed. Now he was angry with me. He took one step and I put the laptop down. At his second step I jumped over the couch putting a physical barrier between us. I had a big smile on my face.

He cocked an eyebrow as he moved like a lion stalking his prey. "Do you really think anything will stop me getting you?"

I smiled coyly. "I was working and keeping my mouth shut as requested."

"I told you keep your feet off the coffee table."

"I told you to fuck me on it but that hasn't happened yet."

He moved quickly and I let him box me in. "You want to be fucked on it? I am going to tie you naked to it while I have this meeting with your husband and Richard, and you are not going to complain."

"You want Richard to see me naked?" I peered around him to see Richard grinning. I looked up at Charlie, "Jackpot."

He pouted because I put the breaks on his kinky punishment. "You know, if we had stayed married, I would have done that to you just to put you in your place."

"And you would have woken up with a steel bar in your urethra." I said bluntly. "I have work to do, you have raging to continue. Can we get back to it?"

He grinned and I went back to the couch, put the lap top back into my lap and my feet back on the coffee table. I smiled at Ian as Charlie shouted at me...

"KATE! Get your fucking feet off the coffee table!" he roared.

I giggled; I couldn't help it. Charlie slapped my feet and I moved them. We really did need to get on top of everything so that we would be ready for the board meeting on Friday when Charlie would officially hand over the reins.

## 70. *Charlie*

"So, you really did leave everything to Kate?" Richard looked surprised.

"Yeah, she is smart. She understands my plans for the company. All of you are doing well for yourselves. I will give you what I want you to have before I go which only leaves the few assets and the company. I knew none of you wanted it and well, this is a little more up Kate's ally."

I glared at her with her feet now on the couch and slapped them off. She gave me a cheeky grin and got back to work. "You are going to get a very red ass for this shit. I have just about had enough of you putting your feet everywhere."

"I am more surprised that you are letting her wear that." Richard pointed at her ripped jeans and t-shirt that said, 'You don't like it, f*ck off'.

"Apparently, she is not going to conform to tradition and is going to wear whatever the fuck she wants."

"Yep and she won't get any respect," Richard muttered.

"Wouldn't you do business with me Richard?" Kate asked mock horror on her face at the thought of him not wanting to play with her.

"No. I wouldn't take anyone seriously if they were dressed like you."

"Take note of the shirt then."

Richard rolled his eyes and shook his head. "You are going to have to wax too."

"She will be doing that anyway." Ian said.

"Actually, I have been looking into laser hair removal. Not sure about it though. Also, you are off topic. I told Charlie he should give the business to you, but he mushed my brain with orgasms until I agreed. If you have concerns, please take them up with him because I am sure I have said everything you are going to say."

Kate was unconcerned, not offended that Richard would be such a shit about the news. I turned to Richard.

"Do you have concerns? Because I am setting this all up so that when I am gone, there is nothing anyone can do. There will be no fighting. You will have what I want you to have. She will be at the top of the business and doing her thing, keeping it on track and you will all be able to move on and live long and happy lives. You do not even have to do anything for my funeral. I have given the funeral director my suit and got everything organised. All you have to do is call him and tell him to come get me."

"Why would you have it organised so that every i is dotted?" Kate asked softly.

"Because I know how much it will hurt everyone and this is my gift so they can relax and grieve."

"That and he is a complete and utter control freak," Ian added making me laugh.

I looked at my ex-wife, whose hands sat on the keyboard not moving. She stared blankly at the screen. I gave her a nudge. She looked up at me as though I had pulled her out of deep thought.

"I am going to go get a coffee. Do you want one?"

I shook my head and she looked around at my brothers who both declined. She got up and left my office and shut the door softly. I turned to Ian.

"How is she when she gets home? Is she letting you into her panties or is sex non-existent because I fuck her?" I asked.

Ian shrugged, "I haven't consummated the marriage with her. She told me that you have not used protection. If she gets pregnant, I don't want any doubt whether it is yours."

I was so shocked, my jaw dropped. I opened my mouth to speak, ran my fingers through my hair and sat back. "Kate is actively trying to get pregnant?"

"Well you haven't used protection with her and according to Emma, she should be ovulating over the last week or so. She is not on any form of contraception. Hence her asking us to use protection."

"I don't want to leave her with children. That would be unfair on her and you."

Ian looked me in the eye. "Do you really think I would leave her if she got pregnant? The kids would be raised as Morrisseys."

"But you haven't had sex with Kate which means one of you can get it annulled. Please tell me now if you are going to just annul it when I die." The guilt on Ian's face gave me the answer I did not want. I shook my head and rubbed my face, "Does she know?"

"I haven't said a word."

"So, you are going to hit her with it when she is vulnerable," I snapped, then sighed. "Whatever Ian. Seriously, it is your life, but if she is not who you want or who you can spend your life with then fine. I hope you find a woman that makes you happy." I glared at him "End it now and save breaking her heart. I need her head in the game for this."

"I need to find out if she is pregnant first."

"Pregnancy isn't a good enough reason to stay married if you don't love her," I snapped. "I told you that when you got Aria pregnant. Ian, if she is not the one, get it annulled, move out of the house then I know. Do not be playing happy families for me if you are miserable."

None of us heard her come back in. She sat down as if nothing had been said, putting coffee on the table. She lifted the laptop and put it on her lap. She looked up at us after five minutes of awkward silence.

She glanced at Ian, "Did you really think I wouldn't know what you were up to when you didn't want to have sex with me on our wedding night?"

Ian looked guilty as sin. "Yes."

"You underestimate me." She smiled at him. "As a friend, I will just keep surprising you."

And just like that, she let him off the hook. I sat in shock. I stared at him and then at her.

"You looked me in the eye and told me he was who you wanted. I asked you as both your father and friend. You didn't lie when you said yes."

She patted my knee. "I am hard to handle, and I am damaged. He deserves beautiful. Now. I am…" She launched into work as if she hadn't just effectively dissolved her marriage and put herself down, saying she wasn't worthy of my brother.

She was worthy of me! Hell, I was punching above my weight with her! She sure as fuck was worthy of being with my little brother.

I put my hand over her mouth, stopping her from talking. She watched me and waited. I was worried about everything I had planned now. What if she did not want my company?

"Do you want my company? Are you going to make it great?"

She took my hand away from her mouth. "I am honoured that you have trusted me with this. I will make it great and build it and keep to your values. There will be no fighting and I sure as fuck won't put up with the shit the current board has been pulling. Trust me, I've got this."

I believed her. "You had other things planned, other things you wanted. I never asked what your dreams were."

"Charlie, you have given me so much. You gave me a Vegas wedding that was so much fun. You gave me the wedding of my dreams. You had me jumping out of a plane and getting head by a woman which is never happening again. I had a threesome that will also never happen again. I won't be getting married again, I think three times is enough. And you have given me a dream job. I couldn't be more grateful because I really did do nothing to deserve it."

She touched my face and smiled. "Now, we have work to do. You have brothers you wanted to vent to."

"Kate, you aren't just CEO," I clarified. "When you put your thumb print on that document, I gave it to you. Everything I have is yours the moment I die."

She froze and there was absolute shock on her face. "What? Why would you do that?"

## 71. Kate

I was curled up on the couch ignoring the TV, trying to sort everything out in my own head. Charlie had bombshells coming left, right and center. I really needed to break it down and comprehend one thing at a time.

Walking in and finding them talking about me. Ian admitting, he didn't want to be married to me and planned to annul the marriage which was why we hadn't had sex. And what did I do? I gave him the out. I didn't fight for him.

The kids were having such a great time in the new house. They seemed to like each other and got along like a house on fire. I wanted nothing more than to ring my family and ask for advice, but I knew what they would say. They had told me in Vegas I would get hurt.

I sensed Ian before I saw him. His mere presence made me tingle. I thought what we had… would get us through, but I was wrong.

He touched my hair. "Are you okay?"

"Just tired."

He sat down beside me. "How much did you hear?"

I couldn't look at him. "Enough to know that I am not married. I am just here to let Charlie think he set up a happy ending. That is okay. I should have realised sooner that it was all for show."

I was going to be an adult and talk if that was what he wanted. I hoped he would not be cruel about ending it.

Ian moved closer. "Are you in love with me?"

*Yes.* "I don't know. Falling, I thought. It's hard to know. I work all day with Charlie. You told me to sleep with him as often as I want because you don't mind sharing only to find out it's because the only way you will stay is if I get pregnant."

I sighed. "I don't want to be in a loveless marriage. I don't want you to stay with me because your brother got me pregnant. If he has, then that is on me to deal with. That is on me for being a slut."

"You are not a slut," Ian reached for my hand. I pulled away. He wasn't having a bar of it and took my hand firmly. "Kate, you are not a slut."

"I knew deep down that it was all an act. I just got caught up in it." I pulled my hand away. "I was a holiday fuck and nothing more."

"Now you are starting to piss me off," Ian growled. "You were not a holiday fuck and you damn well know it. The second our eyes met, we connected." He reached for my chin. I pulled away from him. "Oh no you don't. I am here to talk to you. So that is what we are going to do."

I was on my back under him so fast I didn't have time to take a breath. He had me pinned, my arms over my head, holding my chin firmly so I would look up at him.

"Now, wife. You are mine," he growled. "I am letting you ride out your love for Charlie. When he is gone and that cloud of grief lifts off both of us, then I hope I will find that I am very much in love with you and that you are very in love with me. I just don't think it is fair on you to try and start a relationship until then."

"Ian, we are fucking married! And all I do is cheat on you with Charlie."

"That is why I haven't slept with you. Even though the paperwork is signed, it isn't official, it hasn't been consummated. As far as I am concerned, you aren't cheating. I am happy to share you with him because he has never wanted a woman like he has you. That is why I stepped back. Because, as much as he denies it, he wants you until death parts you. He wanted to fucking collar you! Not because of the bucket list, but because he loves you."

I stared at his beautiful face. "I dreamt he gave me a ring… He called it a collar… I thought it was real…" How could Ian be so impossibly beautiful. I believed he was trying to save a marriage he didn't want.

"Ian, you don't have to explain. You don't want me. I get it."

"Kate, stop it. You are beautiful. There is obvious chemistry."

"Ian, how the hell will I be able to trust you if I am pregnant? You will stay for the children. What about my other two children? What about ME!"

His eyes blazed. "I am giving you time to finish it with Charlie. I am giving you time to get your head around everything he is throwing at you. I am trying to be your friend. I do not know anything about you. I do not know what you do for a living. I do not know what happened to your husband. I know nothing about who you are!"

"Then you haven't paid attention because I have been me the whole time. You said you were okay with crazy!"

"I am!"

"The thing is you say all this, but I know you did it for him. I know you did not marry me because you wanted a future with me. My family were right. I am a fucking idiot!"

*Shorty don't you dare get emotional!*

"Please don't put yourself down. You are not an idiot."

"Ian, please don't be nice. I am. I should have just said no. Charlie would have stopped it and you wouldn't be here pretending you want to work it out."

"I am trying to get to know my wife. I am not pretending to do anything."

"Why when you already set us up to fail? Were you even going to tell me when you got it annulled?"

"Stop. Enough. I mean it. You want me to fuck you, I will."

"I don't want you to fuck me." I tested his hold on me, I was going nowhere. "Please don't."

Ian sighed and put his forehead to mine after seeing genuine fear in my eyes. "I am not a rapist, Kate. I want to take it slow and fall in love. I know how much fun you are in bed. I know how fucking beautiful you are under your clothes. And I know you have a wonderful, brave heart. But I need to know more."

He lifted his head to look deep into my eyes again. "Right now, you have shut me out. I deserve it. I said some stupid things today. Charlie and I have had a fight because of it. Please understand, you are losing your husband and I am losing my brother. It hurts me too. I am going to need you when he goes."

Ian looked upset and frustrated. "It hurt to fight with him. I do not want to fight. I want his last days to be happy but, me being the shit I am, I keep stirring him instead of shutting my fucking mouth."

"I will be there for you and the kids when he goes. I won't let you be alone. But there is a good chance I am not pregnant. I have to prepare for you to tell me our marriage is over."

"Would you know if you were pregnant?" he asked. "How did you find out with the twins?"

Umm... "I found out when I learned Chris had an affair around two months before he was killed."

"What?" His eyes blazed into mine with surprise.

"Things got really hairy, I wasn't there. She was. They fucked, she got pregnant. He died and she didn't want the babies. I adopted them."

"You are kidding, those kids aren't yours?"

"They are mine," I said defensively.

"Yeah, I know, but you didn't give birth to them? Ella looks like you!"

"I didn't give birth to them. I have never been pregnant. We tried but it never happened. I think... the injuries and the rape might have fucked me up so much that I can't have children."

233

"What rape?" He looked confused then murderous. I tried to look away, but he forced me to look at him. "Tell me, Wife."

I took a shaky breath. "It happened around two weeks before Chris was killed. I was drugged and then—well I didn't know anything until I woke up in the hospital after surgery to fix the stab wounds and the anal tearing. I lied when I said three men had touched me. The truth is the police think there were five men. They worked that out from the bite marks."

Ian touched my face with his fingertips, his touch making my skin burn. "Did they catch them?"

"No. The case is still open."

"Won't be for long, I will get Brian to look into it."

"No. Please. Involving my family will have them all put in jail. I don't remember it. I honestly don't. So please leave it be. I don't want to remember it."

He nodded, "Okay. Well if you ever don't feel safe with me please say so."

## 72. Charlie

Little fucking shit. Ian had done it to stir me up. He had me going too. He did want her. He was just letting her finish loving me first. But she had overheard him and not given him a fight, let him off the fucking hook with understanding and a smile. When we had duked it out after work, he and I had had a massive fight. Richard and Ben had watched, shaking their heads. Ben though looked like he was going to hit Ian.

"She will never believe you truly want her if she is pregnant," I shouted.

"It will be fine. I will sort it out with her when I get home." He waved his hand. "I said it to stir you up. Not her."

"Ian, she meant it. She was hurt and she let you go. She thinks this is going to end in divorce." Richard shook his head. "I thought you were getting along."

"We barely talk. She spends time with the kids and the animals, but she avoids me. I find her in the office working or patting that bloody Doberman." Ian sat down "The Doberman doesn't leave her alone."

"That is because it's her fucking assistance dog," Ben snapped. "They got it for her when she came back from her last deployment. The dog will leave her be if she is okay. But when she freaks out the dog will stay by her side until she calms."

We all stared at Ben. "Why does she need an assistance dog?" Ian now looking worried.

"She has been through hell. She keeps her shit together most of the time but in times like now... She needs the support the dog gives her."

It was all my fault. "I should get her settled in the business and step away from her."

"If you do that you are going out with a black eye," Ben growled. "Let her know you, let her love you and when you go, we will let her grieve. She knows what is going to happen which is a damn sight more warning than she had with her first husband. Poor fucker." Ben glared at Ian. "Go talk to her, please. Explain it to her like you just did to us. Tell her you want her in your life."

"Like you have done?" Ian asked.

Ben gave him a look that made me feel a little protective of Ian. Considering how fucking angry I was at the pissant, that was surprising.

"Ian, go home and talk to your wife. You make it right or I will make it right. Every time you think about sabotaging your relationship with her or letting her call it off I want you to think about her four brothers that were special services and the amount of pain they will inflict onto you."

"Are you threatening me Ben?" Ian's eyes darkened.

"Not at all. I just informed you of the consequences." Ben looked completely relaxed and turned to me. "You did tell Brian to beat the shit out of him if Ian went to divorce her, didn't you?"

"I did." I nodded.

"You probably shouldn't have asked that of men who are trained killers." Ben answered thoughtfully. I think the look on my face must have said everything. Now I was worried about Ian's welfare. "I won't let them kill him. Apparently, it's Gerrard that dishes out the pain of a broken heart…"

Ian got up. "I am going to go make up with my wife. See you all later."

He left and Richard smiled. "That was really good. He is a bit scared of Gerrard."

"He isn't the one to be worried about." Ben grinned "Her ex-husband, now apparently he was a piece of work. He actually had a badass reputation that still gives troops motivation."

"What was he?" I asked.

"Chris was a sniper. They called him the Devil of Death. Never missed a shot. Fucking master behind a rifle. Billy was a combat engineer in the bomb disposal unit. Gerrard was a medic, but um don't get in a fight with him because he will rip you apart. Brian is also a sniper. Carrie is in IT and Emma was a nurse."

I had not talked to Kate about any of this. We had been working to get on top of the business. "What did Kate do?" I asked almost fearing the answer.

Ben looked immensely proud. "She started out as a medic and became a sniper."

I stared at Ben, eyes wide. "That little woman killed people."

"Meh, her kill rate is nothing to be sneezed at, it's higher than mine but she saved more people as a medic so it kind of evens out."

I blinked. "How much higher?"

"Oh well I would pick a hide and never seemed to get any action…"

"Ben how much higher? We know yours was sixty-six." Richard said.

Ben now looked shitty. "Just over a hundred."

*KATE SHOT OVER ONE HUNDREND AND SIXTY PEOPLE?! BULLSHIT!* I looked at Richard. "I can't see her doing it."

"I can't either but hey, the woman took off an instructor to save your ass, so I am not completely surprised."

"None of that came up in the background check."

"It won't because what you had was Kate Smith." Ben smiled. "She was smart enough to keep her maiden name during her service, even though she was married. Kaitlyn Henderson was a pure badass."

I do believe the man was proud of his little sister. I grinned and changed the subject. "Have you started making moves on Tammy yet?"

He bit his lip and scrunched up his face "She came over last night."

"What!" Richard and I exclaimed. Ben held up his hands.

"No, not like that. No. She felt like she was being stalked and she just turned up and when I opened the door, she threw her arms around me and she was crying and hysterical… I didn't know what to do so I kissed her."

I cocked my head to the side. "You kissed her, huh? That all?"

"Man, I didn't know what to do. She started talking sense after I did it and—well, she stayed the night."

"In your bed?" Richard asked.

"No." He shook his head "I made her stay in the guest room. Vince is becoming problematic. The smack to the head did not get through to him. I had Brian put a detail for her. She is going to stay with me until it is over. Because of that and if we get a middle of the night call saying you have passed... she won't be alone." He looked a little pained at saying that. "Sorry. That was blunt."

"Hey, she is in good hands." I held up my hands. "I just hope that she will be fine when I go."

"I want to know why she went to you and didn't call her big brothers." Richard looked at Ben who stayed cool. "Something has already happened other than a kiss."

"Nothing. I have kissed her once." Ben shook his head in denial, and I smiled. "I did put her to bed in Vegas because she got really messy. She threw up on herself. Shorty had been feeding her fucking shots. She was so gross I had to give Tammy a shower."

Richard smiled. "You just had to strip her naked and shower her."

Ben looked frustrated, got out his phone and bought up a photo of our sister who really was covered in vomit. Richard and I both made faces as he then blurted out...

"I knew I was going to cop shit for being in love with you sister, but I wasn't going to let her wake up in that mess."

I looked at Richard, then back at Ben who realised what he had said. This was good.

After the meeting when I had eaten and showered, I called Mum and Dad to talk for a while. I wanted to check in with them before bed. I was still feeling surprisingly good.

I was just getting into bed when I got a text from Ian. I smiled as I read it.

'I'm so far in the doghouse it isn't funny. I have lost her trust. I do not think there is anything I could say tonight to make her believe me. We have talked a little. Did you know her husband was killed by a land mine? And she is a fucking sniper. Not was, still is! She has more layers than a large roll of silk. She will not let me kiss her, she would let me touch her and did you know some fuckers raped my wife? I am going to find them and make them fucking pay. I have a lot of work to do to earn her back.'

I smiled. 'Threesome at the office?'

'No, I have serious work to do. You go for it though. I think you need to show her the club.'

'Taking her there next week.'

'😊 Awesome, I will come with you so you can concentrate on that sub that really does need a whipping.'

'I decided on the cane. I am off to bed, go cuddle your wife.'

## 73. Kate

Friday morning came around too quickly. The morning I got to meet the board. Charlie had made it clear to me that no one knew he was sick. So, I kept my mouth shut. But someone had found out. When one man asked a lot of questions other members started asking questions too.

Charlie sat back in his seat with a calm I was not feeling. "You have all been on the board for a long time. Overpaid for very little work. As you understand, this is a private company. This company is mine and you are here for your advice and direction."

Charlie looked at each man in turn. "But I am shaking up the company. I want to take it in a slightly different direction, and I feel you would hold the company back when it takes its next steps forward."

"You are firing us?" the troublemaker exclaimed indignantly.

"I am." Charlie nodded. "And I am retiring so new blood can step in."

"Look Charles. I am a little worried about your mental stability. You ran off to Vegas and apparently got married…"

*Where the fuck was this fuckwit getting his information?*

"Getting married makes me mentally unstable?" Charlie asked, glaring at the man.

"No but getting married to a whore does. We have photos of you with a woman you traipsed around Vegas with. The word on the street is she was well paid for her services. Now you are wanting to retire."

Charlie leaned forward looking dangerous. "So, to clarify, you think I am mentally unstable because I reportedly got married to a whore and want to retire. I just want to make sure I am clear, Rod. Because right now I am completely disgusted at the way you are referring to women in general. Especially when there is a lady in the room."

"We will file an injunction to block your actions until such time as you can be proven otherwise."

I glared at the man; I wasn't going to stay silent any longer. "How are you going to do that when you are fired? As in, effective immediately?"

"You just shut up and stay out of it. I am not leaving this job." Rod pointed at me.

*Game on cunt.*

I relaxed back in my chair. "Because you like fucking your assistants, male or female? Or because you have been embezzling without getting caught?" I asked, then pointed around the table. "You all are. This meeting was just to inform you, all in one place, that you are relieved of your duties before the police take you away."

"You can't fire us! We hold shares!" Rod roared at me, pointing his finger.

I smiled because if he kept pointing his finger at me, I was going to break the fucking thing off and stick it up his arse. "You had shares, yes. But they were only yours while you were employed with the company. None of you hold private stocks. I know because I checked."

The board room exploded with men who thought they had more power than they did. They argued, verbally threatened and abused Charlie and me. Then there were several death threats handed out.

That was when I got up and motioned for Charlie to leave the room.

As Charlie stood up someone threw a glass at his head. I managed to stop it hitting him before getting him out of the room. The police were outside waiting to enter. I motioned for them to take over.

As I walked Charlie to his office, he seemed relatively calm. He took a seat behind his desk, watching me.

"Do you think I am mentally unstable?"

"No, I believe out of the two of us I am the batshit crazy one."

He laughed. "You did well in there." I loved it when his face lit up.

"You think so?"

"Absolutely, you were made for this." He pointed up and down at my button up blouse and jeans. "I don't approve of your work attire but that is no longer my concern."

I grinned. "You are just shitty I didn't wear a skirt today. More effort."

"A pair of tight jeans never stopped me, Kate. And I am glad you wore them because we are not having office sex today, I have too much to do."

"Spend another week here with me, make sure I have got it. I really don't want to fuck up everything you built."

He smiled, "You won't. I have nothing but confidence in you."

"You have too much faith in me." I whispered. "It is too much. You are fine."

He got up and gave me a hug. I buried my face in his chest. I breathed in his scent as I did every time, like it was the last time.

"When I die, Kate you will live a long and happy life with Ian and when you think of me every now and then, I hope you will smile."

"What about your babies?" I asked looking up at him.

Please, let me be pregnant, I prayed silently.

He smiled and touched my face. "You can tell them I was a hard man who didn't believe in love until their beautiful mother bought me to my knees."

## 74. Charlie

Saturday night, I went to the club to burn off some stress. Kate and her nose for trouble had averted disaster. The company would have been bought to its knees by a bunch of greedy fuckheads. It was time for drinking with my friends and saying goodbye to everyone here.

I was a part owner of the lucrative and discreet BDSM club; my share would be split between Ian and Richard. I walked in, surprised when the subs all fell at my feet but not in the normal beat me/fuck me way but on their knees in tower pose, heads bowed, knees spread, hands flat.

I stopped and scanned the room. The Doms stood at the bar with Richard and Ian.

Nathan smiled. "What happens in the club stays in the club so we will all keep your secret. We know that you will probably be back while you still can, but tonight... Tonight, is your big send off. I believe you are due a bucks' night since you didn't have one."

I grinned. "I swore I would never do it. But I found a good girl."

Nathan turned and walked between the Doms coming back with Kate in his arms, bound, gagged, and blindfolded. "We know. We have met her. She is a fiery one. Ian is going to spend a lot of time in the doghouse."

I laughed, walked over to her noticing the buds in her ears, all she had was instinct, smell, and touch.

"What's with the sound deprivation?" I asked.

"She isn't a member." Nathan shrugged as he held her like she weighed nothing, Kate mumbled something, then her head started to bop to the music she was listening to. Nathan looked at her amused, "Pure heart. Bought you to your knees."

I touched her cheek. She giggled and gave a muffled. "Hello Charlie." When Ian touched her, she said, "I wouldn't. You are still in trouble."

Nathan laughed. "Anyone tell you, that you are a really strong cunt?"

It really was amazing what you could understand after years of experience with a gagged sub.

Kate went straight over his shoulder for a spanking. She laughed hysterically. He said to Ian, "You need to get your woman out of here so we can start this party." He threw her to Ian who put her down, held her steady and took the gag out of her mouth. I kissed the hell out of her. She knew it was me and kissed me back as she melted like chocolate.

As was tradition in the club, the head Doms kissed the new wife or collared sub. Nathan always went last and when he kissed her, she fought him for a moment before she gave up. Kate kissed him back and his intention to dominate her went out the window. He took Kate off Ian without taking his mouth off hers and held her tenderly. I looked at Ian who watched with a cocked eyebrow.

"Nathan, mine." Ian snarled softly.

Nathan broke the kiss and gasped. Breathless. He was also dangerously close to fucking Kate senseless. Her chest heaved as she struggled for oxygen. Nathan glanced at me. "Okay, I get it. I so want to fuck her. Ian, you need to get her home."

"I am staying, Joe is waiting for her." Ian took hold of his wife who was a little legless from being kissed.

"Ian?" He kissed her gently and she smiled. "Nathan better have enjoyed that because he is never going to kiss me again. Where is Charlie?"

"Aw man, I even like how she says your names." Nathan muttered softly.

I chuckled. "Careful, you might want to try vanilla." He gave me a nod, realised what he did, then gave me an evil look. I just laughed.

I touched Kate's cheek and she turned her head to me. "Have fun. Lots and LOTS of fun. Enjoy your buck's night. I am going home now. Ian can join in. I don't mind. He has a free pass."

I kissed her and removed a bud from her ear for just a moment so I could whisper "You are the fucking jackpot."

She smiled brightly and Nathan looked away. I kissed her chastely before Ian picked her up like the bride she was. "Have fun you dirty fuckers," she said loudly.

Ian carried her out and I patted Nathan on the shoulder. "She is different."

He nodded, "How come you didn't tell us?"

"She kind of just happened and well the rest… I needed to sort out my family first."

"With any luck, Charlie got her pregnant." Richard added.

Nathan looked at me, "You went raw with her?" I nodded. "You have never gone raw with anyone! Is she pregnant?"

I shrugged then smiled at his excitement. "I don't know. In Vegas, she told me she was, just so I could hear the words." Nathan looked back at the door where Ian had taken her. "She got to you, didn't she?"

He nodded absently, "Yeah, don't you worry. She just made some powerful friends and doesn't even know it yet. We will make sure she succeeds."

I smiled, clapped my hands together and turned to the patiently waiting subs. "Okay so what are we going do with all these wonderfully behaved subs?" I walked to a little woman who reminded me a little of Kate in body shape. I stood in front of her "Look up at me," I commanded softly, when she lifted her eyes, I realised it was Daphne. "What should we do to you all little Daphne?"

"It is your buck's night, Sir. Anything you like, Sir." She smiled; obviously happy I still remembered her name.

I held out my hand to her. "I feel like whipping some nipples. Go get my black and red whip."

She took my hand and I pulled her to her feet. She scampered off. Kate had a nicer arse. I looked at Nathan.

"Right are we going to play some games?"

Nathan looked at Richard and both smiled. So began the best night at the club I had ever had.

Now, this was a buck's night.

## 75. Kate

After spending most of the weekend with the kids and animals. My family had come over and we had spent a lot of time going over the past two weeks, debriefing. I waited to talk to Ian about Friday night. It had been very weird when they cut off my senses and then kissed me like that.

Curious, I wanted to know if Ian touched another woman. I figured he had a regular sub he would see, and he would be able to stop it on a good note. That was fair, considering I was sleeping with his older brother on almost a daily basis.

We lay out on the grass with the family that had kept me sane for the last ten years, the animals lounging around us.

The kids ran about playing. Ian was out and about with Charlie and Richard.

"So, what exactly are they doing?" Gerrard asked.

"Golf." I smiled. "Apparently they try to play once a month."

"You wouldn't even know Charlie was sick," Carrie looking at me. "Is he on a lot of pain relief?"

I shrugged, "I think he might have been in Vegas, but I am not sure since he got home. He flits around doing whatever he feels like he needs to. He officially retired on Friday. He has his retirement party tonight."

"We didn't get an invite. Maybe he doesn't want riff raff at the high end do," Billy smirked, acting hoity toity.

I laughed, "I am not even going."

Brian stared at me like I had lost it. "The new CEO isn't going to the old CEO's retirement party? Shorty, you gotta go. He will have contacts he likes and ones he doesn't, and you should be on Ian's arm."

"He has already given me a list of his contacts. We have covered a lot in the last week."

"So, you have your head around it then?" Emma asked.

I shook my head. "Not by a long shot but he is confident. I think he is insane leaving it in my hands."

"I think it is a smart move." Gerrard said. I cocked my head to the side and waited for him to elaborate. "The man obviously sees you for yourself. A lot smarter than your old life gave you credit for."

I shook my head. "You are all just as smart."

"I am not saying we aren't." Gerrard relaxed, linking his fingers behind the back of his head staring up at the sky. "But watching you with Ben, you naturally have some of your father's traits. You were born an aristocrat."

I laughed, "Aristocrat! What the fuck!" I lay staring at the sky. "I am sure my birth father was a lovely man. But I am the daughter of an Australian SAS sniper and a cop. I was not born to be stuck in an ivory tower."

"Oh, don't you worry, we won't let you get fat. We will need to work out how we are going to keep you on the response team. I am not losing you as a sniper. Because this is not going to be a small job that you are taking on," Brian reasoned. "More so when he dies. I think it is going to hit you harder than you let on. I know you are falling in love with Ian more every day, but you have fallen for Charlie too."

"I don't want to talk about it," I snapped. "He still has a couple of weeks."

"He told me he could go anytime," Billy said.

I bit my lip. "That is what he told me too. It is just a little hard to believe when he is running around like he is perfectly fine." *Certainly, fucks like he is.* I added in my head. "I know he will go; he tells me constantly. He tells me not to cry or to be sad. I don't know how he could even think that I wouldn't." I teared up. "I have only known him what two and a half weeks? It isn't going to hurt as much as Chris."

"No, but it is going to hurt." Gerrard said looking at me with concerned eyes. "I think it will hurt more than you are willing to admit to yourself."

"I know it will hurt Gerrard; I try to prepare myself for it every morning I wake up."

"You can put yourself into tactical work mode all you like Shorty, but loving a brother is different to loving your husband and you know it," Brian said gently. "He might not legally be your husband now but in your heart, you are married to two men."

"And you are holding the one you are legally married to at arm's length," Emma added.

I wanted to punch them all for having this conversation with me. I didn't want to have it. But I knew they were only trying to look out for me. Chris's death had shocked and wrecked me. I had not taken it well at all. I had barely functioned as a human.

But it was also only a couple of weeks before he died that I was abducted, beaten, raped and left on the side of the road unconscious and covered in my own blood. It had been the kids that had finally pulled me out of the rut and saved me.

It was different this time. I knew it was coming. I was healthy. I could prepare and get my head around it. I could plan how to handle the few weeks after his death and support Ian and the kids.

"You do know we are going to be with you the whole way, don't you? You aren't on your own." Emma took my hand. I looked at my friend and nodded. "You just tell us what you need done."

"Thank you."

"Seriously though, we have gone through the house and the office checking security, but I am thinking you need a driver for a few weeks at least." Brian bought up another point I didn't want to discuss. "Joe is good, holding the fort here with the kids, Ian has Jaxon, but I think you need someone with you too."

"I don't need anyone."

"You can't go showing off your moves, Shorty. That is how you get sued. Getting sued is bad." Billy explained it to me like I was two, if he kept up the tone we were going to spar.

I gave Billy a dirty look warning him about his tone. He just smirked. The fucker was an engineer in the army, his job was bomb disarming. Not a lot scared him because he was fucking crazy but then I couldn't really judge. I started out as a combat medic.

We talked for another hour before Ian came home. He chuckled when he saw us.

"Why are you all sprawled out on the lawn. What is wrong with the chairs?"

"Good view of the sky and you don't strain your neck," Carrie told him, turning her neck at a weird angle to look at him. "What is that you are holding?"

"I got you girls dresses for tonight. The men's tuxes are inside. You all need to get up and get ready. We only have a couple of hours before Charlie's retirement party."

"How come we got an invite?" Gerrard wanted to know.

"Because you are a lot of fun to drink with." Charlie came outside. "Hair and makeup will be here any minute ladies, so I suggest you get a wriggle on and go have showers."

I sighed and got up before pulling Emma and Carrie to their feet. "Come on, they will be pissed off if we are late."

"Late? We get dressed faster than the boys," Carrie muttered.

"Oi, that is bullshit and you know it." Billy acted offended, really, truly hurt by Carrie's comment, NOT! *Cheeky prick.*

I went to shower and put on a robe before Ian came to tell us the hair and makeup were being done in the guest bedroom.

"Everything else will be on the bed." He gave my bum a pat. "You honestly didn't think we would leave you home tonight, did you?"

"I thought I talked him out of it," I admitted.

"Mum, where you goin'?" Ryan asked, wrapping his arms around my legs.

"I have to go to a special party with Ian." I said.

"Can we come?" He looked up at me with his father's brown eyes. Ryan was Chris's mini me.

"No, you are going to have a movie night with Rita and Joe." Ian said trying to make it sound exciting.

Ryan looked up at him folding his arms. "I'm not silly Ian. Tell me the truth."

"Well this is a work thing Mum needs to go to. There will be lots of things like this."

"She never had to do this before." Ryan noted.

"Mummy hasn't had a job like this before." Ian smiled, "Want to come talk to Rita and see what will be for dinner while Mum gets ready?"

"Okay." Ryan was happy with any conversation that involved food. Again, just like his father.

I went to the guest room and an incredibly happy stylist, who introduced himself as Hans, was all over me. I sat back and let him do his job. When Emma and Carrie entered, he had his assistants look after them.

"Can you smile please?" Emma giggled after twenty minutes of Hans pulling on my hair. I had gone off in my own head to ignore the hair pins he was inserting into my skull.

I poked my tongue at her and then gave her the bird. She did the same back.

"I have ladies who smile and chatter and enjoy this time being pampered. Never have I had two women act like bratty little girls," Hans finally spoke up.

"You get used to it," Carrie smirked and laughed at Emma's and my protests. She gave us the speak to the hand gesture and grinned.

"You are as bad as these two," Hans told Carrie who laughed.

An hour and a half later we left the room and went to get dressed. I was quick to get my undergarments on then the most stunning dark green dress I had ever seen. It flowed over my curves accentuating everything I had. I slipped on the high heeled shoes and left the room. I wanted to see the kids before I left.

I was halfway down the stairs when I heard a low whistle. I looked up; Billy was waiting at the bottom in his tux. I rolled my eyes and shook my head.

"Don't shake your head Shorty, you look seriously hot," Billy said. I was going to say something sarcastic but when I looked back at him, I saw he was serious and blushed instead. "I think you are going to have to get used to being best dressed."

"I would have to agree with him," Ian stated, "That dress looks like it was made for you."

Billy let off another low whistle. "They might just give her a run for your money, Ian. Far out—the women in my family are hot."

Emma and Carrie giggled. "Aww Billy, time to get yourself a woman."

"Nah, too busy for that shit. I have you lot to look at and I don't mind giving love to a random."

"Looking like that Billy, you might actually pick up tonight." Emma grinned looking him up and down.

"Oh no you don't. Don't you look at me like I am some piece of man candy. Next you will be sitting on my lap telling me you love me. I hate that mushy shit." Billy backed up as we converged on him. "I mean it, stay off me, I don't want to stink of your perfumes. I want to pick up!"

## 76. *Charlie*

I had not planned on having a retirement party. But when Richard suggested it, I ran with the idea. Why not? Kate needed an introduction to the business world, and this would be perfect. Having both sides of her family behind her would make my little random that much more formidable. Not that she was not already.

I had not yet touched pain meds. I think it was the fact I had the best sex I had ever had with Kate. But not just that, I was a lot more relaxed. And, now she had officially taken over my business, I could relax even more. I watched her in-laws walk in and bit my lip; Emma was the hottest redhead I had ever met.

And Carrie—with her dark brown hair hmm, beautiful. Gerrard and Brian were hitting well above their weight class with both women but then so was I when it came to Kate. Ian walked in without her and my heart skipped a beat.

WHERE THE FUCK WAS KATE!

Ian got to me, shaking my hand in greeting. "Ryan called to tell her she looked pretty. She is chatting with the kids. She will be here in a minute."

I let out a breath I did not know I was holding. "How does she look?"

"Wait and see." Ian grinned and ordered a scotch which the bartender handed him a moment later. "You just concentrate on having a good night. You have a lot of people to see."

I nodded and looked back to the door just as Kate walked in. My jaw dropped. "Holy shit. She is beautiful." Her eyes scanned the room until they found me. She smiled and walked my way. She turned heads the whole way. When she finally got through the crowd Ian kissed one cheek and I kissed the other. How the press had not found out I had married her I didn't know. I hoped they would not.

"You look ravishing." I smiled when she blushed. "Ian, do you mind if I steal your wife away to do some meet and greet?"

Ian told us to have fun. I moved through the crowd speaking to some of my long-time friends, mentors and rivals. Of course, they were all business, sizing Kate up as a competitor. She was polite and smiled but not once did she take their shit.

If they said something out of line, she told them, and they apologised. If anything, they treated her like a lady and would respect her as such. Only one man pushed her, and as I was about to step in, she took my hand and patted it.

"It's okay Charlie. You are retired. If I can't handle a little pissant like him then I don't deserve the job you trusted me with." She winked before she turned back to Oscar, no longer smiling.

"Repeat it." She took a step toward him. "That is, if you dare." Another step, she was in his personal space. "I mean, you did just imply," she took another step and he took a step back. "that I was a whore." Another step, he backed up. "Would you like the opportunity to clarify what you said, or would you rather apologise?"

She backed him up, smiling but not nicely. She looked downright dangerous. I managed to keep a neutral expression as he held up his hands.

"I am sorry. I was out of line."

She backed down with a nod. "Enjoy the rest of your evening." She smiled at me. "Should we go get a drink Charlie?"

I walked her back to the bar. "I thought you were going to go a level of crazy that I couldn't handle then."

She grinned before saying in a singsongy voice, "That's what you get for picking up a random."

I laughed, putting my arm around her shoulders. "Yes, I should know by now that you are just full of surprises."

At the bar Ben looked his sister up and down and gave her a nod. "You look nice."

She did the same thing to him. "You do too."

I smiled, "Have you two even spoken since Vegas?"

"Nah you have had her busy with all your stuff." Ben stated, "I was talking to Brian before though and he was talking about having a jam session tomorrow afternoon. I told him he wouldn't have recovered from the hangover."

Kate grinned. "You were feeding him doubles."

"You were feeding me doubles." Ben glared at his sister. "What is this fitness thing you have to do?"

Kate shrugged, "Something we do every six months to make sure we are up to the task."

Did not seem like a big deal, fitness tests happened all the time.

"But this is for renewal of the contract you have with the police," Ben said.

"Yeah, we will run a few drills and stuff, no biggie."

Ben watched his sister, "Mind if I come watch?"

"Miss the old days or curious?"

"Curious."

"You know what happened to the cat don't you?" She looked across the room. "Who is the skank all over my husband?"

I turned to see Ian politely removing Amy's hands from him. She smiled at him, then giggled. He was trying not to make a scene and she was insisting on having one.

Ben gave Kate the lowdown on Amy, who had been in love with Ian for forever and a day, but he couldn't stand her. Kate took a sip of her drink and left us to deal with Amy. I looked at Ben.

"I thought you wanted nothing to do with her?" I smiled.

"Yeah well, I changed my mind," Ben muttered.

"I thought you said she was nothing but trouble." I continued, "Money grabbing bitch was what you called her."

"She is trouble.."

"I am glad she will have you. You are her big brother. I am sure she would love to hear about your father."

"I will show her photos and talk to her in time. I will let her process all this first." He looked at me, "How are you feeling?"

"Oh, I have been really good. Happy to retire. I think the company is in good hands."

"I think so too." Ben nodded. "She is smart. But she isn't good at making friends."

I laughed. "What makes you say that?"

"The consensus is that she is a bitch who is going to run the company into the ground."

"Well you make sure you sit back and smirk when she proves them wrong about the latter. As for the former? She will be respected because she is not a pushover. She will be fine."

Richard wandered over with a smirk. "Your new CEO is causing a stir with the women."

"How so?"

"Oh, they hate her. Yet they are trying to pick apart her makeup and her dress and can't." He chuckled. "I think you need to talk her into a photoshoot. She could literally take the business world by storm. And she sings. Hell, she could be in the movies."

Ben raised his eyebrows. "Are you trying to get your paws on my little sister?"

"What are you talking about Henderson? You don't have a sister." Peter Hollands laughed as he walked past. "If you did, she would be as ugly as you."

Ben watched Peter walk away. "You know, for an old man he has ears sharper than Susan when you screw up."

Richard thought that was funny. "Might be a good idea to keep her a secret Ben. You have a lot of enemies."

Ben nodded then looked over to where Ian was. "Who was the smart ass that invited Amy."

Richard and I both denied it. A moment later Amy screeched, and slapped Kate straight across the face. Amy, was close to six-foot-tall in her heels, but she went over Kate's shoulder with an outraged squeal.

It was the funniest thing I had ever seen. Amy fought and protested and screamed. In her three-inch heels Kate, carried her out the front door like it was just another day of the week. Security was with her a moment later. The room went silent. Kate reappeared a minute later, shaking her head, not even seeming upset. She looked up at the crowd of faces that was solely on her and cocked her head to the side.

"What?" She watched everyone a little longer. "Back to it." She waved her hand dismissing everyone.

It was a simple order, but everyone turned away from her. I though, burst into laughter. Kate looked at me and her face lit up as she smiled.

Her family, then mine burst into laughter and the whole room followed. Kate just shrugged and walked back to Ian who gave her a chaste kiss and checked her cheek.

"She just carried Amy out!" Richard laughed holding his stomach. I nodded because I could not answer for the laughter. Richard pointed at me. "You're crying!"

I wiped my eyes as I got control of myself, shaking my head. "Fucking Jackpot!"

## 77. Kate

Monday should have been my first day at the top of Charlie's company but instead I was doing my fitness test and running drills while Ben, Ian, Richard, and Charlie watched. I had shaken my head and tried to discourage it, but they insisted. Before the day started, we had our medicals and blood tests. We went through the driving course and shooting at the range before we did the physical.

The obstacle course was five miles all up. The obstacles were designed to test agility and strength. After I got through, we changed into the full tactical gear that we wore into the field. I ignored the fact that the boys were here watching, glad Emma and Carrie were babysitting them.

I was not ready to give up this part of myself. I was still fit and healthy and fast enough. We were given a brief and had worked out our plan of attack. This would be quick.

## 78. Charlie

We watched from the sidelines for most of the day. It moved quickly and it was extremely exciting seeing Kate in the world she had been trained for. Today she was not playing the princess, she was the warrior. Now it was easy to see how she had managed Amy so easily.

She drove the car like she stole it, she went sideways around the corners. I was glad I was not in the car with her because I would have been screaming as much as the instructor. Then the weapons.

Amazing. She was cool, calm and confident and a wicked shot. Ben muttered a couple of times, making me grin.

"What's wrong?"

"I miss this shit." He sighed, "I need to go to the range more often."

I watched him for a moment longer. "There is something else."

Ben clenched his jaw. "I think she might be better than me."

"You were a fucking SEAL; how can general army be better than you?"

Billy laughed. "Shorty's father was SAS. He taught her to shoot."

I watched my little random. She was humble. Her brother was slightly green with jealousy. Sibling rivalry, I chuckled.

"I was never special forces. Don't go getting jealous," she smirked as she went past to get ready for whatever the hell she had to do next.

"I'm not jealous." Ben got up. "Shoot again. I can beat you."

She turned to Billy.

"Alright, Ben. We will time you both." Billy smirked. "Are we having a match of brother vs sister or Australia vs America?"

"Australia vs America," Ben said, "I don't want to feel bad for beating my little sister."

Richard teased, "I think you might like having a little sister, Ben."

Ben shook his head as the range was set up. He checked his weapon and sighed. It was interesting seeing the man he was years ago. He was competent and it was easy to see that in a shitty situation he would be an extremely dangerous man. "I really do miss this shit sometimes."

"You shot alright on the long range, so let's see what you got." Kate grinned before giving an up nod to Billy. "You got my times there?"

"You want to use them?" Billy nodded.

"If he doesn't beat me," she grinned.

"That is all the motivation I need," Ben said as Billy stood behind him with the timer. He pressed it and Ben let off his shots with speed and precision. I was impressed. I met Ben after he did his stint in the SEALs. He had gotten out after his father had gotten sick and he had taken over the family business. Weirdly, our fathers had been friends since they were boys.

I had never seen Ben shoot. He was good. I watched Billy looking at the times.

"You might want to shoot again," Billy grinned at Kate.

She cocked an eyebrow and got in position. Same process. When she put down the gun only a few seconds later she waited for Billy's verdict, bored. Ben folded his arms.

Billy held up the timers. "Ben," he showed the timer in his left hand. "Shorty." He held up the timer in his right. Both looked at it and neither looked impressed. "Dead heat."

"What was my score before this?" Kate asked.

Billy held it up and Kate smiled, patted Ben, who looked pissed off, on the shoulder and walked away. "Aussie for the win! Don't worry Bro, you are out of practice, better luck next time."

I laughed at the look Ben gave her before he shot a glare at me. "Shut up Charlie. It isn't funny."

"You are competitive but retired from this and she is not. She should be better than you. For the sake of her job."

"Doesn't make it hurt less."

Richard and Ian laughed.

Next, we watched her go off on a run, then the last of the obstacles. Richard and Ian continued to give Ben shit. He just shook his head and muttered he was going to get back in shape. When he got more shit, he dared them to do the training with him. Both took Ben up on the challenge.

"You mother fuckers don't know what you just signed up for," Ben smirked.

"Are you having fun?" Emma asked as she sat beside me handing out bottles of water.

"Yes, we are having a ball." Ian grinned.

"They are about to do the scenario. Then they will be done. Shorty was saying she wanted to stop in at the office afterward and get some work done. She wants to make her presence felt."

"She will be exhausted. She will be going home," Ian said firmly.

Emma cocked an eyebrow. "You just want to fuck her cause you are seeing the side of her that we know. Shorty has a job; she is going to at least make an appearance."

"What are you her PA now?" Ian asked.

"Oh fuck no. I am telling you that if you start trying to dictate to her when she is going home when she has a job to do, all because you want to fuck, you are going to get cock blocked."

"Now you are just setting me a challenge," Ian grinned.

"She is trying to find her feet, let her do it. She has had a lot of change in the last few weeks and if you don't let her get her head around it you are going to make it worse when Charlie…" She stopped and bit her lip "Sorry."

"Don't be. I am going to die. That is a given. I agree. She needs to work things out. But I am not going to let her hide. Ian won't either." Trying to relax and talk about it hurt, but I wanted them to be open and say what they needed to.

I wanted to seem fearless in the face of death when secretly I was shitting myself. I did not want to die. I loved my family and friends. I loved life. I loved Kate.

"Kate is hiding. She barely talks to me," Ian said. "She does try but she seems to be just trying to sort it out in her own head."

The conversation ended because there were people head to toe in black tactical clothing, they were moving fast and were all armed. Ben sat forward watching. I sat back, to enjoy it.

I did not enjoy it. It scared the shit out of me.

They were in formation when two were pretty much thrown through a second story window to gain entry. The door was breeched, then there was gunfire.

Then silence. Eerie quiet. Emma sat forward with a walkie talkie.

"Brian, are you clear?"

It was probably only a couple of seconds, but it felt like a lifetime. "Show clear, doing a quick debrief."

"Well that was scary," I said softly.

"That was just about perfect except I have never sent a guy through the window," Ben muttered. "Breached walls but never gone through the window."

"That was Shorty and Jimmy," Emma smiled.

It amused me how she called Kate, Shorty. "How did she get the nickname?"

"Well when Chris first laid eyes on her, she was in a bar for the first time. He said "Hey Shorty, wanna dance? She looked up at him and smiled before taking his hand. It stuck. The next day when he saw her on base he called out 'Hey Shorty!'" Emma sighed. "I miss him." She gave me a shoulder bump. "I'm going to miss you too."

I smiled and shoulder bumped her back. "You haven't known me long enough to miss me." That was sweet.

She shrugged. "I don't think you realise how easy it is to like you, Charlie. You are a good man."

I studied her. She was upset but keeping her composure. She meant what she said. I put my arm around her shoulder and kissed her temple. "I let you see me because it's all I have ever let Kate see. If you knew the other me—you would think I was a cunt."

"We are not having a threesome, Charlie." Brian's voice came over the radio. "Please stop pulling moves on my wife."

I laughed and Emma giggled. Then said to me, "If you saw how Shorty gets sometimes, you would be scared."

"She already has scared me. Her doing this scares me. But this is part of her. I just hope Ian can accept it."

"I'm good. I will not bitch about this and she won't bitch about the clothes I put her in or the events we attend. This has been a rather good insight into her. It explains why she is such a controlled little wench."

## 79. Kate

Today was my first official day at the top. I sent out an email to everyone in the company as a formal introduction, I wanted to see what the staff morale was like. Especially with a new boss at the top of the company. I also wanted to see who had been here the longest, who had gotten promoted, who had not, and what their managers were like and had done up an informal survey so I could gather the data I would need to implement changes.

After last week's investigation and the dismissal of the board, I wanted to ensure that everything else was hunky-dory before I moved forward. This was always an incredibly good way to get the staff to know that I will fuck up anyone who tries to screw with Charlie's business.

I had a meeting with Sam to explain what I wanted to do, and made it clear I couldn't do it without her and needed her to guide me since Charlie had thrown me in the deep end. Sam promised to help me. We would meet again when we had a few answers.

Charlie turned up at lunchtime with sushi, dressed in jeans, a t-shirt and running shoes. He looked happy and relaxed. He shut my door and locked it.

"How is your day going?" he asked with a cheeky grin. "Mine has been fucking awesome. I slept in, had pancakes for breakfast, and had a massage for the first time in forever. It was amazing.

Then I got sushi and my girls gave me a hug when I came in. Now I get to have lunch with you before Billy teaches me to shoot like you. I already drive well enough to put you to shame."

I smiled as he got out the food and put it on the coffee table. I sat down beside him. "Sounds like you have had a busy day." I loved that he was so relaxed.

"I have. It's great not having any responsibility." He put some sushi in his mouth and chewed. Charlie's eyes rolled as he groaned in appreciation. "This is so good." He offered me a bite, I opened my mouth and he smiled as he put it in. I sucked his fingers making him grin. "You are in need of a spanking."

I chewed the delicious food in my mouth. "I am, am I?"

He nodded. "You are. You are shaking up my company."

Instant guilt. "How do you know?" I hoped I wasn't upsetting him.

"I just do." He gave me his wise old man impersonation. "I like what you are doing. I just want to spank you because I like touching your butt."

I giggled, picked up another tasty bite and popped it in my mouth before lying over his lap. He laughed and lifted my skirt, palmed my arse before giving it a squeeze then a little slap.

"This is turning into a very enjoyable lunch date."

"Yeah it seems to be going well." I grabbed another bite. "Do you think I am doing the right thing?"

"I know you are. It is exactly what I do when I take over a company. But I wait to see who will cause trouble and who will suck up for a pay rise." He put some sushi on my arse and popped another bit in my mouth. "Never straight up after."

"Why?"

"Because I like people to think I am a fool and kind."

"Well I am already a woman, so people already think that." I made a point. "Doing it now or later, it won't make a difference."

262

"That is true," Charlie admitted. "I would have played you for a fool. I would have had a rude surprise, but I would have done it. Hey, I like these panties."

"Do you?"

"Hmm, but I like it better when you don't wear any."

I smiled as we ate in silence for a few minutes. It was nice, not uncomfortable at all. When he was done eating, he massaged my bum with firm hands.

"You are an incredible woman Kate."

"I am?"

Slap! He landed the first of my spanks, hard. I grunted, glad I didn't have food in my mouth 'cause, it would have landed on the couch. I laughed and got another for my effort.

"Why am I getting spanked?"

"It will get all the happy chemicals happening in your brain."

"Put your face between my legs and it will do the same thing." I grinned back at him.

"You know I have done a lot of things on that desk, had many women under it giving head. But I never gave head. Hmm. Want to be the first?"

I was excited at the opportunity to be naughty. "Like I would pass that offer up."

We got up and I sat in his chair. "Stand in front of me," he ordered as he took back his seat. I did as he asked, and his hands slid up my skirt and pulled down my panties. "No teasing, I am just going to bring on this orgasm. I told Billy I would be there by 1:30."

He sat me on the desk, arse on the edge before laying me back. He placed my legs on the arm rests and lowered his chair. I took a breath as he parted my legs.

"Why do you always want to cover up?" he asked as he kissed my thighs "Your flower is the most beautiful I have ever seen."

I blushed. "You are just saying that."

"No, I'm not. And I have not tasted anything sweeter than the juice I get from your honey hole."

His tongue was wicked. He knew the right spots to get me lost. His growls and grunts were a turn on. It didn't take me long to hit that orgasmic high. I stared at the ceiling, taking a few deep breaths to bring myself back to center as he put my panties back on.

He helped me sit up and kissed me deeply, my essence on his lips. I touched his chest, neck, and face. I ran my fingers through his hair.

He broke the kiss and smiled at me. "I have to go."

"You don't want me to get you off?"

"I got off watching you cum." He delivered a chaste kiss. "Have a good day."

I nodded, watched him leave then went to the bathroom and straightened myself up. As I looked at myself in the mirror, I wondered how Ian really felt about me still being with Charlie. I pondered it and, at four when he walked through my office door, I was ready to talk.

I don't know how people had affairs. Ian and Charlie had shared me from the very first night. I had sex with both together and Charlie on his own. I understood Ian's logic for waiting and I was grateful. I never lied to Ian, I always told him when I had slept with Charlie. But I wasn't really communicating with him.

Ian sat on the couch with a huff. "I had to get out of my office." Then launched into a rant about work and idiots who wouldn't do their jobs. I got up and sat across from him and heard him out. He was so wound up that he had a vein popping in his forehead. I got up, sat in his lap and hugged him. He kept ranting so I stood up and put his face between my boobs. Ian's arms went around my waist.

"Why is my face in your boobs?"

"I am hiding you from stupid people." His eyes peeked up at me as he started to laugh.

"You are such a good listener. Thank you, I needed to lose my shit in a safe place."

"It's okay. It's what a good wife should do."

"You are a very good wife." He nuzzled my tits and then sat me on his lap. It felt natural and not at all strained. "How was your day?"

"Oh, getting to know the company more intimately. Charlie bought me lunch and then went for a play date with Billy who was going to teach him how to shoot tactically."

Ian chuckled. "What did Charlie bring you for lunch, other than an orgasm?"

I blushed. "Sushi. He used my butt as a plate."

"I will have to do that." Ian looked inspired. "I will lay you out with three courses and work my way down."

"Maybe I could do that to you."

His eyebrows went up. "I love the idea of being laid out for you, to have you feast on me. It puts all kinds of ideas in my head."

"Does it bother you that I am still sleeping with Charlie?"

"Nope." He shook his head.

I watched him, searching for a lie. "Why?"

He watched me for a moment and then stroked my face. "I knew you were mine when our eyes met in the casino. I know you pretended not to see me, but I know you did." I blushed again. "But I saw the moment you and Charlie connected, and I won't deny him that."

"But I am your wife."

"You will be 'til death do us part. But Charlie refused to have you go through that part of your vows. Like everything, he did it on his terms and divorced you. He didn't want you to mourn him like you did Chris."

I looked into my husband's eyes and teared up. "I think it is going to happen anyway. I know he tells me he is dying but I look at him and he looks perfectly fine. He bounces around and seems so happy."

"That is because he is happy. He is in love for the first time in his life, he has freed himself from responsibilities and is doing things that he never thought he would do. He got to retire and have his company in capable hands, he got to see us both move on. He got to play Dad and give his daughter away. He could be out slutting around, but since the first night, he has only slept with you. Well except for Friday night. He is faithful to you and trust me when I say he has never been faithful in the bedroom to anyone."

"How can you put up with it. I am married to you. I should be faithful to you! And I can't! I am in love with him, Ian. I am in love and as much as I am falling for you every day... I feel like I am being the shittiest wife because I have been avoiding you. I... I haven't lied to you about being with him. I am trying to be honest, but I am so conflicted! How can I be what you need?"

Ian took my face between his hands and gazed into my eyes. *How could his eyes be so blue!* "You are what I need because I am falling for you too...I know you are struggling. I hate that you don't let me in here." He pointed to my heart and then my head. "But I know you are only trying to protect yourself to a certain extent. And I can't blame you."

"Is he really dying?" I asked, hoping he was about to tell me that Charlie was a perfectly healthy 40-year-old male whose arse I could go kick for lying to me. The look on Ian's face was like a kick in the guts. Confirmation that Charlie had been telling the truth from the beginning.

"Yeah. He is. He had four opinions before he showed Mum and Dad the test results. There is nothing that can be done. The cancer is all through him, stage four."

"He is the healthiest looking cancer patient I have ever met."

Ian looked at me and then got out his phone and showed me a picture of a very healthy-looking Charlie who was fucking drop

266

dead gorgeous. "This was taken twelve months ago." He swiped to another. "This was six months, and this was a month before he told us, and we ended up in Vegas and met you."

I looked at the photos with disbelief, "He has gone downhill so fast. I mean he still looks really good, other than the weight loss and even that isn't a lot."

"And other than suffering some really bad hangovers and getting a little bruised from skydiving and paintball, he says he isn't in pain, he lied in Vegas thinking it would make it easier on us. He thinks it's because of all the awesome sex he has been having."

I smiled, but only a slight one. "Isn't it weird having a threesome with your brother?"

"He was adopted, he isn't my blood brother. Technically he is my cousin, but in my heart, he is my brother. It was weird when he suggested it but so long as swords don't cross, I don't mind."

I smiled, I figured that would be a problem for a lot of men. "Are you okay? Have you accepted it?"

"No. Not at all. I fear the phone ringing. I fear going to sleep." He put a little bit of hair back behind my ear. "You make it better being beside me. You love him and you love me. I know when he goes it's going to hurt us both, but I won't let you stay broken. I know you will not let me either. We will just get out the superglue and put our hearts back together again."

That was so sweet I kissed his cheek. "We are going to be okay, aren't we?"

He nodded and hugged me to his chest "Yeah, we will be. Just have to be patient. And please stop stressing about sleeping with him. He calls me every time he is planning sex with you and asks."

"Would you tell him no?"

"No, because he looks at you with so much love. I told him to stop asking and just do it when he wants to fuck you. If he were fucking you just because he could, then I would stop it. As I said he was a real man whore. But he loves you, Kate. Just like I do.

Life is short and we must make the most of it. So please, relax and enjoy him. It makes me happy to see him happy."

For the first time since I married Ian, I felt like I had made a good decision. That we would work together, that this was going to be long term. Then I realised, Ian just told me he loved me for the first time.

## 80. Charlie

Who knew shooting could be so much fun? Or that killing targets could be so satisfying? Seriously, I wish I had found this sport sooner. It would have made hard, shitty weeks at the office so much better. And the Smith men, they were rough and uncultured, and man could they swear. Until now, I had only ever seen them with the girls around. They had been nice and all, but apparently, they had been on their best behaviour.

Everything was a joke. They would literally 'take the piss' out of anything and anyone. And crude. I now understood how Kate could have rolled with us in Vegas and not batted an eyelid. They made me feel like a brother. I had not had a lot of male friends, mostly because I was a competitive dominant. I liked women who, to a certain extent, I could control.

Ben was my closest male friend, Nathan a close second. I felt a little bad that I had not invited Nathan to Vegas but drinking with him would sort that out. Like the Smiths, they did not bullshit me, gave me shit and listened when I talked which made me sit up when they spoke.

I sat drinking beers with them at my place which was a first because I never had anyone over to my place socially. Then Ben arrived with Ian and Richard and we drank more beer. I told them about shooting.

"He is surprisingly good. He keeps up training, he will be better than Ben." Gerrard had a dig at Ben who grinned while he opened another beer.

"Next he will be joining the military." Ben grinned at me. "You could be a sniper like your ex-wife."

"I think that is a skill she can keep." I looked at my brothers. "How goes the workout Ben dared you to do?"

"What workout?" Brian asked putting another beer to his lips.

Ben told him about the dare and Brian smirked as he listened. "You know. to do that right you gotta do hell week."

"Nah, not fair on them, Ian especially, four kids at home and Katie. He needs to be able to give them time," Ben said and every man there looked at him "What?"

"You just called her Katie. I don't even call her Katie." Ian grinned.

"I thought you didn't want to know her. Now you are giving her a nickname only her parents would give her." Richard chuckled.

Ben sighed and shook his head. "I haven't really talked to her since I got back."

"Yeah, so give her a call, or go see her." Ian gave him a 'duh' look. "She is your sister."

"One, I didn't know about until she contacted me. Only had it confirmed when the Will was read."

All eyes snapped to Ben who looked like he just had the cat let out of the bag. I smiled slowly.

"She didn't know anything about her father, nothing but a photo and a name." Brian watched him. "Are you telling me your old man knew about her?"

Ben took a breath and nodded. "One-night stand in Vegas, quickie marriage even quicker divorce and a pregnancy. He thought he had made a mistake. He thought she was a stripper."

"He didn't know she was a young police officer. She contacted him and told him she was pregnant. He had women he never even slept with tell him that. He ignored it. She sent him a photo of Kate after she was born. Told him a friend had married her, so she wasn't born a bastard, but she was given his name. Said he could see her if he chose to. He got a photo of her every year on her birthday. I found them when I was cleaning up the house. She was a cute kid. No denying that she is his daughter. She has his eyes."

"So why never meet her then?" Billy exclaimed. "That was all she ever wanted. She wrote to him twice to tell him her parents had passed and when she moved over, she wanted to meet him…"

"He died before he could read the last letter." Ben shook his head. "He left some things in the Will for her though."

All eyes went back on Ben, I cocked my head to the side. "Why haven't you given them to her then?"

Ben frowned. "Well, it just doesn't seem like the right time. He gave her my grandmother's rings and jewellery and a twenty percent share of his business. She has had a lot going on and when things quieten down and she settles, I will sit her down nice and quiet like and give it all to her."

"A couple of rings and what a few necklaces? You want to wait to give her that?" Gerrard scoffed and took a drink of his beer.

"The jewellery and rings are worth more than 70 million," Ben said flatly.

Gerrard's sprayed his beer in shock. I laughed, enjoying the surprise on his face as he roughly wiped his mouth with the back of his hand. I did the math in my head and quickly worked out that, when Ben handed all that over to Kate, with what I was giving her, she was going to be richer than Ian and Richard combined. She might just do what I hadn't and hit the top ten of the Forbes list. I wasn't going to tell them that though.

"You are kidding?" Gerrard still couldn't believe it.

"Grandma was from old money. The jewellery has been handed down through generations to the first-born girl. No, I am not kidding."

"If you are old money what they fuck were you doing running around in warzones?" Brian muttered shaking his head. "You were your father's heir. Why didn't he talk you out of it?"

"Because he was a SEAL too." Ben smiled proudly.

I smiled at Ian and Richard; Ben was getting himself another set of brothers. Ian and Richard would have their support too. Why hadn't I had more boys' nights?

They went home to their wives a couple of hours later. Ian stopped as he was leaving and looked back at me.

"Come home with me. I was thinking about covering Kate in food and licking her clean."

I smiled broadly. "Really?" I went to my cabinet and got a bottle of Bollinger. "Let's go."

## 81. Kate

I had gotten all the kids to bed after Ian went drinking with Charlie for the afternoon. I wasn't pissed off; I was happy to have a shower and time to think. I got out of the shower and was drying myself, completely off in my own world. I didn't see the door open but when I stood up I saw in the mirror, Ian behind me with a smirk on his beautiful face and not a stitch of clothing on his gorgeous body.

For a moment, we just stared at each other. I grinned then bent over to finish drying my legs. His hands went on my hips a moment later.

"Charlie is here, would you like to play?" He used that deep sexy, seductive voice of his that made me wet. His hand landed on my bum with a playful tap. "You are a very naughty girl bending over like that." Another slap on my other butt cheek. "You need a spanking to get you warmed up I think."

271

I smiled; I didn't mind getting spanked. It didn't hurt and was kind of relaxing if I was to be honest. There was a rhythm to it. I stood up, put the towel on the rack and his hand went into my nape under my hair.

"Come wife, your ass is going to glow a pretty pink. And I want to fuck your face."

I grinned as he walked me from the bathroom to the dungeon where Charlie was waiting with rope. He smiled and took hold of my wrists, binding them behind my back as Ian effectively kissed me blind. I moaned and surrendered myself to these two beautiful men.

I didn't really consider myself a submissive person. I loved control, but I loved what these two had done for me so far. Ian took my face between his hands, gave me his neck so I kissed and nipped at it before he directed my head down his chest to his nipple which I gave a good nip. He yelped and my arse stung a moment later. My arms were pulled up behind my back and my legs were kicked a little wider apart. I was bent at a ninety-degree angle.

I was spanked and face fucked by both men, and when they were certain my arse was red enough, I was tied to a table and blindfolded. They turned on the music, all I had was touch, and smell. I couldn't see or hear anything, and I couldn't move. It was sensory overload like nothing I had experienced before.

## 82. Charlie

Ian and I did not talk as we ate strawberries and chocolate off Kate's body. We dribbled hot chocolate over her and licked her clean. We ran ice over her just to chill her before going back to the chocolate. Ian got the bottle of champagne and pointed at her glistening cunt. He poured a glass as I got down and planted kisses on her.

I ran my tongue up her slit and then pierced her because I loved the way she tasted. Ian poured the champagne down her slit. She cried out and jerked, fighting the restraints as I lapped the champagne up like a thirsty dog. The bubbles and the cold would have tickled and chilled her.

Ian poured more on her body and as he lapped it she cried out, writhing against her restraints. Hot and cold. Hot and cold. Ian drank from her and I could see that he would spend a lot of time doing that in future. Ian got the flogger and bought it down on her to change up the sensations. She cried out but he hit her three more times before kissing every red mark.

I stood up, pumped myself a couple of times and put the top of my cock just inside her. Ian pinched her nipples hard then gave them a tight twist as I slammed into her. Her cry was ecstasy. Her pussy was a tight, wet haven. Heaven on earth.

Ian grabbed her hair and kissed her mouth and jaw. "Charlie loves to fuck you, Kate. Feel him inside you. Feel his cock. Feel how wet, how tight you are around him." Ian poked his tongue in her ear, she whimpered. Ian whispered filthy words in her ear, caressing and stroking her skin.

Then he put her head back and fucked her face, pinching at her nipples. I fucked her and spanked her ass hard.

She came hard and me, being even more of an ass than normal, led her into a couple more orgasms before her body dropped. Ian and I both saw the moment it happened and fucked her 'til we both came. I came inside her. Ian came on her tits. Twice in a week, Kate was in subspace. Ian inspected his wife as we untied her restraints.

As a Dom, my biggest job was the aftercare. Bathing, rubbing cream into the welts I caused. Cuddling and telling my sub how fucking proud and honoured I was to have her put her trust in me. Ian planned to do the aftercare tonight, but one of the kids woke up so he went off to put them back to bed while I cared for her.

Kate watched me with exhausted but sated eyes. But it was the love that she had in them just for me that made me want to protect her. I lay down beside her spooning her body against mine.

"Are you coming for lunch tomorrow?" she asked softly, holding my hand.

I shook my head. "No, I am going to have lunch with Tammy and Susan, maybe take them shopping. Then I am going to Mum and Dad's for dinner. And on Friday night I am going to get everyone together for a jam session because I think we sounded awesome in Vegas. Sunday we have family lunch with Mum and Dad and then it's the beginning of a whole new week where anything can happen."

I kissed her hair and felt the moment that she fell asleep, mumbling she loved me as she did. Ian came back a couple minutes later and climbed into bed. I kissed the base of Kate's neck and went to get up. I did not want to leave but it was the right thing to do.

"Stay." Ian said softly in the dark. "You have never run out on a sub. Don't start with her."

"Thank you," I whispered with tears in my eyes. I nuzzled her hair. Then Ian did something we had not done in Vegas. I was holding her hand and he put his hand over ours.

"Ours." Ian whispered.

"Yours." I whispered back.

"Only when you are gone. Kate is Ours."

It only took him thirty-two years, but Ian finally learned how to share.

## 83. *Kate*

The week dragged on. Charlie didn't come back in for lunch which kind of sucked because I liked my lunch time fuck time. But I got a lot of answers to my email and with them, a heap of problems to sort out. Charlie's company was in great shape but there were changes going to happen hard and fast. I may not have worn a suit to work, but the company was getting the message that I would not be fucked with.

I did enjoy going home and spending time with the kids and with the animals. I used my time wisely, getting to know Tim and Evie and giving Ryan and Ella some much needed attention. I needed to learn how to juggle my new life. I needed to learn fast. I had four children, a massive business and a husband I barely knew anything about.

Of course, that was all my fault. I had moments when I opened up to him, but I don't know, he was beautiful, smart, and funny. He'd played my body like I had known him forever in Vegas but there hadn't been anything except a little kissing and cuddling since then. Well except in the dungeon the other night but I am not sure that oral sex counts as consummation of a marriage.

I guess I got shy when I tried to talk to him. I needed to snap out of it. He was my husband. If we were going to work, we would have to communicate openly. But, with Charlie, I could talk about anything and everything.

I sat on the grass brushing the dogs with the kids.

"Mum, Ebie does nastics. I do nastics too," Ella told me."

I looked at my little girl "Okay. You can go to Gymnastics with Evie."

"Then we go to baseball?" Ryan asked.

I smiled. "That sounds like fun"

The boys both seemed happy about that.

"Shorty, the dogs really like being brushed but not as much as the tats," Evie smiled.

"The cats do really love being brushed." Evie was pretty with her dark curls which contrasted with Ella's blonde curls. I liked it when Tim and Evie would sit close but not touch, as if they wanted attention but were shy. I decided to let them come to me.

I needed to get to know them and I hoped I would be a good mother to them. Although I knew little about Aria, I guessed she would not have approved of my parenting style.

"Hello, my minions," Ian said from behind us, making me jump. The kids, of course, found that funny. Ian chuckled as he sat down on the grass, picked up a brush and began brushing one of the Shepherds. It lay there and sighed. "How was everyone's day?"

The kids told him how I had agreed for them to go to gymnastics and baseball and how excited they were. Then they wanted to do all sorts of other stuff like dancing; all of us, as a family. I sat there, looking at the kids like they were off their heads. I had agreed to baseball and gymnastics. But Ian stayed engaged and agreed to it.

It was good that they wanted to do things as a family, it would be good for bonding. I would just have to juggle it all.

It was then that I realised just how thankful I was for Joe and Rita living here, doing the housework, sorting out the gardens and animals when we weren't here. They kept the household stable.

I made a note to thank them both. My kids had settled in because they had a solid routine and Joe and Rita were firm. I was thinking about a lot of things when a big hand touched my shoulder. Ian was watching me.

"Are you okay?" he asked, his eyes always watching me, seeing me, reading me. "You were quite chatty before I announced myself."

"I am okay, I am just thinking." I tried to smile and failed.

He moved closer and I hugged him, his big arms a cocoon of safety and comfort. "You aren't doing this alone."

"The bits I talk to you about are what I need to talk to you about. The rest is mental notes to do things and getting my shit in order."

"You know I don't mind listening if you just want to tell me what shit you need to get in order. Maybe saying it aloud will help you sort it."

I stayed silent, I didn't really want to talk but I had to give him something "I only agreed to the baseball and the gymnastics. Everything else they come up with on the fly."

Ian chuckled "Sounds fun though."

## 84. Charlie

I had spent the day with Tammy walking through her design house before we had lunch and went shopping. I spoilt my little sister rotten with clothes, shoes, and diamonds. Not that she needed them. The woman had a wardrobe the size of a large bedroom. I listened to her hopes, her dreams and when we were finished, I took her home so I could really talk to her.

She sat with me on the couch, she had been cuddly as a child. She was still like that now.

"I want to talk about Vince," I began and she rolled her eyes. I slapped her leg. "Don't be a petulant little bitch, Tammy. I want to talk about Vince."

"There is no Vince," she spat, rubbing her leg. "Ben made him go away. Why did you slap me!"

"Because you rolled your eyes. You know that is rude."

"Kate does it all the time and you don't slap her!"

"If she were mine Tammy, that woman wouldn't sit down for a week from the cane marks on her ass. Now tell me about your

277

trouble with Vince. Do not sugar coat it. I want to know exactly what is going on."

"I don't want you to worry." She teared up; this was her go to when she didn't want to talk about something. "I want you to be stress free."

"I am more stressed not knowing." I took her hand. "Why did you go to Ben and not come to us?"

"Because Vince said he would kill you if I did," she answered softly. "He didn't say anything about going to Ben."

We sat and talked and when she said Vince had been stalking her for six months, it made my blood boil. The fact that he had broken into her apartment and had attempted to rape her only to be stopped by Ben… Well, I was damn near explosive.

"Have you told Ben about all of this?" I asked gently, controlling my anger. *Only. Just. Controlling. My. Anger.*

She nodded, "He made me report it. Vince was interviewed and he has an alibi. Ben said he would sort it out."

Inner me smirked before wondering if I had left myself enough to hire Larry and put him on a retainer for Ben, Kate, and the family for the rest of his working career. The man was a legal weapon. I decided that I would do that regardless. If Ben was sorting it out, he might just need a good lawyer himself.

Tammy sat quietly while I hugged her then bought up the subject of Ben.

"How do you like living with Ben?" I asked.

"He is a clean freak. Everything has a place. If it does not have a place, it goes in the bin. He does not really have a lot of stuff though. He just has what he needs. Not like my place. I have lamps and rugs and pictures on the walls. He has three photos up in his room. One of his Dad, one of his Mum and last night he put a cute photo of Kate when she was little beside them."

Ben had people over as often as I did. He was a very private man. I did not realise he was so minimalist.

"So, when I am gone, do you think you might move in with Ben on a more permanent basis?"

"I am just staying there because I am a wreck and he is worried about me. There isn't anything going on."

"Come on Tammy, are you seriously going to tell me that he is doing all this for you while you are effectively living with him and there is nothing going on?"

"I can't tolerate the thought of being touched. When this is over, I will go back to my flat and be fine."

"So, you aren't attracted to Ben at all?"

"NO! Of course not! He is so big and a little scary. No, I do not want a man like that. He is nice and he kisses..."

"He kisses you?"

"Just once. I was upset and I don't think he really knew what to do..."

"What does he kiss like shit?"

"No, not at all. It was nice..." Tammy bit her lip. "I guess I just do not see him like that. You know? He is such a slut."

"He isn't a slut. Are you thinking that is why he hangs out with me? Because I am a Dom and a slut?"

Her face said yes, I sighed. "Ben isn't a slut. I like him because he is a good man. He is a friend and my equal. Maybe not as smooth, but deep down a good man. Are you seriously going to tell me that his kiss didn't give you a little tingle or make your panties wet?"

Tammy blushed scarlet. "Charlie!"

I laughed. I loved teasing her. "Seriously, if he can't make you wet with a kiss then he is not the man for you."

She smiled and shook her head. "I was too upset at the time. I was too shocked when he did it to even enjoy it. I just know that afterward I was breathless, and my heart was beating really fast."

I waited for Ben to pick her up before I said anything more about the kiss. I mentioned it again just as they were leaving. I decided to be an asshole, but it was something I wanted to see.

"Can you both do me a favour?"

Ben turned to me. "Yeah, what do you need?"

"I will never see Tammy go down the aisle. I would like you to kiss her like you just took her as your wife."

Tammy looked at me wide-eyed before she glanced at Ben, then back at me as if to say 'what the fuck are you up to?'

"I won't force a kiss on her." Ben held up his hands.

"You already did," she snapped.

"I apologised. You were hysterical, and I didn't know what else to do." He faced her and touched her hand but did not take it. "Say no and I will take you home."

Tammy looked up at him. He really did love her but would not push her and would let her make up her own mind. And he knew he was solidly in the friendzone. I was hoping he would take this opportunity to get out of it. When she looked at me with sadness in her eyes, I knew I was about to get my way.

"Do you Ben take Tammy to be your wife, to have and to hold from this day forth, 'til death do you part?"

"I do," Ben said without hesitation, meaning it.

Tammy looked up at him, the surprise on her face clear. She teared up as he took her hand and pretended to put a ring on her finger. She bit her lip.

"Tammy do you take Ben to be your husband, to have and to hold from this day forth, 'til death do you part?"

She swallowed hard and nodded, "I do."

She took his hand and pretended to put a ring on it, her hands trembling. She looked up at Ben nervously. He gave her a nervous 'I know you do not want me' smile. I think for the first time she saw that he was helping her because he was in love.

"I now pronounce you man and wife. You may kiss your bride."

Ben touched her face gently and then stroked her neck, she shut her eyes for a moment before she met his eyes. He cupped the back of her neck and then put his hand on her waist. Gently he pulled her against him.

Her breathing heightened as she touched his chest. He lowered his head and brushed his mouth over hers. He looked at her, giving her the out. I smiled when she nodded. Ben put his lips against my sister's.

After a moment he growled, and the kiss became more intense. He held her to him and she melted in his arms. He kissed her 'til they both needed to breathe...

I bet she could not tell me she wasn't wet after that.

He put his forehead to hers to catch his breath. She took some shaky breaths.

"Charlie, shut up." She said softly.

I grinned as Ben lifted his head. "Huh? He didn't say anything."

"I told her if a kiss didn't make her wet then you were not the man for her."

Ben looked at me wide-eyed and then at Tammy, still not letting her go. "Oh, I am glad." He pulled her pelvis against his and she looked up at him eyes wide. "It's only fair."

I laughed as he grinned and Tammy blushed. He let her go. "Congratulations."

"It is just pretend Charlie," Tammy gathered herself.

"You forget that I am able to perform marriages." I smiled, "If you handed me paperwork, I could make it official." I moved toward them. "But I won't. If you choose this later when I am gone, then I would be more than happy to have Ben as my brother-in-law."

I patted him on the shoulder. Tammy hugged my waist and buried her face in my chest. "If you don't choose him, that is okay too, Tammy. I got to see it. That is all I wanted." I hugged her. "Take her home Ben. She needs to rest after all the shopping we did today."

## 85. Kate

I was showered but I couldn't seem to wind down. I was curled up on the couch again, staring at nothing. Ian was on a phone call in his office. I just hoped it wasn't bad news. Charlie had left me to work his company and was off living life. He had only stopped in to see me a handful of times. Not since the dungeon had we had sex, and that was nearly two weeks ago.

"Well that was fucked." Ian walked in and flopped onto the couch beside me.

"What was?"

"Oh, some poor fucker managed to electrocute himself on a jobsite. He didn't look properly and cut through a live power cord. He is alive but he will be in hospital for a few days."

"That is fucked. Electrocutions can cause heart arrhythmias."

"That is exactly why he is in hospital." Ian looked at me. "You look beautiful and you smell good. But you look sad. Are you okay?"

I nodded. "Work is going well. I like Sam. She and I seem to be on the same page. I am still coming to terms with the sheer scale of the company. Charlie has fingers in so many pies. My calendar is insane so I am splitting all these fucking events he generally goes to with Sam. I just can't do it alone, and with her little one, nor can she." I sighed. "All Charlie has done in his life is work."

Ian watched me for a moment. "No, he hasn't. He had a lot of play time too."

"Going to the club isn't living. It is getting off. Charlie has worked. He has set up his company to ensure job security and growth. He has so many charities to support that they are coming out of his ears."

Ian shrugged. "You work it how you see fit. He didn't have kids."

"That is because he was too busy."

"Because he never found the right woman."

"Because he was working all the time."

Ian laughed. I took in his beautiful features then turned back to the TV.

"What is wrong now?"

"Just thinking about getting a nanny for the kids when you dissolve the marriage."

"I am not dissolving the marriage, Kate. I told you I said it to stir up Charlie." He took my hand and played with the rings on it. "When I put these on your finger, I meant my vows. I like living with you. I like having someone to come home to."

"The sex?"

"When we first moved in, I didn't think I would be able to handle having so many animals inside all the time. I thought that they would drive me insane. But they do not. You are good to my kids. My kids like you. Your kids are freaking cool. I am trying to be their Dad without replacing theirs…"

"They never met him."

"Doesn't matter. He is still their Dad. You get it. You are letting my kids come to you. You can't replace Aria and I can't replace Chris, so it's new territory."

"Can you tell me about the club the other night? Why wouldn't they let me see inside? And what was with all the bondage and crap."

"Smooth transition into another conversation Kate." He nudged me. "You don't want to talk about the kids, but you want to talk about kink."

"I am doing the best I can. I am just trying to find my feet. You aren't yelling at me saying you don't like what I am doing so I figure I am doing okay. Now tell me about the club."

"Well." He lay down and put his head in my lap, his eyes playful. "Nathan wants to fuck you."

"I figured as much. Did you see your sub?" I ran my fingers through his hair giving him a head massage.

"I don't have a sub. I did not fuck anyone that night. Well not with my tongue or cock."

"Why not? I gave you a free pass."

"Because you were feeling guilty about Charlie."

"Because I thought you had a sub and that you would want to finish it properly."

"Well I don't have a sub, so I didn't have anything to finish. I did use toys and floggers and things on a couple of subs but that was it. Charlie took a sub he has used for years back to his private room and came back out two hours later. Her body was full of welts and her hair was a mess. She looked happy and he looked like he had finished it on a good note."

So, he fucked one. I felt a little jealous.

"He told me yesterday he used toys on her but did not fuck her. He is faithful to you." He shut his eyes and sighed. "Did I ever tell you that I love my head being massaged?"

"Which head?" I asked without censorship before I bit my lip. "Sorry."

"Both actually." I touched his face then scratched his hair. "Woman, you are going to get fucked if you keep that up. Damn, that feels good."

I stopped moving my hands. "Sorry."

"Why are you sorry? I am your husband. If you want to seduce me, by all means do so. I am already semi-hard."

"We should find out if I am pregnant first."

He sighed and sat up. "Okay. But you need to understand something."

"What is that Ian?"

He took my face between his hands, brushing his lips over mine. "You are MINE." He growled. "You are my wife and I am not divorcing you. We are in this until we are old and grey. Pregnant or not."

Ian's blazing eyes stared into my soul. My heart beat fast. He was fierce and dominant. It was hot. I took a shaky breath. It was in that moment I realised I would not always have to be the strong one. That I could share the burden. He was mine.

"How does it feel to have that little epiphany?" he whispered, brushing his mouth against mine but not kissing me. "How does it feel to know that I am yours?"

I took another shaky breath, "I am not in this alone?"

"No. We are in it together."

Ian fucking meant it! Not alone, not an idiot!

"What are you going to do when I want to go back to work with Brian?"

"Get hard." He nuzzled my nose giving me a butterfly kiss. "I like that you are tough like a diamond. We really should spar sometime." His mouth was a little firmer as it brushed mine but he still didn't kiss me.

"I am not tough. Charlie is going to break my heart."

"Yeah, you and me both. We will be okay." He rubbed his nose against mine again then pulled back a little. My heart dropped, thinking this was the end of our discussion. "I like what you are wearing."

Huh? I was in pyjamas; I couldn't look frumpier if I tried. "No, you don't."

"You are right." Ian smiled and stood up. I looked up at him shocked. "You look much better naked." Then he scooped me off the couch and walked toward the stairs.

"Ian? What are you doing?"

"I want to see you naked."

"Um, why?"

"Because you are my wife and we are about to consummate the marriage. You will not be doubting me when I am done. Also, there's a possibility you may not be able to walk for a couple hours after."

"Are we going to the dungeon?"

"No. We are going to bed. I am going to not hold back for a change."

That took a moment to sink in. "You were holding back?"

"I didn't want to make Charlie look bad." Ian carried me into the bedroom and put me down. "Get naked Kate." He locked the door with a wicked look in his eye. "Now."

"Kiss me first and get me motivated." I backed up a little.

Ian cocked an eyebrow and pulled his shirt over his head. "You need some motivation?"

I nodded shyly. "You want this to be our wedding night."

He dropped to his pants to the floor and I stared wide-eyed at his hard manhood. "Get naked, my wife."

I blushed, looking away shyly. "Are we really doing this?"

Ian let out a sigh of exasperation and took two steps before grabbing the back of my head in one hand pulling my waist to his with the other as his mouth crashed onto mine. I saw stars as my heart pounded and my breathing went out of control.

I put my arms around his neck to hold on because my knees went weak. Ian moved a little, stepping on the hem of my pants, he pushed my pants down below my bottom and then grabbed my arse and lifted me. The pants dropped to the floor.

My feet went back on the floor and he broke the kiss to almost tear my shirt over my head. I pulled him back to kiss him again as I ran my hands over his body.

# 86. *Ian*

I had finally seduced her. My wife. My beautiful little diamond-tough woman. Her mouth drove me wild, her hands on my body burned like she was dragging a live powerline over me. Yeah okay enough of that. I picked Kate up, threw her on the bed grabbed her legs and spread them, licking up her center. Her juices on my tongue made me stop and eat her for a minute before getting on top of her. I was not going to hold back. Not tonight. I needed to win Kate over so she would never doubt me again.

I had only held back before because Charlie had been in the lead. He was not here now. I sucked Kate's nipples and then kissed her 'til I was damn near blind with hunger.

"How could you think I didn't want you?" I whispered as I massaged her clit, watching her eyes. She went to speak, and I pressed a finger inside her wet and ready and oh so fucking tight pussy. Her mouth went slack instead. "Mine."

I kissed her mouth, "Mine." I sucked her breasts and nipples, "Mine." I moved and then slammed my cock home into her, she cried out her body bowing, "And I am all yours. Don't you ever doubt it." I slammed into her again. "I am yours." I slammed into her "All of me is yours. Do you believe me Kate?"

"No." She whimpered. Her trust was so fragile, I would have to be careful, I had an epiphany of my own.

"You will." I kissed her jaw and her neck as I gentled my strokes, I did not want to bruise her. I just wanted to claim what was mine and make love to my wife.

Now that Charlie had told me that his dick did not work anymore, it was up to me to truly win over Kate over. No more stupidity, no more playing. Charlie would still have her until he died. I had made sure of it… But I needed to make sure I would have Kate when he was gone. For the first time in years I let my animal off the chain and was not at all surprised when Kate's inner sexual goddess came out to play and said, 'bring it'.

## 87. Charlie

I had been meaning to go to church since finding out I was sick. Today was the day. I walked in and stared at the cross on the wall. At the top of the aisle I admired the beauty.

"Are you okay, my son?" a priest asked, scaring the shit out of me... I never even heard him. He chuckled, "Sorry."

I smiled at him. "It's okay. And no, not really. How much time do you have?"

"How much do you need?"

"I want to confess a lifetime of sin. In my case, we might be here a while."

"Well then, I am not sitting in the confessional booth that long."

"Can we sit in there for a while? It is a bucket list thing." I said.

He watched me for a moment then nodded. "Okay, why are you ticking off your bucket list?"

"Cancer. If the doctors are right, I have minutes to live. They gave me a month seven weeks ago."

"So, you are here to make peace and yell at God for being unfair?"

"No, I am not angry. Not at all." I bit my lip and looked at him with tears in my eyes. "I am sad. I will not get to see my children grow or my sister in white. Nor will I grow old with my brothers and be grumpy old men together. I am really gutted that I am going to make my parents bury a child. But I am not angry." I wiped my face and shook my head. "Come on, this is going to take a while."

"I have got as much time as you need."

I got in the booth and looked around. "It stinks in here."

"Yeah a little."

"One sin and we will get out."

The priest chuckled. "Okay."

"Everything I say will be kept between you, me and God won't it."

"Absolutely."

I sighed and sat back. "Lots and lots of premarital sex. I divorced the woman I love so she wouldn't have to bury a second husband."

"They are two big ones."

I smirked. "Yeah but I never had any complaints. I made sure they all got off first." I frowned. "Except my wife. She would have been mine 'til the end. I wanted her so much. I couldn't have her watch me die."

"Would that have been a sacrifice she would willingly make?"

"She is still making it. I see her most days. But I have stopped sleeping with her."

"Why?"

"My dick doesn't work anymore. Annoying, but I had a good run." I sighed. "Is there somewhere we can sit without ears listening, or paparazzi?"

We got out of the confessional booth and he walked me outside to a small courtyard. The stars were out. I looked up. He took a seat on the bench and I sat beside him and just talked through everything. I felt no shame when I broke down.

It did not feel creepy either when he touched my shoulder to comfort me. But telling him my life story, telling him how I had gone from a haunted lost little kid to employing 70,000 people, running charities, was a weight off my chest. I told him about Kate and her family. I told him about mine. He laughed and asked questions.

"So, is she pregnant?"

"I don't know," I shrugged. "I want to know and at the same time... I do not. I would be even more upset at not being here then. I mean, in Vegas when she pretended, I felt like I had managed it. Still, the world will never know they are mine. I don't want the world to know either."

"Reputation to keep?"

"Safer for my children," I said. "With power come security problems. Especially since I made Kate my sole heir."

"Have you written your eulogy?"

I nodded and pulled a couple of pages from my pocket. The priest sat in silence to read it. I looked at the stars.

"This sounds like a press release."

I laughed, "Really?"

"Yes. How about we go to my office and rewrite it?"

"Okay. But you will have to read it."

The priest smiled, "Anything to make it easier on your family huh?"

I nodded.

I had never really been true to my religion and I had admitted that to him. But I had always believed in God. I spent the night at the church. Talking and getting my ceremony together. He never once complained of being tired. He made me feel like a friend. When the eulogy was done, he made it sound like he had known me for a lifetime. He absolved me of all my sins. And I felt as free as I did when I was skydiving.

"Thank you, Father." I shook his hand.

"Charlie, it has been an absolute pleasure. And your secrets are safe with me."

I nodded and looked around. "The next time I am here I will be dead."

The priest nodded. "Beautiful isn't it."

I nodded "Yes. It is. 'Bye Father."

"God is with you Charlie."

## 88. *Kate*

I was at work and feeling like shit. I had been nauseous for days and it was getting on top of me. Sam came in for our meeting.

She took one look at me and stopped in her tracks. "You look like shit. What's wrong?"

"Nothing, how did you go with the reshuffle?"

Sam sat down. "Well there are a few pairs of panties in a bunch, but they will suck it up."

I smiled, I liked her. She was tough and business minded. "And how are you dealing with the new bitch boss?"

"I have no issues." She grinned, "She and I are on the same page and that will help us continue to grow the business and make Charlie's legacy live on."

I nodded and a wave of nausea hit me. I covered my mouth and took a couple breaths. She observed silently. When it passed, I sat back, feeling green.

"Go home and don't you dare be giving the office a bug," she said flatly. "I am serious Kate; you give me a bug and I will kick your ass."

I laughed weakly. "You could try."

She and I talked for close to half an hour before I had a dizzy spell that had me cold sweating in my chair. I leaned back and took a couple of breaths.

"You are not alright." Sam stated, getting up. "Come, lay on the couch. You are white as a ghost."

I shook my head. "If I move, I am going to faint. Or vomit."

She picked up the phone and dialled out. "Ambulance."

I groaned, fucking hell. The last thing I needed was a trip in the wham-bulance. When she did that, she called in Katerina. When she came in Sam was quick with instructions. I felt worse. When I opened my eyes a moment later, I was looking at medics.

"When did you get here?" I asked as they moved me out of the chair to the stretcher.

"You have been out for five minutes," Sam said. "Ian is waiting at the hospital."

Dizziness and nausea overtook me as I was about to be put on the stretcher. My knees collapsed and the medics held me as my body went limp. They lay me on the stretcher and fussed as I proceeded to throw up.

## 89. Charlie

I was sitting with Dad and Ian having a coffee at the hospital. I had a check-up, only because I was alive when I should have been dead. The test results revealed I was dying. No shock, just not as quick as I had been told. I was on borrowed time. I had lived a month longer than expected.

Ian's phone rang and frowned when he saw the number. "Kate?... Oh, hi Sam... Huh? What do you mean she is unconscious?... I am at the hospital... having coffee with Dad. I will meet her in the ER... Okay thanks." He hung up and stared at his phone. "Kate collapsed."

He put his phone down and took a sip of his coffee. "Not surprised. She has been off colour for three days. She works too much. I picked her up last night and tied her to the bed so she would go to sleep early."

Ian looked calm. Meanwhile, I was having a mild heart attack at the thought of my precious Vegas random being ill. Ian glanced at me.

"Relax. She won't be here for another ten minutes; the ambulance had just arrived," he said calmly.

"Ian, why is she sick?"

"I don't know Charlie. She works stupid hours. She is probably tired. Relax. I am sure it is nothing to be worried about." The fucker had a little smile on his lips that I wanted to wipe off his face.

Ian sat and finished his coffee like nothing was wrong. I wanted to kill him. "Aren't you at least a bit worried?"

"Of course, I am. But you must remember I was married to Aria so… I am used to drama."

That made me smile as Dad's pager went off. He stood up. "She has arrived."

In the ER, Kate was hooked up to machines and a nurse was taking blood. She was white as a sheet under her oxygen mask, her eyes shut. Dad barked a couple of orders and she waved her hand dismissing him. He cocked an eyebrow.

"I am sick, stop fussing," she mumbled. "And please stop spinning the bed or I will vomit again."

Dad clenched his jaw before he ordered up anti-nausea medication. "You my dear Kate, will just let me sort out what the hell is going on."

"You are fussing like an old hen."

Dad put the cannula in personally before he gave her the drugs. He put a rush on the blood work.

"What is wrong with her?" I asked, freaking out.

"Oh relax. I have a stomach bug." She opened her eyes and looked at me, "I am fine." She turned to Ian. "Don't fuss."

Ian smiled. "I'm not. Charlie is."

"If you don't stop smiling, I am going to put you in the bed beside her," I snarled. "Why is she sick."

Ian smiled at me. "I have no idea. Dad a word?"

They left the cubical and I took Kate's hand. "Is the stress too much? Is it making you sick?"

"No Charlie. I promise you, that it is nothing like that. I am upsetting some people with the reshuffle but meh, they will get over it." I will never get sick of seeing the love in her eyes. "Come over for dinner. The kids would love to see you."

I nodded. "I would love to."

"Good. I miss you."

"I have been running amuck." I grinned and she smiled then I whispered in her ear. "My dick doesn't work anymore."

"I love you for more than your dick," she whispered back, putting her little hand over my heart. I held it there.

"I know. Has Ian done the right thing yet and sealed the deal?"

"Yes, I believe he is very keen on keeping me."

"He will make you happy. And you will make him happy."

"No, I will send him grey, but he did say he was okay with crazy."

I laughed as Dad came in with Ian and a nurse. They said they were moving her, and I just about had another heart attack. We were wheeled into a private room where Mum was waiting. The nurse left and shut the door leaving Ian with Mum, Dad, and my Vegas random. Dad picked Kate up and she protested.

"John! I am not a bloody cripple!"

He smiled and put her on the examination bed. Ian sat down and patted the chair beside him, inviting me to sit. I did because by now I was feeling sick.

"I need to pee," Kate said.

"Good." Mum said, then lifted Kate's shirt and opened the fly of her jeans before tucking in a little towel. "That will make this scan easier."

"What the hell am I having a scan for?"

Mum squirted some gel on her belly "When you were pregnant with Ryan and Ella…"

"I adopted them. I have never been pregnant," Kate snapped as Mum put a probe on her belly.

She moved the probe a couple of times and then smiled. "Well Charlie, you can tick kids off your bucket list."

"Huh?" Kate and I said in unison eyes drawn to each other's. Ian chuckled and I punched him in the arm. He laughed harder. I hit him again.

Mum pointed at the screen. "One jellybean, two jellybeans. Kate is pregnant and you are going to be a father."

Kate and I looked at the screen. Then back to each other.

"You told me in Vegas."

"I know."

"You told me in Vegas!" I said, taking her face in my hands and kissed her lips chastely before moving so I could look at my children. I watched their heartbeats. For just a split second, I could see them being born and then growing to play with their siblings, going to school and to their formals. Me having a drink with my son and walking my little girl down the aisle. Seeing them with their own children, a life I would never see.

I knew already that they would forgive me for not being here. That they knew I was watching over them from the other side. "They are beautiful. A boy and a girl, just like I asked. I don't think I have ever seen anything more perfect."

"I am pregnant?" Kate asked weakly. "Ian, am I pregnant?"

"Yes, you are."

"Oh. Okay." I would have looked at her, but I was watching my children. Imagining a wonderful future for them that I would never get to see. "I am going to have a baby."

"Not just one baby. You are going to have two." Ian told her; I could hear him smiling.

That little fucker knew and did not say anything! *Well played Ian. Well played.*

"Oh. They told me I couldn't get pregnant. Too much damage when I got shot. They had to take out an ovary. And the other one was polycystic. They said I couldn't... Chris and I tried for years and I couldn't do it."

"Charlie, I want to move the probe and have a look. Would you like me to take a couple of extra photos for you?"

I nodded. "Just another minute. I want to hear their hearts beat a little longer."

I would remember their heartbeats for the rest of my life. Mum handed me a couple of pictures. I handed one to Kate and sat down beside Ian. I stared at my babies.

MY BABIES! I WAS A FATHER!

## 90. Kate

Charlie was quiet at the hospital but the second I was home and through the front door, he hooted like he won the bloody lottery. He hugged Ian who smiled and hugged him back. Then he picked me up and carried me upstairs. I looked at Ian who just smiled. In the two moments we had to ourselves, he had told me to just go with whatever Charlie wanted to do.

Charlie put me in the bath and bathed me like a child. I had the cleanest belly in history. He dried me off and put me in bed. He touched me gently. He looked at me with awe and every time he looked at my belly, he was more in love with his babies.

He fussed, getting me dressed into my favourite pyjamas and then lay beside me touching my belly, kissing it. Talking to his children. I played with his hair and neck. After an hour, Ian appeared at the door. He leaned against the doorway and smiled.

"I am the luckiest man in the world," Charlie said, looking up at his brother as Richard appeared beside Ian. "Richard, I am a Dad."

"I heard," Richard said, coming in. "What are their names?"

"Charles Johnathon and Alexia Rachael," Charlie said with so much love, I bit my lip so I would not cry. "CJ and Lexie."

Richard nodded. "I like it. Feeling like a million bucks then, huh?"

"I am over the moon."

Ian and Richard sat down on the bed with me and I smiled. "Oh well Richard, it happened. All three of you in my bed."

Richard laughed. "Not like I wanted, Kate my dear. I have been informed that my beloved wife is not up for any threesomes."

I giggled. "I don't blame her. One insatiable man is more than enough. Two—well that is just madness."

Ian chuckled. "You loved every second of it."

"I loved the men I was with," I said softly and took Ian's hand while I continued to play with Charlie's hair. "I want Charlie to sleep with us tonight."

"Absolutely." He kissed the back of my hand. "Rita is making you some broth. Richard came over to drop off some medication to hold off the nausea."

I looked at Richard who was watching his big brother with mild amusement. "Thank you, Richard."

"Hey, when I saw the news about you getting carted out of work…"

"Oh FUCK!" I exclaimed. "Where is my fucking phone. I have to ring Brian and Gerrard and Harry and Billy before they fucking kill me."

"I already spoke to them." Ian grinned. "The whole family is coming over tomorrow night for a jam session. They are going to let you rest tonight."

I kissed the back of his hand and thanked him. "Charlie? Are you hungry?"

"Nope. But you have to eat." He turned to look at me. "I know you aren't well, but you need to eat."

I stroked his beard. "I am pregnant. Not ill. I just had a sissy moment at work. I am okay."

More like I had just had the fucking shock of my life if I was completely honest. PREGNANT WITH TWINS! HOLY FUCK! Just like we had said in Vegas.

The only thing I was worried about now, was whether I would be able to carry them. If I couldn't and lost them, then when Charlie passed it would be a million times worse. I had sustained a lot of damage over the years.

Years ago, I was told I would never get pregnant. I had told them this at the hospital. What I didn't tell them was that if I did, there was a good chance I would die birthing them.

I was a lot stronger than I was back then. My injuries had healed. I would stay silent and seek advice when no one was looking.

Charlie talked to his brothers until he fell asleep with me in his arms. Ian smiled and kissed my forehead.

"Are you okay?" He whispered.

"Just tired."

## 91. *Ian*

She lay asleep in Charlie's arms. As a father he would have been an overprotective bastard. The kids would not have gotten away with anything. He would have protected them with his last breath. Just as he was now. It was nearly sunrise.

Kate moaned and then shot up out of bed nearly kicking Charlie off as she did. She ran into the bathroom and vomited. Charlie woke up, rubbed his face and looked toward the bathroom then at me.

"Does she do that every morning?"

"Yes, she does."

"That sucks." He said looking back at the bathroom. "Where is her medication?"

"It is morning sickness Charlie, it is normal."

"I don't like it. I do not like her being sick. Make her better."

I chuckled. "She will be okay in a moment. Then I will get her some water and medication and hopefully she will still enjoy the smell of coffee."

The toilet flushed and she wandered to the sink looking wrecked. She washed out her mouth and came out. "Fuck me dead. That was terrible."

"I don't want you to be sick," Charlie told her and she smirked. "I am serious. I don't want you to be sick."

"It's okay, all part of the experience." Kate kissed his temple and then kissed mine. "I am going to go have some toast."

She left the room and Charlie lay back and looked at the ceiling. "I love that woman. She is the mother fucking jackpot. I am so glad I collared her."

*Wait what?* "When?"

"That night at my place." He told me what happened and looked sad. "It is for the best. Still, I love her."

"I love her too." He turned his head, looked at me and I nodded. "Yes. I love her."

He smiled and sighed. "Good. Look after her."

"I will. I will make sure they know who their very awesome Daddy is too."

He nodded and swallowed. "Thank you, Ian."

I patted his shoulder and got up. "You are more than welcome."

## 92. *Charlie*

I was going to be a father. It was the best news ever. We had a jam session to celebrate. Playing, singing, dancing. And Kate, although under the weather, was beautiful. I told my Vegas random every moment I had, how much I loved her and thanked her for giving me this gift.

I was a little shitty though on Saturday that I had booked matinee tickets for a Broadway show for my parents. I wanted to spend as much time with my babies as possible. The Lion King had been booked out for months. But I got three tickets and was glad I did. Mum had wanted to see it for so long.

The show was incredible. But it was the look on Mum's face that made me glad that I did come. She had asked so little of me over the years. This was one thing I could do for her. There was pure enjoyment in the visual but I think it was the music and singing she enjoyed most. She would shut her eyes, take a breath and just listen. Taking it all in.

I took her hand. She squeezed it and looked at me with a sad smile.

"The Lion King was the first movie you wanted to watch when you came to live with us."

And that was why she wanted to see it. Why it was important to her to see it with me. I remembered watching it between them and feeling loved, wanted, and safe.

Dad was simple. He just wanted time; hence I had been going to the hospital when he was on break, having coffee or dropping by to have a scotch with him. That was all he wanted. When I took them home, I had a night cap with them before going back to Ian's. Ian was holding a sleepy Ella in his arms when he opened the door.

"She wanted to stay up to see her Charlie." He smiled and handed her to me. Her little arms wrapped around my neck and I hugged her tight.

"Hello my Charlie."

"Hello, my Ella, why aren't you asleep?" I asked, kissing the top of her head.

"Because I wanted to cuddle you and give you kisses."

"Okay," I sat on the couch and she rained kisses all over my face. I looked at Ian who smiled and indicated he was going to have a drink of water. I nodded. "You give lovely kisses, Ella."

"'Cause we love you." Then at the top of her voice she yelled. "Charlie's HOME!"

Seconds later, there were running footsteps and I was mauled by three more kids. Hugs, kisses and so much love. They asked me about the show, and I told them all about it with as much animation as I could muster.

A kiss on the top of my head and a soft touch on my skin and beard had me looking into the eyes of the love of my life. She gave me a tired smile. She was a little pale, her hair was a mess, but she was still the most beautiful woman I had ever seen in my life.

She sat down on my lap at my direction and the kids told me how Ian had said they must be very gentle with her tummy because there were babies inside. They lifted her shirt.

"They are your baby's and we are going to love them and play with them and bash them up when they are naughty, and we are going tell them about Charlie Daddy all the time," Ryan told me.

"Because they are our sissy and brother," Tim added.

"Can we watch Lion King? With all our Daddy's and our Mummy's and our babies?" Evie asked, batting her eye lashes at me.

I smiled. I was so tired. I just wanted to go to bed and hold Kate. But I nodded. Ian put it on, we put the pillows on the floor and lay down. Kate between Ian and I and the kids all over us. My hand on her belly.

It was how I fell asleep. Feeling very loved. Praying that my children would know how much I loved them, that they be healthy and grow up into good people.

## 93. Ian

Charlie had gotten up and had breakfast with the kids. Kate vomited so he had fussed over her too. Then he decided that he wanted to go to Mum and Dad's to help set up for Sunday lunch. The kids were running around happily like little nutters.

I liked watching them like this. Happy, carefree, and full of life. Kate though looked ill. She gave me a little smile and I went to give her a hug.

"We don't have to go if you aren't up to it."

She shook her head. "I am okay. That medication does jack shit."

"Talk to Mum about another one," I suggested, stroking her hair as the kids ran past laughing. "They are all nuts today. Did Charlie give them red cordial?"

She laughed softly. "They are just happy."

I kissed the top of her head. "How about we get them showered and go to Mum and Dad's?"

She nodded and we started the process of getting ready. I chuckled as we all got in my newest car. I had an excuse to buy another car now. Having six kids would be crazy. Rita and Joe had decided to come with us. Sometimes they liked the afternoon off. Either way they were welcome.

We walked into Mum and Dad's, and the kids ran to Charlie. Again, they showered him in kisses and love. He lapped it up. He had never really liked kids before. But now it seemed he could not get enough. I greeted him with a hug and managed to whisper a secret in his ear that I had been keeping since Vegas.

He looked at me with surprise and I was sure nobody would ever wipe the smile off his face as he went to Kate, pulled her into his arms, kissing her so passionately that her knees gave out as she melted against him.

Charlie took his time before he broke the kiss. Then he dropped to his knees and planted kisses all over her belly. She stroked his hair. She looked up at me and I gave her a wink.

## 94. Charlie

We had Sunday lunch out in the garden at Mum and Dad's. It used to be such a fucking tedious time of the week. I was generally hungover and tired after a night at the club. Now, I wish I had appreciated it more.

I was a lucky man to have been adopted by Mum and Dad. To have siblings who accepted me as one of their own even though I was a lot older. As I watched them interact, I did not feel out of place, for I was part of the family.

This was my family. Which was not something I felt often. Today though, the feeling was strong.

I had managed to talk to everyone separately. And even play with the kids. Oh, and give lots of kisses for my babies. And one awesome kiss to my wife. Her knees had buckled and everything. It had been the perfect day. Now I just wanted to watch them all while the sun set.

I had always loved sunsets. And this one was turning into the most beautiful one I had ever seen. I sighed as I admired it.

"It was a good day, Son," Dad said coming out on the porch, handing me a scotch as he sat beside me. I had my arm around Mum who had been fussing over me all day. Dad handed her a glass of white wine. Dad settled with his shoulder to mine. This was us being affectionate.

"It has been a great day," I agreed then laughed at my brothers picking on Tammy as they played tag with the kids. "She totally loves being the center of their attention."

Mum giggled. "She admitted to me that she might be falling for Ben."

"I saw it coming," Dad stated with a nod. "He is a good man. I approve, for once."

I nodded. "Yeah, I hope he mans up and marries her. Even I managed to man up and marry the woman I wanted."

Mum looked at me. "Are they yours?"

"Yes, Ian wore a condom and I didn't." I looked at her and gave her a one-armed squeeze. "She was the only one I ever went raw with. No, fib."

Kate stood off to the side smiling as she watched the games, a protective hand over her belly and my babies. "She was the only woman I ever fell in love with. Well other than my Mummy." I grinned at Mum who looked up at me with a bright smile.

"You never called me that, not even as a boy. It was always just Mum."

"You were never just Mum." I kissed her forehead as she beamed with pride. Then I nudged Dad. "You were never just Dad either. I

304

would have been fucked without both of you keeping me on the right path."

Dad nudged me back then chuckled. "You weren't just a son to us either." I looked at him and he looked at me. "You are our son."

I smiled at him. "I know." For now, I really did know.

We looked back at the family playing chatting and drinking our drinks. I watched Kate who seemed distracted staring off into the distance.

I followed her line of sight to see a man and a woman walking toward me. As they got closer, I recognised Aria and smiled. She smiled back. I recognised the man from the photos on Kate's walls. It was Chris.

It was my time. It had come... I looked back at the sunset. Beautiful.

"I love you all so much. Don't be sad when I go."

"We can't make any promises." Dad said cuddling me.

I took a last look at Kate who was staring at me with so much love as her heart broke. I gave her my best smile as goodbye. "Tell Kate she is the fucking jackpot."

Kate ran toward me looking like she was screaming as my scotch glass slipped from my hand and shattered on the tiles. I heard my heart stop. Breath left my body with a sigh.

I watched as my family realise, I was gone. For each one it was different, but it was Kate, the love of my life, my little wife who shattered like the most fragile glass.

I was glad I did not hear her scream. It was a relief when Ian took hold of her, pulling her into his arms as he broke down, looking back at me in shock.

"She will be okay," Chris said beside me. "Ian will look after her."

I shook his hand as I left my body. Then I kissed Aria's cheek. "Hi Princess."

"Hey Charlie. You are going up Charlie. I don't know why you would have ever thought you were going down." She patted my arm.

I smiled and looked back at my family. Chris crouched down and stroked Kate's cheek, Aria ran her fingers through Ian's hair like she used to. I kissed the top of Kate's head and stood up.

"What happens next?" I asked as we walked toward a light in the distance.

"Peace." Aria smiled.

"Will we get to watch?"

"Yeah. We have a great seat." Chris nodded.

I concluded that for my life to end on such a good note, to have it end and not be terrified, just as Jet had told me—this was the end of a perfect life.

I had achieved business success and given jobs to people, I had a wonderful family, had fallen in love with a brilliant woman and had left two children behind as my true legacy.

All because of a Vegas random, I could see now how truly rich I had been.

# 95. Ian

I think that, if Kate had not been pregnant, she would have just broken into a million pieces. I still wake hearing her scream as she realised he was gone. I think it will haunt me 'til the day I die. I was sure I heard her heart break.

Charlie died on what anyone could only describe as the perfect note. No pain killers, no fights, surrounded by his family, with a scotch in his hand, just like he wanted.

Two hours after his death, after the funeral home had come to collect his body, Larry and Sam arrived at Mum and Dad's for Kate to sign off on the press release. I was watching the news when the story broke two minutes after the release went live. The TV presenter read it and then looked around and said, "Has this been confirmed?" The shock in his eyes, "In breaking news, Charles Morrissey has died at home surrounded by family after a short battle with cancer."

I do not think Charlie believed the world would care, the press release was just a public service announcement to say Kate will be taking your calls now… I do not think he could have imagined what happened next. In under thirty seconds, all our phones started ringing off the hook and the media went insane with an outpouring of grief.

Charlie's funeral was huge, the members of the club turned up in clothes which was strange, considering I had only ever seen them in various stages of undress. Representatives of his charities, businesses, and then there were those extremely high ranked in both society and government who made an appearance. Thank God Crosshairs was overseeing security. The priest gave the perfect ceremony. He had us laughing and crying. The eulogy was as if Charlie were there reading it himself.

The priest smiled as he looked around and pointed at the paper he was reading from. "Charlie bet that his last words would be something stupid, so I found out before the service what they were." He smiled as he looked around then his eyes settled on Kate, "They were 'I love you all so much, don't be sad when I go.'" He paused as Kate broke down as did what sounded like everyone in the church.

Halfway through the service, I felt at peace. Like the weight was off my chest. This had been the perfect send off for a good man.

At the graveside, there were close friends and family only. We committed his body to the ground as it started to rain. My little wife was shaky. The crowd dispersed but she did not make any move to leave despite getting saturated.

"We are going to take the kids to your parents'," Brian said softly at my side. "Will you be okay?" I nodded and they left. I knew that over the years they would become brothers. They had been fantastic in the last week.

The cemetery became deserted quickly and still Kate stood there. Wet footsteps got my attention, Nathan returned with something in his hand. He touched Kate's face and showed me Charlie's favourite whip.

"I couldn't let him go without it." Nathan grinned and put it on top of Charlie's coffin. He touched the coffin. "'Bye old friend." A strangled sob escaped Kate and she covered her mouth as though to keep her pain in. Nathan turned to her, pulling her into his arms. I had tried that ten minutes earlier and she did not want a bar of it. "Don't keep the pain in, Little Random. He is gone and at peace. Let the pain out."

"I can't. I need to keep my blood pressure under control. I...I don't want to hurt the babies," Kate sobbed into his chest.

Nathan gaped at her then at me. Slowly a smile spread across his face "He got her pregnant?" I nodded. "He got her pregnant! Why is she standing in the rain! She will get sick!"

"I have morning sickness; I am already sick!"

"He is right Kate; we should get out of the rain," I said gently.

She shook her head stubbornly. There really was no depth of stubborn in this woman. You would think she reached her limit and nope. She was just playin'.

Nathan scooped her up. "Come, Little Random, there are only a few people in the world that know who you were to him. He protected you to the last. You are pregnant with his child and this is where your self-care comes in."

"Children. He is getting twins," I whispered.

Nathan stopped walking and stared at me. "Twins?" I nodded. "Right, well we are going to get this beautiful woman out of the rain, healthy Mum equals healthy babies."

"I couldn't agree more."

"I want to stay with him." Kate sobbed into Nathan's chest.

"He is in your heart and your womb, Kate. He is with you." Nathan kissed her forehead and put her in the back of the car. He stood up. "See you at the wake. Would you like me to get her some dry clothes?"

Nathan never offered to do anything. I nodded my thanks. He patted me on the shoulder and walked away while I got in the car to care for my broken-hearted wife.

## 96. Kate

Carrying twins was a challenge. I really didn't like not seeing my toes. Or not being able to bend over. Or not being able to have sex. Yes, I know, funny coming from the woman whose status was nun seven months ago. I also did not like cotton wool or bed rest.

Ian was wonderful. We both had moments in the early days where not having Charlie in the world was more than we could bear but we shared the load and took the strain when the other broke so we could grieve. Five months had passed since I watched Charlie smile at me and die.

Yesterday, I had nearly met the grim reaper myself. I was hanging out at home; the babies had been quiet, and I was feeling like shit. The whole family were there just chilling out, laying on the grass. Richard and Ian had found a new appreciation for it. I was loving being outside in the sun enjoying the fresh air.

"Guys, I feel weird." I said.

"How do you mean?" Gerrard asked.

"Um… I don't know, like I want to squat."

Gerrard and Emma sat up and looked at me. "Like you want to squat?" Gerrard had said. "Are you having contractions?"

"No. I just want to squat. I am not comfortable. My back aches," I grumbled. "My back never ached before I became pregnant."

"Rachael!" Emma called. "Get some gloves!"

"Why are you fussing?" I asked. "I am fine. I just feel like shit."

"I have gloves. Who hurt themselves?" Rachael came out.

"Do an internal on Kate. I think she is about to have the babies." Emma stated.

"She is booked in for a caesarean in two days. She had better not be." Rachael came downstairs "Get her panties off."

I looked at Ian, "Tell them to stop fussing." He ripped my knickers off me. "Hey! They were my comfy ones."

"Shh, you. I will get you another set."

"She does have a pretty pussy." Richard said and I lifted my head to see him looking.

"RICHARD!" I shouted at him. Ben punched him in the arm. "Thanks Benny." I felt fingers and then I was very wet. "Did my waters just break?"

"Yes, all over me. JOHN! GET AN AMBULANCE!"

"Oh, you have to be fucking shitting me." John said coming out. "Seriously Kate? Can't wait two more days?"

"Nope, this is Shorty. I told you her belly dropped three days ago," Nelly said.

"I told you she was in labour when we arrived." Harry muttered.

I laughed and then moaned as the need to bear down took hold. "I need to sit up. I need to sit up."

There was movement from Gerrard, John, Emma, and Rachael. Brian and Ian helped me get to my knees. Now, I was panicking. I was okay until I was on my knees and now, I was in pain.

I looked at Brian. "It hurts."

"Yes, having a baby generally does." Brian tried not to laugh. *Arsehole.*

"This is Charlie's fault." I groaned.

"Yes, it is." Brian smiled as Ian chuckled.

"It's always our fault." Ian said.

I punched Ian and shouted, "Shut up!" He fell back and Brian grabbed my hand to stop me hitting him too. I groaned as I pushed. I could hear laughter.

"Breathe Kate, you are doing great." I heard Rachael say.

"Why are they laughing?" I took a couple of breaths and glared at Brian.

"You knocked Ian the fuck out." He laughed.

"I what? Oh God…" I pushed. "WAKE HIM UP!"

"Kate, you have a head out. Just breathe for a moment and don't push." Rachael instructed calmly.

I moaned. "Ian, Ian I am sorry. I need you."

"I'm here. I'm here," he said and then he was beside me, touching me, holding my hand firmly. I looked up at him, in the most pain of my life. "I have to push."

"Another moment," Rachael said firmly.

I had looked at Ian who was looking okay. Rachael told me to push and I looked Ian in the eye as I did.

A couple of pushes later, and I had felt relief. For a moment. For just a couple of blissful moments. Rachael held the child, a boy up for me to see. I smiled.

"Hello CJ." I whispered. Then there was a bone crushing pain. For a moment, I swear I went blind.

I pushed. I breathed and I pushed. I opened my eyes when the pain stopped. Charlie and Chris were there. I gave them a weak smile. Both were so proud. I collapsed. I was lay back on the grass. I was numb and exhausted. I stared at the sky as I heard Rachael tell me it was a girl. As I shut my eyes someone shouted at me not to.

That was my yesterday. Giving birth to Charlie's twins on the back lawn. Today, I was feeling a lot better and eating jelly in my hospital room.

Ian smiled as he walked in pushing a bassinette. I put the jelly down and held my hands out.

"CJ is strong enough to be out of special care for a visit with his Mummy." He passed CJ to me, and as I examined him my heart swelled.

I smiled up at Ian, "He looks just like Charlie."

"Spitting image." Ian sat on the bed and touched my face. "How are you feeling today? You scared the shit out of me yesterday."

I swallowed and wet my lips. "Charlie and Chris were there. I think I died for a minute or two."

"You did die for a minute or two. Gerrard and Emma were busy resuscitating you while Mum and Dad looked after the twins. Brian sorted me out and well everyone else tried to calm the kids."

I shook my head. "I am sorry I scared you."

He moved closer. "The medics sedated me. I was a mess. But our babies, they were strong and wonderful." He touched CJ's cheek. "You say you saw Charlie and Chris."

"They were there." I nodded. "They looked happy."

Ian nodded.

* * *

I was in hospital two weeks before we could go home. The twins were strong and healthy despite being small. I was stronger and tired, but I could not wait to sleep in my own bed.

On the way home, I asked to visit Charlie's grave. I took the babies with me and sat on the grass with them. I felt I needed to bring them to their father since I had seen him when they were born. I spoke to him as I tidied up his grave. But I stopped when I saw a line of small writing on the bottom of the tomb stone. It looked like there was also a piece of ribbon... I gave it a tug out from under the headstone. On the end of the ribbon was a diamond ring. I stared at it in shock. This is the ring I dreamt about. His collar for me because we were not married anymore... I held it against my heart as I read what was hidden on the bottom of his headstone.

*My Vegas Random, the love of my life.*
*You are the fucking jackpot. C.*

I covered my mouth to hide the massive smile on my face. One message, just for me. I took a moment to wipe my teary eyes. Charlie had meant every word. Every kiss.

"Yes, you will be forever in my heart Charlie. Thank you for your gifts." I smiled then kissed his head stone.

I picked up the babies and went back to the car, the breeze gentle on my cheeks. It felt like soft kisses from Chris and Charlie. My heart felt strong. I felt strong. I had been dearly loved by two great men and somehow still managed to have one by my side.

I was the luckiest woman in the world. I would love Chris and Charlie until my dying breath. I would tell their children about them and ensure their legacies lived on. I would love Ian without guilt. Without fear. For he was here, and he loved me.

Despite me being batshit crazy.

Ian was waiting, leaning against the car. He was happy.

Seriously how was it legal to be that beautiful? And how come he never had a hair out of place?

"Happy?" he asked smiling that megawatt smile that could and would every now and then get him out of the doghouse.

I nodded, "Yeah. I am. Are you?" He put the babies in the car before he answered.

"Yes, I am. More so when you are cleared to have sex."

I laughed, *dirty bastard*. I hesitated and then showed Ian the ring. He took it from my hand and inspected it.

"This is the collar he bought for you in Vegas."

"I thought he gave it to me, but he said I dreamt it." Ian took the ribbon off the ring and took my hand gently. I pulled my hand away when I realised what he was about to do. "No. I won't wear his collar now. He didn't give it to me for this reason."

Ian shook his head and took my hand.

"The inscription says, '*Our JACKPOT xoxoxo*'." I think the stones are Chris, Charlie, and me. The three loves of your life. You should honour us by wearing it." Ian slid the ring onto my finger and as if on instinct, my hand made a fist and I put it over my heart. "Come on, let's go home."

We got in the car and I looked back to Charlie's grave and smiled. His Vegas Random. His love. His Jackpot. Just for a night... or two.

"You know I am yours. All this crazy just for you." I turned to Ian with a big smile on my face.

"Yes Beautiful. Just like I am all yours." He took a fistful of my hair and pulled me to him over the center console and kissed the hell out of me. When he broke the kiss, I collapsed back in my seat breathless. Lusty eyes on my beautiful husband.

Ian smirked as he turned on the car, put it into gear and put his hands on the steering wheel.

"I love you. Don't for a second think that I will ever let you forget it."

I smiled as I watched him drive. "I love you too."

# 97. Amy

I watched her leave the hospital with my babies. Now she had been to Charlie's grave. I hated her. Ian looked happy as though he were wearing rose-coloured glasses. That bitch wasn't who he wanted. She would never be who he needed.

When I watched him drive away after kissing her, anger and hatred for her had me wanting her to die... painfully.

After she embarrassed me so badly and stole my man... I hated her more.

Just like Aria. Fucking bitch. Ian only loved her because she could sing. She was nothing but an injured bird, crying in distress.

I smiled as I thought of Aria, so eager to please. So easy to manipulate.

*So easy to kill...*

I would bide my time, plan it carefully. I do not want it to look like Ian did I already knew the perfect person to do the job...

I went to Charlie's grave and pulled down my panties and pissed on his grave. He was the reason I wasn't with Ian. He had always been in the way. Not anymore.

I walked from the cemetery. Planning my new life with Ian.

Minus Kate and her little bastards.

\* \* \*

Ellie Gerrard

That's it for now! Thank you for hanging in there
and for reading The Vegas Random. I hope you enjoyed it.
I guess now you see why readers lovingly call me
Ellie 'Fucking' Gerrard.

Read. Review. Repeat!

XO

*Ellie Gerrard*

P.S. Not So Random is COMING SOON! (Excerpt below!)

## Stalker Links!

**Website:** https://www.elliegerrard.com/
**Facebook Profile:** https://www.facebook.com/EllieGerrardAuthor/
**Facebook Group:** https://www.facebook.com/groups/369628090139915/
**Instagram:** https://www.instagram.com/elliegerrardauthor/?hl=en
**Twitter:** https://twitter.com/elliegauthor

# About the Author

Ellie is a born and bred Queenslander from her proud beginnings as the daughter of a farmer who calls her "Number 1" out of frustration when he has called her all of her sibling's names and sometimes the grandkids names (there are advantages to being the firstborn), and a Mum who spent most of Ellie's teen years driving her to choir and music practice.

Ellie is the wife of a man who loves to tinker in the backyard like a mad scientist, mother of one daughter who is her pride and joy.

Ellie's first memories of reading are from grade one, discovering Grug. But writing—that came after the sheer frustration of watching a movie for which there was no sequel.

Yes, she wrote her first script at 13. Believing she would never write again, she burned it in a pile of rubbish around four years before she released The Vegas Random.

Ellie has a love for police shows, chocolate, reading and of course sitting at the computer and being the vessel for her characters to take over so their stories can come to life on the page.

Her favourite thing about writing is to be as surprised as her readers when the book is being written. She guarantees that if you cry, she cried first.

She has sometimes got the attention span of a goldfish and is easily distracted by shiny things.

If Ellie could live on chocolate, she would. This all makes Ellie sound as sweet as the ice cream you will probably be eating at the end of the book. Ellie is a bitch who will attempt to press every emotional trigger you have after lulling you into a false sense of security. Leaving you a blubbering mess with a pile of tissues, a bad case of cry face and a book hangover. She will sit and listen to you as you tell her you cried, with a smile on her face.

It is why she got dubbed by her readers as "Ellie 'Fucking' Gerrard"

To date her favourite review is: "I have never loved a book so much and hated the author."

Her response to that review was: To laugh and say, "Awesome. I did my job."

Excerpt from:

# *Not So Random*

## *Kate*

The house was quiet, everyone was asleep. Ian had gone to bed
an hour ago dead on his feet when CJ and Lexie finally settled and
went to sleep. I had gone to bed with him. But the second my arse
hit the mattress, they started screaming again. Both were having
trouble with the split feeds they were having because I couldn't
produce enough breast milk to keep up with their demand. So,
tummy aches were the problem tonight.

The thing was, I was so tired. I didn't remember the last time I
slept. I had been sleep deprived with Ryan and Ella but this was
something far beyond that. I was so emotionally fucked. It was as
if being tired had bought everything I had been through in the last
twelve months to the boil and I was a pressure cooker that was
about to explode.

I would tell everyone I was fine. Even when I wasn't. Hell, I had
been shot to shit and told my team I was fine while I reloaded my
gun. Right now, I was not fine. I wanted Charlie and Chris to come
back just for a day so they could meet their children. I wanted them
to be able to hug and to kiss their babies and hear their beautiful
little giggles. I wanted them here for me to hold one more time…

I had never admitted it before but sometimes it was hard to look
at my kids. The heart break their fathers had given me was so
much that I sometimes felt like my heart was like a fine glass
ornament that was put on the top shelf for safety… Sometimes I
felt like I was just waiting for the cat to push it off and for me to
shatter completely.

I couldn't get CJ and Lexie to settle and it upset me because I
knew that they would just have to adjust to the formula. But
tonight, it was too much. Every ounce of my baggage and stress
came out to head fuck me. I sat in my rocking chair with the babies

safely in their cots and cried with them. I felt like I was the worst mother and wife in the world. I wanted Ian to be here to help me but at the same time, I wanted him to get some sleep because one of us had to be sane in the morning. I felt so selfish because he was so good to me and right now, I didn't feel like I deserved it.

I was up with the twins doing my best to feed them on time, to change them and to make sure they were warm all while I cried like a fucking sook. Wishing I could just get ten minutes of sleep. When they finally went to sleep, I stayed in the rocking chair sobbing until I finally stopped. I was so tired. I had so much I wanted to do when I woke up… I would just have to embrace the suck and get on with it like I always did.

Warm hands touched my cheek. I opened my eyes to see Ian dressed for work. His eyes asked questions but his mouth stayed silent. I couldn't help it when I shut my eyes again. A moment later, I was in his arms and we were moving. "I am fine Ian. You don't have to do this."

He lay me on the bed, tucked me in and kissed my forehead. "Get some sleep. I will stay until Nelly arrives."

"No Ian, I got a couple hours." I went to sit up and he lay me down again.

"Bullshit. You have been up all night because you were too stubborn to come get me to tag out for an hour or two."

"You have to go to work. You needed the sleep."

"No, I need to help my wife look after our babies." He lay down beside me and threw his leg and arm over me to keep me under the covers. "Do you want to tell me why you were crying for four hours?"

My lip started to wobble; I couldn't look at him as I shook my head.

"You never grieved Charlie like I thought you would. Is that why you were crying?"

I nodded, "I am fine, honestly. I am just tired, and it got the better of me."

Ian stroked my hair and sighed. "Fine is a fucking dangerous word." He kissed my temple as I felt like I was sinking into the mattress. "Sleep well." My eyes fluttered shut.

CPSIA information can be obtained
at www.ICGtesting.com
Printed in the USA
BVHW072256170123
656503BV00012B/195